30,000 on the Hoof

ZANE GREY

30,000
On the
Hoof

WALTER J. BLACK, INC.

ROSLYN, NEW YORK

30,000 on the Hoof

Chapter One

GENERAL CROOK and his regiment of the Western Division of the U.S. Army were cutting a road through the timber on the rim of the Mogollon Mesa above the Tonto Basin. They had as captives a number of Apache Indians, braves, squaws, and children, whom they were taking to be placed under guard on the reservation.

At sunset they made camp at the head of one of the canyons running away from the rim. It was a park-like oval, a little way down from the edge, rich with silver grass and watered by a crystal brook that wound under the giant pines. The noisy advent of the soldiers and their horses and pack-mules disturbed a troop of deer that trotted down the canyon to stop and look back, long ears erect.

Crook's campaign was about over and the soldiers were jubilant. They joked with the sombre-eyed Apaches, who sat huddled in a group under guard. Packs and saddles plopped to the grass, the ring of axes echoed through the forest, blue smoke curled up into sunset-flushed pines.

The general, never a stickler for customs of the service, sat with his captain and a sergeant, resting after the hard day, and waiting for supper.

"Wonder how old Geronimo is going to take this," mused Crook.

"We haven't heard the last of thet redskin," replied Willis emphatically. "He'll break out sooner or later, and then there'll be hell to pay."

"I'm glad we didn't have to kill any of these Apaches."

"We were lucky, General. I'll bet McKinney will burn powder before he stops thet Matazel an' his braves. Bad youngsters."

"Do you know Matazel, sergeant?" inquired Crook.

"I've seen him. Strappin' young buck. Only Indian I

ever saw with grey eyes. He's said to be one of Geronimo's sons."

"Wal, McKinney won't stand any monkey business from thet outfit," added Willis. "He's collared them by this time. Huett knows the country. He'll track them to some hole in the woods."

"Good scout, Logan Huett, for so young a man. He has been invaluable in this campaign. I shall recommend him to my successor."

"Huett is through with army scout service after this campaign. He'll be missed if old Geronimo breaks out an' goes on the warpath. Fine woodsman. Best rifle shot I ever saw."

"What is Huett going to do?"

"Told me he wanted to go home to Missouri for a while. He's got a girl, I reckon. But he's hipped on the West an' will soon be back."

"He surely will," added the other officer. "Logan Huett was cut out for a pioneer."

"The West needs such men more than the Army. . . . Hello, I hear shouts from above."

"Bet thet's McKinney now," said Willis, rising.

"Sure enough. I see horses an' army blue through the trees," added the sergeant.

Presently a squad of soldiers rode down into the glade. They had three mounted Indians with them and another on foot, a tall lithe brave, straight as an arrow, whose bearing was proud. These captives were herded with the others. Sergeant McKinney reported to General Crook that he had secured Matazel and three of his companions. The others got away on foot.

"Any shooting?" queried the general.

"Yes, sir. We couldn't surprise them an' they showed fight. We have two men wounded, not serious."

"I hope you didn't kill any Indians."

"We didn't, to our knowledge."

"Send Huett to me."

The scout approached. He was a young man about twenty-three years old, dark of face. In fact he bore somewhat of a resemblance to Matazel, and he was so stalwart and powerfully built that he did not look tall.

"What's your report, Huett?"

"General, we made sure of getting Matazel alive," replied the scout, "otherwise none of them would have escaped. . . . I guessed where Matazel's bunch was headed for. We cut in behind them, chased them into a box canyon, where we cornered them. They had but little ammunition, or we'd had a different story to tell."

"Don't dodge the main point, as McKinney did. Were there any Indians killed?"

"We couldn't find any dead ones."

"Willis, fetch this Apache to me."

In a few moments Matazel stood before the general, his arms crossed over his ragged buckskin shirt, his sombre eyes steady and inscrutable.

"You understand white man talk?" queried General Crook.

"No savvy," replied Matazel, sullenly.

"General, he can understand you an' speak a little English," spoke up the sergeant who knew Matazel.

"Did my soldiers kill any of your people?"

The Apache shook his head.

"But you would have killed us," said the general, severely.

Matazel made a magnificent gesture that embraced the forest and the surrounding wilderness.

"White man steal red man's land," he said, loudly. "Pen Indian up. No horse. No gun. No hunt."

General Crook had no ready answer for that retort.

"You Indians will be taken care of," he said presently.

"It's better for you to stay peaceably on the reservation with plenty to eat."

"No!" thundered the Apache. "Geronimo say better fight—better die!"

"Take him away," ordered the general, his face red. "Captain Willis, according to this Apache, it sounds as if old Geronimo will break out all right. You had it figured."

Before the sergeant led Matazel away the Indian bent a piercing glance upon the scout, Logan Huett, and stretching out a lean red hand he tapped Huett on the breast.

"You no friend Apache."

"What do you want, redskin?" demanded Huett, surprised and nettled. "I could have shot you. But I didn't. I obeyed orders though I think the only good Indian is a dead one."

"You track Apache like wolf," said the Indian, bitterly. His eagle eyes burned with a superb and piercing fire. "Matazel live get even!"

It was Autumn before Logan Huett was released from his military duties, once more free to ride where he chose. Leaving the reservation with light pack behind his saddle he crossed the Cibeque and headed up out of the manzanita, scrub oak and juniper to the cedars and piñons of the Tonto Rim.

The trail climbed gradually. That same day he reached the pines and the road General Crook had cut along the ragged edge of the great basin. Huett renewed his strong interest in this mesa. From the rim, its highest point some eight thousand feet above sea level, it sloped back sixty miles to the desert. A singular feature about this cliff was that it sheered abruptly down into the black Tonto Basin on the south while the canyons that headed within a stone's throw of the crest all ran north. A few miles from their source they were deep grassy valleys with heavily timbered slopes. The ridges between the canyons bore a growth of pine and spruce, and the open parks and hollow swales had groves of aspen and thickets of maple. The region was a paradise for game. It had been the hunting grounds of the Apache, and they had burned the grass and brush every year, making the forest open.

Back toward the Cibeque several cattle combines, notably the Hashknife outfit, ran herds of doubtful numbers on the lower slopes. At Pleasant Valley sheepmen and cattlemen were at odds over the grazing. Sooner or later they would clash.

Huett left that country far behind to the east. He traveled leisurely, camping in pretty spots, and on the third night reached the canyon-head where he had brought Matazel and his Apache comrades to General Crook, which service practically ended the campaign.

He found where the soldiers had built their camp-fires. little heaps of white and lilac ashes in the grass. He thought of the sombre-eyed Matazel and remembered his threat.

At this lonely camp Huett fell back wholly into the content of his pondering dream. He had not enjoyed the military service. The range life he had led before his campaign suited him better. But he had long dreamed of being a cowboy for himself. The hard riding, the camp fare, the perilous work and adventure were much to his liking, but he had revolted against the noisy, bottle-loving, improvident louts with whom he had to ride.

He broiled turkey over the red coals of his dying aspenwood fire. With salt, a hard biscuit, and a cup of coffee he thought he fared sumptuously. In that still autumn close of day, in the whispering forest Logan Huett found himself. He might have been aware of the surpassing beauty of the glade, of the giant pines and silver spruce, of the white and gold aspen grove on the slope, of the spot of scarlet maple higher up, but he did not think of it that way. He was alone again. Slowly the pondering thought of his long-cherished plan faded into sensorial perceptions. The gusto with which he ate the hot turkey meat, the smell of the woodsmoke, the changing of the colored shadows all about him, the tinkle of the little stream, the crack of deer or elk horns on a dead branch up the canyon, the whisper in the tips of the spruce, the watching, listening sense of his loneliness,— these he felt with singularly sweet and growing vividness, but he did not think of them. He did not know that they accounted for his content. He never established any relation between them and the life of his ancestors or the primitive heritage they had left him.

He slept in his clothes, between his saddle-blankets, with his saddle for a pillow. When the fire burned down, the cold awakened him and he had to get up to replenish it. At dawn crackling white frost covered the grass. Going out to procure firewood he saw bear tracks in an open place. These had been made by a cinnamon, as he could tell by the narrow heel. A cinnamon bear was not the most welcome visitor a camper could have in those hills.

Huett made an early start and headed north down the canyon. Deer, elk, coyotes melted up the slopes at his approach. The tips of the pines high on the western ridge-crest turned gold and gradually that bright hue descended. Not until the sun was on the grass in the canyon did he see any turkeys. After that he came upon flock after flock, one in particular being composed of huge old bronze and white gobblers, with red heads and long beards, wild from age and experience.

All this continual sight of game quickened his interest and speculation in a canyon he knew and which he was going to visit. For three years this canyon had been a subject of intensive thought.

He was not certain he could reach it that day, for he had much travel up and down the ridges which lay between. When he had journeyed perhaps a score of miles down from the rim and the canyon was widening and growing shallow, he took to the slope and headed west. Travel then was slow, up through brush and across ridge, around windfalls and down into another canyon. He kept this up for hours. Most of the larger canyons had seldom-ridden trails along the brooks that traversed them.

When the giant silver spruce trees that flourished only at high altitude began to fail Huett knew he was getting down country and perhaps too far north. He swerved more to the west. Dusk found him entering one of the endless little grassy parks. He camped, and found the night appreciably warmer. Next morning he was off at dawn.

About noon, in the full light of sun, Huett came out upon the edge of the canyon that he had run across while hunting three years before and had passed twice since, once in early winter. Compared to many of the great valleys he had crossed this one was insignificant. But it had peculiar features, no doubt known only to himself, and which made it of extreme interest.

He had never ridden completely around this canyon or from end to end. This part that he had hit upon happened to be toward the south, and it was impossible to ride down into it from where he worked along the rim. He came at length to the great basin with which he was familiar. It had no outlet. The sparkling stream, shining like a ribbon, disappeared in the rocks under the south wall. Huett circumnavigated the basin, which, as far as he could determine, was the largest open pasture in the Mogollon forest. It was oblong in shape, of varying width. and miles long. All around the top ran a rim of gray or yellow limestone, an insignificant wall of rock: crumbling, of no particular height, and certainly something few men would have looked at twice.

But for Logan Huett that band of rock possessed marvelous interest. It was a natural fence. Cattle could not climb out of this canyon. Here was a range large enough to run twenty, probably thirty thousand head of stock, without the need of riders. This canyon had haunted Logan Huett. Here his passion to be a cattleman could be realized, and without any particular capital he could build up a fortune.

Huett rode around the south side and up along the west, finding a few breaks that would have to be fenced. Heavy pine forest covered this western slope. Scarcely a mile back in the woods ran the road from Flagstaff into the little hamlet of Payson, through the rough brakes of the Tonto, down to the Four Peak Range, and out to Phoenix. Settlers looking for ranges to homestead passed that point every summer, never dreaming of what Huett now saw—the most wonderful range in Arizona.

Apaches had once used this beautiful site for a hunting camp. Huett had found arrow heads there and bits of flint where some old savage had chipped his points. The brook made several turns between the gradually leveling slopes. Scattered pines trooped down to the deep blue pools. The bench on the east side had waited for ages for the homesteader to throw up his log cabin there. It was a level bit of ground, above the swift bend of the stream, and marked by a few splendid pine trees. A magnificent spring gushed from the foot of the slope. Deer and elk trails led up through a wide break in the rock wall. This opening, and a larger one at the head of the canyon were the only breaks in the upper half of the natural fence.

"I'll come back," soliloquized Huett, with finality. For

so momentous a decision he showed neither passion nor romance. He had a life work set out before him. This was the place. He wasted no more time there, but rode across the flat below the bench, and climbed the west slope. At the summit he turned for one last look. His glance caught the white and bronze of the great sycamore tree shining among the pines. In honor of that tree Huett named his ranch Sycamore Canyon.

The early afternoon hour gave him hope that he could make Mormon Lake before night. The dusty road held to the levels of the dense pine forest, and Huett did not know the country well enough to try a short cut. Trotting his horse, with intervals of restful walk, he made good time.

A new factor suddenly engaged Logan's mind. He wanted a wife. The life of a lonely ranchman in the wilderness appealed strongly to him, but a capable woman would add immeasurably to his chances of success without interfering with his love of solitude. While he was employing the daylight hours with his labors and his hunting, she would be busy at household tasks and the garden.

Lucinda Baker would be his first choice. She had been sixteen years old when he left Independence, a robust blooming girl, sensible and clever, and not too pretty. She had told him that she liked him better than any of her other friends. On the strength of that Logan had written her a few times during his absence, and had been promptly answered. Not for six months or more now, however, had he heard from Lucinda. She was teaching school, according to her last letter, and helping her ailing mother with the children. It crossed Logan's mind that she might have married some one else, or might refuse him; but it never occurred to him that if she accepted him he would be dooming her to a lonely existence in the wilderness.

Thinking of Lucinda Baker reminded Logan that he had not been much in the company of women. However, she had always seemed to understand him. As he rode along through the shady silent forest, he remembered Lucinda with a warmth of pleasure.

By sunset that day Huett reached the far end of Mormon Lake, a muddy body of surface water, surrounded by stony, wooded bluffs. On the west and north sides there were extensive ranges of grass running arm-like into the forest. The Mormon settler who had given the lake its name had sold out to an Arizonian and his partner from Kansas.

"Wal, we got a good thing hyar," said the Westerner Holbert. "But what with the timber wolves an' hard winters we have tough sleddin'. You see its open range an' pretty high."

"Any neighbors?" asked Huett.

"None between hyar an' the Tonto. Jackson runs one of Babbitt's outfits down on Clear Creek. Thet heads in above Long Valley. Then there's Jeff an' Bill Warner, out on the desert. They run a lot of cattle between Clear Creek an' the Little Colorado. Toward Flagg my nearest neighbor is Dwight Collin He has a big ranch ten miles in. An' next is Tim Mooney. Beyond St. Mary's Lake the settlers thicken up a bit."

"Any rustlers?"

"Wal, not any out an' out rustlers," replied Holbert evasively. "Rustler gangs have yet to settle in this section of Arizona."

"Wolves take toll of your calves, eh?"

"Cost me half a hundred head last winter. Did you ever hear of Killer Gray?"

"Not that I remember."

"Wal, you'd remember thet lofer, if you ever seen him. Big gray timber wolf with a black ruff. He's got a small band an' he ranges this whole country."

"Why don't you kill him?"

"Huh! He's too smart for us. Jest natural cunnin', for a young wolf."

"I like this Arizona timber land," declared Huett, frankly. "And I'm set on a ranch somewhere south of the lake."

"Wal now, thet's interestin'. What did you say yore name was?"

"Logan Huett. I rode for several cattle outfits before I worked a scout and hunter for Crook in his Apache campaign."

"I kinda reckoned you was a soldier," returned Holbert, genially. "Wal, Huett, you're as welcome out hyar as May flowers. I hope you don't locate too far south of us. It's shore lonely, an' in winter we're snowed in some seasons for weeks."

"Thanks. I'll pick me out a range down in the woods where it's not so cold. . . . Would you be able to sell me a few cows and heifers, and a bull?"

"I shore would. An' dirt cheap, too, 'cause thet'd save me from makin' a drive to town before winter comes."

"Much obliged, Holbert. I've saved my wages. But they won't last long. I'll pick up the cattle on my way back."

"Good. An' how soon, Huett?"

"Before the snow flies."

All the way into Flagg next day Logan's practical mind resolved a daring query. Why not wire Lucinda to come West to marry him? He resisted this idea, repudiated it, but it returned all the stronger. Logan's mother had not long survived his father. He had a brother and sister living somewhere in Illinois. Therefore since he had no kindred ties, he did not see why it would not be politic to save the time and expense that it would take to get him to Missouri. He had already bought cattle. He was eager to buy horses, oxen, wagon, tools, guns, and hurry back to Sycamore Canyon. The more time he had in Flagg the better bargains he could find.

Flagg was a cattle and lumber town, important since the advent of the railroad some half dozen years previously. It had grown since Huett's last visit. The main block presented a solid front of saloons and gambling halls, places Logan resolved to give a wide berth. He was no longer a cowboy. Some man directed him to a livery-stable where he turned over his horse. Next he left his pack at a lodginghouse and hunted up a barber shop. It was dusk when he left there. The first restaurant he encountered was run by a Chinaman and evidently a rendezvous for cowboys, of which the town appeared full. Logan ate and listened.

After supper he strolled down to the railroad station, a rude frame structure in the center of a square facing the main street. Evidently a train was expected. The station and platform presented a lively scene with cowboys, cattlemen, railroad men, Indians and Mexicans moving about. Logan's walk became a lagging one, and ended short of the station-house. It seemed to him that there might be something amiss in telegraphing Lucinda such a blunt and hurried proposal. But he drove this thought away, besides calling upon impatience to bolster up his courage. It could do no harm. If Lucinda refused he would just have to go East after her. Logan bolted into the station and sent Lucinda a telegram asking her to come West to marry him.

When the deed was done irrevocably, Logan felt appalled. He strode up town and tried to forget his brazen audacity in the excitement of the gambling-games. He suppressed a strong inclination toward drink. Liquor had never meant much to Logan, but it was omnipresent here in this hustling, loud cow town, and he felt its influence. Finally he went back to the lodginghouse and to bed. He felt tired—something unusual for him—and his mind whirled.

The soft bed was conducive to a long restful sleep. Logan awoke late, arose leisurely, and dressed for the business of the day. Presently he recalled with a little shock just how important a day it was to be in his life. But he did not rush to the telegraph office. He ate a hearty breakfast, made the acquaintance of a droll Arizona cowboy, and then reluctantly and fearfully went to see if there was any reply to his telegram. The operator grinned at Logan and drawled as he handed out a yellow envelope: "Logan Huett. There shore is a heap of a message for you."

Logan took the envelope eagerly, as abashed as a schoolboy, and the big brown hands that could hold a rifle steady as a rock shook perceptibly as he tore it open and read the brief message. He gulped and read it again: "Yes! If you come after me—Lucinda."

An unfamiliar sensation assailed him, as he moved away to a seat. Then he felt immensely grateful to Lucinda. He read her message again. The big thing about the moment seemed the certainty that he was to have a wife—provided he went back to Missouri after her. That he would do. But it flashed across his mind that as Lucinda had accepted him upon such short blunt notice she really must care a good deal for him, and if she did she would come West to marry him. Under the impulse of the inspiration he went to the window and began a long telegram to Lucinda, warm with gratitude at her acceptance and stressing the value of time, that winter was not far away, the need of economy, the splendid opportunity he had, ending with an earnest appeal for her to come West at once. Logan did not even read the message over, but sent it rushed up town.

"I've a hunch—she'll come—and I'm dog-gone lucky," he panted.

That day he spent in making a list of the many things he would need and the few he would be able to buy. Rifles, shells, axes, blankets, food supplies and cooking utensils, a wagon and horses, or mules, he had to have. Then he hurried from his lodginghouse to make these imperative purchases. Prices were reasonable, which fact encouraged him. During the day he met and made friends with a blacksmith from Missouri named Hardy. Hardy had tried farming, and had fallen back upon his trade. He offered Logan a wagon, a yoke of oxen, some farming tools, and miscellaneous hardware for what Huett thought was a sacrifice. That bargain ended a day that had passed along swiftly.

"My luck's in," exulted Logan, and on the strength of that belief he hurried to the railroad-station. Again there was a telegram for him. Before he opened it he knew Lucinda would come. Her brief reply was: "Leave to-morrow. Arrive Tuesday. Love. Lucinda."

"Now, there's a girl!" ejaculated Huett, in great relief and satisfaction. Then he stared at the word love. He had forgotten to include that in either of his telegrams. As a matter of fact the sentiment love had not occurred to him. But still, he reflected, a man would have to be all sorts of a stick not to respond to one such as Lucinda Baker. Logan recalled with strong satisfaction that she had not been very popular with certain boys because she would not spoon. He had liked her for that. All at once his satisfaction and gladness glowed into something strange and perturbing. The fact of her coming to marry him grew real; he must try to think of that as well as the numberless things important toward the future of his ranch.

The next day, Saturday, saw Huett labor strenuous hours between daylight and dark. Sunday at the blacksmith's he packed and helped his friend rig a canvas cover over the wagon. This would keep the contents dry and serve as a place to sleep during the way down. Monday, finding he still had a couple of hundred dollars left, Logan bought horse and saddle, some tinned goods, and dried fruits, a small medicine case, some smoking tobacco, and last a large box of candy for his prospective bride.

This present brought him to the very necessary consideration of how and where he could be married. Here the blacksmith again came to his assistance. There was a parson in town who would "hitch you up pronto for a five dollar gold piece!"

Two overland trains rolled in from the East every day, the first arriving at eighty-thirty in the morning, and the second at ten in the evening. On board one of these today would be Lucinda Baker.

"Hope she comes on the early one," said Logan aloud, when he presented himself at the station far ahead of time. "We can get the 'hitch pronto' as Hardy calls it, and be off today."

It did not take Logan long to discover that the most important daily event in Flagg was the arrival of this morning train. The platform might have been a promenade, to the annoyance of the railroad men. Logan leaned against the hitching-rail and waited. Obstreperous cowboys clanked along with their awkward stride, ogling the girls. Mexicans, with blanketed shoulders, lounged about, their sloe-black eyes watchful, while handsome Navajo braves with colorful bands around their heads, padded to and fro with their moccasined tread. Lucinda would be much impressed by them, thought Logan.

The train whistled from around the pine-forested bend. Logan felt a queer palpitation that he excused as unusual eagerness and gladness. Small wonder—a fellow's bride came only once!

Presently Logan saw the dusty brown train, like a long scaly snake coiling behind a puffing black head, come into sight to straighten out and rapidly draw near. The engine passed with a steaming roar. Logan counted the cars. Then with a grinding of steel on steel the train came to a halt.

Chapter Two

LUCINDA BAKER's dreams of romance and adventure had been secrets no one had ever guessed; but none of them had ever transcended this actual journey of hers to the far West to become the wife of her girlhood sweetheart. Yet it seemed she had been preparing for some incredible adventure ever since Logan had left Independence. How else could she account for having become a school teacher at sixteen, working through the long vacations, her strong application to household duties? She had always known that Logan Huett would never return home again, and that the great unknown West had claimed him. For this reason, if any, she had been training herself to become a pioneer's wife.

She was thrillingly happy. She had left her family well and comfortable. She was inexpressably glad to be away from persistent suitors. She was free to be herself—the half savage yearning creature she knew under her skin. Steady, plodding, dutiful, unsentimental Lucinda Baker was relegated to the past.

Kansas in autumn was one vast seared rolling prairie, dotted with hamlets and towns along the steel highway. Lucinda grew tired watching the endless roll and stretch of barren land. She interested herself in her fellow-passengers and their children, all simple middle-class people like herself, journeying West to take up that beckoning life of the ranges. But what she saw of Colorado before dark, the gray swelling slopes toward the heave and bulk of dim mountains, gave her an uneasy, awesome premonition of a fearful wildness and ruggedness of nature much different from the pictures she had imagined. She awoke in New Mexico, to gaze in rapture at its silver valleys, its dark forests, its sharp peaks white against the blue. But Arizona, the next day, crowned Lucinda's magni-

fied expectations. During the night the train had traversed
nearly half of this strange glorious wilderness of purple
land. Sunshine, Canyon Diablo were but wayside sta-
tions. Were there no towns in this tremendous country?
Her query to the porter brought the information that
Flagg was the next stop, two hours later. Yet still Lucinda
feasted her gaze and tried not to think of Logan. Would
he disappoint her? She had loved him since she was a
little girl when he had rescued her from some beastly
boys who had dragged her into a mud puddle. But not
forgetting Logan's few and practical letters she argued
that his proposal of marriage was conclusive.

What changes would this hard country have wrought
in Logan Huett? What would it do to her? Lucinda
gazed with awe and fear out across this purple land,
monotonous for leagues on leagues, then startling with
magnificent red walls, towering and steep, that wandered
away into the dim mystic blue, and again shooting spear-
pointed, black-belted peaks skyward; and once the vista
was bisected by a deep narrow yellow gorge, dreadful to
gaze down into and justifying its diabolic name.

After long deliberation Lucinda reasoned that Logan
probably would not have changed much from the serious
practical boy to whom action was almost as necessary as
breathing. He would own a ranch somewhere close to a
town, perhaps near Flagg, and he would have friends
among these westerners. In this loyal way Lucinda subdued her qualms and shut her eyes so she could not see
the dense monotonous forest the train had entered. Surrendering to thought of Logan then, she found less
concern in how she would react to him than how he
would discover her. Lucinda knew that she had grown
and changed more after fifteen than was usual in girls.
What her friends and family had said about her im-
provement, and especially the boys who had courted her,

was far more flattering than justified, she felt. But perhaps it might be enough to make Logan fail to recognize her.

A shrill whistle disrupted Lucinda's meditation. The train was now clattering down grade and emerging from the green into a clearing. A trainman opened the coach-door to call out in sing-song voice: "Flagg. Stop five minutes."

Lucinda's eyes dimmed. She wiped them so she could see out. The Forest had given place to a ghastly area of bleached and burned stumps of trees. That led to a huge hideous structure with blue smoke belching from a great boiler-like chimney. Around it and beyond were piles of yellow lumber as high as houses. This was a sawmill. Lucinda preferred the forest to this crude and raw evidence of man's labors. Beyond were scattered little cabins made of slabs and shacks, all dreary and drab, unrelieved by any green.

As the train slowed down with a grind of wheels there was a noisy bustle in the coach. Many passengers were getting off here. Lucinda marked several young girls, one of them pretty with snapping eyes, who were excited beyond due. What would they have shown had they Lucinda's cue for feeling? She felt a growing tumult within, but outwardly she was composed.

When the train jarred to a stop, Lucinda lifted her two grips onto the seat and crossed the aisle to look out on that side. She saw up above the track a long block of queer, high, board fronted buildings all adjoining. They fitted her first impression of Flagg. Above the town block loomed a grand mountain, black and white in its magnificent aloof distance. Lucinda gasped at the grandeur of it. Then the moving and colorful throng on the platform claimed her quick attention.

First she saw Indians of a different type, slender, lithe, with cord bands around their black hair. They had lean clear-cut faces, sombre as masks. Mexicans in huge sombreros lolled in the background.

Then Lucinda's swift gaze alighted upon a broad-shouldered, powerfully built young man, in his shirt sleeves and with his blue jeans tucked in high boots. Logan! She sustained a combined shock and thrill. She would have known that strong tanned face anywhere. He stood bareheaded, with piercing eyes on the alighting passengers. Lucinda felt a rush of pride. The boy she knew had grown into a man, hard, stern, even in that expectant moment. But he was more than merely handsome. There appeared to be something proven about him.

Lucinda suddenly realized she must follow the porter, who took her grips, out of the coach. She could not resist a pat to her hair and a readjustment of her hat. Then she went out.

The porter was not quick enough to help her down the steep steps. That act was performed gallantly by a strange youthful individual, no less than Lucinda's first cowboy, red-haired, keen-faced, with a blue dancing devil in his eyes. He squeezed her arm.

"Lady, air yu meetin' anyone?" he queried, as if his life depended on her answer.

Lucinda looked over his head as if he had not been there. But she liked him. Leaving her grips where the porter had set them she walked up the platform, passing less then ten feet from Logan. He did not recognize her. That failure both delighted and frightened her. She would return and give him another chance.

She walked a few rods up the platform, and when she turned back she was reveling in the situation. Logan Huett had sent for his bride and did not know her when she looked point-blank at him. He had left his post at the rail. She located him coming up the platform. A moment later she found herself an object of undisguised speculation by three cowboys, one of whom was the redhead.

Lucinda slowed her pace. It would be fun to accost Logan before these bold westerners. This was an unfortunate impulse, as through it she heard remarks that made her neck and face burn.

Logan had halted just beyond the red-haired cowboy. His gray glance took Lucinda in from head to foot and back again—a swift questioning baffled look. Then Lucinda swept by the cowboys and spoke:

"Logan, don't you know me?"

"Ah!—no, you can't be her," he blurted out. "Lucinda! It *is* you!"

"Yes, Logan. I knew you from the train."

He made a lunge for her, eager and clumsy, and kissed her heartily, missing her lips. "To think I didn't know my old sweetheart!" His gray eyes, that had been like bits of ice glistening in the sun, shaded and softened with a warm glad light that satisfied Lucinda's yearning heart.

"Have I changed so much?" she asked, happily, and that nameless dread broke and vanished in the released tumult within her breast.

"Well, I should smile you have," he said. "Yet, somehow you're coming back. . . . Lucinda, the fact is I didn't expect so—so strapping and handsome a girl."

"That's a doubtful compliment, Logan," she replied with a laugh. "But I hope you like me."

"I'm afraid I do—powerful much," he admitted. "But I'm sort of taken back to see you grown up into a lady, stylish and dignified."

"Wouldn't you expect that from a school teacher?"

"I'm afraid I don't know what to expect. But in a way, out here, your school teaching may come in handy."

"We have to get acquainted and find out all about each other," she said, naïvely.

"I should smile—and get married in the bargain, all in one day."

"All today?"

"Lucinda, I'm in a hurry to go," he replied, anxiously. "I've bought my outfit and we'll leave town—soon as we get it over."

"Well . . . of course we must be married at once. But to rush away. . . . It isn't far—is it—your ranch? I hope near town."

"Pretty far," he rejoined. "Four days, maybe five with oxen and cattle."

"Is it out there—in the—the . . . ? she asked, faintly, with a slight gesture toward the range.

"South sixty miles. Nice drive most of the way, after we leave town."

"Forest—like that the train came through?"

"Most of the way. But there are lakes, sage flats, desert. Wonderful country."

"Logan, of course you're located—near a town?" she faltered.

"Flagg is the closest," he answered, patiently, as if she were a child.

Lucinda bit her lips to hold back an exclamation of dismay. Her strong capable hands trembled slightly as she opened her pocketbook. "Here are my checks. I brought a trunk and a chest. My hand-baggage is there."

"Trunk and chest! Golly, where'll I put them? We'll have a wagonload," he exclaimed, and taking the checks he hailed an expressman outside the rail. He gave him instructions, pointing out the two bags on the platform, then returned to Lucinda.

"Dear! You're quite pale," he said anxiously. "Tired from the long ride?"

"I'm afraid so. But I'll be—all right. . . . Take me somewhere."

"That I will. To Babbitts', where you can buy anything from a needle to a piano. You'll be surprised to see a bigger store than there is in Kansas City."

"I want to get some things I hadn't time for."

"Fine. After we buy the wedding-ring. The parson told me not to forget that."

Lucinda kept pace with his stride up town. But on the moment she did not evince her former interest in cowboys and westerners in general, nor the huge barn-like store he dragged her into. She picked out a plain wedding-ring and left it on her finger as if she was afraid to remove it. Logan's earnest face touched her. For his sake she fought the poignant and sickening sensations that seemed to daze her.

"Give me an hour here—then come after me," she said.

"So long! Why, for goodness' sake?"

"I have to buy a lot of woman's things."

"Lucinda, my money's about gone," he said, perturbed. "It just melted away. I put aside some to pay Holbert for cattle I bought at Mormon Lake."

"I have plenty, Logan. I saved my salary," she returned, smilingly. But she did not mention the five hundred dollars her uncle had given her for a wedding-present. Lucinda had a premonition she would need that money.

"Good! Lucinda, you always were a saving girl. . . . Come, let's get married pronto. Then you come back here while I repack that wagon." He slipped his arm under hers and hustled her along. How powerful he was and what great strides he took! Lucinda wanted to cry out for a little time to adjust herself to this astounding situation. But he hurried her out of the store and up the street, talking earnestly. "Here's a list

of the stuff I bought for our new home. Doesn't that
sound good? Aw, I'm just tickled. . . . Read it over.
Maybe you'll think of things I couldn't. You see we'll
camp out while we're throwing up our log cabin. We'll
live in my big canvas-covered wagon—a regular prairie-
schooner, till we get the cabin up. We'll have to hustle,
too, to get that done before the snow flies. . . . It's
going to be fun—and heaps of work—this start of mine
at ranching. Oh, but I'm glad you're such a strapping
girl! . . . Lucinda, I'm lucky. I mustn't forget to tell
you how happy you've made me. I'll work for you. Some
day I'll be able to give you all your heart could desire."

"So we spend our honeymoon in a prairie-schooner!"
she exclaimed, with a weak laugh.

"Honeymoon?— So we do. I never thought of that.
But many a pioneer girl has done so. . . . Lucinda, if
I remember right you used to drive horses. Your Dad's
team?"

"Logan, I drove the buggy," she rejoined, aghast at
what she divined was coming.

"Same thing. You drove me home from church once.
And I put my arm around you. Remember?"

"I must—since I am here."

"You can watch me drive the oxen, and learn on the
way to Mormon Lake. There I have to take to the saddle
and rustle my cattle through. You'll handle the wagon."

"What!—Drive a yoke of oxen? *Me!*"

"Sure. Lucinda, you might as well start right in.
You'll be my partner. And I've a hunch no pioneer ever
had a better one. We've got the wonderfullest range in
Arizona. Wait till you see it! Some day we'll run thirty
thousand head of cattle there. . . . Ah, here's the parson's house. I darn near overrode it. Come, Lucinda.
If you don't back out pronto it'll be too late."

"Logan—I'll never—back out," she whispered, huskily.

She felt herself drawn into the presence of kindly people who made much over her, and before she could realize what was actually happening she was made the wife of Logan Huett. Then Logan, accompanied by the black-bearded blacksmith Hardy, dragged her away to see her prairie-schooner home. Lucinda recovered somewhat on the way. There would not have been any sense in rebelling even if she wanted to. Logan's grave elation kept her from complete collapse. There was no denying his looks and actions of pride in his possession of her.

At sight of the canvas-covered wagon Lucinda shrieked with hysterical laughter, which Logan took for mirth. It looked like a collapsed circus-tent hooped over a long box on wheels. When she tiptoed to peep into the wagon a wave of strongly contrasted feeling flooded over her. The look, the smell of the jumbled wagonload brought Lucinda rudely and thrillingly to the other side of the question. That wagon reeked with an atmosphere of pioneer enterprise, of adventure, of struggle with the soil and the elements.

"How perfectly wonderful!" she cried, surrendering to that other self. "But Logan, after you pack my baggage in here—where will we sleep?"

"Doggone-it! We'll sure be loaded, 'specially if you buy a lot more. But I'll manage some way till we get into camp. Oh, I tell you, wife, nothing can stump me! . . . I'll make room for you in there and I'll sleep on the ground."

"Haw! Haw!" roared the black-bearded giant. "Thet's the pioneer spirit."

"Logan, I daresay you'll arrange it comfortably for me, at least," said Lucinda, blushing. "I'll run back to the store now. Will you pick me up there? You must give me plenty of time and be prepared to pack a lot more."

"Better send it out here," replied Logan, scratching his chin thoughtfully.

"Mrs. Huett, you'll change your clothes before you go?" inquired the blacksmith's comely wife. "That dress won't do for campin' oot on this desert. You'll spoil it, an' freeze in the bargain."

"You bet she'll change," interposed Logan, with a grin. "I'd never forget that. . . . Lucinda, dig out your old clothes before I pack these bags."

"I didn't bring any old clothes," retorted Lucinda.

"And you going to drive oxen, cook over a wood fire, sleep on hay and a thousand other pioneer jobs? . . . Well, while you're at that buying don't forget jeans and socks and boots—a flannel shirt and heavy coat—and a sombrero to protect your pretty white face from the sun. And heavy gloves, my dear, and a silk scarf to keep the dust from choking you."

"Oh, is that all?" queried Lucinda, soberly. "You may be sure I'll get them."

Hours later Lucinda surveyed herself before Mrs. Hardy's little mirror, and could not believe the evidence of her own eyes. But the blacksmith's good wife expressed pleasure enough to assure Lucinda that from her own point of view she was a sight to behold. Yet when had she ever felt so comfortable as in this cowboy garb?

"How'll I ever go out before those men?" exclaimed Lucinda, in dismay. A little crowd had collected round the prairie-schooner, to the back of which Logan appeared to be haltering his horses.

"My dear child, all women oot heah wear pants an' ride straddle," said Mrs. Hardy, with mild humor. "I'll admit you look more fetchin' than most gurls. But you'll get used to it."

"Fetching?" repeated Lucinda, dubiously. Then she

packed away the traveling-dress, wondering if or when she would ever wear it again. The western woman read her mind.

"Settlers oot on the range don't get to town often," she vouchsafed, with a smile. "But they *do* come, an' like it all the better. Be brave now, an' take your medicine, as we westerners say. Yore man will make a great rancher, so Hardy says. Never forget thet the woman settler does the bigger share of the work, an' never gets the credit due her."

"Thank you, Mrs. Hardy," replied Lucinda, grateful for sympathy and advice. "I begin to get a glimmering. But I'll go through with it. . . . Goodbye."

Lucinda went out, carrying her bag, and she tried to walk naturally when she had a mad desire to run.

"Whoopee!" yelled Logan.

If they had been alone that startling tribute to her attire would have pleased Lucinda. Anything to rouse enthusiasm or excitement in this strange, serious husband! But to call attention to her before other men, and worse, before some wild, ragged little imps—that was signally embarrassing.

"Hey lady," piped up one of the boys, "fer cripes' sake, don't ya stoop over in them pants!"

That sally elicited a yell of mirth from Logan. The other men turned their backs with hasty and suspicious convulsions. Lucinda hurried on with burning face.

"Jiminy, she'll make a hot tenderfoot cowgirl," called out another youngster.

Lucinda gained the wagon without loss of dignity, except for her blush, which she hoped the wide-brimmed sombrero would hide. She stowed her bag under the seat and stepped up on the hub of the wheel. When she essayed another hasty step, from the hub to the high rim of the wheel she failed and nearly fell. Her blue jeans were too tight. Then Logan gave her a tremendous boost. She landed on the high seat, awkwardly but safely, amid the cheers of the watchers. From this vantage point Lucinda's adventurous spirit and sense of humor routed her confusion and fury. She looked down upon her glad-eyed husband and the smiling westerners, and then at those devilish little imps.

"You were all tenderfeet once," she said to the men, with a laugh, and then shook her finger at the urchins. "I've spanked many boys as big as you."

Logan climbed up on the other side to seize a short stick with a long leather thong.

"Hardy, how do you drive these oxen?" called Logan, as if remembering an important item at the last moment.

"Wal, Logan, thar's nothin' to thet but gadep, gee, whoa, an' haw." replied the blacksmith, with a grin. "Easy as pie. They're a fine trained brace."

"Adios, folks. See you next spring," called Logan, and cracked the whip with a yell: *"Gidap!"*

The oxen swung their huge heads together and moved. The heavy wagon rolled easily. Lucinda waved to the blacksmith's wife, and then at the boys. Their freckled faces expressed glee and excitement. The departure of that wagon meant something they felt but did not understand. One of them cupped his hands round his mouth to shrill a last word to Lucinda.

"All right, lady. Yu can be our schoolmarm an' spank us if you wear them pants!"

Lucinda turned quickly to the front. "Oh, the nerve of that little rascal! . . . Logan, what's the matter with my blue-jeans pants—that boys should talk so?"

"Nothing. They're just great. Blue-jeans are as common out here as flapjacks. But I never saw such a—a revealing pair as yours."

The oxen plodded along, the canvas-covered wagon

rolled down the side street. It must have been an ordinary sight in Flagg, because the few passers-by did not look twice at it. Lucinda felt relieved at escaping more curiosity and ridicule. What would that trio of cowboys have said? Logan drove across the railroad, on over a rattling wooden bridge, by the cottages and cabins, and at last by the black and yellow sawmill.

"Darling, we're off!" exclaimed Logan, quite suddenly, and he placed a powerful hand over hers. With the whip he pointed south beyond the hideous slash of forest, to the dim blui of range beyond. His voice sang deep and rich with emotion. "We're on our way to my ranch-- to our home in Sycamore Canyon."

"Yes, Logan. I gathered something of the kind. . . . I'm very happy," she replied, softly, surprised and moved by his term of endearment and the manifestation of strong feeling.

"I've just lived for this. It's what I worked for—saved my money for. Down there hides my canyon—the grandest range for cattle—grass and water—all fenced. And here's my outfit all paid for. And last and best the finest little women who ever came out to help build up the West!"

Lucinda settled back happily. She had misjudged Logan's appreciation of her and her sacrifice if not his absorption in his passion for the cattle-range. But she could forgive that, respect it, and cleave to him with joy now that she knew he loved her.

The road wound through the denuded forest-land, dry but not dusty, and down-grade enough to make an easy pull for the oxen. A sweet musty fragrance came on the slight warm breeze. It grew from pleasant to exhilarating, and Lucinda asked her husband what it was. Dry Arizona he replied—a mixture of sage, cedar, piñon and pine. Lucinda liked it, which was all she did like on that six mile drive out to the forest. Here the cabin

and pastures, with their crude fences of poles, appeared
to end. Driving into the forest was like entering a green-
canopied brown-pillared tunnel. It was still, shadowed,
lighted by golden shafts, and strangely haunting. Lucinda
was affected by a peculiar feeling she could not define.
It had to do with a strange sense of familiarity when she
had never before been in a forest.

Before sunset Logan drove into a wide open place.
"We'll camp on the far side," he said. "Water and grass.
And firewood—well, Lucinda, we'll never be in want
for firewood."

They halted under great pines that stood out from the
wall of forest. Wrecks of trees that Logan called windfalls lay about, some yellow and splintered still, others
old and gray, falling to decay. Logan leaped down, and
when Lucinda essayed to follow he lifted her down with
a hug. "Now, tenderfoot wife, tight pants and all, you
can begin!" he said, gayly. But he did not tell her what
to begin, and Lucinda stood there stupidly while he
unyoked the oxen, turned them loose, then started to
lift bags and boxes out of the wagon. He lifted her trunk
down with such ease that Lucinda marveled, remembering how her father had to have help in moving it.

"That'll go under the wagon," he said. "Don't worry.
I'll cover it. But the rains are past, Lucinda. What we
get next will be snow. Whew! Does it snow and blow!"

"Logan, I hate wind and I don't like snow."

"I daresay. You'll get over that in Arizona. . . .
Now, Lucinda, you watch me and learn." He spread a
heavy canvas on the grass. Then from a box he took
canvas bags of varying sizes, which he set down side by
side. He emptied a burlap sack of jangling things that
proved to be funny little iron kettles with lids, coffee-
pot, skillet, pans and plates, cups of tin, and other
utensils. Then he loosened several buckets that fit one

into the other. These he plunged into the brook to swing out brimming full of water. All his movements were quick, vigorous, yet deft. It was wonderful to watch him ply an axe. Chips and splinters and billets flew as if by magic. He built a roaring fire, explaining that it must burn down to a bed of red coals. Next, like a juggler, he produced washbasin, soap and towel, and thoroughly washed his hands. . . . "Most important of all," he said with a grin. "Now watch me mix sourdough biscuits." She did watch the procedure with intense interest. Here was her husband encroaching on the preserves of a house-wife. But she was fascinated. He was efficient, he was really wonderful to a tenderfoot girl. To see that brawny-shouldered young man on his knees before a pan of flour and water, to watch his big brown hands skillfully mix the dough was a revelation to Lucinda. With the further preparation of the meal he was equally skillful. She sat down cross-legged, despite the tight breeches, and most heartily enjoyed her first supper in Arizona. She was famished. Logan had forgotten to take her to lunch. Ham and eggs, biscuits and coffee, with canned peaches for dessert, and finally the big box of candy that Logan produced from somewhere, as an especial present on that day—these certainly satisfied more than hunger for Lucinda.

"Logan, you amaze me. You're a splendid cook," she said. "It's just fine to think *I* won't have to cook and bake."

"Ha! Ha! No you won't atall!" he ejaculated, gayly. "But I'm glad you see I can do it. . . . Now we'll clear up. I'll wash and you dry."

After these chores were finished Logan went into the woods with an axe, to come forth burdened under an immense load of green fragrant boughs. This he threw down beside the wagon. Then he unrolled a canvas to take out blankets.

"There's hardly enough room in the wagon for you to sleep, let alone me," he said. "I'll make my bed on the ground. If skunks and coyotes, scorpions, tarantulas and sidewinders come around they'll get me first. Ha! Ha! But really they're not to be laughed at. I won't take any risk of you being bitten, especially by a hydrophobia skunk. You're too dog-gone precious. I'd never find another woman like you."

Lucinda said nothing. His words, like his actions, were so natural, so inevitable. Yet he showed fine feeling. She was a bride and this was her wedding-night. Dusk came trooping out of the forest. She heard a sough of wind in the pines, an uneasy breathing melancholy sound. How lonely! She shivered a little. Logan's observations were keen. He fetched her heavy coat. Then he threw a bundle of the green pine foliage into the wagon, and some blankets, and climbed in the door after them. Lucinda heard him rummaging around at a great rate. Presently he leaped out, his hair rumpled.

"There! All you got to do is use your coat for a pillow, take off your boots, crawl under the blankets, and you'll be jake. . . . Well, the day is done. Our first day! . . . Now for a smoke. Lucinda, better stretch your legs a little before we turn in."

She walked under the pines, along the brook, out into the open. But she did not go far. The windfalls, the clumps of sage might harbor some of the varmints Logan feared. She looked back to see he had replenished the camp fire. He stood beside it, a tall dark stalwart figure, singularly fitting this unfamiliar scene. There appeared to be something wild and raw, yet thrilling about it. The flames lighted up the exquisite lacy foliage of the pines. Sparks flew upward. The great white wagon loomed like a spectre. Black always depressed Lucinda, but white frightened her. Logan stood there spreading his hands. . . . He was splendid, she thought. She could well transfer the love she had given him as a boy to the grown man, for Logan had matured beyond his years. In repose his face showed fine stern lines. He had suffered pain, hardship, if not grief. Lucinda's fears of Logan vanished like the columns of smoke blowing away into the darkness. She had vague fears of this West and she divined they would be magnified and multiplied, but never would there be a fear of Logan Huett. Whatever it would cost her she was glad she had answered to his call for a mate, and she would try to make herself a worthy one.

She returned to the fire and warmed her hands over the blaze. How quickly the air had chilled!

"I never knew how good fire could feel," she said, laughing.

"Ha! You said a lot." Then he drew her to a seat on the log nearby. He removed his pipe and knocked the ashes from it. "Lucinda, I'm not much of a fellow to talk," he said, earnestly, with the light from the fire playing on his dark strong face and in his clear gray eyes. "Sure, I'll talk your head off about cattle and range, bears and cougars, Indians and all that's wild. But I mean the—the deep things—the things here—" and he tapped his broad breast. "I've got them here, only they're hard to say. . . . Anyway, words would never tell how I appreciate your leaving your people, your friends, and civilized comforts, to come out to this wild Arizona range. To be my wife—my pardner! It's almost too good to be true. And I love you for it. . . . I reckon I was selfish to make you come to me and rush you at that. But you'll forgive me when you see our ranch—the work that's to be done—and winter coming fast. . . . You're only a young girl, Lucinda. Only eighteen! And I feel shame to think what you must have overcome—before you accepted. But, my dear, don't fear I'll rush you into real wifehood, you know, like I did into marriage. All in good time, Lucinda, when you feel you know me as I am now, and love me, and want to come to me. . . . That's all, little girl. Kiss me goodnight and go to your bed in our prairie-schooner."

Lucinda did as she was bidden, relieved and comforted as she had not thought possible except after long trial. She peeped out to see Logan in the flickering firelight. Then she crawled under the warm woolen blankets. How strange! How marvelous to be there! She would not have exchanged that bed, and the canvas roof with its moving weird shadows, for the palace of a princess. But the wind moaned through the pines—moaned of the terrible loneliness, the distance, the wildness of this West.

Chapter Three

LUCINDA awakened sometime in the night, coming out of a dream of a strange pale place, where she wandered down empty echoing streets, fearful lest she should be seen in her boy's garb. The night was pitch dark and silent as the grave. The crickets, the wind, the brook had all but ceased their sounds. She was cold despite the blankets. She lay there shivering while the black canopy of the canvas changed to gray. Soon she heard sharp weird piercing yelps, wild and haunting.

Dawn came. The ring of an axe and splitting of wood told her that Logan had begun his work. Lucinda sat up with an impulse to go out and join him. But the keen air made her change her mind. When she heard a fire crackling, however, she threw back the blankets and hunted for her boots. By the time she had the second one laced her fingers were numb. She donned her coat, took her little bag and crawled out.

Logan was not in sight. Lucinda made for the fire. If it had felt good the night before what did it feel now? She had not known the blessing of heat. While she warmed her hands she gazed about. The grass was gray-white with frost; far across the open Logan appeared astride one of the horses, driving in the oxen. The sky in the east was ruddy, but the all-encompassing wall of pines appeared cold, forbidding. Logan had been thoughtful to put on a bucket of water to heat. Before he arrived at the camp Lucinda had washed her face and hands and combed her hair. This morning she braided it and let it hang.

"Howdy, settler," she called to Logan.

"Well! Hello, red-cheeks! Say, but you're good to see this morning. . . . How'd you rest?"

"Slept like a log. Awoke once, after a queer dream. I

was in a deserted town wandering about in these pants.
What made those barks I heard?"

"Coyotes. I like to hear them. But wolves make me
shiver. I saw the track of a big lofer out there."

"Lofer?"

"That's local for wolf. Perhaps that track was made by
Killer Gray. He's got a black ruff, Lucinda. I'll shoot
him and cure his hide for a rug. We must live off the
land."

Lucinda helped him prepare breakfast. Afterward, while
Logan hitched the oxen to the wagon Lucinda went after
the second horse. He was not easy to catch and the best
she could do was to drive him into camp where Logan
secured him. The exercise made her blood tingle, but
she was glad to warm hands and feet at the fire. The
red in the east paled and the sun arose steely. Logan,
remarking that the day was not going to be so good,
advised Lucinda to procure her gloves and put a blanket
on the seat.

Presently the oxen were swinging on, tirelessly, their
great heads nodding in unison. Lucinda marveled at
them. How patient, how plodding these gentle beasts
of burden! She had her first inkling of the value of such
animals to the settlers in the wilderness. Thick woods
swallowed up the wagon and claimed it for hours. But
Lucinda was more at ease because the cold wind was shut
off and the sun shone now and then.

"Move over here and take your lesson," said Logan,
at length, and put the whip in Lucinda's hands.

"What'll I do?" she asked, breathlessly.

"Drive," he replied, laconically.

Before she realized it Lucinda was piloting a prairie-
schooner. The oxen went along as well for her as for
Logan. But what would she do when he left the wagon

to handle the cattle? "It's easy," said Logan. "Much easier than driving a team."

"But suppose they do something," protested Lucinda.

"Yell 'whoa' when you want them to stop, 'gee' when you want to go to the right, 'haw' to the left, and when you start up—a crack of the whip and 'gidap,' " replied Logan, with suppressed mirth.

"It's not so funny," said Lucinda petulantly. "It looks *too* easy. They do go right along—but it's straight road. What if a herd of buffalo or band of Indians broke out of the woods. . . ."

"That sure wouldn't be funny. But the buffalo are gone, Lucinda, and we put the Apaches on the reservation. Reminds me of Matazel."

"Who was he?" asked Lucinda a little fearfully.

"Young Apache buck. Said to be one of old Geronimo's sons. He sure didn't favor that ugly old devil. Matazel looks a noble red man if ever an Indian gave reason for such a fool idea. Lucinda, the Navajo braves caught your fancy. Matazel would have done that and more. He had gray eyes—the most wonderful eyes! Wild, bright, fierce! I'll never forget the look in them when he tapped me on the breast and said: 'Matazel live—get even!' "

"My word! Logan, what ever did you do to incur his hatred?"

"Huh. I did a lot. I was one of General Crook's scouts. Crook sent me out with some soldiers to round up Matazel and his braves. I trailed them across the mesa and cornered them. We had a skirmish. Nobody killed. We captured Matazel and sent him back to the reservation with the rest of Geronimo's outfit. They'll break out some day."

"Won't that be bad for the settlers?"

"I reckon it will. But no danger for us. We are a long way from the Cibeque."

The wind increased until it began to blow the dust.
This, added to the cold, induced Lucinda to crawl back
over the seat and wrap herself in the blankets. Lucinda
propped herself against the packs and gazed out, thinking wearily of the women who had crossed the plains in
caravans. What incredible hardship and privation they
must have endured! The dim, dark forest, with its
threshing foliage, the open range with its flying dust,
the lowering sky, the slow steady roll of wheels, the dry
permeating pitchy odor that filled her nostrils—these
held Lucinda's senses until she fell asleep.

When she awakened Logan informed her that the lake
was in sight. Cramped and stiff Lucinda crawled back
on the seat with Logan. Gray pastures fringed by pine
led to a wide sheet of water, dark as the clouds. She saw
fences running up to cabins on the shore. The west side
of the lake sheered up in a bold bronze bluff, while the
road ran along the east shore, a ragged, rocky slope,
desolate and uninviting to Lucinda's gaze.

"Will these settlers want to take us in?" she asked.

"Sure. We'll eat with them, but we'll sleep same as
last night. They're crowded in those log shacks. You'll
be more comfortable in the wagon."

"I'd like that better," said Lucinda, with a sense of
relief.

Lucinda found herself welcomed by Holbert and his
womenfolk. If she had not been so cold and hungry and
miserable she might have regarded that poor cabin and
its plain inmates in some such way as she had the long
day and the hard country. But she realized that what
counted were protection and nourishment, and the kind
hearts that furnished them. Holbert's wife, two daughters, and a sister lived there with him. She gathered that
one of the daughters was married and lived in an adjoining cabin. They seemed to take Lucinda's advent as

a matter of course. The married daughter was younger than Lucinda and had a baby. None of them had been to Flagg since spring—six months—and they were hungry for the news that was easy for Lucinda to furnish.

Presently the son-in-law came in, accompanied by a gray-furred, wild-looking dog. He at once joined Holbert and Logan in a discussion of cattle.

"What a strange dog!" exclaimed Lucinda, who loved dogs. "Is he a shepherd?"

"Half shepherd an' half wolf," replied the settler's wife. "Her mother is John's best cattle dog."

"How interesting! Half wolf? I never saw a wolf. What's her name?"

"Reckon she hasn't none. She's no good because she won't run cattle an' fights the other dogs. John would be glad to get rid of her."

"Logan," asked Lucinda, eagerly interrupting the trio of men, "may I have this dog, if Mr. Holbert will give her to me?"

"Why, sure. How about it, Holbert?"

"You're welcome, if you can get her to go with you," replied the settler.

Lucinda made overtures to the unwanted wolf-dog, and they were accepted. When presently Lucinda grew so drowsy from the hot fire that she could scarcely keep her eyes open, Logan came to her rescue. They bade their new friends good-night and left for their wagon. The dog came readily with Lucinda.

"Rustle up to bed before you freeze again," said Logan, helping her along. "And here's your dog. I liked his looks. I'll bet he sticks to you."

"It's a she, Logan. What'll I call her? . . . Come, doggie, you can sleep right here at my feet."

"A good name always comes. . . . Luce, I'll go back and finish my deal with Holbert. He'll sell me some stock very cheap and give me more on credit. The drawback is there's no one here to help me drive the cattle. But by gosh! If you'll drive the oxen I'll drive all the cattle Holbert will let me have."

"I'll try," rejoined Lucinda, suppressing her fears because of his eager hope.

"There's an old homestead half way to our place. If we can make that tomorrow night and turn the stock inside the fence we'll be jake. Next night we'll be home!"

Lucinda pulled off her boots, and folding her coat for a pillow crawled under the blankets. The dog nestled close to her. Outside the wind was blowing a gale. As Logan had laced up the front flaps of the wagon Lucinda was protected. But to hear it was enough. It whistled hauntingly around the canvas and roared through the trees overhead and swept away scattering the pebbles and propelling the dust along the road. Finally Lucinda's drowsy spell ended in sleep.

Logan's voice penetrated Lucinda's deep slumbers. "Daybreak, Luce! Pile out and get going. . . . Did your dog stay with you? . . . Well, she did, by gosh! No man or varmint who ever pleased you would quit."

"Compliment so early?—Oh, Logan, I can't get up. It's so nice and warm in here. Ughh! . . . I guess I'm a tenderfoot."

"Well, Luce dear, you won't be one by nightfall, that's a good bet," replied Huett, grimly. "I'm going to start you out with the oxen and follow you with the stock. Then I'll be close to you. So you can't stop to pick flowers by the roadside."

The day promised better than yesterday. Clouds were wanting in the brightening sky and the wind had abated. Still Lucinda's fingers ached again when she had laced her boots. After breakfast the womenfolk detained Lucinda for a little, while Holbert accompanied Logan out to the wagon. But Lucinda soon followed, promising to stop on her first trip into Flagg.

"Hope thet'll be soon. But winter's comin'," called Mrs. Holbert, after her. "Don't get in front of thet bull John sold your man. He's wilder'n a skeered jack-rabbit!"

Lucinda's breast felt as if it had suddenly been crushed. She was glad the Holberts could not see her face as she ran off with the dog leaping at her side. Her husband and Holbert were not in sight, but she heard a halloaing over in the corral. Presently Logan appeared riding one horse and leading another.

"Climb aboard, Luce," he said, briskly, in a matter-of-fact tone. "Better keep the dog with you. Here, coyote —say! there's a name for her."

"Coyote? Oh, it's pretty," replied Lucinda, as she climbed up. "Here, lift her up . . . Well! She doesn't need to be packed. Logan, I believe she won't have to be tied."

Huett leaped up to the seat and yelled: "Gadep!" The oxen moved away with the wagon creaking. "*Gee! Gee!*" They turned into the main road. "Now, Luce, it's all plain sailing, without a turn-off for fifteen miles—to the old homestead. We've got to make it before dark. . . . Put on your gloves. . . . Gosh! if we make it with all my stock—one brindle bull, a mean cuss, eight cows, six two-year-old steers, and five heifers—Oh! I'll feel rich. But I'll have to ride some."

With outward composure Lucinda took the whip he tendered her, and averted her face. Was the man stark mad to set her this task? Or was he paying her the tribute due the women of the Oregon Trail? She chose not to let him guess her perturbation. Logan leaped off while the wagon was moving.

"Good luck, old girl!" he called, happily. "If this isn't

great? Luce Huett, ox-driver of the Arizona range?
Whoopee!"

Lucinda failed completely to share his enthusiasm,
although she was glad to find that a really momentous
occasion could pierce his practicality. She was left
alone on that high driver's seat, too high to leap off
without risking life and limb. Coyote regarded her with
intelligent eyes, as if she understood Lucinda's predicament. Lucinda held the whip with nerveless hand. The
wagging beasts plodded on unmindful of her tightly
oppressed breast and staring eyes. Ahead the road followed the lake shore for miles, as far as she could see.
Her ponderous steeds could not turn to the left, but
suppose they turned to the right? The wagon and she,
with her trunks of pretty clothes and her chest full of
even more precious and perishable belongings, and
Logan's utensils and supplies for his great enterprise—
these must all go toppling down into the lake. But while
Lucinda watched with uncertain breath the oxen traveled
along, slowly and steadily, ponderously, as they had done
the day before. Probably they were not even aware that
a woman-driver now held the whip. Lucinda hugged that
comforting thought to her heart. She determined not to
yell "gee," "haw," or "whoa" until necessity compelled
it; and gradually her fears subsided. She could look at
the slope and out upon the lake, and far ahead with a
growing sense of something beside the risk of the situation. She was doing an unprecedented thing. Driving a
prairie-schooner drawn by oxen! Here was an amazing
fact that should have indulged her primitive side to the
full. But that part of her seemed in abeyance.

"I had an idea school teaching was hard," she soliloquized. "But this pioneer game! . . . Oh, I *do* love
Logan!"

The sun came up glaringly hot. Lucinda removed her

heavy coat. When she looked back she thought she saw the dust-obscured cattle running the other way, and before she realized disloyalty to Logan she hoped they were.

The time came, however, when she realized her mistake. A breeze from behind brought a smell of dust, then the sound of hoofs. Peering back Lucinda saw that Logan's stock was not far behind. Then through the dust she espied him, and on the moment he appeared to be throwing stones with a violence that suggested impotent fury. Lucinda had it in her to laugh. "Serves him right—the cowboy cattleman husband who does not have time even for a honeymoon!"

Almost before she realized it she had reached the end of the lake, where the road turned across a bare flat to enter the forest. The oxen apparently saw nothing save the road, and they kept on it, oblivious of the cattle behind. Lucinda also made the surprising discovery that the sun stood nearly overhead. She was hot and thirsty, and she could not find the canteen that Logan had stuck somewhere under the seat.

As the wagon rolled around a bend in the road Lucinda looked back. The cattle were strung out. On the moment Logan was chasing some wild heifers that had swerved far off the course. The cows looked dusty and tired. Then Lucinda saw the bull. In fact he bellowed on the instant. She had to see him. So close behind that he had driven the haltered horse right on the wheels of the wagon! A dusty beast with wide horns and a huge head with eyes of green fire and a red tongue hanging out! Lucinda conceived the fearful idea that he would frighten the horse, charge the wagon, and perhaps gore the oxen into a stampede.

This direful catastrophe failed to materialize. The oxen

gained the woods, where the wide canvas top brusned the foliage on each side.

Meanwhile the hours had been passing. Soon the character of the woods gave way to scaly ground covered with brush and scattered oaks, then a large oval open gray with sage, and centered in a depression which had at one time held water. Lucinda's quick eyes caught sight of a band of fleet gray-rumped graceful animals fleeing behind a coal black leader. They flashed into the forest on the far side.

Some time in the afternoon Logan passed her to the left, making a cut off across the sage. He was at full gallop in pursuit of some of his stock. He rounded them up and turned them back with the others. After a while, far in the distance, Lucinda espied an old cabin and a fence. Logan drew far ahead. She saw him drive his stock through the fence or around it.

Lucinda was half an hour covering the intervening space. She needed all that time to recover her equanimity. But she need not have concerned herself about Logan. It transpired that at sunset when she drove up to the old cabin and yelled, *"Whoa!"* she came upon Logan sitting on a log, grimy with dust and sweat, red as fire where he wiped the black off, and manifestly possessed by an elation that had just banished a very ignoble rage.

"How'd you make it—when I wasn't close?" he asked.

"Just fine. But that bull gave me a scare."

"I reckon. I'll kill him yet. Of all the damn ornery muddle-headed beasts I ever had to do with—he's the worst. . . . Wife, I worried myself sick about you, all for nothing."

"Yes, you did," scoffed Lucinda, secretly pleased. She got off with Coyote leaping down after her. The ground felt queer—or else her legs were insensible. "Where do we camp? And where's the water?"

"Holbert said there's a spring behind the cabin. Reckon we'll camp right here."

Lucinda untied the swinging buckets and with two of them started to hunt for water. Disillusion and weariness hung on her like wet blankets; nevertheless some feeling antagonistic to them worked upon her. A few plaintive flowers, primrose and dahlia, growing out of the weeds beside the cabin, eloquently told Lucinda that a woman had tended their parent roots there once upon a time. Perhaps a tenderfoot woman like herself! There was tragedy in the vacant eye-like windows. She was crossing a level grassy place when Coyote sprang back with a bark. *Bsszzz!* A loud buzzing rattle sent Lucinda's nerves tingling.

"That's a rattler. *Look out!*" shouted Logan, from behind. He came on a heavy run. "There! See him? A timber rattlesnake."

Lucinda saw a thick snake black and yellow, scaly and ugly, glide under the cabin. "That's all right," she said to the perturbed Logan. "I'm not afraid of snakes."

"Well, don't go kicking one of those boys in the grass. . . . Here's a trail."

They discovered the clear bubbling spring of cold water, which made the difference, Logan stated, between a good and a poor camp. On the way back Lucinda peeping into the log-cabin became virtually obsessed by wonder and dread. The littered, earthen floor, the blackened fireplace, the rude shelves and the bedstead of poles, told a story that saddened and shocked her. What had happened there? How little eastern people realized the crude living of those who set their faces West! Lucinda did not want Logan to find out how strongly she felt. She asked him if he had seen the beautiful black horned animal leading the white and tan ones across the open.

"Sure did. Golly, I wanted my rifle. That was a black

antelope, king of that herd. Holbert has seen him for years."

"Logan, you wouldn't kill him, would you?" she asked, gazing at him in horror.

"Reckon I would. Wild animals sort of excite me. I like to hunt. I'll bet we make the acquaintance of Gray, that black-ruffed lofer."

"I hope not, if you must murder everything," returned Lucinda sharply. Logan stared at her then stomped away with a puzzled frown on his face. Lucinda remembered how she used to fight her brothers and their comrades for chasing chipmunks along the rail-fences. How they would yell and run, wild as any young savages! But she must conquer her disgust at Logan's passion to kill, she knew, regardless of her own feeling in the matter.

Supper was soon over and the chores finished. The lonely night clamped down upon the forest. Lucinda was glad to crawl into her wagon-bed and stretch out—glad that weariness inhibited thought. Her slumbers were punctuated by dreams of an enormous bull and a huge snake. Logan routed her out in the gray of dawn. Before sunrise the wagon was packed and the oxen ready for Lucinda.

"I'll follow, same as yesterday," said Logan, imperturbably, as she climbed up to the seat. "I'm not sure about all the road. But it's most as good as that we've come over. There's a long down-hill stretch through the woods. When you hit that you'll be getting near home. But I'll be on your heels before we get there. Good luck."

"Let me try to start them," said Lucinda, after she had helped Coyote up. She uncoiled the long whip and tried to crack it. She did make a noise, but that was the end of the leather thong lashing her back.

"Gadep!" she shouted, at the top of her lungs. The

oxen obeyed at once, to her surprise, and relief, and the wagon was on its way.

"Turn left," called Logan. He waved his hat.

"Haw! . . . Haw!" yelled Lucinda. They wagged to the left and straightened out on the road, headed south.

"Say," shouted Logan, gleefully, "let me drive the oxen and you drive that bull!"

"I should say not!" retorted Lucinda, refusing to allow her husband's flattery to inflate her egotism. Something was bound to happen—she just knew it.

The morning was warm, compared to the others before it. There was no frost. When she drove into the forest she had an agreeable surprise. Jays were screeching, squirrels were chattering. Gray deer with white tails up bounded away from the road. Presently Lucinda came upon a flock of wild turkeys, scratching in the grass under the pine saplings. Those near the road ran with a put-put, put-put-put. But most of them let the wagon go by without taking flight. The sight greatly pleased Lucinda.

As the day progressed, the heat poured down from the sun and rose like transparent veils of smoke from the ground. Lucinda grew unbearably hot and wet. Then she ran into the stretch of dust that Logan had mentioned. It appeared to be half a foot deep on the road, and every step of the oxen sent up great yellow puffs, thick and dry, that rolled back upon Lucinda. Her clothes became as yellow as the roadside; the dust ran off her sombrero; her gloves filled; she gasped and choked and nearly suffocated. "Whoa!" she finally yelled in desperation to her oxen. They stopped, as if glad for a respite. The dust pall rolled back, so that Lucinda could breathe. Her nostrils were clogged. She could smell no longer. Then she remembered the silk scarf which Logan had advised for this very emergency. She tied the ends around her neck and drew the wide fold up over her nose. This was stifling, yet not so unendurable as the dust. At her call the oxen lurched on and again she was enveloped. Then followed an almost insupportable period, the length of which could only be computed by slow hateful miles. The tears that Lucinda shed saved her from being blinded.

Presently the oxen floundered into dust that was so suffocating that they halted of their own accord. Lucinda coughed and choked miserably. Would this horrible day never end? She felt that she could not bear it longer. The afternoon must be waning, and when the air cleared somewhat, she looked around for the position of the sun. It was low in the sky and shone dark red through the pall. Their destination could not be far off now, but despite her misery, she hoped that Logan's Canyon was not located in this terrible country. Where was Logan? Suddenly a distant yell quickened Lucinda's pulse. She looked back. Dust clouds far behind!

"Gadep!" she called. But the oxen did not budge. She called louder. Then she yelled. But the gentle long-suffering beasts of burden had rebelled at last. Lucinda did not blame them. She looked back. That terrible bull was coming at a gallop. Swift terror shook Lucinda. Suppose he ran into us, she thought wildly. She yelled hoarsely and cracked the whip, but the drooping oxen never swung an inch under the wooden yoke.

A bawl and pound of hoofs behind elicited sharp barks from the dog. Coyote leaped to the ground and dashed back. Lucinda thanked her stars that she was high up on the wagon seat. The bull, his hide as yellow as the road, dashed about the wagon, his huge head lowered at the snapping dog. He lunged this way and that. Coyote nipped him on the nose. Then with a bellow he charged and in blind fury or by accident ran into the oxen with a terrific crash. The shock nearly upset the wagon. Lucinda screamed. The bull sprawled as the oxen, leaping ahead, struck him with the yoke. Down the road the oxen galloped madly, Lucinda holding on to the seat, terrified. They were running off, going faster every moment. The wagon rolled and swayed, but careened along fast enough to keep ahead of the great stream of dust which rolled from under the oxen's ponderous hoofs.

Lucinda realized she must leap for her life. Sooner or later the oxen would run off the road into a log or a ditch; but every time she essayed to get a hold and a footing which would enable her to spring clear a bump would throw her back. The yellow road flashed under her; the trees blurred; the ground appeared like moving sheets of gray. A heavy clattering thud of hoofs mingled with the rolling creaking roar of the wagon. Alas! for her trunks and Logan's treasured possessions!

The oxen sheered off the road toward brush and trees. They were slowing down of their own accord or the soft going retarded them. Lucinda made up her mind to leap into the brush. She stood up, leaning out, holding desperately to the canvas-covered hoop. But before she could jump the oxen plunged into a wash, the wheels hit a bank with a tremendous shock, and Lucinda shot as if from a catapult far out into the brush. Thick branches broke her fall. Still she landed on the ground hard enough to make her see a shower of sparks.

She struggled to her feet, dizzy, scratched, torn, but sound in limb. A few rods beyond the wagon stood upright with the heaving oxen halted by the brush. The extra horse that had been haltered was missing. Lucinda staggered out to a log at the edge, and there she sank down, panting, scarcely able to believe her good fortune, suddenly freed of mingled terror and anger.

Then she saw that Coyote had stopped the bull a short distance up the valley. Logan appeared beyond urging on the spent straggling bunch of cattle. He chased the bull in among them, and riding from one side to the other shunted them off the road on Lucinda's side, passed her with a wild shout and drove them into the woods. Because of that move Lucinda knew gratefully they had not far to go.

She rested endeavoring to remove some of the travel stains and the blood on her wrists where the brush had scratched her. Coyote sought Lucinda out and sank to the ground, her red tongue protruding, and her heavy coat yellow with dust. Presently Lucinda espied the horse that had been tethered behind the wagon. She secured it and led it back to the oxen. Oppression from her exertion and fright weighed heavily upon her.

At length Logan rode back to her, black as a coal-heaver; yet nothing could have hidden his triumphant air, his grim mastery, his gay possession of success.

"Done!" he cried, ringingly. "Not a hoof lost! But oh, what a hell of a drive! . . . What happened to you, Luce?"

"Oh, nothing—much," she answered, calling upon a sense of humor that eluded her.

"But you look queer. And the wagon there—in the brush! . . . But say, Luce, your face—it's all scratched."

"That awful bull! He butted into the oxen. They ran off. Down here they turned off the road, hit a bank and pitched me into the brush."

Logan leaped off to approach her with earnest solicitude. "You poor kid! I was afraid something had happened. I shouldn't have left you so far ahead. But are you hurt, dear?"

"No. Only a scratch or two."

"Thank God for that!" He shook his head in wonderment. "I can't get over how my luck holds." He ran to the wagon, then examined wheels and tongue and the oxen. Evidently no damage had been done, for he mounted the seat and with yells drove the oxen out of the brush.

"All right. Come on, honey. Get up while I tie the horses behind . . . It won't be long now, Luce. Sycamore Canyon! My range! Our home!"

Lucinda had lost her hopes and what little curiosity she might have had. Logan drove into the woods, along what appeared to have once been a road. Oxen and wagon jarred heavily over saplings. After about a mile or less Lucinda saw a light space through the woods. The green failed, and far beyond and above appeared again, only dimmer. There was an opening and a valley—a canyon Logan had said—just ahead. On the left side of the road a rocky ledge rose. Logan drove through a gap between the ledge and a brushy bank, halted and dismounted to carry poles and small logs with which to improvise a gate closing the opening. How energetic he was and tireless! There seemed a growing passion within him. Lastly he hauled a log that two men might well have found burdensome, which he placed across the gap.

"Luce girl," he said, intensely, as he mounted beside her. "Our stock is down in the canyon. Fenced in, all save a few holes in the rock rim they'll never find before I close them. Aha! . . . I'll show you pronto." A great weight seemed lifted from his shoulders.

Lucinda could not look just yet. She watched Logan jump off the wagon, untie the horses at the back and drive them past the wagon, down what appeared a narrow overgrown road. She saw him take an axe and chop down a small pine as thick at the base as his thigh. The whole bushy tree, by prodigious effort, he dragged behind the wagon and secured with a chain.

"What's that for?" she asked him as he returned.

"Just a drag to hold us back. Pretty steep. Hold on

now and look. You'll see the greatest valley in all the West!"

In spite of herself Lucinda was compelled to gaze. A long, winding, apparently bottomless gorge yawned beneath them. As the wagon lurched down the grade this thing Logan called a canyon gradually became visible. It struck Lucinda with appalling force: a gray granite-walled abyss widening to the south, yawning up at her as if to swallow her. It appeared narrow just below, but it was not narrow. As all this deceitful West it was not what it appeared. A ribbon of water and waste of white sand wound through the center of it, to disappear round a bend; beyond the canyon widened out into a great basin inclosed by yellow slopes and pine-fringed rims.

Lucinda had to hold on tightly to keep from being thrown off the seat. As the wagon rolled deeper into the declivity, brush on one side and bluff on the other obscured Lucinda's view. The grade steepened. Screeching brakes and crunching wheels increased their clamor. Despite the oxen holding back and the drag of the pine tree behind, the wagon rolled and bumped too fast for safety. Lucinda held on to her seat although she wondered bitterly why she clung to it so dearly. Then suddenly the pine tree behind broke or pulled loose; the wagon rolled down upon the oxen, forcing them into a dead run, and swaying dangerously one side to the other. Barely in time for safety it rattled out upon the level open of the canyon floor and came to a jarring stop. Manifestly unable to control his elation, Logan drove across a flat of seared, bleached grass, across a shallow brook and bar of sand, up a considerable grade to a flat where big pines stood far apart and a white-barked tree shone among them.

"Whoa!" he yelled, in stentorian voice of finality, that echoed from the black looming slope above. He threw away his whip and giving Lucinda a grimy, sweat-laden embrace, leaped to the ground, and held out his arms to help her down.

"Sycamore Canyon, sweetheart!" he said, with husky emotion. "Here's where we homestead."

But Lucinda did not move nor respond on the moment. She gazed about spellbound, aghast. The drab, silent rocks, the lonely pines shouted doom at her. The brook babbled in mockery. There was no view, no outlook except down the gray monotonous canyon with its terrible, forbidding walls. Savage wilderness encompassed her on all sides. Solitude reigned there. No sound, no brightness, no life! She would be shut in always. A pioneer wife chained irrevocably to her toil and her cabin! A low strange murmuring, the mysterious voice of the wild, breathed out of the forest. The wind in the pines! It seemed foreboding, inevitable, awful, whispering death to girlish hopes and dreams.

Chapter Four

HUETT, seldom prey to strong feeling, expected Lucinda to share his joy at their safe arrival in the canyon which they were to homestead, but he was somewhat taken back by his wife's pale face and the strange gaze that seemed to see beyond the pines. When she had no word to say he divined that his vague fear of her reaction to Sycamore Canyon had been justified. But, he reflected, women were queer and beyond men's understanding. What difference did it really make where they began to live their lives together? The essential thing was that they were together, mated, facing the great project. He stifled his disappointment.

"Come down and let's rustle," he said, and helped her out of the wagon, aware that she was heavy on her feet. "Rest a bit. Or better walk about. I'll throw supper together in a jiffy."

As she walked slowly away, not looking, Logan felt sorry for her. But what had he done that was amiss? This was the finest place he had ever seen. He threw off his coat and filled all the water pails. What a wonderful spring—cold as ice, straight from granite rock, soft as silk, and even now late in the fall flowing a hundred gallons a minute! That spring was priceless. As Logan carried the pails he gazed about for firewood. Up the canyon on the slope stood an aspen grove, burning vivid gold in the sunset. There would be dead aspen wood there—a wood next best to dead oak for a corking fire. He fared forth with an axe and dragged down some long poles. He noted with pleasure that beaver had been cutting the live aspens, and he wondered where their dam was. He built a fire with pine, and split the aspen to burn afterward. Lucinda had not come back.

While Logan was rushing the supper Lucinda returned, carrying a handful of flowers.

"Purple asters!" she exclaimed, her pale features animated for the first time. "My favorite flowers! These are wild—so much larger and lovelier than cultivated ones."

"Lots of wild flowers in these woods," he replied. "I like best that yellow one, like a bell in shape, that nods at you in the creek bottoms."

"I saw golden rod along the road. That's something," she said thoughtfully. She helped him get supper, ate without appetite, and wiped the utensils after he washed them. Logan felt full of thoughts and feelings. He was not given to voluble expression, but if she had encouraged him now he might have formed the nucleus of a habit to talk. But she said only that it was much warmer down in the canyon. This night she did not put on her heavy coat, nor stand eagerly by the fire.

"I'll make your bed before it gets too dark," he said.

"What will we use for lights?" she asked, curiously.

"Campfire. I can get some pine knots presently. There's a box of candles to use in the cabin, when we throw that up." When Logan emerged from his task in the wagon Lucinda was standing with her dog watching the afterglow fade in the west. He made his own bed under the great pine nearby. Dusk fell and then began the gloaming hour Logan liked best. He lighted his pipe. Lucinda came back presently.

"I'm tired," she said. "I'll be—all right tomorrow. Good-night, Logan."

"Good-night, dear. You've sure been game." He patted her shoulder awkwardly with his hand, but did not attempt to kiss her.

Night closed down upon the canyon. Logan sat smoking. He saw the fading red embers of his fire, the great looming pines, the black shadowy wall; he smelled the smoke and the tang of the forest; he heard the sough of the wind, the brawl of the brook, the wail of coyotes. But he did not waste thought on these external manifestations which measured his contentment. He had made the drive from Flagg in three days, with a heavy load, the latter half of the distance with a score and more of cattle and a wild bull. That stock, his oxen, and horses were safe in the canyon. It seemed incredible. Even with less than that he would have had a splendid start. His ranch was an established fact, and his range would be the envy of cattlemen some day. Yet he did not dream; he had no illusions. He was assured of the fact that he would have a great herd. Holbert had had trouble with a grasshopper plague one year, but such a contingency did not worry Logan here.

He looked impartially toward success in the long run. As he would not require cowboys for many years he could manage the ranch himself. Lucinda would cook and take care of the children when they came. He would do the thousand and one tasks that fell to a homesteader's lot. For the immediate present he had the log cabin to throw up speedily—a job for one man; then the gaps to close in his natural fences around the canyon; and after that the winter's supply of firewood and meat. He would never have to kill any beef—not in this forest. Such a reflection afforded him double satisfaction. He would be able to indulge in his one and only pleasure, and besides that, save many calves and yearlings.

It did not occur to Huett, as he stretched out under the blankets, that he was a happy man. Nevertheless he felt a great sense of accomplishment—to have won Lucinda Baker for a wife, to have driven safely into Sycamore Canyon with supplies and stock sufficient for the long task ahead—this seemed as much of a miracle as he ever dared hope for. The rest depended upon him, and he was positive that he was equal to the task. He had never tested his powers, but he felt that they were unlimited. Sleep glued his eyelids the instant he closed them.

At dawn he was up, wading through the dewy grass to fetch in his horse. He saw deer with the cattle and wished he had brought along his rifle. Venison was tasty after the first frosts and would keep if hung up in the shade. Returning to camp he put his heaviest saddle on Buck and left him standing bridle down. Logan next applied himself to putting up a tarpaulin shelter in a convenient place. He had a camp chair somewhere in the wagon. This and a box for a table would do for Lucinda.

The sun struck down early into Sycamore, another of the many desirable features of this canyon. In summer it would be hot, but in winter the more sun the better. Huett anticipated much from those ample south slopes and walls, which would not only melt snow off promptly but reflect heat down upon the level. What corn, beans, cabbage, hay, grapes, peaches, he would raise! While mixing the biscuit dough that morning Logan located certain spots for gardens and fields.

Lucinda appeared, her face sunburned and slightly swollen.

"Mawnin', settler," she said, with a brightness that he was quick to grasp.

"How are you, Luce?" he greeted her, heartily.

"Fine. Only burnt to a crisp, lame in one leg, and sore from sundry scratches," she replied wryly. She had brushed her hair and left it to hang in a braid, a way that made her look more girlish, and pleased Logan. "I'm afraid to wash my face, it's so sore."

"Don't. Be chary of water in this country till you're broken in."

"Heaven!—What'll we do for a bath?"

"There's the brook."

"Be sensible, Logan. Besides, I felt that water last night. Cold—why, it made me jump. Can't you fix a place for us?"

"Sure I can. And I'll do it pronto. The brook will be good enough for me yet a while."

"Where's my dog?"

"I haven't seen her."

"She went out before daylight."

"Coyotes! By gum! I hope she doesn't run true to form. These half-wolf dogs are queer. She might go back to her kind. For she's more wolf than shepherd."

Lucinda made a face. "Oh dear!—I suppose I mustn't let myself love anything out here, because I can't keep it."

"I reckon, Luce. Nothing except me," he replied, not realizing the jest.

"You? Why—er—of course, Logan. But can't I keep pets?"

"Sure. But I won't swear how long. You can have bear-cubs, fawns, anything I can catch for you."

"A bear-cub? Oh, how darling! I'd love that."

While they sat at breakfast Coyote came back, her long fur full of burrs, her tongue hanging out. Lucinda was delighted at her return, while Logan was manifestly not displeased. The dog evidently had been chasing some wild animal, but apparently knew when to return home.

"Well, Luce, you clean up while I tackle the big job," drawled Logan finally.

"What?"

"Our cabin."

"How thrilling! Let me help."

"I should smile you will help."

"Where'll we put it? How big?"

"Right there, in the center of the bench. I reckon those pines are good to stand a hundred more years. How big?

—Doggone, that stumps me. I guess I can manage twenty-four foot logs, if they're not too big around."

"Twenty-four feet! How many rooms?"

"One. We'll have to live in one room. After a time, as our needs grow, we can add a section."

"But, Logan, that Holbert cabin was awful," cried Lucinda impetuously. "Small, dark—no floor, no porch. . . ."

"Don't worry, Luce. I've thought of that," Logan assured her. "We'll have a floor and a flat stone hearth. I'll extend the roof beyond the cabin wall—say twenty more feet . . . Like this," he drew a rude plan on the ground, "with posts to hold it up at the corners. And a loft to store things."

"Logan, can you do all this alone?" she queried, as if suddenly appreciating the enormity of his undertaking.

"Sure can. You'll have to help though. Our tough job will be to lift logs one above the other, after we get so high. But I'll cut a forked sapling, heave up an end of the log in that. You'll hold the sapling while I tend to the other end."

"But suppose the log should slip," suggested Lucinda fearfully.

"I won't let it. Shall I move your things under the shelter? I've a chair and a box. Then you can find something to do until I come back."

"Yes, please. I've plenty of sewing."

"Good. Can you knit, Luce?"

"That is one of my few accomplishments."

"I'll bet you have a lot of them," Logan declared pridefully. Then having moved her belongings and the boxes to the shelter he took his axe, and, mounting Buck, rode up the canyon. Round the bend and conveniently half way up the slope stood a dense grove of pines which Logan had remembered from a former trip. He could

drag what he needed down-hill all the way, a factor saving of labor and time.

It took less than half an hour to cut and trim the first
log for snaking down to camp. How deep the heavy axe
had bitten into the pine and how satisfying the feel of
swinging it! Logan took a half-hitch with his rope round
the log's end and mounting, looped the pommel and
started at a long angle down hill. The log slipped along
as if greased. As he neared camp the dog barked, and
Lucinda ceased her work to watch him. It was something
deeply exhilarating for Logan to see her there.

"Making out fine, Luce," he called in a cheery tone, as
he dragged the log into camp. "What have you been
doing?"

"Chastening my spirit, Logan," she returned cryptically.

Riding back up the canyon he wondered what Lucinda
had meant. But he did not ponder long over her com-
plexity.

In the following hour Logan snaked down the three
other logs, and by the time Lucinda called him to eat
he had the four foundation sides of his cabin squared,
leveled, and blocked up with flat stones.

"I'll cut logs this afternoon and tomorrow," he told
Lucinda. "Maybe it'll take another day. Fine crop of
small pines to choose from. But the shakes have me
stumped."

"Shakes?" inquired his wife.

"Yes. Shingles for the roof. They're called shakes in
the West. You split them out of a big pine log. It's got
to be straight grain and not too sappy. Maybe I can find
a lightning struck pine. Ought to for lightning sure strikes
in this forest."

"Thunderstorms, you mean?" asked Lucinda fearfully.

"I'll say. Terrible electric storms. Trees crashing all
around you—rain, wind. . . ."

"I'm afraid of storms," said Lucinda in a troubled voice. "When I was a child Mother used to shut me up in a dark hall."

"Don't worry, Luce. It's too late for that kind of storm." He glanced at the sky, shaking his dark head. "Lord, I hope the snow holds off till we're under a roof. But the weather here is fine till Thanksgiving, mostly."

When Logan finished his work, supper was almost ready and would have been earlier, Lucinda explained, but for the biscuits. She had burnt the first batch.

"Luce, it's no easy job," said Logan, hastening to excuse her. "Did you remember to heat the lid while you were heating the oven?"

"No. But I put a shovelful of coals on the lid."

"Always heat it first. . . . Well, this has been a doggone good day. Only too short."

"It was long for me—and lonesome," she replied wistfully. "You'll always be at work, won't you?"

Logan nodded gravely. "I reckon so, Luce, come to think of it. But I like work. That's what I want. And presently you will be so busy the days will fly."

Lucinda did not seem to share his optimism. The thought struck Logan that he must be kind and attentive to her. He helped her with the work after supper, talked about the cabin, and afterward persuaded her to walk with him along the brook. He felt affection and solicitude, and warm yearning, but he was clumsy about expressing such feeling. Still his presence and his attention had a brightening effect upon her that he was glad to see. Lastly he kissed her good-night and was amazed at her wet eyes, shining in the firelight.

Before sunrise next morning Logan shot and dressed a deer, cut and stacked firewood, and had breakfast ready when Lucinda arose. He then put in a prodigious day with the logs, cutting and trimming fifty, and peeling most of them. He did not know where the hours went, but that one spent with Lucinda after supper seemed to bring them closer. She was beginning to display interest in his work, to ask about the future. Yet she seemed to have a dread of being left alone and she hated the cold. Logan vowed he would make their cabin snug and warm, and as if the daylight hours were not enough, working by firelight, he notched and laid the second square of logs

"But there's a space between," protested Lucinda when she noticed their arrangement.

"Sure. We can't get the logs perfectly flat one on another."

"What will we do, then? The rain and wind would blow in."

"Tenderfoot! What's dobe mud for if not to fill in the chinks? This kind here in Arizona sets like mortar."

"I used to build mud houses—and now I'm to live in one," said Lucinda dreamily, then, "But where'll the doors be?"

"Only one door. Opening on the porch to the east. Storms usually blow from the southwest. I'll strain a point and put in a window for you—in the south wall. That'll let in sun and light."

Without any help the following day Logan notched and lifted and squared four sections of logs on top of the two already laid. This, he told Lucinda, was getting somewhere, but he would need her assistance from then on. His mode of procedure might not have been original, but it was effective. He leaned a forked sapling against the cabin wall and lifted the end of a log to rest in it. Then Lucinda held the sapling while he performed a like service with the other end of the log. He managed to hold it, too, while he climbed up on the wall. Then he set his notched end in place, after which he crossed to Lucinda's side and placed hers. Logan was delighted with his ingenuity and could not see why his wife was not the same.

The fifth day bade fair to be hardest and most trying of all. Log after log Logan notched and set in place, one on top of the other. The fragrant yellow wall went up. Once Lucinda came near to disaster. A log slipped at Logan's end, while he was climbing and holding at the same time. It fell. Only by remarkable strength for a girl did Lucinda hold her prop in place.

For once Logan lost his characteristic reserve.

"Luce girl, are you all right?" he cried anxiously as he swung down from the ladder. "My God! If that had come down to hit you. . . ." he could not finish the sentence.

After the log had slipped into place, Lucinda leaned against the wall, her face white. "I'm all right—I guess," she said.

"Lord! what a jackass I am! After this I'll use the rope and haul my end up!" exclaimed Logan fervently. "But then, you haven't got those square shoulders and round arms for nothing." Coincidentally his pride in her grew.

They worked late that night and completed the walls. Logan was jubilant. He relieved the weary Lucinda from the supper task and laughed at her sore hands, although he tenderly picked the splinters from them. Then he gave her a good-night embrace and sat up long beside the fire pondering the problem of the roof. Before he went to bed he solved it; and the following morning, putting the simple plan into effect, he flattened poles laying them across from wall to wall, giving him a foothold from which to erect the roof structure. He wanted a high peak for two reasons: first to make a steep slant from which the snow would slide, and secondly to give the loft room for a man to stand.

That brought Logan to another problem—to find a suitable pine, cut it down and split out the shakes. But his good fortune attended him further. He found a fallen pine, riven at the top by lightning. It lay at the ^dge of the pines above the cabin. Another down hill haul!

Logan's first few bundles of shakes would make excellent firewood and no more. Presently, however, he got the knack of it and made up for lost time by putting on extra muscle. Packing the shakes down proved a harder job than he had expected. His initial attempt was to drag down a bundle in a canvas. This proved a poor way. Then he tried packing bundles on Buck, an equally ineffectual task because Buck was a poor pack horse and displayed temper. By using a burlap bag as a pad on his shoulders, Logan carried a bundle of a hundred or more shakes down at a trip. The climb up was short, and unburdened he made it quickly. Sunset of that day saw his roofing piled neatly beside the cabin.

The weather had been fine, even too hot in the afternoons, but on the last day a change threatened. A haze overspread the sky. The golden Indian summer was at an end. The wind moaned in the pines; November was at hand.

That night Logan was awakened by dull rumbling thunder away to the southwest. He groaned. Then he swore. Pattering rain fell upon his canvas. The first fall storm always began in that way: usually it rained a little, turned into snow, and then into a blizzard. It would be serious indeed if Lucinda and he were caught without their cabin completed.

Morning came, drab, raw, with misty cold rain falling. Logan built a fire, cooked breakfast, and then carried firewood for Lucinda to burn while he worked. It heartened him that she still preserved a cheerful spirit.

Logan tackled his job grimly. He placed bundles of shakes along the wall, so that he could heave them up with a rope. Lucinda slipped the noose under the bundles as fast as he could loft them. He laid as many along the rafters as he thought he would need on that side, then while Lucinda repaired to her shelter to get warm and dry, he set to work.

With the cold rain falling, the slippery rafters hard to straddle, and the nailing to be accomplished with benumbed hands, Logan had as grievous a job as even he wanted. But he stuck doggedly at it without time wasted at noonday. Lucinda called him, but he kept on. Every shake meant so much. Another few inches of roof! About midafternoon the rain ceased, to Logan's grateful surprise, the clouds broke up a little, and a pale sun shone through. Logan finished a whole side of the roof by evening in a tremendous burst of energy. Then wet and starved and half-frozen he clambered down the pole ladder to a warm fire and a hot supper.

"Logan, you *are* wonderful," said Lucinda with enthusiasm. "But giant though you are, I fear you'll kill yourself."

"Ha! Work never hurt any man. . . . I don't know, though. If I'm not tired I'm damn near froze! . . . Golly! Venison and mashed potatoes. And gravy! Whoopee! . . . Luce, I'll have a roof over us by tomorrow night."

On the morrow the sun shone again and before it set Logan made good his boast.

"There! She'll shed—water," he panted, huskily, as he came down, a flame in his gray eyes. "Our homestead cabin is up—and roofed. Now let's move in."

"I see," replied Lucinda. "But Logan, how do we move in? There's no door—no window."

Logan stared. His jaw dropped. "Holy mavericks!" he exclaimed in consternation verging on mirth. "I'm a son-of-a-gun if I didn't forget to cut either. . . . Luce, I guess we don't move in tonight, after all."

Huett kept up his mighty pace of labor. He began his
floor from the foundation log of the cabin. Here his pro-
ficiency with an axe asserted itself. To rough hew logs
and lay them close and flat, with level sides uppermost
called out all his skill. He laid the floor in two days,
leaving a large open square against the north wall for
the stone hearth and fireplace.

Logan built a bough bedstead in the corner, framing it
so it would hold a goodly mattress of evergreen foliage.
He wanted to use balsam for this, but he did not believe
that species of evergreen could be obtained as low down
from the rim as Sycamore Canyon. Therefore he chose
fir, which was as springy as balsam, if not so sweet-
smelling. He packed huge bundles of fir boughs down
from the slope, and cut them, using only the tips, in
short lengths. When he had a sufficient quantity he carried it in. He folded a piece of canvas and laid that over
the bed. "Here, wife, is a job for you," he said cheerfully,
and he showed her how to lay the tips of fir with the butts
down, one upon another, in layer after layer. While she
labored at this task Logan spread the blankets in the warm
sun, then sat down for his first daytime rest. This was
not through weariness—he never acknowledged such a
weakness as that—but because he became conscious of
something no longer possible to put aside. Once released
it surged over Logan, warm, imperious, staggering—his
love for his wife and his need of her. Of late she had appeared less strange and no longer aloof. She had worked
willingly at whatever task he gave her, and sometimes she
laughed. This isolation, he could see, was tremendously
hard for her, being used to family and friends, to the
social life of a town; but he believed she would grow used
to solitude and become engrossed in their great task.
Strong emotion, so seldom actuating Logan and never
before like this, came over him. He had been considerate

of Lucinda, far more than most husbands would have been, and during these days of toil he felt that she had grown dearer for his restraint. He packed in the warm woolly blankets and threw them in a bundle at Lucinda's feet.

In the subdued light of the cabin she looked pale and her dark eyes met his questioningly. Logan took her in his arms. "Dear wife," he said, "I love you—and I want you. Will you make our bed—and let me come to you—tonight?"

"Why, Logan! Of course," she answered, shyly. "I'm your wife. And I—I love you too."

If Huett had been happy before he was happier now. The still smoky warm days persisted. He laid his hearth-stones and built his fireplace and chimney. It was a serviceable job, though wanting the finish he had been able to put upon his carpentry. But he was not a mason. When he found that his chimney would draw and not fill the cabin with smoke he whooped his delight. Then with boards he had brought in the wagon he built shelves and a table. He drove pegs in the logs upon which to hang utensils. In his mind's eye he saw a fine head of elk antlers on the wall for his rifles. In an opposite corner he constructed shelves for his ammunition, of which he had a large amount, and his few personal belongings. For Lucinda he built a wardrobe with a canvas curtain, and a box-like affair she could use as a bureau. Above this he hung a little mirror.

The hour came when Logan fared out on horseback to attack another important job—the fencing of the gaps on his canyon walls. It took him a week of arduous labor, but was labor in which he reveled for many reasons, not the least of which was the sight of deer and elk, and lion tracks and flocks of wild turkeys, and his cattle grazing

below. One day he sighted a newly born calf, and thought
of that as a herald and a promise of the great herd to
come.

His anxiety over the possibility that snow would come
before he had rolled and snaked down sufficient firewood
for winter was without warrant. November days stayed
clear and warm with pale sun. Dead aspen wood by the
cord, hard as iron, lay, already felled by the beaver. Huett
had but to drag it to the cabin—cut, split, and stack it on
the windward side of the wide porch. Dead oak he snaked
down from the woods above. And he sawed many sections of pine, to roll them down the slope. Before he
completed the cutting, however, the weather changed.
The pale sun faded behind gathering cloud, the air lost
its warmth, the wind sang the knell of Indian summer.
A cold fine rain began to fall.

"Luce, she's coming and we almost got her beat," announced Logan, stamping in at noon that day.

"Who's she?" interrogated Lucinda, in mild surprise.

"Winter, by gosh! Just let me hang up some meat to
freeze—then we're jake."

The drizzle turned to sleet, and when Logan awoke
during the night he heard its soft patter and seep upon
the cabin. How good it felt to be housed, snug in this
strong abode made by his own hands, warm under the
woolen blankets beside his young and hot-blooded wife!
Logan had no fear of wind or snow or cold. But before
he went to sleep he heard the wild bay of hunting wolves.
That was different. Wolves were the bane of settlers.

In the morning there was a thin sheet of snow on the
ground and white flakes were falling scantily. His horses
favored the lee side of the canyon, where under the high
shelving wall neither wind nor snow reached them. Logan
saddled Buck and rifle in hand rode up the canyon.
"Well, varmints," he said to the tracks in the snow, "you

better keep off my range." Before Logan had ridden two
miles up the draw he crossed tracks of beaver, fox, marten,
deer, and cat, but none of cougar or wolf. While building
the fences at the upper end of his range he had barred
two elk trails, with the satisfaction of realizing that the
elk which had come down could not get back. At length
Logan came upon a small herd, feeding in one of the
offshoots of the canyon. They were as tame as cattle, but
Logan had no compunction about shooting a fine bull.
He hung it up from a strong branch, dressed it and cut
off the antlered head. This he stuck safely in the crotch of
a sapling. The carcass he loaded over his saddle. Buck
snorted under the heavy load, and packed it unwillingly
back to the cabin.

Logan chose the big pine nearest the cabin, and therefore unexposed to sunshine, upon which to hang this
meat. He skinned the carcass first, and nailed the fine
hide to the wall of the cabin. Then he cut out the
haunches and hung the several parts high over a branch,
out of the reach of all beasts but the cat family.

Lucinda fried elk liver for Logan that night for supper.
She had learned how to bake fine sour dough biscuits.
Logan thought he fared sumptuously and he told Lu-
cinda so.

"I'll hang up a couple of deer to freeze and some wild
turkeys," he went on. "Then if I can only track a fat
bear that hasn't holed up we'll be jake. Bear fat renders
fine grease and oil. Best to cook with. As good as butter.
And a bear rib roasted—um umm!"

As luck would have it Huett shot his complement of
game without traveling three miles from his cabin. The
brakes in the lower end of the canyon appeared to be
winter quarters for all kinds of animals. These ravines
were choked with splintered cliffs and windfalls and

thickets of oak. Buck came in for some hard packing before Logan brought all the meat home.

On the last trip, late one gray November afternoon,
Logan came upon the half eaten remains of one of his
heifers. Cougar tracks in the thin snow! Logan sustained
a strong shock. This was an abrupt break in the happy
and fortunate sequence of events. The big cat had rolled
the skin back and eaten the liver, hardly taking any more.
Coyotes had consumed about half of the carcass.

Logan vented his rage vehemently to the leaden skies.
It was his first set-back. No doubt the cougar had killed
other heifers and calves. Logan had no time that night to
search, but he swore he would trail that cougar to its
lair.

It was dark when he returned to the cabin. He un-
packed and unsaddled Buck, to turn him loose. The load
of meat he lifted up on the wood pile. Then he burst
into the cabin, where for the first time a bright blaze of
fagots in the fire, and steaming pots on the hearth, and
Lucinda's pale pretty face warming at his entrance, failed
to elicit a glad shout.

"Wife, what do you think?" he began, his face red and
heated, "I found a cougar kill. One of our heifers! Damn
cat ate only the liver. I'll bet he's killed others. . . . Why
in hell don't cougars stick to deer meat? But when the
snow flies they want beef. . . . By God, I'll kill him!
Here's a chance to use your dog. Coyote will trail that
varmint if I can't. . . . Luce, wolves and lions are the
curse of cattlemen on wild ranges. I knew that, yet I over-
ruled the warning. . . . But, I see now—and it's war on
the meat eaters!"

Lucinda looked at him with what seemed surprise and
compassion.

"My dear husband! Has it taken that to show you the
terrific truth of your trial? I have known it since we got

here. All the time I've known it. . . . Don't be discouraged by this loss, or by what it threatens. You will conquer all obstacles."

"Why—bless your heart!" exclaimed Huett, turning his big cold hands to the fire. He felt amazed, ashamed, and something else he did not quite grasp. "Sure, you're right. It's nothing. . . . But how good to feel the fire—to smell that stew—to see you here!"

Chapter Five

LUCINDA watched the drifting snow. It was late in the afternoon of a winter day. A steely brightness showed where the sun hung over the western fringe of the canyon, and black patches stood out on the south slopes where the snow had melted. The dry scattered flakes swirled down; ceaselessly the wind moaned in the pines. During these winter months that ghostly wind had been the cruelest of Lucinda's trials. She hated it. She feared it. Forever it haunted her with the specter of loneliness and isolation. When the storm-king raged out of the north sometimes it drove her frantic. In the dead of night when Logan slept beside her like a log it was endurable, but she could not refrain from listening. There would come a lull and then a faint moan far off. It would grow and swell, and sweep through the forest, mounting to a tremendous roar. She could feel the cabin move over the roots of the great swaying pines. The roar would move on, dying to a moan.

Twilight was creeping out from under the walls. It would soon be dark. When Logan did not come home by nightfall she would fall prey to uneasy worry. It was nearly time to begin supper. The fire was red, the kettle beginning to sing.

The months had dragged by. Logan Huett was not only a natural hunter, but also a rancher who had conceived a passion to kill predatory beasts. Day after day he left Lucinda by herself in the cabin. At first she nearly died of loneliness, but she never let her husband see that. She had her housework, her sewing, and her knitting—tasks she left numberless times to look out as she was gazing now, unseeingly across the cold white black-tipped ridge to the outside world. Logan had killed nine cougars, and many coyotes. The wolves, however, had so far been too keen for him.

His herd, his poor little herd of cattle—had dwindled to the brindle bull and three cows. Calves, heifers, steers all gone, except the furry bags of bones! That had been heart-rending for Logan. He dreaded this would defeat his cherished hopes, yet he was a man that nothing could stop. His one consolation was the growth of Lucinda's respect and love for him. In many ways Huett was wanting. He was neither callous nor selfish nor indifferent, but his great fault was his blindness to the martyrdom that he had nailed upon his wife. Long since, however, Lucinda had given herself to his project and nothing could have swerved her from it now. She had resolved to make herself the helpmate of the pioneer. She had every qualification, but her one weakness was her sensitive mind, her emotional nature.

Hours on end she had pondered over the lives of the women who had come before her to this devastating West. What had happened to them? If they had been delicately organized as she was they had become hardened to meet the callousness and brutality of the wilderness; or else they had died.

Lucinda was heavy with child now in this last winter month, and the feeling of life within her had been the best resistance to the morbidness of the early weeks of that season. She had always loved children. She longed for some of her own. She wanted passionately to give Logan the sons he would need in this long fight to success, but giving birth to them in this desolate hole in the forest appalled her as nothing else ever had. The nursing and caring for them as babies did not loom so terribly; nevertheless, it struck her deeply. When they grew old enough for her to teach—that would be her happy task; and when they were lads, big enough to ride and shoot and plant and chop, to do all Logan talked so fondly of—that would be wonderful.

She fought loyally against the tragedy that seemed inevitable, against the disillusionment which hung in the balance, against the magnifying fears that beset her.

Down across the pale track of daylight upon the snow Lucinda made out the dark figure of Huett, bowed under a burden, with the dog trotting beside him. Turning away from the window she threw wood on the fire, lighted a pine cone, and set about her neglected supper task. Presently she heard a crunching of snow and pattering sounds, then the thud of a heavy pack upon the porch. The door opened letting in a cold blast of air and flying snow. Logan came stamping in, virile and forceful, followed by the whining dog.

"You're late, Logan," said Lucinda, "so I thought I'd better wait till you came before getting supper."

"Hello, girl!—Late nothing. I'm early to what I expected," he replied, cheerfully. "Luce, this dog of yours will trail a cougar—any kind of cat, and bear, too. But she won't take a wolf track."

"Blood tells, you know. What did you do today?"

"Lord, let me see. What didn't I do? . . . First off Coyote chased a lioness up a tree—the biggest cat I've killed. After I skinned her out I visited my traps. Had a mink, marten, or beaver in each one of them. I skinned those out. Then I shot and hung a buck. We'll have fresh meat again. Coming home I had a look at the place we drove down to get in here. Snow all off. Think I'll begin work on that road we need so bad—I can cut trees and brush away, build a fence and a gate where I piled those poles, and be ready when the ground gets soft to grade a road out."

"How soon will that be, Logan?"

"I reckon pretty soon, if signs can be trusted. We must

we well into March. Funny I couldn't find that calendar. I stuck it some place. . . . It's getting time we should keep track of days on your account."

"Logan, I told you the baby would come in July."

"No you didn't. . . . Maybe I forgot. Anyway, I'm glad it'll be midsummer."

"You must have the doctor from Flagg for me."

"Well, I will if it's possible. But I'll sure have some woman to see you through it. . . . Pour me a basin of hot water, Luce, and rustle supper."

Day by day the sun grew higher and warmer. The snow, except that which lay under the walls facing north, melted away, yet it seemed to Lucinda that spring came all at once. The turkey gobblers must have thought the same, because one day they began to gobble from every hilltop. It was a chorus Lucinda never tired of hearing.

The brook ran bank-full of smoky snow water; the jays came back to squall in the trees; the warm winds began to dry up the boggy places.

"Got the road all graded out tip-top," said Huett, one evening. "Reckon tomorrow I'll mend harness and grease the wagon."

"You'll be leaving for town soon?" queried Lucinda, anxiously. She would be left alone—the bitterest test of the pioneer's wife.

"Not very soon, much as I'd like to," replied the homesteader, seriously. . . . "We're most out of supplies. Holbert told me the road would be good here a month sooner than up beyond Mormon Lake. But there's a heap of work. I'll plot out the fields and gardens—clear them up and get ready to plow. My! what rich soil we have, Luce. We can live while we're starting that herd."

"Have you any money, Logan?"

"Not much. But my credit is good. Besides I've got a

pack of pelts to sell. If I'd known last fall what I know now I'd have trapped a wagonload of furs. That's a dodge I'll work next winter."

All too soon for Lucinda the time arrived that Huett had set to leave for Flagg. If he had been less practical and less engrossed with his important journey, the condition of roads, the prices of cattle and merchandise, he could not have failed to see Lucinda's vain effort to hide her agitation at this first parting; but he took his leaving as a matter of course and evidently thought she did also. After he had gone Lucinda wept nearly the whole day. When night came she barred herself in the cabin, and stayed up late, busying herself at various tasks in the dim light. Coyote slept by the hearth. At times, involuntarily, Lucinda stopped her work to listen. At night it never rested—that awful wilderness wind. It rustled along the ground outside, moaned under the eaves, mourned in the pines. After she went to bed it kept her awake until she buried her head under the blanket.

Compared to the night the day was blessed relief, yet even the light had its drawbacks. She could see the frightening loneliness then—the long winding gray-walled canyon without a sign of life. She wanted some hunter or settler to happen along, although she feared even that. She worked the long hours away.

Doggedly she kept count of the days. On the afternoon of the tenth she heard the grind of iron wheels upon stone, and then Logan's trenchant call to the oxen. The dog flew out of the open door. Lucinda thrilled to her depths. She saw Logan driving down to the level and felt that at last all was well with her once more.

Logan was clean-shaven. How handsome his tanned lean face! His dark eyes beamed upon her. Lucinda felt weak with her relief, her happiness, her sense of utter dependence upon this man.

"Oh, Logan—I'm so glad—you're back!" She almost wept with relief of the strain that had burdened her.

"Hello, wife. You and home look mighty sweet to me. . . . Six months' mail for you. Heaps of it. And a whole canvas pack of bundles. Got all on your list and added some on my own hook. . . . How'd you manage without me?"

"I worked far better—and slept less," she said with an attempt at levity as she received the heavy pack he handed down.

"Any hombres show up round here?" he queried, halting in his task to fasten intent eyes on her.

"I haven't seen man nor beast since you left. Darling, I would have welcomed an Indian—or even a grizzly bear."

"Well, maybe. . . . Here, I better lift this pack down. It weighs a ton." He balanced the long bundle on the wagon-wheel and leaping down carried it into the cabin. "Luce, I had some durn good luck. That explains the big load. You know those pelts I had and how you complained last winter because I killed and trapped the poor dear beasts? Well, I got eight dollars for beaver hides, five for mink and three for marten. What do you say to that? Saved me from going into debt! I've got supplies to last till fall, corn and beans and potatoes to plant. No end of seeds. And some much needed farm tools. Best of all I bought another little bunch of cows and heifers from Holbert. I'll have to rustle after them some day soon. . . . All paid for, Luce!"

"That's wonderful, dear. I'm so glad you didn't need to go in debt," exclaimed Lucinda.

"We'll begin all over again. Believe me, I wasn't the only rancher south of Flagg to lose stock last winter. Bad winter for varmints! That gray wolf ran amuck up Holbert's way. . . . Lots of other news, but I'm not much

of a hand to remember things. Reckon it'll come to me
bit by bit . . . but one thing I do recall—old Geronimo
broke out of the reservation with his braves, and made
south for Mexico, killing and burning. By God, Crook
should have hanged that old devil. I reckon my redskin
friend Matazel was one of them."

"Matazel! You mean that gray-eyed Apache who swore
he'd live to get even with you?" queried Lucinda, her
face paling. "But isn't he dangerous?"

"You needn't be afraid, Luce," Logan assured her. "I'd
love to have a bat with him, but General Miles with a
regiment of soldiers are hot- footing it on the track of the
Apaches. They'll get Geronimo eventually. It'll be a long,
hard, bloody chase, though. Apaches are light steppers
and they cover ground."

"But wasn't this forest once their hunting-ground?"

"They ranged all through the Mongollons and the
Matazels once upon a time. But that is past. We needn't
worry about them, dear. . . . Well, you read your mail
while I unpack."

Lucinda felt an inexplicable reluctance to open her letters and bridge the measureless gap between the present
and the past. But after the poignant plunge she gained
some nameless solace and strength. Life had gone on
without any particular changes to her loved ones. It was
and interesting and an awesome thing to read the gossip
of old friends. She received a melancholy pleasure in
hearing about the vicissitudes of the teacher who had
succeeded her with that unruly class. Lucinda's sister, having attained the mature age of sixteen, wrote that she
would be happy to come West and marry a pioneer like
Logan—if Lucinda would find him for her. Lucinda
whispered, "God forbid!" under her breath and then
felt amazement and shame. Had she come to such intoler-

ance as that? But she decided she would nip in the bud any such growing sentiment. One Baker girl sacrificed to the vast empire of the West was enough! Altogether then Lucinda's letters reestablished relations and renewed memories that were good for her.

Lucinda was glad to get outdoors with Logan. She found that being penned indoors for months had contributed much to her inclination toward morbid thought. Her energy came back and with it something of enthusiasm. At least she found some satisfaction in her yielding to work in the open. She labored steadily at the planting, though not violently, and appeared to grow less heavy and loggy for the exertion.

To plant things in the earth seemed to Lucinda a happier and safer way to expend labor than to use it on the raising of cattle. In the main, the soil was sure. Lucinda loved the smell of the freshly tilled loam. She loved to get her hands in it.

Logan's especial pride was in the cornfield. Only a man of such enormous strength and endurance as he possessed could have plowed and planted such a big field, alone and in such short time. Besides that, with Lucinda's help, he put in an acre of beans, a large plot of potatoes and many rows of cabbage, and lastly a considerable area of turnips. He had a leaning toward produce that could be fed to stock.

Lucinda planted sunflowers and golden-glow on the porch side of the cabin. These homely flowers would be reminders of her mother, with whom they were favorites.

Huett's estimate of the fertility of that canyon soil had not been without warrant. There was one section rich with black leaf mold, where seeds sprouted as if by magic, and potatoes and cabbage came up almost over night. Corn and beans followed as if loath to be left behind in the race for fecundity. Logan raved to his wife that Sycamore Canyon was a land of milk and honey.

However, he had reckoned without his host! The crows and gophers began at once to contest with Logan his right to the soil. Once more he became a hunter. Lucinda heard his carbine popping all day long. He planted props with old coats and hats all around the fields. He made scarecrows of dead crows, and it was only by the greatest vigilance that he saved his crops.

In June he took two days off to ride to Mormon Lake and drive back the new stock he had purchased from Holbert. When he turned these cows and heifers loose in the canyon no one would have guessed that he had suffered a grievous loss. Lucinda heard him laugh and whistle as he had while building the cabin. Then presently she heard him swear as never before. When his corn and beans attracted the deer his rage knew no bounds. He did not want to shoot the deer; and every dawn and every dusk he and Coyote had to chase the four-footed destroyers out of the fields.

As Lucinda's time drew nearer she fell prey to the morbid old fears. Logan had assured her that Mother Holbert had brought forth a troop of children, counting her own and her daughters', and that she would come the instant Logan rode after her. Holbert had a light buggy in which the trip back could be made in four hours. Nevertheless neither Logan nor this experienced old mother could still the voice that whispered to Lucinda. It was like the voice in the pine-tops, that whisper of tidings from the unknown. Lucinda had all the yearnings, the hallowed anticipations of a mother, the vague feelings of fulfillment to come; and these were beautiful, all satisfying, strong and sweet and rewarding. Nevertheless they did not preclude the dark forebodings nor the instinctive blind terror of childbirth. All these distressed her despite Logan's assurances that a woman would be with her. A presentiment that she would be left alone filled her with uneasiness.

Huett did not see this. He was kind, even loving, but he was stupid. Lucinda felt that she wanted to fly into a rage and flout him with his preoccupation in his practical tasks. Here she was about to go down into the valley of the shadow for him, for his offspring, and he felt no concern.

Logan rose at daybreak and rushed out to shout and shoot the deer out of the fields. All day he toiled in the fields; at night he ate like a wolf, smoked a pipe, and if he conversed at all, it was about his new-born calves, or his corn. He then tumbled into bed to sleep the sleep of honest toil. In the darkness of night, while Lucinda lay awake, helpless in the loneliness he had failed to break through, she almost hated him. Then when day came again she would reproach herself for such black thoughts. This burden was something a woman must bear alone.

Then one day she sustained a pang which instinctively warned her that the crucial time had come.

"Logan!—Go after Mrs. Holbert! Make haste!" she implored.

Her husband gave her one comprehending look and rushed out. A few minutes later Lucinda heard iron-shod hoofs cracking the rocks on the road. She sat down, composing herself with the courage of despair. Logan could be depended upon to return with some one in six hours or less. But that might be too late. She was but a woman whose intelligence grasped the inevitableness of the time, whose delicately sensitive nature shrank in terror from a repetition of that terrific first pang. It did not do any good to try to think how she would meet the situation alone. She felt the slow ascendency of the animal. She was in the clutches of nature. The pang recurred, to be prolonged into a paroxysm of agony. At its conclusion Lucinda heard voices and footsteps and Logan entered with a man and two women.

"Luce! talk about—luck," panted Logan. "I run plumb —into these good folks. . . . Tom Warnock—his wife and mother—traveling south. . . . They'll see us— through this."

Lucinda smiled a welcome to the kind-faced eager women. Then she was seized again—dragged down to the primitive verge, where her last conscious thought was that she did not care for sympathy or help or even for her life that was begetting life.

The Warnocks stayed three days at Sycamore Canyon, until Lucinda's condition was satisfactory to the women-folk, and then they drove away, leaving Lucinda immeasureably grateful, and Logan a prey to doubt and gloom. He told Lucinda that Warnock, a rancher and cattleman of long experience thought that this natural-fenced canyon was a delusion and a snare. True, it would keep cattle from straying and it was wonderfully fertile, but that was all the good he could say for it. He advised Logan to homestead some other range.

"What would you do, Luce?" he asked, appealingly.

Lucinda was sure Logan would never give up his canyon. He had dreamed of it for years; he had set his heart upon it; and no matter what the obstacles were he would rise superior to them. She knew that her part was to encourage and sustain.

"What do you care for Warnock's opinion?" she said sharply. "He was either envious or mistaken. He admitted you had a fenced range and a fertile one. Your strength and industry will make up for the drawbacks."

She had never before seen her husband respond so

markedly to words from her. He brightened and cast off his pondering dark mood.

"Right! I should have come to you sooner," he declared. "I have my homestead, my cattle range. My dear wife and son! Surely I can work to deserve them."

The baby made a vast and inexplicable difference to Lucinda. When she recovered her strength, so that she could go about her duties, she was as happy as she had been miserable. Logan named his son George Washington Huett and worshipped him. Lucinda could never have been convinced that her husband had it in him to waste time over an infant in a basket. But eventually she divined that this tiny son was Huett's self repeated, his perpetuation. Huett might be thinking that George would grow into a sturdy son to help conquer this wilderness. Whatever it was that went through the father's mind, it made Lucinda rejoice.

The canyon took on a transformation in Lucinda's eyes. Daily it grew in her sight until the long gray sweep of range, the sloping black-fringed walls were bearable. The great tall pines, never silent, always mournful, began to whisper a different language to her. The brook sang by day and the crickets by night that she must find herself and content her heart there. Such possibility had come with the baby.

In six weeks she was working with Logan in the fields. Many times they were driven indoors by the sudden electrical storms. As the days grew more sultry these storms increased in frequency and intensity. The sky would be azure blue with cloud-ships of white sailing across. Then some would show with darkening mushrooming centers, followed by an inky pall. Jagged forked lightning and splitting thunderbolts, peculiarly Arizonian in their intensity and power, awakened Lucinda's old fear of storms. And it grew in proportion to the vastly sharper and more numerous zigzag flashes and the looming thundering volume of sound. The splitting shock and the crash of a struck pine added materially to the threat of the storm, as well as the hollow slamming of echoes from wall to wall. The smell of brimstone always preceded the smell of electrically burned wood. Rain poured in torrents upon the cabin roof.

"Nothing to be afraid of, wife," Logan said stolidly, as he watched from the open door. "Lightning never strikes down in a canyon. That's another good feature about our homestead."

This period of storm lasted less than a month. For Logan its worst feature was that it beat down his corn and washed the soil from the roots of his beans. It was followed by hot weather. Day after day grew hotter. The heat reflected from the stone walls and proved that Logan had planted his corn and beans in the wrong place, and had made no provision for a blasting torrid spell. His patch of beans burned up; his half-matured cabbage wilted as if under the blast of a furnace; his turnips withered, and at last the ten acres of corn, over which he had toiled early and late and which had been his pride, drooped sear and brown, leaf and ear dead on the stalk.

Huett took this sickening destruction of his crops bitterly to heart. It hurt him as had the depredations upon his cattle. His first herd—his first season's planting—all for naught!

"But, husband dear, look at our baby. Look at little George Washington!" exclaimed Lucinda, praying to say the right thing, to renew the courage of this headstrong defeated man.

Huett shouted, as if to the skies. "It was nothing. Only a lesson! . . . George and you are all that count—bless your hearts!"

Chapter Six

SEPTEMBER came with its fringe of golden rod and its clumps of purple asters. The hot spell slowly surrendered to the cooling nights.

Holbert had brought Lucinda a neighborly gift in shape of a setting-hen and a dozen eggs, which he vowed were worth their weight in gold on the range. Lucinda diligently watched the hen, and when the twelve little fluffy chicks hatched out her delight was unconfined. She had developed a deep satisfaction in the birth of living things. The hen was a great pet and kept her brood round the cabin. Lucinda feared the prowlers of the night and shut up her little feathered family carefully at sundown.

Toward the end of September, when the chickens had grown to a respectable size, Lucinda missed one, then another, both of which disappeared during the daytime. Logan took the matter seriously. It seemed that whatever they attempted was destined to failure. He told Lucinda that he believed a coyote or fox was to blame for the depredations. Lucinda's chickens continued to vanish and she was unable to discover the source of their disappearance until one day she heard the mother hen squawking at a great rate. She hurried to the door just in time to see a wide-winged hawk flying towards the treetops with a struggling pullet in its talons. Then if never before in her life Lucinda experienced the blood lust mounting dangerously within her. She watched the hawk fly to a dead limb and there calmly begin to rend and devour the chicken. Logan was close at hand, working on a fence with which he intended to inclose a large area under the opposite wall. At Lucinda's call he came running.

"Logan! It's a murderous hawk," she cried, in rage, pointing at the bird of prey. "It's eating my chicken—right before my eyes. Kill it!"

"Hen-hawk," muttered Logan. He dashed indoors to emerge with his rifle. "If he sets there a second longer it's Katy, bar the door!"

Logan elevated the rifle and appeared to freeze into a statue. Lucinda clapped her hands over her ears, but she watched. At the sharp crack of the rifle she saw a puff of red-brown feathers drift away on the wind, and the hawk, releasing its prey, pitched off its perch to sail heavily downward.

"He's hard hit, Luce," said Logan, grimly. "But we won't take any chances." As the hawk came along overhead, sagging, Logan shot again to bring it hurtling to the ground across the brook. He went to fetch it while Lucinda returned to the cabin a little surprised at the fierceness of her feeling and its weakening reaction. It was a death-dealing place, this awful wilderness of pine ridge and grassy canyon. Now she clearly saw that it was well that Logan possessed as unerring an aim as he did and an unrelenting heart. Not for days did she recover completely from the sickening spectacle of that hawk calmly devouring her pullet alive. Logan had told her that both wolves and cougars loved hot blood—to tear down their prey and glut themselves while the deer or heifer was dying. Before, this would have shocked her, but gradually she was growing insensible to all but the most devastating crises.

October came with a promise of the quiet, purple, smoky days of autumn. The leaves appeared to be slow in coloring. Logan said there had been slight frosts and that if rain came with the equinox, which was late that fall, there would be a riot of gold and scarlet and purple.

Every day Lucinda carried the baby in his basket across to where Logan was at work, and while he slept in the shade she helped her husband. He was on a big job which he hoped to complete soon so that he could drive to Flagg for winter supplies. He was building a fence of poles, high enough to shut out any beast but a cougar, and here he meant to keep the seven calves born the past summer. Shed and corral had already been completed under the wall.

After Logan finished the fence he began to cut the unmatured corn. It would make good fodder, he said. Lucinda laid the stocks in bundles, as they were too short to stack. Logan hauled two wagonloads to the shed and stored them for winter.

"Won't you take me to Flagg with you?" she asked pleadingly, one evening, after their field work was done.

"And take the baby?" he asked, in surprise.

"Of course. I couldn't leave him here."

"Wouldn't it be hard on the kid?"

"That is what has worried me. Would it be—very?"

"Would it? Well, I guess. Hard on you both. You've forgotten how rough that road is. I'll have a big load coming back. Reckon you better not risk it."

Lucinda did not quite understand the gravity of her desire to visit Flagg, but she did not press Logan further. She wanted to go to town, see people, make purchases with which Logan could not be trusted; she hated the thought of being left alone again—but none of these reasons accounted wholly for her intense wish to accompany him. At length she reluctantly decided to remain at home, and kept to herself one of her vague, queer intimations.

"I'll have heaps of work when I get back," Logan said. "If we should have an early winter I'd just be out of luck. And I'm afraid we will. I see birds dropping down here on their way south, and every varmint I've run across has thicker fur than last year. That's good, because I'm going to trap a lot of fur this winter. The acorns have thick hulls and they're falling already. . . . By gosh, I was so sick about the corn and beans and cabbage that I forgot about the potatoes. Reckon they newer grew at all. But that patch was planted in the black soil. Never saw such rich ground. . ."

"I'll look, and if there are any I'll dig them," rejoined Lucinda.

"Good. You'll find sacks in the shed. . . . But doggone, I kind of hate to go this trip." He scratched his head. "No money. Six months of supplies. I need traps, and so many other things I haven't even counted them. . . . Heigho. I'll need my credit this trip sure."

"Why do you dislike taking credit?"

"I don't. All farmers and ranchers live on it. But they have crops and herds coming on. My crop failed, and it'll be long before I raise any cattle. I must depend on the pelts I can trap. Last fall when I was hunting over across the ridge I ran onto a beaver dam that was a humdinger. Lake as big as this bench. Lots of beaver there. I'll work it this winter, till the snow gets too deep on top."

Still Logan lingered on at the ranch finding odd jobs to do. One of these was deflecting the outlet of the spring to run it down close by the cabin, a task that could well have been left, but Lucinda had found it handy to fill a bucket right at her door. About mid-October when the weather was at its best she advised Logan to go. She resisted sending for things she thought she needed, although she had begun to realize how she could do without almost everything. What she could not improvise, she dispensed with. Clothes, medicines, luxuries—these she had forgotten. And when she remembered, she thought of her trunk full of bride's dresses and flimsy garments. How useless here on the range! But she vowed she would not give up yet and grow old and never care about her appearance.

It dawned upon Lucinda after a day longer that Logan wanted to ask her for money, but was ashamed. She thought it best to keep that five-hundred-dollar marriage gift intact, for there would come a time when she would need it more than now. So she pretended not to guess his feeling, and when he finally asked her outright she evaded both consent and denial. Nevertheless Logan left in a huff, perhaps because he had weakened to ask her. How sure she was that he would be glad some day for her strength!

As the weather had cooled, Lucinda's energy had returned full tide. She felt that she would develop into a fit mate for Huett, if she could only learn to subjugate her thoughts to the practical tasks that confronted settlers. But she always thought and felt too acutely.

The morning of Logan's departure, she left Coyote to guard the baby, and she went up the canyon to gather wild grapes. This was the first time she had ever been round the bend. Here the canyon did not have the characteristics that marked it below. The walls were hidden; the forest covered slope and floor; the brook poured out from a green-gold bank to leap over a ledge; the aspens blazed in golden glory and the maples burned scarlet. The grapevines hung from oak trees along the brook and their mingled foliage of bronze and russet added to the prevailing color. The pines were scattered, allowing the sun to shine through in broad rays. Lucinda stopped to gaze in surprise and what was almost consternation. It was lovely there. She had never until that moment accorded any beauty to Sycamore Canyon. She had seen it first at the drab end of autumn, when her receptiveness had been blunted by her terrible disappointment.

A flock of wild turkeys scattered as she approached the grapevines. The big birds had been feeding there. Lucinda heard the put-put-put of a hen calling young ones. She felt an affinity with that mother. Lucinda filled her basket in short order. The large purple grapes made those with which she was familiar in Missouri look insignificant.

She rested several times on the way back to the cabin. The basket was heavy. And she kept looking back. The wildness and loneliness of the solitude did not prohibit beauty. Really they enhanced it, as Lucinda saw with clearer eyes. Logan's ruthless axe had not desecrated here.

Lucinda resolved to go back often to that colored glen. It grew upon her. Whatever had enlightened her or removed the scales from her eyes, she must trust and cultivate. She had found melancholy happiness in the tending of her sunflowers; surely there was a relation between that and this new-found pleasure in the woodland. Since the coming of the baby she divined that it was a deeper and more motivating power than she had felt before. Huett's salvation depended upon lusty sons.

Upon arriving at the cabin again Lucinda set the basket of grapes upon the porch and curiously looked down the canyon. It appeared that she looked through a transformed medium. Gray field and winding brook, forbidding walls of stone and yellow, red-spotted slopes, high ravines choked with wild growth, and black-fringed ridges against the blue sky—all had become invested with a glamor as real as the purple haze that hung over everything like smoke.

"Oh, if this—this only lasts!" cried Lucinda, and turned to her work. It was to find that her task did not prohibit visual and mental study of the changed wilderness.

She built a fire outdoors and put the large iron kettle upon it. How vividly this outdoor fire, the smell of smoke, and the kettle, recalled the autumn days at home when her mother made peach jam and apple butter to preserve for winter! And hard on that succeeded the poignant pinch of her poverty. She had nothing to preserve for winter except the wild grapes she had stolen from the turkeys.

While these grapes were stewing Lucinda happened to think of the potato crop, long given up by Logan as a failure. She took the forked spade from among Logan's few tools, and hurried out across the canyon to the shaded swale of black soil. It was a long narrow acre lined by some big pine trees. The shriveled potato-plants were hardly to be found in the grass and weeds, but the outline of the long rows could be discerned.

Lucinda shoved the spade deep under some dead vines and pried upward. The spade stuck in something hard. Pulling it out she uncovered the hill, to expose great brown potatoes, one of which showed the wet marks where the fork had pierced. Lucinda fell upon her knees in virtual rapture to dig energetically with her hands. Potatoes! Could she be dreaming? In that single hill she unearthed nineteen, all solid, perfect, and some as large as quart measures. Missouri could not boast of such potatoes as these. That black soil, mast, Logan called it, a mold of leaf and pine needle, accounted for such growth. But Lucinda could not trust to this one hill. She dug up another to exhume half a dozen enormous ones. Then she tried a hill in another row, and then another, with a like result. Evidently they had matured early in the rich soil before the hot spell came.

"Oh, it isn't all bad—Logan's luck!" she exclaimed, gladly. "What a pity he didn't find out before he left! He could have hauled a whole wagonload to Flagg."

She carried some of the potatoes back to the cabin, thinking that she would endeavor to dig and sack the crop before Logan's return. By midafternoon she had filled all her crocks with the grape-jam. Then she milked the two cows Logan had put in the pen, after which she got her supper.

Sunset blazed gold and red down in the canyon, and when it faded the cool wind breathed down from the heights.

At dusk Lucinda barred herself in the cabin. Coyote had been her only companion before, but now she had the bright-eyed, crowing baby. The mother side of her felt like a lioness; there remained, however, that stifled but resurging nature of Lucinda Baker which she feared would never grow callous to loneliness, to solitude, to dread of elemental things and the worse ones of the imagination.

The wind did not rise and no wild beasts prowled about the cabin. Lucinda went to sleep and did not awaken until the hungry baby proclaimed his wants. When the smoky still morning came and Lucinda saw the white on the grass and the blanket of fog far down the canyon she thought she had gained a victory over herself.

That day, in addition to her other tasks, Lucinda dug three rows of potatoes, and spread them out to dry. Before she stopped she found it back-breaking toil. Yet it had made her happy as cooking and washing and mending never had. The dank odor of the black soil, the feel of the potatoes, the hot sun pouring down and the sweat on her brow—all proof that she had the vigor and the will, that she was indisputably a pioneer wife—these raw sensations, added to the uplifting ones of yesterday, made her perceive her lot in a stronger clearer light, made her begin to build against the outrageous shocks that she knew must ensue.

Hour after hour Lucinda labored in the field. If she halted occasionally to catch her breath or straighten her aching back she gazed out at the ever-changing canyon scene. Sometimes she saw Logan's cattle down the gray stretch; often deer and turkeys watched her without fleeing; once a herd of elk, some with great antlered heads, rolled and cracked the stones on the slope. And every day the smoky veil of autumn deepened, the stillness grew more pronounced, the colors took on more fiery hues, the plaintive notes of birds heading south accentuated the silence. A living breathing presence in the great forest seemed to hang suspended over them, waiting for a voice.

At last, on the eighth day, Lucinda sacked the final pile of potatoes; and she viewed the field with more than satisfaction. Huett's amaze and gladness would be divided between sight of this abounding yield of potatoes and realization of his wife's prodigious labors.

Lucinda finished strong, but ruefully looked at her calloused palms and the capable hands that had once been tender. She would never again see them white and soft even if the dirt could be scrubbed out of the blistered skin. Her round arms were as brown as the oak leaves, and her tanned face had become impervious to the sun. The little wall-mirror told Lucinda that she was a handsomer woman than she had been a girl. But who was there to see her now? Logan never looked at her that way. Lucinda experienced a poignant return of the old yearning for friendly faces, gay voices, for the life that she had been brought up in. The old revolt against loneliness, against this bitter, forsaken range where she had blindly expected to find neighbors, women, close at hand, lifted its hydra-head and had to be cudgeled down. Neighborly settlement of this land would never come in her day. She must resign that longing, she must make work, baby, and Logan fill her life. There was always compensation for loss. She believed in time she would find consolation in toil such as she had just ended.

That afternoon the sun had faded under a gray haze. Lucinda marked the change only at sunset, when she missed the rose and gold colors. She feared it might mean a change in the weather. Wet heavy roads would slow Huett if not detain him. Probably he was far on his way home now. She refused to be depressed by the untoward sign, did her chores as usual, and went to bed early.

Sooner or later Lucinda awakened. Apparently no sound had disturbed her rest. The child was asleep beside her. Coyote did not move. She listened. And she became aware of such silence as had never before lain upon that cabin. She could not tell where the window was, which proved that the night outside was as black as pitch. The air felt appreciably warmer.

After a prolonged moment of suspense and uncertainty a low rumble, almost indistinguishable, came up out of the southwest. It sounded far away. Lucinda wondered if it was a landslide somewhere in one of the canyons. Avalanches were heard infrequently, though they occurred in the spring or rainy season.

Moments dragged on. It came again—a faint rumble, as if made by a rolling rock. Then a long interval ensued before the next disturbance which seemed closer, louder, and was unmistakably thunder. Could it be a belated thunderstorm, at the end of October? Then she remembered Logan's telling her that some of the worst storms known to the canyon country of Arizona slipped up at night heralded by a few insignificant rumbles of thunder.

Ah! Her arch-enemy, the wind! A long strange sigh seemed to sift through the forest, on over the cabin, and down the canyon. It ceased. Lucinda strained her sensitive ears. Even the tips of the pines were silent. Then the still oppressive heaviness and impenetrable blackness warned Lucinda that she had not sensed these before. Dread clamped down upon her.

Suddenly lightning flared, weird and pale outside the window, to be followed almost instantly with an angry short clap of thunder. Lucinda gathered her endurance to withstand more; but there was no continued flash of lightning and roll of splitting clouds.

Instead the wind gained strength in volume. Its soft low moan swelled to a steady wail that grew, seemed swallowed up in an oncoming roar. Lucinda trembled under her blankets. This storm could be no less than the belated equinoctial disturbance—in that latitude a dreadful onslaught of the elements.

A mighty roar of gale swooped over the canyon. Lucinda could sense that the fiercer stratum of wind passed over her cabin, missing all but the tops of the lofty pines. Above the tumult, up on the ridges, crash after crash split the din, witness to the fact that old and dead pines were falling like leaves before the blast.

But Lucinda knew that the autumnal hurricane was no respecter of pines even like those in the prime of life which surrounded the canyon. She heard them creak, she felt their sway in the lift of the cabin. That one giant with the blasted top—she was positive that one would crash. What was happening up on the ridge-tops was now of no moment to her. The menace was close at hand.

A terrible splitting crack that drowned the uproar ended in an earth-jarring crash. Stones rattled down from the chimney. The cabin settled down from its leap, and the wind roared on as before, high up, with its steady whine punctuated by more shocks low down in the canyon. Then the floodgates of the black sky opened to add a roaring deluge of rain to the frenzy of the wind.

All the rest of the night Lucinda lay there stiffly, clutching her baby to her breast, until she was deaf and numb, insensible to pain and terror; the storm raged by and gray dawn broke.

Arising wearily, she uncovered the red coals of her fire and replenished it with chips and cones. She made breakfast and fed the baby before gathering courage enough to look out. She heard the sullen chafe of the flooded brook. When she unbarred and opened her door the sun had arisen, bright and steely.

Lucinda gazed out upon a changed canyon. The great pine had fallen so close to the cabin that some tips of its branches had broken against the wall. The other trees adjacent had withstood the gale. High up on the slopes windfalls were scattered about. The brook was a yellow river, swirling slowly down the canyon, its muddy surface covered with driftwood and leaves. She would not be able to cross to milk the cows that day; and if Logan returned he would be compelled to camp on the other side. The glorious golden groves of aspen, the scarlet ravines, the patches of sumach, the thickets of oak and maple, only yesterday a mosaic of bronze and russet and purple, all appeared devastated of beauty and stood shrunken and drab under the cruel morning light. The drenched pines loomed dark, their foliage thinned of all their lacy brown. It was as if a blight had passed over the wilderness. Something was gone. The wind moaned its requiem in the tips of the pines. The still warm smoky glamorous days, that seemed always afternoon, were as irretrievable as the fallen leaves.

Lucinda did not see how the sun could shine so brightly. The elements of nature were as relentless as the beasts that clawed and ripped live flesh. Another season had come, the herald of winter. These changes had to be. The days and weeks and months rolled on in their unscrutable cycle. Life also had to go on; and human beings were like leaves tossed about in the turgid flood. A nameless imponderable force lay heavy upon her.

Her depression wore away during the day, like the flooded brook which gradually ran down to normal. With her endless tasks before her and the prospect of Logan's return nearing, Lucinda recovered from the shock. Every vicissitude was leaving her stronger. She began to divine that there was a lesson to be taught through all this, if only she could find the courage and necessary intelligence to absorb it. Still she feared blindly that she might be beaten down into the submissiveness and lethargy of an ox, although her common sense repudiated this.

Next morning the brook had fallen low enough for Lucinda to ford it and milk the cows. At noon the sun was bright and warm. She emptied the sacks of potatoes and spread them to dry. Every few minutes she would halt in her task to gaze yearningly at the road to see if Logan was coming. He was long overdue. There was scarcely anything left to eat in the cabin. . . .

That night she slept poorly and was restless when awake. The dawning of a fine clear day usually cheered Lucinda, but this morning she seemed distraught. Her work did not take her mind off Logan's failure to arrive. From anxiety she passed to dread.

He would be coming soon; she felt that. But she surrendered to an impulse to climb from the canyon to watch along the road.

She did not mind the journey, although little George was growing heavy. When she reached the top and drew out on the main road she sank to rest on the same log where she had waited for Logan that day the oxen ran away with her. The spot appeared unfamiliar. After gazing about she decided a better view could be obtained up on the rocky bluff above the canyon road. Pantingly she climbed the short distance.

From this location she could see the yellow road winding along the edge of the forest, and several miles beyond where it cut up over a bare ridge. As she watched a moving white spot appeared. It was a prairie-schooner.

The slow snail-like movement attested to the team of oxen.

"Oh! it's Logan!" she cried, breathless with relief and joy. "Baby, here comes your daddy now!"

All at once Lucinda's queer undefined dread vanished like a shadow over which the sun rose. How glad she was that she had come up to see him before he could reach home! It would be an hour yet before he turned off to descend into the canyon, and with so heavy a load he might be longer.

"But he mustn't see me here!" exclaimed Lucinda, suddenly confronted by her childish anxiety. She hurried down the bluff and into the weedy road. Coyote had gone off chasing some animal. She called, but the dog did not return. As Lucinda went on leaving the gate open, she wondered what would Logan say to the great fallen pine that had so nearly crushed the cabin? Probably he would take it practically as he did nearly everything: "Gosh! that equinox laid a winter's firewood right at my door!" None the less Lucinda felt that all was well again. It would be six months before he could leave her in the spring. Six long months without the dreaded lonely oppressiveness that had weighed upon her so heavily.

She felt young and happy again, and her love for Logan welled up from an overflowing heart.

When she surmounted the bench to the cabin she espied the numerous piles of huge potatoes shining out there in the sun. That unexpected stroke of good fortune, as well as her work must fetch something really extravagant in the way of compliments from Logan Huett.

Hot and panting Lucinda went indoors to lay the sleepy baby in his basket.

Suddenly she heard a sound outside. A padded step! Could that be Coyote? She would have run to the door, but something hindered swift movement. From the threshold she saw several ragged ponies. Two of them bore riders. Lean, dark, wild! They were Indians. And on the instant a tall savage strode from one side to confront her.

Lucinda saw a handsome somber visage lighted by piercing eyes of gray. Before her mind worked beyond sensation the Indian shoved her back into the cabin. He spat across the threshold and entered.

"Me Matazel!" he announced, impressively, and he struck his beaded breast with a sinewy brown hand.

That Apache! Lucinda was rooted to the floor. Logan's mortal enemy, the Apache who had sworn to get even—he was here! She seemed to grasp his lithe magnificent presence, his ragged buckskin garb, though his eyes held hers with the hypnotic power of a snake. They were gray eyes, something like Logan's, and as they swept her body they grew terrible with a hot searing blaze.

"What do you want?" she cried.

"Matazel get even! Matazel take Huett squaw!" he hissed, snatching at her. "Say no, me kill—burn cabin!"

Suddenly Lucinda heard the shrill squeaking of wheels on Logan's wagon, coming down the steep road beyond the corrals. The Apache heard, too. With a piercing look at her, Matazel wheeled and strode silently from the cabin. Lucinda saw him join the Apaches. Avoiding the trail, they rode up the canyon, quickly out of sight.

Lucinda's legs wobbled under her and almost she sank in collapse. Logan, the woodsman, would surely see the tell-tale signs of the Apache's visit. He would take up his rifle and trail Matazel. The Apaches had heard Logan. They would ambush and kill him. Logan must never know. As she heard the oxen splashing through the brook, Lucinda grasped a broom to run out and sweep away the moccasin tracks on the hearth.

Chapter Seven

HUETT went out in the gray of dawn, glad to feel a light sifting snow almost damp in his face. That meant moderation of the bitter cold. The hard winter with deep snows on the ridge-tops had ruined his cherished plan of trapping abundant beaver and other animals. He had cleaned out his canyon of valuable fur. Deep snows had driven an old cougar down into the protected places, and Huett's little herd had suffered severely.

With his milk pail Huett strode for the cowsheds. In the pale gloom the brook made a black belt down the white canyon. Only in the most severe weather did the water freeze. He was thinking that a thaw would be most welcome. His hay was all gone and the fodder would not last another month. The cows and heifers, and the three calves he still had left, must soon be turned out in the pasture. There was abundant feed on the south slopes, but the risk in the open canyon was greater.

"Well, I don't know," pondered the homesteader. "That old Tom cougar has come right into my pen to kill stock. Reckon it's about six for one and half a dozen for the other. But by jiminy! I've got to kill that cunning old cat. But for him I'd come through the winter with little loss."

He carried a bundle of fodder to Bossy and threw it under the shed. He was about to sit down on his box-seat, preparatory to milking Bossy, when he heard a thumping of hoofs and the bawl of cows in the far pen.

"That cougar—I'll bet!" muttered Huett, and he stood up to listen. Then followed a scratching of claws on the high fence, a soft thump and a growl, followed by a strangled cry of a calf, suddenly cut short.

Huett looked about for a weapon. Foolishly he had forgotten his gun. There was a pitchfork in the stall, but close at hand he espied a spade, which he caught up as he ran to the gate of the next pen. He was in time to see a dark convulsive blur on the snow, to hear a rending of flesh, and a gasping intake of air. The next instant a big cougar, gray in the dim light of dawn, left the calf and bounded for the fence.

Huett yelled and ran, brandishing the spade. The cougar leaped, catching the fence about two thirds up. Then he climbed like any cat. The beast hooked his fore-paws over the top and was drawing his body up when Huett, with terrific sweep of the spade, knocked him off the fence. The blow was so powerful that it propelled the cougar almost twenty feet into a corner of the pen. It disabled him also, as Huett was quick to see.

The homesteader leaped to take advantage of this opportunity, hoping to put in a telling blow before the giant cat recovered. He was an instant too late. The cougar spun around, sending the snow flying, and backed into the corner, crouched to spring, spitting explosively, his eyes blazing balls of green fire.

"Aha, I got you now!" roared Huett, swinging the spade. "You bloody calf-eater! You'll never eat another calf of mine. . . . I'll split your head!"

The cougar sprang. Huett met that onslaught with a vigorous thrust of the spade. He hit straight into the open mouth of the beast. The cracking of teeth was followed by a snarling roar, then a grind of bone on steel. Huett wrenched the spade free and struck the cougar another blow that sent it sprawling again into the fence-corner.

"Fightin' cornered cougar, huh?" shouted Huett, fierce in his anger. "You've got a man to deal with now, cat. . . . Take that—damn your yellow hide! . . . Spit—roar. . . . I'll separate those sneaking eyes!"

Beaten down, the cougar rolled up on its back, emitting frightful hisses, snapping at the spade, clawing with four striking paws. Huett swung the spade edgewise and the blade caught in the fence. In the next instant the cougar whirled to seize Huett's left arm in its jaws. Luckily the heavy leather sleeve saved his arm from being crushed. Wrenching out the spade he struck savagely at the eyes of green fire. The blade glanced off the skull, but one of the terrible eyes went out like a light extinguished. The spade broke, leaving the handle in Huett's grasp. With that he beat the beast over the head until the wood flew into bits. But he had freed his arm. With lightning speed he seized the big cat around the throat and brought to bear all his wonderful strength. A fiery elation ran along his veins. He muttered grimly at the clawing beast. Insensible to the rip and tear of claws, he lifted the animal high, crashed its head on the fence and choked it until it sagged limp in his grip.

Huett held it a moment, gloating with the sheer savagery of his victory. Then he let it fall and staggered back to lean against the fence and look about with glazed eyes. Daylight had come. The snow had ceased. The corner of the pen displayed a ploughed area of blood-stained snow. Huett's left arm and his legs down to his boots had withstood the clawing attack of the cougar, but his sleeve and jeans were torn to shreds and soaked with blood.

Realizing that he was seriously clawed and bitten Huett hurried back to the cabin. Lucinda was up, bending over the fire, which was burning brightly.

"Logan!—What's happened?" she cried, standing up pale and staring.

"Don't worry. I'm all right. Just had a hell of a fight with a cougar. That old Tom! And I killed him, too. . . . But he cut me up bad!"

Lucinda could only gasp as he threw off his coat, the left sleeve of which hung in ribbons. Then he took off his shirt.

"Luce, don't look so scared," he said, with grim humor. "You should see old Tom! . . . We'll want hot water and some clean linen. . . . They tell me a cat bite in this hospitable land is most as bad as that of a hydrophobia skunk. Danger of blood-poisoning. Have we anything to put on—any medicine or strong salve?"

"No. I used the last. . . . There's some turpentine. But you can't use that."

"Just the stuff. Get the basin, Luce. Let's see. . . . Water not too hot. . . . Now, wash off the blood. Make a clean job of it, Luce. When I was scout for Crook I used to watch the Doc fix up cuts and gunshot wounds. To wash 'em clean was the trick. . . . Yow! there's where Kitty got me with a big canine tooth! Reckon I broke off the other with the spade. If I hadn't had my leather coat on—whew!"

"Does it hurt, Logan?"

"Hurt? No. I was just thinking over what he might have done to me. . . . Get some bandages before using the turpentine. . . . He scratched this arm pretty bad. . . . All right. Now! . . . Auggh! . . . Get some in that bite. Deep."

Logan thought he sweat blood during the application of the fiery turpentine, but he would have undergone it again to get rid of such a flesh-eater as the cougar. After Lucinda had bound his arm, she examined his leg to find long deep scratches, but little laceration of flesh. When all of them were treated and bandaged Logan felt immersed in a bath of fire. He paced the floor restlessly, his black eyes gleaming, while Lucinda turned her hand to breakfast. The dog Coyote sat on the hearth, grave-eyed and watchful.

"Luce, that tom-cat was our worst enemy," said Logan with strong relief in his tones. "With him out of the way I can raise some calves. . . . That reminds me I didn't look to see if he'd had time to kill the calf."

Throwing a blanket around his shoulders Logan went out. Snow was falling again. The air felt raw and damp. He found the calf dead. Judging by the tracks, which were printed words to Logan, the cougar had leaped nearly twenty feet on his last jump, and, landing on the calf, had buried his fangs in the back of its neck and with both paws had pulled its head back thus breaking its neck.

"He was a killer! . . . Dammit, that means I'll have to butcher this calf," Logan mumbled to himself. Then he turned his attention to the cougar. He had sliced off one side of its head, taking an eye and an ear. Other wounds did not show. . . . "Here's a hide I won't sell. . . . Biggest cougar I've seen. This was a good morning's work, in spite of losing a calf."

Logan returned to the cabin, dragging the cougar over the snow, and indoors, much to Lucinda's disgust. "Here's the son-of-a-gun, Luce," he exclaimed. "Isn't he a beauty. I'll make a rug out of that hide. . . . Back, Coyote. If you'd been a real dog you'd have smelled this cat, and saved me God knows what."

After breakfast Logan skinned the cougar, and nailed the hide up on the wall outside. Then he went out to butcher the calf. He felt extreme dizziness, and such pain from the burning turpentine and wounds that it made him weak. His movements lacked their customary vigor and speed. He was long at the task, but finally got the calf hung up to a rafter. Then he returned to the cabin.

"Luce, I can't milk this morning," he said, sinking into a chair. "You'll have to do it."

"All right, Logan. . . . You must be suffering torture. You're white and drawn."

"Reckon I feel pretty bad. Loss of blood—and this

damned burn. . . . Be careful how you walk, dear. It's slippery this morning and you're getting heavy again." He shook his head mournfully. "I'm afraid I'll be laid up a bit. . . . And you with child doing all the work! We don't have much good luck, Luce."

"It could be worse. We'll manage, Logan. If only you weren't in such pain!"

"I reckon that'll wear off presently," he replied, heavily. However, it did not wear off, but grew worse. Logan endured the most agonizing night of his life. Morning found him feverish, with swollen throbbing limbs. The burn from the turpentine, however, had abated.

Logan lay awake in the gray of dawn. Always a slow thinker, he was additionally inhibited by his condition, but he realized that the situation called for extreme measures. His faithful wife must not have thrust upon her all of the work from cabin to corrals. She had not been well for months, if to be strange, brooding, wholly unlike her old self, were ill. It was the new child. For him to succumb to his wounds, to be victim of blood-poisoning, to lie useless for weeks and more—these were absolutely impossible. At this juncture he began his fight.

Logan did not go out of his head. His will compared markedly with his great physical strength. Many times during the next three days, especially in the dark of night, he was forced to sit up to keep his senses. Even then the darkness, the silence, rolled over him like demons. He endured the pain without betraying it to Lucinda, although her constant attention and solicitude gave him cause for concern. Three long days and three ghastly nights he fought to get off his back. All the while he was aware that Lucinda cared for his wounds and tried to ease his sufferings. She was required to chop wood because, owing to the unusually cold winter, the supply had been exhausted. This labor galled Logan to exasperation and passionate maledictions concerning his neglect, but stoically she went about her tasks ignoring his protests. While breakfast was cooking she fed the baby, now a lusty and growing boy. During the day there was no rest from her unending toil. This evening and the succeeding one she kept the fire burning all night: winter was dying hard.

On the fourth day Logan forced himself to get up. He staggered. It seemed his strength had vanished completely. He could not use his left arm nor scarcely move his left leg; but doggedly he chopped wood, built a fire, carried water, milked the cows, packed the fodder to the corrals. Silent, plodding, unbeatable he refused to allow his muscles to cease their unremitting labor.

Gradually the hard days and awful nights passed. Logan well knew when the fever left him. A dark and terrible force at work upon his mind, a slow boil of his blood, a dizziness and constant dancing spots before his eyes, the hot fire in his flesh—these fled with the endless days, and he was on the mend.

Logan could not remember a spring so welcome. The snow faded off the ridges, the turkeys began to gobble, the bluebells to nod under the pines; jays returned to squall and the squirrels to chatter, bear tracks showed in the open spots, and the sun shone daily warmer—these portents of summer could not be denied: they were a fulfillment of promise. Lucinda had quoted an ancient maxim one early winter day: "If winter comes can spring be far behind?" Lo! here it had come and Logan's doubts fled. He would soon be himself; he would beat this pioneer game; soon he would have sons to help him ride and drive and shoot and chop with him. He envisioned the day in the years to come when his canyon and the one below would be full of grazing cattle—the thirty thousand head these magnificent grassy valleys could support.

That spring Logan did not go to Flagg. Lucinda begged him to wait until after the baby came so she could ride in with him. How somberly she had vowed she would never stay alone at Sycamore Canyon again! But Logan was tolerant with her. She could well be ex-cused during the burden and travail of child-bringing. She was a wonderful helpmate. Her uncomplaining steadfast loyalty did not escape him. Lucinda Baker could have married a better man than he—one who could have given her the comforts which she had been brought up to expect. Logan Huett never forgot that. It was a spur to goad him on.

Logan's horses stayed in the vicinity of the cabin, al-ways hanging around for a little hay, or the measure of grain he doled out to them. He had acquired the habit of training horses while with the soldiers. No rider ever needed to follow the tracks of a trained horse. His oxen, however, he kept with the cattle down the canyon. Logan found six steers and the bull. Again his herd had dwindled. Instead of feeling badly about more loss, Logan was glad it was so small.

The frost thawed out of the soil and the water dried up. Logan began his spring ploughing. It was slow work because of the snail-like pace of the oxen. Some day he would buy a good farm team. His poverty did not in-terfere with his old dreams and plans. He knew his tre-mendous assets—his strength, his endurance, his un-quenchable optimism. No range could destroy these forces. Besides, it was to the future that he looked for results; and only his slow beginning filled him with dogged wrath at the seasons and the obstacles.

He ploughed all the ground he had farmed the year before except the sandy ten acres he had planted in corn.

For the cornfield he chose a plot lower down, near the brook, where the grass grew abundantly. He trebled the area for potatoes. He would sell two hundred bushels that fall.

Planting was labor he loved best of all with the exception of work pertaining to cattle. Mistakes indulged in during the preceding year he carefully avoided. From dawn until dark he sowed, planted, waded through the rich dark soil, but when he arrived at the cornfield he had scarce begun sowing when the flight of crows arrived. A black crowd of cawing crows!

"All the damn crows in Arizona!" ejaculated Logan, in a rage. "You black buzzards; why don't a few of you call on some other farmer?"

This spring he gave up killing them. All the corn he laid that first day they ate behind him. Next day he covered the precious kernels and so outwitted them. Crows were not diggers at least.

"If it gets dry this summer, I'll irrigate," soliloquized Logan, surveying the land, and its relation to the brook. By going up the canyon he could dam the stream and run water all over his farmland. He scarcely gave a thought to the prodigious labor involved. After planting the cornfield he set to work with the beans. In a country where beans were supposed to flourish he had failed signally. He had one sack left which was enough for a dozen long rows. He had no turnip seed.

One morning at breakfast Lucinda said: "Logan, it is July."

"July?—Well!—How do you know?"

"I've kept track of the months. . . . My time is near."

"Aw! I almost forgot, dear. I wish I could stand it for you. . . . Another boy! Gosh, I hope he comes on the Fourth of July. Anyway I'll name him Abraham Lincoln Huett."

"Husband, we should wait until we get him." Lucinda's tone was strange and far away, but Logan failed to notice it.

"Hadn't you better take it easy, Luce?" he asked earnestly. "You're on your feet all the time, even when you're not helping me."

"I feel strong—restless. I don't get tired. If I idle, I brood."

"I know so little about such things. . . . Can you tell any ways near when?"

"Not very closely. But when the hour comes a woman knows. . . . You must be ready to hurry after Mrs. Holbert."

"I can get her here in five hours."

"That's reasonably quick, I'm sure. But it might be all over in far less time than that. We'll hope not . . . only you must have your horse ready."

"I'll keep Buck in the corral. Don't worry, dear. It'll be all right. I'll be within call any time."

"Logan, you forget I'm alive while you're at work," she said, somberly.

Several days went by with Logan ever thoughtful of Lucinda, neglecting his work to make frequent trips back to the cabin, and never going far away. However, she went about her tasks as usual and gradually his anxiety lessened. He expected another word from her to prepare him.

There was a long narrow ravine opening down into the canyon, a favorite place for cattle to stray in hot weather. It was shady and the grazing was green. Logan had not fenced the upper end of this, as he had never tracked any cattle that far. One afternoon, however, happening along near this spot, he found to his dismay that several of his steers had worked out onto the ridge above. He discovered them up an aspen swale and drove them back carrying poles and logs to obstruct the opening for the time being. When he had completed this job and started home he saw that the afternoon was spent. The shade of the deep ravine where he had worked had failed to warn him of the approach of sunset and dusk.

Darkness had settled down by the time he reached the fields. The night hawks were flying about with their weird cries, the insects had begun their buzzing chorus, and the drowsy summer warmth of the day had begun to cool. Logan was surprised not to see a light in the cabin. He hurried on, a sudden fear assailing him. Reaching the open door he found the cabin dark.

"Luce," he called, anxiously. She did not answer. He went in, repeating his call, this time sharply. She was not in the cabin. He rushed out to shout. If she had gone out for wood or water she could hear him; but there was no answer. The only other place she could possibly be was at the cowshed. His neglect to come back early to milk the cows might have induced her to do those chores herself—she was queer about such little things.

Logan strode down the path. Stars had begun to twinkle. He heard a pattering on the ground, and the dog came running to him, leaping up and whining. Coyote would not be far from Lucinda. Nevertheless Logan's sense of something amiss did not leave him.

He hurried to the sheds. All dark! Still it was nothing for Lucinda to finish milking after nightfall. Logan heard the rustle and munching of hay. Coyote had left him, but he noticed that Bossy was in her stall.

"Lucinda—are you there?" called Logan hesitantly, peering into the darkness. Fear knifed him with a swift, sharp pang.

"Here—I am," Lucinda replied, in a voice from which it seemed all life had drained.

Logan felt his way to the next stall. It had been used

to store hay, of which only a lower layer was left. He called again huskily.

"Here," she replied, almost under his feet.

"Luce—Girl!" he cried, falling on his knees to feel around for her. "What has happened?"

"I wanted—to milk—before dark. . . . But I never got to it . . . my time came. . . . Your son, Abraham Lincoln, has just—been born. . . . He was in a hurry to—come into this world."

"Son! Abraham—Oh, my God! . . . Luce, this is awful . . . what shall I do?"

"Leave me here. . . . Go for Mrs. Holbert."

"Let me carry you up to the cabin."

"It wouldn't be safe. . . . You'd better go . . . and hurry! . . . The baby is alive."

Logan struck a match with shaking hands. The light flared up. He saw Lucinda lying on the hay, white as a corpse. Her face appeared small—shrunken—her eyes too large—somehow terrible. Tucked under her arm, half covered, lay a strange little mite with a mop of black hair.

"Well!—Howdy there—Abe!" he said, in a strangled voice.

But he did not look at his wife again. He extinguished the match with fingers which did not feel the burn.

"Luce, I hate to leave you. But I'm helpless. . . . If only I ——"

"Go, Logan. Don't waste time."

Huett left her with a husky utterance, and running clumsily in the dark to the corral, saddled and bridled Buck with hands that shook in spite of his intense efforts to control them. Mounting he was off up the hill. He found that Buck was not a racer, but was strong and tireless and could lope indefinitely. Except on the grades where Logan was forced to walk or trot, the homesteader kept his horse in open gait.

The hard action gradually steadied Logan, but he could not remember having known such agitation before. However, his practical habit of thinking out obstacles soon enabled him to apply all his faculties toward the ride through the forest. Where the pines grew dense it was darker and the road was full of pits and roots; but in the open stretches Logan made better time. Vigilant and intense in his concentration over the lay of the land Logan hardly realized the passing of time. At last he swung out of the deep wood and into the open where the south end of Mormon Lake gleamed under the stars. In less than half an hour he hauled Buck up in front of Holbert's ranch.

The rancher and his womenfolk were astounded at Logan's onslaught upon their door; particularly his panting relief at finding them home, and his frantic appeal for help.

"Hitch up pronto, John," said the older woman calmly. "Mary, you come help me get ready. . . . Don't worry, Huett. It'll be all right. There was once a great and good man born in a manger."

Logan unsaddled Buck and turned him into the pasture. Then he ran to the barn, where Holbert was readying the wagon by the light of a lantern.

"Won't take a jiffy," announced the rancher. "Bill went after the hosses. I had them in to water no more than an hour ago. . . . It's a down-hill pull. You can drive it in three hours. My wife is an old hand at birthday parties. Don't be upset, Huett. This is kinda common in the lives of settlers."

Logan had a fleeting idea that he lacked something these pioneers like Holbert possessed, but their assurance and kindliness heartened him in this extremity. For the first time he echoed Lucinda's wish that they might have had near neighbors. Presently Holbert drove the buckboard up to the cabin, Logan following with the son-in-law, Bill, who was solicitous and helpful. When they arrived at the cabin, the women were emerging.

"We'll take the lantern," Mrs. Holbert was saying. "But put it out. Give Huett some matches. Put some blankets under the seat. . . . Mary, have I forgotten anything?"

"I reckon not, maw."

They climbed into the back seat. Holbert gave the reins over to Logan and jumped down. "Easy team to drive, Huett. Hold them to a fast trot, except on the grades. . . . Good luck!"

"I'm much obliged, Holbert," said Logan, gratefully. He drove out and turned south on the main road. A half moon had risen over the black forest and gleamed softly on the lake. That would be a help, he thought. The women wrapped blankets around their knees and lapsed into a silence welcome to Logan. He attended to the road, forcing into abeyance his acute anxiety while his sense of dragging time eased away under the influence of swift movement. Holbert had spoken modestly of this team: they trotted on tirelessly rolling the light buckboard; the lake passed, the moon soared, and the sections of black forest gradually grew longer as the miles went by.

Before Logan thought such a thing possible he reached Long Valley and soon was clattering down into moonlit Sycamore Canyon.

Halting at the corrals, he leaped out to dash toward the cow-stalls. He could dimly see Lucinda lying on the hay. The moment was exceedingly poignant. His voice almost failed him, but she heard and answered.

"Aw!" he exclaimed, fervently. "They're here, Luce." And he ran back to the buckboard. "She's alive, Mrs. Holbert!" he cried, boyishly. "She spoke!"

"Shore she's alive. What was you thinkin', man? Light the lantern an' hand out thet bundle."

Logan heard the cheery pioneer woman talking solicitously to Lucinda. He halted the team near the corral fence to pace the moonlit path. After an endless interval the younger woman sought him.

"Maw says to tell you it's a strappin' boy an' favors you," she said. "Both doin' fine. In the mawnin' they can be moved to the house. We'll stay heah with them. . . . An' you can go to bed."

Logan mumbled his profound gratitude to her and to something more of which he was only vaguely conscious. He unhitched the horses and turned them loose to graze. Then he went up to the cabin and sat down outside the open door, wiping the cold sweat from his brow. The silent canyon with its silver winding ribbon seemed to rebuke him.

"Reckon there was something I didn't figure on," he soliloquized, grimly. "And that's been Luce's part in this lousy cattle range deal of mine. My idee of a husky mate and some strappin' sons! . . . I reckon now I sure see the cost to a woman."

Logan worked in the fields. Before August was out Lucinda was helping him with the harvest. The rain and heat for summer season held to normal; Logan raised no bumper crop, but he was satisfied with a yield that looked great compared to the failure of the years before. He sacked more potatoes than he would be able to haul to town in one load. The corn did not mature well, but there would be enough to take care of the young stock he wanted to keep inclosed during the winter. By mid-September the harvesting was finished. Then Logan was eager to make his fall trip to Flagg. Upon his return

October would be well advanced—the one season he had any leisure to roam the woods with his gun.

Lucinda kept to her vow regarding the next trip to Flagg. She went, despite the heavy load, and carried the baby on her lap, letting George hang on as best he could. They camped the first night at Turkey Flat, and the next afternoon late made Mormon Lake, where the Holberts welcomed them.

"Abe Lincoln Huett, huh?" ejaculated the rancher, as the baby was placed on his knee. "Wal, if he ain't a kid! Got your eyes, Huett, only a little darker."

Logan slept under the wagon with Coyote. At breakfast the following morning Holbert asked more questions about Sycamore Canyon.

"Thet's a good place, if you ever get started," he said, thoughtfully: "My herd is growin' fast. I'm drivin' a hundred head to the railroad next month. Don't forget to find out the latest price."

"I won't. Holbert, I'm wondering if you could spare me some stock this fall and let me pay you when I do get started."

"Shore glad to oblige you, Huett. . . . Have you proved up on your homestead yet?"

"Not till next year."

"Wal, I'd make application for a patent to the land. Government awful slow. When the land's yours, wal, it's different. You'll own your homestead allotment an' have right of way over a big range. But in case you cain't make it go down there, I'd advise your locatin' over here north of me. There's a fine range thet some feller will locate sooner or later. An' he might not be a good neighbor. We got to expect rustlin' in this wild country."

"Rustling! You mean cattle thieves?"

"Shore do. Wait till more settlers drift in an' we all raise enough stock. Then we'll ketch it hot, I'll bet."

"Last thing I'd ever thought of," replied Huett, somberly.

Soon he was driving on, with Lucinda beside him, more animated than she had been for months. Logan decided that in the future, when he went to town, it would be the right thing to do to take his wife along.

"Wife, we'll stay a couple of days," said Logan, upon their arrival at Flagg. "I haven't any money. But I'll trade in this load of potatoes and arrange for credit this time."

"Logan, are we forced to go in debt?" asked Lucinda.

"I reckon so. But not much."

"A little is too much. . . . I'll lend you a hundred dollars."

"Luce!—Say, have you got that much money?—Well, you just spend it on yourself and the children."

Babbitt's gave Logan a dollar a bushel for his potatoes and claimed they were the finest ever brought into that store. This pleased Logan and made him thoughtful, although he did not deviate in his ambition to be a cattleman, not a farmer. Nevertheless, he saw clearly the value of good crops while his herd was growing. Logan purchased food supplies, seed, tools, and clothes and boots for himself, of which necessities he was sadly in need. He renewed old acquaintances and made new ones. Flagg, a wide-open frontier town, had begun to grow rapidly, especially in undesirable citizens. Hard characters from New Mexico and Colorado had come to Arizona, and were drifting about looking for a place to lodge.

Logan hardly saw his wife that day. They took supper at the blacksmith's, where Logan scarcely recognized the new, gayer Lucinda. Next morning he packed his supplies, leaving a space under the seat for Lucinda's purchases, but it developed that he had not left enough room for her numerous bundles. He had to tie many of them on the wagonside; and about a few Lucinda was both particular and mysterious, refusing to allow him to handle them. Then she surprised him by announcing that if he was ready she would be glad to start home.

"I've had a wonderful time," she said gaily. "Everybody was nice—and crazy about the babies. I'm ready if you are. We mustn't waste money. And if I stay another hour I'll spend. . . . Well, it's time to go home, Logan."

Logan opined she had meant that she might spend money she did not have, as he had done. He had further cause to appreciate this wonderful wife.

Logan had reason to rejoice for more than good credit in Flagg and at the prospect of an addition to his herd. Lucinda appeared to have changed, to have lost a somberness that had come so gradually that Logan had scarcely perceived it. She was more like her old self. The ride into Sycamore Canyon after Logan had arranged with Holbert for the new stock, was almost as thrilling for her, it appeared, as her first one had been. The golden rod and the purple asters had bloomed during their absence. The canyon was beginning to blaze with scarlet and gold and purple.

"I'm glad to get back," Lucinda announced as if telling herself something new and exciting. "After all, it's home!"

Three weeks later Holbert's sons drove in the score and more of lately purchased cows and heifers. All too soon, then, Logan's short fall season for hunting ended with deep snows up on the ridges. Again he was disappointed that he could not trap beaver. He must wait for an open winter. When he completed hanging up the winter supply of meat, he attacked the firewood job. This he made a long and hard one, goaded by the unforgettable fact that Lucinda had been forced to chop wood during her delicate condition while he lay helpless in bed from the cougar wounds.

Day by day the snows crept down into the canyon, limiting Logan's activities to chores and the killing or frightening away of the predatory beasts that preyed on his herd. The winter passed swiftly, giving way to an early spring and a warm summer. Lucinda persuaded Logan to wait until fall for the trip to town. Their third boy, whom Logan named Grant Huett, after General Grant, was born at Flagg in October. When they again returned to their ranch the snows were whitening the forest ridge-tops.

Logan toiled early and late. He had a growing trio of youngsters now—the lusty boys he had prayed for—and prosperity still held aloof. The Government finally gave Logan a patent for his homestead, and now the land was his as well as the rights of water, grass, and timber for all the canyon area. But Logan's draught of sweetness was rendered bitter by Holbert's demanding a mortgage on the property for the cattle he had advanced—the little herd, which instead of increasing in number toward the long-deferred fulfillment had dwindled to a quarter. In spite of his dreams, Huett was a better farmer than a cattle-raiser. But he never faltered, never lost sight of his vision; and while he toiled, his giant frame bent over plow or furrow or axe, the months and years rolled on.

Chapter Eight

ONE early fall afternoon Logan returned from down the canyon with a pale cast of countenance and fire in his gray eyes. He did not vouchsafe any explanation and Lucinda thought she had better not question him.

She knew something unusual had happened, but without betraying any curiosity she managed to observe things that sent the slow, icy constriction to her veins. There was blood on Logan's hands and a bullet-hole in his shirt! He left almost at once, carrying his rifle, and climbed the ridge into the woods instead of returning down the canyon. As she knew it was impossible to stop him, she felt a little less concern about his going that way rather than in the open.

"Logan has been shot!" she reasoned, with a sudden sensation of faintness that she thrust off with an effort. An intuition dark and ominous quickly flashed over her. . . . "That Apache! . . . *Matazel!*"

She was as certain that it was the Indian as if she had witnessed the actual deed. Very probably Logan had not seen his assailant, but considering that he had no other enemy, would he not suspect Matazel? Lucinda spent uneasy, anxious hours until Logan returned, some time after dark.

After this incident Lucinda observed that Logan carried his rifle with him whenever he went out, even if only to milk the cows. He grew silent, somber, watchful, and preoccupied. Lucinda did not intrude her great fear upon him. Despite it she had great confidence in her husband. He had been a scout in the Apache round-up years before; he was a woodsman and a hunter; he had been forewarned against peril and he had answered it with extreme caution.

The smoky warm languorous days passed. The leaves

began to carpet the grass with gold and brown. Again the purple asters bloomed along the path to the brook. The wind moaned of the coming of winter. The sun sloped farther toward the south.

Lucinda lived in constant dread. Always when Logan was absent she had expected another visit from Matazel; she imagined she had heard his stealthy moccasined step on the path. But now added to this was the fear that Logan might not come back from one of his hunting trips.

"How is it you don't bring in any game?" she asked him.

"Too early. Not cold enough. But soon," he replied, gruffly.

He was indeed roaming the forest, canvassing the game trails, but he was not hunting any four-footed beast. One evening he returned with all his strain and tenseness gone. Lucinda saw drops of sweat on his dark brow. For once his appetite was poor. When she inquired anxiously if he were sick, he replied: "Kinda off my feed at that." But he smoked a pipe before the fire—something he had not indulged in a great deal, formerly. Afterwards Logan was his old self, chopping wood with cheerful vigor, stamping in and out of the cabin, breaking his silence. Soon after that the snow whitened the ridges and he began to pack down game meat for winter use. At last the drifting curtain of white trailed down into the canyon. Lucinda rejoiced, her fear somehow mysteriously abated. They were isolated now for months.

With two growing youngsters and a baby Lucinda had her hands full, irrespective of cooking and baking and sewing. But when she did not think, she touched happiness again. What a difference the children made! George was getting big enough to teach. In fact his father had already begun to interest the boy in guns, knives, tracks, and all pertaining to his wilderness home. Huett's sons would be hunters—Lucinda could not gainsay that, and at length she decided it was well. On her side, however, she made up her mind to give them a good education.

Late the following spring Lucinda took her children as far as Holbert's with the intention of leaving them there while she accompanied Logan on into Flagg.

Already Holbert had been south to Payson that spring, and he was full of news. Lucinda seldom gave heed to the conversation of the men, because it invariably had to do with range, cattle, grass, calves, and all pertaining to ranch life. At the very outset, however, Holbert sent a chill shock to her heart.

"Huett, you knew thet Apache runaway, didn't you?" he queried.

"Which one?" asked Logan, and Lucinda felt his wariness if he did not show it to the others.

"Thet one said to be Old Geronimo's son. He used to hang around Payson. His name was Matazel."

"Sure. I remember him. Helped round him up when I was scout for Crook. . . . What about Matazel?"

"Wal, some Tonto Basin deer-hunters found him daid last fall. Down below your canyon somewhere. He'd been caught behind a pine too small to cover him an' he'd been shot to pieces. Put up a fight, though, they said. Empty shells layin' all around his body!"

"Well! . . . So that was the end of Matazel," ejaculated Huett.

"Folks down Payson way was plumb glad. Thet Apache had a bad name. He'd escaped from the reservation several times. Shore hated white people."

"Who'd he fight with?"

"Nobody knows. But it was hinted thet the Horner boys might have an idee. Their sister fought off an In dian once, when she was alone at home. An' they had a hunch he was the Apache."

"Good riddance, I'd say," replied Huett, forcibly.

"Yes. Thar's varmints enough around without renegade Indians. . . . How'd you come off with the lofers?"

"Wolves, you mean?—They didn't kill any of my stock last winter."

"Wish I could say thet. Our old friend Gray shore did us dirt. He's got a pack now, an' they shore left a bloody trail across this range."

"I got most of the cougars cleaned out down at Sycamore. All the same I can't raise calves."

"Man alive! If you cain't, you'll never be a cattle-raiser."

"I'm not licked yet," said Huett, doggedly.

Lucinda in bed and wakeful was now sure of two tremendous facts. Logan had killed the Apache. The other was that she seemed to have been freed from an awful burden; a haunting uncertainty that she had never named to her consciousness but which was now dissolved forever before the dawn of another and a happier day.

On the way to Flagg they passed several wagons that bore semblance to the old prairie-schooner. What a thrill they gave Lucinda!

"Settlers going south," explained Logan exuberantly. "Holbert told me there was a lot more travel on the road this spring. Some Mormons and a few Texans. That's good. We need settlers."

That visit to town was one for Lucinda to store up and remember for many a month. She felt so happy again, and excited at being near people, at the stores displaying their spring goods, that she spent half of her long-saved money before she realized what she was doing. But she could not regret it. Most of her purchases were for the children. She treated herself to one luxury—a long-wished-for lamp, which would enable her to sew at night, and to a necessity almost as greatly needed—a case of jars to put up preserves.

Back at Sycamore Canyon once more Lucinda saw the lonely log-walled home with clarifying eyes.

Logan's toil claimed half the days, and there were not hours enough left, even after dark, for her own. Yet, her healthy precocious children would have been compensation and joy for any toiling mother. The habit of work grew so strong, so necessary and satisfying that Lucinda would not have been without it. Years had been required to mold her into a pioneer wife, but she had achieved that height.

Lucinda loved her children, but in time she seemed to realize that the dark-haired, grey-eyed Abraham was her favorite. She had suffered most carrying and giving him birth; she had kept him at her breast far too long, Mrs. Holbert said; and he was the handsome one of the trio.

"Dandy bunch of boys, wife," said Logan, one night, as he played with the blond baby. "Wherever did Grant get that fair hair? Well, I don't wish he was a girl, but I wish we had a girl. . . . But, Luce, three is enough. God has sure been good to me."

The hot summer, with its sudden black storms, the still autumn with its blue haze and lingering sadness, the gray days and then the white months—these passed as if time were not. Then again spring, summer, autumn rolled around.

The ragged, sun-browned urchins were at once the despair and the joy of Lucinda's full days. It was utterly impossible for her to keep track of them. George had a propensity for falling into the brook, but though some of the pools were quite deep he seemed to bear a charmed life. Abe was fond of slipping out of his garb, which was scant enough, to hide naked among the sunflowers or the willow-patches. Grant did not appear to have any annoying traits, except to imitate his elder brothers when they were mischievous. However, at that time he was only two years old.

One trying fall day, when things simply would not go right for Lucinda, she quite forgot the children—a matter of self-preservation. However, she had never before neglected them for hours on end; when she finally remembered them and they did not return at her call, she went out to look for them.

The spots where they usually played were vacant. Logan had gone off with the dog somewhere down the canyon. Lucinda called frantically: "Abe! . . . George! Come here this minute!", wholly unconscious of the fact of calling Abraham first. She stifled alarm and hurried down across the brook, following the little barefoot tracks in the dust. Among the many pioneer accomplishments she had mastered was the art of trailing. She read a record of their play along the sandy brook, around the corrals and in the sheds, and at last up the road toward the gate. Before this time they had never appeared so big, although they certainly were enterprising enough to leave the canyon. However, it appeared that now they had grown sufficiently large to try such an adventure. Still Lucinda did not become thoroughly alarmed until she tracked them to the spot where they had crawled under the gate and gone on. Then she gave way to her fears.

It was a good quarter of a mile from the gate up to the level. Lucinda pushed on, calling out whenever she gained enough breath. Sunset was not far away. Visions of her children lost in the dark woods tormented the distracted mother.

"Abe—the little savage—he's to blame—for this!" panted Lucinda. "Won't he catch it!"

Ahead of Lucinda the road curved out of the scattered pines onto the open grassy ground. Suddenly she espied the youngsters scattered around and on top of the very log upon which she had once sat years before waiting in despair for Logan. But what had that despair been to this pang she had just sustained? Overjoyed at finding them safe she quite forgot the punishment she had intended to mete out to Abraham. Suddenly she halted to rub her eyes. Could she be seeing aright? There were four children!

Lucinda hurried on. "Boys, what are you up to? And who's this?" she demanded. The fourth member of that quartet, to her utter astonishment was a little flaxen-haired girl about the same age as Grant. Her dress was ragged and dirty, but of a fine texture. She wore shoes, also, which further removed her in garb from her companions.

"George, where did you find this little girl?" asked Lucinda, attempting to suppress her excitement.

"I dunno. Abe found her."

"Abe, you tell me," ordered Lucinda, sternly.

"She was by the road—cryin'," replied Abraham, his hazel-gray eyes solemnly uplifted.

Lucinda was profoundly struck by something she did not understand.

"But isn't there a wagon somewhere?" she queried and stepping up on the log assayed a better view of the road and the long green open. There was neither wagon nor camp in sight.

"I saw wheel tracks," said Abe blandly.

"Didn't you see anybody?"

"Nobody 'cept her."

Lucinda hurried out to the road. She found fresh horse

and wagon tracks in the dust pointed south. She could
see a mile down in that direction, but there was no sign
of cart, horse, nor man! The sun had gone down behind
the forest.

"Strange," she muttered. "There must be a wagon
near, of course. Perhaps driven back off the road to camp.
. . . The child must have strayed."

Lucinda returned to the log, and sitting down on it
she said: "Come here, little girl." The child turned
beautiful violet eyes. She was very pretty and well-
nourished. After a moment of hesitation she came shyly
to Lucinda.

"Little girl, what's your name?" asked Lucinda, softly,
taking the child's hand.

"Bar'bra," she lisped.

Lucinda could not extract another word from her. Seeing that the child began to appear frightened Lucinda
desisted from further inquiry, still pondering as to what
to do with her.

Meanwhile the last gold of sunset faded off the pine
crests and dusk came trooping out of the forest. The stillness of the hour was such that Lucinda could have heard
a voice, the thud of a hoof, or especially an axe a very
way off; but she heard only a melancholy bird note and
the wail of a distant coyote.

Soon the boys began to get hungry and were not backward about voicing it. At last Lucinda took the little girl's
hand and sending the boys ahead walked slowly homeward. The canyon had become dark, but she could see the
road without difficulty. Once again Lucinda questioned
the little girl as to her identity and where she had left
her mother but received no answer.

A light in the cabin assured her of Logan's return. The
boys ran in ahead, clamoring. Logan whooped at them.
When Lucinda appeared he said: "Where you been?

Milking late? . . . Supper's most. . . . But say. . . . Who's that?"

Lucinda told of her hunt for the boys and the result. Logan was amazed.

"Sure there was no wagon close?"

"No wagon, nor camp anywhere near. I went out to the road, looked up and down. Then I sat on that log for a while. It was very quiet. I could have heard voices or camp sounds for a mile."

"Well, I'll be damned . . . but that's funny. If there was any one looking for her he'd never get down here after dark. . . . Abe, come here . . . where'd you find this kid?"

"By the road, Paw."

"What you mean, by the road? Talk sense now, boy. This is important."

"She wuz sittin' in the grass, cryin'. I heard her first."

"Where? How far from our road?"

"Way off."

"Ahuh. Up or down the road?"

"I dunno."

"You do know. Tell me or I'll lick you."

"Up by that windfall where you chased the rabbit for me."

"Way up there. Luce, I reckoned as much. The youngsters went a mile from our road. . . . Don't worry any more. I'll find her folks in the morning."

"Oughtn't you to go tonight? Think how distressed I was that night till you found Abe the first time he ran off."

"Well, so I should. Rustle supper while I milk the cows. . . . Say, isn't she a pretty, shy little thing?"

"Indeed she is. Says her name's 'Bar'bra.' I couldn't get another word out of her."

"Little girl lost!—Seems strange, but it's simple enough

Wagons go by often now," replied Logan, and banging his pails he stamped out.

Lucinda ordered George and Abe to wash themselves. She performed this task for Grant and the newcomer. When the tear-stains and dirt had been removed from Barbara's face she turned out to be the loveliest little girl Lucinda had ever seen. Lucinda left them to their play while she hurried supper. By the time she had it ready Logan returned, his buckets full of foamy milk. Logan bolted his own supper, and taking his rifle and a lantern, and calling the dog went out to try to locate the camp.

Grant fought sleep valiantly but it overcame him. George and Abe had to be driven to bed. Barbara fell asleep on Lucinda's lap. Fashioning a little bed beside the boys' in the corner of the cabin, Lucinda tenderly laid the little girl in it, and then went thoughtfully about her tasks, listening for Logan's footsteps.

He was gone more than two hours. When he returned treading softly, his eyes flashed keen and bright in the firelight. Lucinda sensed before he spoke that he had found nothing. He laid his Winchester across the elk antlers on the wall and extinguished the lantern.

"Luce, this has a queer look," he announced, shaking his shaggy head.

"Queer?" echoed Lucinda.

"It sure has. I went down the road a mile, then back up, clear to the end of the open. Not a sign! No wagon or camp. Then I took to the road to see what I could make out of tracks. Dust just right for tracking. Two wagons, one hauled by horses, passed here some time after midday. . . . You say it was way in the afternoon when you missed the kids?"

"Yes. They might have been gone a couple of hours. Less than that out of the canyon, because I saw where they had played all around and inside the corrals."

"Then Abe run across the kid late in the day, that's certain. . . . Well, I trailed Abe up the road to the windfall. Then he sheered off. A good ways beyond that windfall, where he said he went, I hit upon signs of the little girl. . . . Don't miss the significance of what I say —you know tracks are like printed words to a hunter. . . . She had fallen down in the dust, right on the wheel-tracks of the second wagon. She must have lain there a bit, probably exhausted, because she crawled off into the grass. No more tracks down the road. Those leading up from where she fell were running tracks. The kid had run after that wagon!"

"Why, Logan! Of all things!" cried Lucinda.

"She must have run several hundred yards before she fell. I forgot to tell you that the horses were trotting. Little down grade there, you know. A kid could not keep up long with a trotting team. . . . I found the tracks where she had been let down off the wagon, on to her feet. She didn't fall or climb off. She was dropped off by some one holding her. Two little standing footprints in the dust! That's all. From these she broke into a run. After the wagon!"

"Logan, what in the world do you make of all this?"

"Some one wanted to get rid of the kid. He saw Abe and maybe our other kids. Figured there was a settler nearby. Lonesome country. Just the place!"

"Nonsense!" exclaimed Lucinda, aghast. "Who'd ever want to get rid of such a lovely child?"

"Human nature has a queer look sometimes," replied Logan, grimly. "Probably I'm wrong. But that's what the tracks say tonight. I'll try again tomorrow in the daylight. . . . You put her to bed with the boys?"

"Right next to them. See." Lucinda lifted the lamp and carried it over to disperse the gloom of the cabin corner. Four curly heads all in a row! Abe's dark and striking, against the fair hair and pale face of little Barbara. They scarcely took up four feet of the cabin. But what a precious treasure! They were for her the difference between happiness and misery, between death and life; for Logan they meant the balance separating achievement and frustration, between something to work for and endless vain oblation. No man could realize failure looking upon such children.

"I wonder!" he ejaculated, his eyes bright. "We wanted a girl. There she is. . . . Luce, all we've gone through is nothing."

"Not quite, for *me*, darling. But they are wonderful recompense. . . . Isn't the little girl lovely? . . . Oh, if we could keep her! But we are silly, Logan. You'll find her mother tomorrow, I hope and pray."

Logan saddled his horse at dawn and did not return until night. Not only had he worked out the problem of the little footprints even more plausibly than on the evening before, but he had followed the wheel tracks clear down over the Rim to Payson. Two wagons had passed through Payson in the dead of night—an unprecedented occurrence according to Logan's informants. It was this news which caused Logan to keep silent as to his motive. Let him who owned the child return and trail her as he had!

However Lucinda took exception to this, and they had their first argument, almost approaching a quarrel.

"Luce, you're thinking of her mother," declared Logan, with finality. "I say she hasn't got any mother. She hasn't had one for so long she can't remember. Well, let's accept gratefully what God puts in our way."

"Logan, I thought that tonight, when the child went to sleep on my lap . . . Poor little dear!—I just can't get over it, nor the conviction that some one will come after her. But if no one does . . . we shall keep her."

No one came. In a few days Barbara was a happy provocative little sister to the boys. The summer passed. Logan put the boys to work with him and Lucinda at the harvest of beans and potatoes, of which he had a large yield. It was all Grant could do to carry some of the largest potatoes. The boys, except Abe, treated the work as play. Abe was willing and obedient, but his heart was not in such pastimes. He watched the birds, the hawks, the crows, the chipmunks; and Lucinda noted more strongly than ever Abe's leaning toward the woods and wild creatures. Barbara had her share in the general work, of her own free will.

When fall arrived George and Abe had their first hunt in the woods with their father. That night George was much excited, proudly showing where the gun had kicked a black and blue spot on his arm and gleefully exclaiming how it had knocked him flat. Abe was quiet, but his great eyes were luminous and haunted. He could not sleep that night.

"Might as well start them early," said Logan through Lucinda's complaint. "You know this'll be our life here till these boys are grown men. Lucinda, I want them to be hunters, woodsmen like their father. They'll make all the better cowboys. We've got to live off the land and fight, Luce, fight! . . . You teach them to read and write —to be fine—to love and obey their parents—to respect women—to believe in God. Leave the rest to me!"

Lucinda surely felt she could trust him with that. When the snow came again, and the homestead was shut in for another half year, Lucinda began her teaching of the two eldest boys. George was quick, intelligent; Abe slow to take up anything mental. But he was sweet, patient, plodding, and he would do anything for his mother. Grant and Barbara played the long winter away on the floor of the cabin.

"But the groundhog saw his shadow and we'll have six more weeks of winter," remarked Logan pessimistically, late in the season.

"Logan, that old folk adage may do for Missouri or back East where they have groundhogs," replied Lucinda.

"But we've got gophers, skunks, and a lot of other varmints that have holes. I can show them to you. We're not through with winter."

Convinced of this aphorism the homesteader kept his young stock in the corrals, feeding them the fodder he had saved from earlier months. Then one night in early March true to his prediction the storm-king roared down through the forest. When dawn came a blinding blizzard was raging. It snowed all that day and the next night, then cleared off to zero weather, freezing a crust over the deep snow. Logan had to shovel paths to the cowsheds and corrals.

"Heard wolves baying last night," announced Logan, noncommittally, when he came stamping in, white-booted, to pull off his woolen mitts and spread his hands to the hot fire. "Bet they've been on the rampage with my cattle. Soon as I eat a bite I'll go see."

"Paw, you gonna take your gun?" asked George, eagerly. " 'Cause if you are I wanta go."

" 'Course, you ninny!" ejaculated Abe scornfully. "Paw, you take me. I'll track them."

"Not this time, my brave buckaroos. Snow's over your heads," replied Huett.

"But it's froze. It'd hold me up," added Abe.

"Luce, don't worry if I'm not back soon. Slow job. But I reckon I'll find easy going under the wall."

The short belated winter day soon passed. A cold white moon followed the sunset. Several times Lucinda looked out to see if Logan was coming—the stock had to be fed and the cows milked. Finally she bundled George and

Abe in their warm woolens, to their great glee, and quitted the cabin with them, jangling the buckets. She had to drive Grant and Barbara back and scold them for leaving the door open.

The cold moon had just tipped the black-fringed wall to flood the canyon with silver light. Weird shadows gloomed under the cliffs. Never had the solitude and isolation of Sycamore Canyon seemed more encompassing and terrible. The black pines sheered up to the cold, blinking, pitiless stars; a moan breathed through their branches. The air held a bitter, nipping tang.

"Boys, you carry fodder while I milk," said Lucinda, taking the buckets.

"Listen, Maw," spoke up Abe, tensely.

"What do you hear, Abe?" she asked, quickly, suddenly fearful.

"Sounds like Mr. Holbert's hounds bellarin'. Paw says thet's the way wolves howl." replied the lad, his wondering eyes shining as he pointed down the moon-blanched canyon. "They're way down."

"Heavens, I hope your father is safe," exclaimed Lucinda, anxiously turning her face in order to listen.

"Aw, he's safe, you bet. Paw can lick all the lofers in Arizona."

"Abe—I hear them!" cried Lucinda, with a cold chill knifing her. The sounds were indeed like the baying of hounds, but deeper, wilder, more prolonged and blood-curdling. Then they ceased, to her immense relief. She admonished the boys to hurry with the fodder and she hastened to her task of milking. She tried desperately not to listen while she milked, attempted also to entertain Abe's opinion of his father's prowess. When she had filled one bucket and had begun the other, Abe, white-faced, came running into the shed.

"Maw, come! *Them wolves*—all around!" he shrieked fearfully, tugging at her.

"Oh, my God—no! Abe, you're . . ." she was stricken mute by the sound of a rush of swiftly pattering feet outside of the shed. Leaping to her feet, she seized a pitchfork and with one hand grasping Abe ran for the corral. The calves and heifers began to bawl and thud about against the fence. She heard George screeching with terror. At that instant, she became a lioness.

"*Where are you?*" she screamed wildly.

"George's up there," yelled Abe.

Lucinda saw the boy then, straddling the high pole fence, his chubby face gray with horror. She reached the open gate a moment before the rush of soft-thudding feet rounded the corral. Abe darted inside, Lucinda after him. Frantically she shoved the gate. It swung—scraped in the snow—caught, leaving an aperture a foot wide. At that instant gray, furry beasts padded up, swiftly scattering the snow. They resembled dirty white dogs, bounding, leaping, like silent ghosts.

"Shut it, Abe! . . . *Shove!*"

A gaunt beast with green-fire eyes leaped at the opening, breaking half way through before Lucinda thrust the pitchfork into him. With a vicious snarl and a grind of teeth on the implement he fell backward. The shock of his onslaught almost upset Lucinda, but she righted and braced herself when another beast leaped. She gave this one a powerful stab which caused him to let out a mad howl. But Abe was not strong enough to close the gate. Lucinda leaned her shoulder against it, still holding the pitchfork low, and shoved with all her might. The gate jarred shut except for the handle of the pitchfork. Then a bigger brute, furry gray with a black collar, leaped up, snapping at George. The boy screamed and fell off into the corral. At that moment Lucinda with-drew her weapon and barred the gate.

On the instant, as she sagged there, she panted audibly: "Thank God—Logan built—this fence!"

Gray forms sped to and fro, bounding with incredible agility, circled the corral, but farther away, and presently thronged into a pack to run up the canyon.

"Maw, they're gone," cried Abe. "You sure stuck a couple of 'em."

"Oh!—are you—sure?" gasped Lucinda, ready to collapse if the peril was over.

Abe peeped between the poles. "Maw!—they're across the brook! . . . Runnin' round the cabin." The lad must have had eyes as sharp as the wolves'. "Shore Grant left the door open!"

"Oh my God! . . . Grant! Barbara!" screamed Lucinda, dragging the gate open.

"Wait, Maw—they're runnin' by—up the hill . . . up that break where Paw slides down our wood."

"George, are you hurt?" queried Lucinda, relaxing for an instant, as the other boy came to her.

"I dunno. I felt his teeth—on my foot."

"Listen, Maw," called Abe, shrilly.

From the black and silver ridge floated down the wild mournful hungry bay of a wolf. It was answered by a deeper one, prolonged, haunting. A weird beast-sound that fit the wilderness canyon.

"They might come back," said Lucinda, fearfully. "Boys, let's run for the cabin. Hurry!"

They dashed ahead of her, without looking back. Thought of Grant and Barbara lent wings to Lucinda's feet. She ran as never before. To her horror the cabin door stood wide open; the bright fire blazed in the fire-place. Lucinda staggered transfixed in the doorway, with Abe and George clinging to her skirt. Playthings were scattered before the hearth. A chair lay overturned. Dirty wet tracks on the floor! With awful suspension of heart Lucinda's terrible glance swept the cabin. Empty! Those gray demons had carried the children away!

"Hey, Maw," piped up Grant's treble voice, from the loft, "Bar'bra an' me run back an' clumb up here!"

Chapter Nine

ONE warm sunny day afterward, when the snow was melt-
ing swiftly, Logan was nailing the gray wolf hide up on
the wall of the cabin.

George was not interested. He had had enough of
wolves. But Abe stood by with shining eyes.

"Paw, where'd you hit him?" asked the lad, sticking his
finger in a hole in the raw skin.

"Not there, Son. That's where your mother stuck him
with the pitchfork. Here's where I hit him, Abe."

"Plumb center," marveled Abe. He never forgot any
words his father used pertaining to guns, animals, and the
forest.

"Sure, Son. But it wasn't a running shot, and your
mother had crippled him. So I don't deserve a lot of
credit. . . . Now we'll rub some salt on. . . . Luce,
fetch me a cup full of salt."

Lucinda came out, followed by the younger children.

"Wife, you broke my only pitchfork on this hombre,"
complained Logan.

"Did I?" shuddered Lucinda. She had only begun to
recover from the devastating horror of the wolves' attack.

"Look ahere, Paw," spoke up Abe, who always took
his mother's side. "Maw kept two of 'em from gettin' in
the corral. They'd et all your calves."

"I reckon, Son. And chewed you up besides. That
bunch was starved all right. . . . Luce, this hide will
make a fine rug. We'll have to get use out of it. Old Gray
cost us dearly. He and his pack cleaned out our herd,
except the bull, and our young stock in the corrals."

"Oh, Logan! That is a terrible misfortune. I'm afraid
we can never start a herd in this wild canyon."

"Yes, we can—and we will," he replied, grimly, then

. . . "Youngsters, I'm sorry to say Coyote went off with the pack."

They were grieved and amazed. Abe said: "What'd she do thet for, Paw?"

"Well, she's half wolf anyway. I always distrusted her, but I took her with me three mornings before daylight. I hid in the pines and watched. About daylight this morning I heard them. They'd killed something. They came out of a side canyon—must have got Coyote's scent. Anyway they stopped to nose around. . . Then's when I shot old Gray. I crippled another before the rest got out of sight. There were only six left. I reckon we've seen the last of them. . . . Coyote double-crossed you, youngsters. She ran out to where old Gray lay, and then she went kind of wild, and let out the queerest yelps. She trailed the pack, looked back at me. I yelled. But she went on. . . . And that's the end of your pet."

Barbara wept. Abe tried to console her by averring he would catch her another pet.

"It's too bad," said Lucinda, with a sigh. "I always felt easier when Coyote was with the children."

"Things happen. We've got to make the best of it," said Logan imperturbably. "I'll get another dog . . . and some more cattle."

"Where and how, Logan?" asked Lucinda.

"Ha!—We'll see."

In a few more days the snow was gone. The brook again ran bank full and Logan was forced to fell another tree to make a higher bridge. Spring was at hand with its manifold tasks. The wild turkeys began to gobble from the ridges. Logan took Abe, and with his rifle, climbed the slope. When they returned Abe packed a turkey larger than himself, holding its feet over his shoulder and dragging it behind, head and wings on the ground. Barbara had an eye for the beautiful bronze and black feathers. Grant remembered turkey from the preceding fall, and whooped: "Maw, can I have the drumstick?"

Another day Logan trudged down the hill with a little bear cub under each arm. Then there was pandemonium in Sycamore Canyon. The children went wild with delight.

"Doggone!" ejaculated Logan. "I didn't know they loved pets so well. That's one thing I can get them."

"Such dear little black shiny things! Not at all afraid!" exclaimed Lucinda. "They can't be very old."

"I should smile not. You'll have to feed them with a bottle."

"And their mother?" asked Lucinda, with a ghost of that old shock which would not wholly vanish.

"She's up on the hill. I'll go back up there, skin out some meat, and pack it down. Hide's not so good."

Not long after that Lucinda at her work heard the children talking about their kittens. At first she thought Barbara and Grant meant the little bears. But she soon ascertained that they did not. When Logan came in from the fields she told him. It was noonday, and the two youngsters were not in sight.

"Little imps! They're up to something. . . . Abe, what about these kittens? Your mother heard Grant and Barbara talking."

"I know, Paw. But I'm not gonna tell," replied Abe.

"Well! I'll be damned," ejaculated the nonplussed father. Whereupon he set off up the canyon in search of the two youngsters.

Lucinda observed that Abe watched with great interest, and this stimulated her own. "They're comin', Maw," he said, intensely. "An' Paw's got 'em."

It developed that Abe did not mean Barbara and Grant. They came ahead, running, babbling, too excited to be coherent. Logan followed carrying two furry tan-colored little cats.

"For heaven's sake, what now?" ejaculated Lucinda mildly.

"Cougar kittens, Luce!—The kids are making friends with my bitterest enemies," replied Logan, in grim humor. "Barbara said Abe found them in a cave. He took her and Grant up there. They've been playing with these kittens every day. While the old cougar mother sat up on the ledge above and watched them. I saw her tracks."

"Why, Logan! I think that's wonderful. She wouldn't harm our children because they didn't harm hers."

"Yeah. It's wonderful how quick they'll grow up and eat my calves. I'll have to kill their maw. But we'll keep the kittens for a while. . . . Never heard of cougar pets."

He built a pen for the little cats. These pets, added to bear cubs, interfered with work and lessons, but Lucinda had not the heart to refuse the children. What else had they to play with? A few primitive bits of stone, some pine cones, and queer knots.

Logan must have reacted in the same way to Barbara's and Grant's rapture, for from that day onward he kept bringing home pets from the woods. Lucinda suspected that he went purposely to hunt for wild creatures, taking Abe with him. Before hot weather set in two baby chipmunks, a black squirrel, a white-spotted fawn, and a blinking little gray owl had been added to the menagerie.

Having but little stock to tend, Logan put most of his labors into the fields, cultivating more land. This season he tried alfalfa. It seemed to Lucinda that her husband worked harder than ever, if such a thing was possible, but without the old cheer and all-satisfying hope for the future. Without cattle his precious ambition languished. He deferred the trip to town until fall. Holbert drove back with him, and it took little perspicuity for Lucinda to see that the rancher was interested in Sycamore Canyon. He appeared friendly as usual, but he bluntly told Huett that in the spring he would require the amount of money he held as a mortgage or he would be compelled to take over the property.

"Luce, the alfalfa crop is what fetched him," said Logan, after the neighbor had gone. "He sees the possibilities in this ranch. And he'd like to get it. . . . I'd just about croak to lose this place. And I can't see how in hell I can save it."

"Well, I can," returned Lucinda, vigorously. "There was a time when I'd have been glad to lose it. But not any more. It's home. The children love it. They will grow up somehow all the more wonderful for this lonely place. . . . Don't worry, Logan."

Logan shook his head grimly. "I owe Holbert three hundred dollars. He's been decent about it, although when I took the cattle I had an idea he'd give me all the time I needed to pay."

"He was amazed at your alfalfa and potato crops," said Lucinda, thoughtfully. "What did Babbitt say?"

"Humph! A lot. He'd take a hundred tons of alfalfa and all the potatoes I could raise. Big talk. But he might as well ask me to cut and haul the lumber off my range."

"Nevertheless we do have an asset here."

"We do. I always saw it. We can live off the land. We can make money on our farm products. We can raise and run thirty thousand head of stock here."

"But Logan, admitting this may be true, we are farther away from that than when we started."

"So far as cattle are concerned. Why, if I ever get a wedge in here my herd will double—quadruple—multiply beyond calculation."

"You have convinced me," said Lucinda. "But without

capital and help you have undertaken the impossible
. . . Logan, we must approach the problem from another
angle."

"Angle? Wife, what do you mean?" he asked, with
dubious interest.

"I don't know that I can answer yet. But my mind is
working. The facts are simple. We have the land and
water and grass. We will not starve. Our boys are growing
like weeds. . . . It's something like a problem I used to
give my school class."

"Luce, I never was any good at arithmetic."

"You let me do the figuring," she suggested.

Lucinda pondered over their situation for days. Holbert's wanting their ranch inspired her as it had alarmed
Logan. One night after the tired children had gone to
bed, and she and Logan were sitting out on the porch
in the soft summer night, Lucinda broached the subject
that had become so important to her.

"Logan, I've worked it out."

"What?" he queried.

"Our problem. But let me ask a question or so before
I tell you. How long can you keep alfalfa?"

"I reckon as long as I could keep it dry."

"How much can you raise a summer?"

"I don't know. Two cuttings, sure. I'm beginning to
see that alfalfa does amazing good here, same as your
potatoes."

"We can't haul alfalfa to town, not in quantity to pay
us. But we can haul enough potatoes to trade for the
flour, sugar, dried fruit—all that we need to live on.
Our wants will grow as the children grow. We must have
clothes, and shoes, books, and many things."

"Luce, don't forget guns, ponies, and saddles. We've
got to have them soon."

"Oh, I never thought of them. Indeed the boys are

growing up. . . . But is there immediate need for those things?"

"No. Only the sooner the better. Abe can ride bare-back like an Indian now. And George's not so bad."

"Perhaps an open winter, such as you've been hoping for, will give you good luck with the beaver hides."

"It would help out wonderful."

"Let's hope for that. Now here's my plan. You've got ten acres of alfalfa in, almost ready to cut. And room in the cow-sheds to store it. Build a large shed—just a peaked roof on posts. Something you can store tons and tons of alfalfa in."

"Wife, that's a great idea," replied Logan, enthusias-tically. "With George and Abe, and a little help from you, I can throw that up in a week. . . . Well, go on."

"Run a high pole fence out from that deep break in the wall below the road. Just two lines of fence meeting across the brook. That will inclose four or five acres of pasture."

"I can do that before the snow flies. But what for? I don't need it."

"You will need it. Let us begin to raise our calves to *save* them. Let's keep them penned in till they are grown. Feed alfalfa as well as fodder in the winter. In summer have the boys graze them like Indian boys do flocks of sheep. All to start a herd while you're killing off these cougars and wolves. In a few years we can turn them loose in the canyon."

"Wife, that's another good idea," declared Logan, thoughtfully. "But so much work—so slow in results!"

"Logan, you're in too much of a hurry. Remember the fable of the hare and the tortoise. We really don't need a big herd of cattle until the boys are old enough to ride with you."

"That's so. Never occurred to me. . . . If I had five

thousand head, say in ten years, when George is eighteen, why in five years more I'd have my thirty thousand head."

"Yes. Meanwhile we'd be living. By then the children will have as good an education as I can give them. They'd be growing up with our herd. . . . It all means prodigious labor, much poverty, perhaps some hard backsets, but in the end success. . . . Logan, that is absolutely the only way we can attain it here in Sycamore."

"Years—years—years!" ejaculated Logan, hollowly, shaking his shaggy head.

"We can count on them. The rest depends upon our preparation and our unremitting toil. . . . Now as to Holbert's lien on our property. I have the money to pay that off."

"Lucinda!" he exclaimed, hoarsely. By that she saw how this debt had dogged him.

"Yes. It'll take almost all of the money I saved out of my wedding gift. We'll get rid of it all in one swoop. . . . I'll go to town with you this fall, taking the children. We'll pay Holbert on the way. Then I'll buy things for the children and myself—we're sadly in need, and so are you, for that matter. Come home and never go in debt again!"

"Lucinda, you're a pioneer wife!" he burst out huskily, as if that was the greatest compliment he could pay her, and with this rare exhibition of feeling, he left her. Lucinda made a mental note of the fact that he had not promised never to go in debt again.

She sat there in the darkness, listening to the babble of the brook, the chirp of crickets, the weird cries of the night-hawks—sounds that seemed to have become a part of her. The stars burned white in the velvety-dark sky. All around, the black fringe of pines on the rims loomed protectingly. The white Sycamore that had given the canyon its name gleamed like wan marble in the star-

light. From the great forest breathed down the leagues on
leagues of pine and spruce—the warm sweet dry tang of
the evergreens. How strange for Lucinda to realize that
her horror of the wilderness had vanished! Only one
dread, one threatening haunting drawback to this pioneer
life remained to vex her, and that was winter—the storm-
demon who roared in the pines and brought the terror of
a white change to the wilderness, the drifting palls of
snow, the cold ghastly windrows down the canyon.

The days went by, too short by hours for the tasks of
the housewife of the pioneer, the helper in the fields, the
milk-maid and the teacher. Winter fled apace and the
seasons rolled on.

Lucinda's vision of the unremitting toil and the set-
backs with their consequent poverty, had been a true
presagement of the future. But the toil and the privation
did not obscure the rest of that vision—the crown of
success in the years to come, the reward and the blessing
of the boys and the girl.

Huett lost sight of that. Like a galley-slave he toiled at
his round of endless tasks. The bitter pill for him was
that he had become a farmer, living from hand to mouth,
when his heart was set on cattle. If he had any happiness
it was in the way his boys took to hunting, woodcraft,
riding. Lucinda always felt glad for Logan when the fall
season rolled around, and he could follow the game trails
with the boys.

For three autumns Logan had upward of fifty head of
stock in the fenced pasture—cows, steers, heifers, calves;
and as many times that fair start toward a herd had been
ruined by the cougars, deep snows and cold of this in-
hospitable wilderness. Always after a set-back like one of
these, it took time to make another beginning. During
another instance a sudden thaw and spring flood depleted

his herd of their calves. He deserted that pasture and in. closed another on higher ground taking up acres of slope where browsing on the oak thickets was good all winter.

Still, no matter what he gained in bitter experience, no matter how unflaggingly he carried on, Lucinda saw the hard years wresting the heart of hope out of his life. Once a year he went to Flagg, traded his produce for supplies, and returned sick and brooding for days over the progress of the Arizona ranges, the influx of new settlers.

Then followed several years—just as swift but harder than ever—which tried Lucinda's soul. Toward the close of that period they had no flour, no sugar, and very few of the necessities of life. They lived on meat and beans— the stable product of that wilderness when all else, even the potato yield, failed. The boys went barefoot in all seasons except winter, when they wore moccasins. In fringed buckskin Barbara was a delight to Lucinda's eyes. She grew up strong, brown, beautiful despite poverty, happy at study as at work, loving the boys she believed to be her brothers, and worshipping the dark, silent, gray-eyed Abe, who had become straight and lithe; handsome as a young pine. They were all of the woodland, and they loved and kept wilderness pets, as they had when they were children. Lucinda's compensation lay in the fact that she had been able to give them an elementary education, to instil in them ideals and loyalties, and belief in God. No poverty, no suffering, not even a permanent failure of Huett, could have robbed Lucinda of that joy. She had given them of herself, of her mind and heart. For the rest, for that physical prowess Logan put such store in, their infinite labors from childhood to youth, Lucinda thrilled to her depths at what she saw they would grow to be.

But Huett sustained a growing bitterness as great as his pride, and it was that he could not give this wonderful

family the bare necessities of life, let alone the pretty
things a girl loved, and the implements, the guns, the
equipment that boys should have had in wild country.

Lucinda watched Logan with misgivings that she had
to fight with all her courage and intelligence. She feared
the iron that might enter his soul. She saw the hair whiten
over his temples. She saw his great frame, grown heavier
with the years, begin to bow a little across the broad
shoulders. She saw him sit beside the hearth without the
pipe of tobacco that had been his one extravagance, and
ponder everlastingly over the problem of his cattle.

His vigor and his will seemed to withstand all inroads
of toil and defeat. With the boys he planted more corn,
more potatoes, more alfalfa, more beans each succeeding
summer. Lucinda had worked with him until the boys,
laughingly yet imperiously, had sent her back to her
manifold tasks at the homestead.

Still she saw Logan at his work. She saw him from afar,
and when he came stamping in at sunset, smelling of the
earth and wiping the sweat from his furrowed brow,
she was there to greet him. She often carried his lunch
into the forest where it appeared he could cut wood
faster than his sons could drag and stack it behind the
cabin. The flashing axe, the ring of steel, the odorous flying chips, the stalwart backwoodsman at his best—these,
with the gray windfalls all around, the brown fragrant
mats under the junipers, the giant pines towering black-
stemmed to spread into a canopy of green far overhead,
the patches of gold and white aspens, and the scarlet
maples—how these at last satisfied a nameless longing in
Lucinda's heart! This wilderness was Logan's place. He
fitted it. And he would have been happy save for that
obsession of the cattle herd.

Lucinda at last faced a winter which daunted even her
fortitude. Logan's load of potatoes went to apply on a

past debt and future credit was denied. He had come home without the supplies so necessary to any semblance of good living. She really worried more about her husband's gloom that time than about the lack of food and other supplies. A long hard winter would reduce the Huetts to wretched condition.

But Logan went into the woods with his rifle and returned to say there were signs foretelling a mild and open winter. That night, while talking to the boys, he seemed changed, more like he used to be. Lucinda took heart. Her prayers, her hopes, her visions could not be utterly futile.

Indian summer held on long, a lovely interval, with frost at night and warm sun all day—the still, dreamy, smoky autumn time that Lucinda loved. Snow did not whiten the ridges until Christmas. And there was a merry Christmas at last for the Huetts! Logan and the boys had already tacked up a hundred beaver hides on the cabin walls, and marten, mink, and skunk hides too numerous to count. These already assured Huett of money to pay his debts and have some left over. Then there was the prospect of still better hunting and trapping during the balance of the winter.

That belated stroke of good fortune carried on to great fulfillment. The wilderness yielded much to Logan Huett that mild winter. It paid him back in fur for much of his loss.

In the spring, before the road was dry, he started for Flagg on the last trip for the faithful old oxen. He returned driving a new team of sturdy farm horses, drawing a new wagon loaded and piled high, with three mustangs haltered behind. His weather-beaten face wore the happiest mien Lucinda had seen there since the day she married him.

The boys, whom he had not taken with him to Flagg.

stood around the wagon wide-eyed, staring at the shaggy mustangs, fat and woolly from a winter pasture. Barbara forgot herself in awe and joy over the ponies she had heard the boys talk about for years. And Lucinda could have wept.

"Well, you moon-eyed Huetts," said Logan, "from this day on you're cowboys!"

"Aw, Paw, which is mine?" queried Grant, eagerly.

"Grant, yours is the buckskin. And that's his name. . . . Abe, the wild sorrel there, rarin' back on that rope, is yours. . . . George, the bay belongs to you—if you can ride him."

"Huh! I'll ride him all right," declared George, raptly.

Abe did not have anything to say, but the look in his gray eyes was enough.

"Tie them to the fence, there, and help me unpack this wagon," went on Logan, practically.

Presently Logan lifted a huge pack, sewed up in burlap, and threw it at Lucinda's feet.

"For you and Barbara. Every item on your list—and every doggone thing I could think of!"

Barbara squealed with delight and pounced upon the pack, but she could not even budge it. Lucinda was not speechless so much from surprise and pleasure as she was at the unusual feeling exhibited by her husband. She watched him.

"Saddles and bridles and spurs and chaps—all Mexican. Navajo saddle blankets. Manila ropes. Rifle-sheaths and gun-belts. . . . Here, cowboys, lift down this heavy one. Shells, plenty! I haven't seen so many since I was Indian scout for General Crook. . . . Look at these. Colts. Forty-fives! . . . And here. Ha! Ha!—Winchester rifles! —Forty-fours! Light, hard-shooting, easy to pack on a saddle! . . . Now, cowboys first and hunters second, the Huett outfit starts this day. And it's a bad day for varmints of this range. Cougars, lofers, grizzlies, cinnamons, take notice! . . . And Outfit, listen to this news from Flagg. Rustlers have come in from New Mexico. Cattle-thieves! They're working the ranges east of Flagg. And rustling will grow in Arizona as the cattle increase. It's hard lines. Something I never reckoned on. I've fought the four-footed meat-eaters all these years. And snow and ice and blizzards and heat and drought and flood. But now comes the worst enemy of the cattlemen. The maver-ick hunter—the calf thief. . . . Let that sink in deep, sons. But rustlers won't stop us. We've got this walled range, and grass and water. Nothing shall ever stop us from raising that thirty thousand head!"

Chapter Ten

LOGAN HUETT took no stock of the passing years. He did not count them, but he saw his sons grow into tall, broadshouldered, small-hipped, round-limbed riders, leanjawed men, with intent clear eyes and still, tanned faces. He saw them grow into the hunters and cowboys he had vowed to make them when they were little boys tumbling about the green bench with their pets. George was the born cattleman, Abe the woodsman, the keenest tracker, the best shot in that section of Arizona. Grant became the cowboy, the hardest rider, the most unerring roper from the Cibeque to the railroad.

Likewise, and with almost as great satisfaction, Huett saw his little band of carefully guarded and nourished cattle grow into the nucleus of a herd. He counted them from calving time to the snows, and from the first white fall to the thaw in spring—jealously, morosely, sorrowfully in lean years, hopefully in those seasons that favored him.

In the same terms he saw and counted the new homesteaders, the settlers that drifted in, the cattlemen who opened up the wide range from Mormon Lake to Flagg, the squatters who located at a spring or water hole, to eke out a bare, miserable existence in log shacks, always looking toward making a stake out of their water-rights. Nor did Huett miss any of the men who drifted in to make their homes back in the great forest. They lived on meat and beans, holed up in the winter, rode the trails in other seasons, and idled away fruitless hours in the few little hamlets that sprang up across the vast rangeland.

Huett's failure for so many years was due to a one man fight against too many obstacles. As his sons grew up, this condition imperceptibly diminished until it was overcome. If any one factor more than another contributed to this victory, it was the winter trapping of fur-bearing animals. But Huett developed his farm. This and the sale of pelts provided them with a living while his herd slowly grew.

His habits of restless energy and indomitable purpose were transmitted to his sons. They were Logan Huett all over again. And as the bitter ordeal of the past years gradually faded and he saw the physical manifestations of his vision take shape before his eyes, he touched happiness almost as great as his pride in his boys.

One late afternoon in the early spring Huett returned from the corrals to the cabin. His wife and Barbara had put the dining-table out on the porch for the first time that season, perhaps a little too early considering the cool evenings. But Huett liked to eat out where he could see the garden, the alfalfa, the pasture, and the cattle dotting the long valley.

Abe had just come down from the rim and stood leaning on his rifle talking to George and Grant. In buckskins, compared to the blue-jeaned, high-booted garb of his brothers, he appeared shorter, but the fact was that he equalled them in lithe six-foot manhood.

"Dad, here's good news," spoke up George, his intent eyes alight. "Abe trailed that bunch of wild horses down into the head of Three Spring Draw."

"Ahuh. Well, he's always trailing something," replied Huett, with a laugh. "But what of it?"

"We can drive them down into the canyon."

"Trap them," added Grant, eagerly.

"It could be done, if they're in that draw. I reckon, though, during the night they'll work out."

Abe said he did not think so. Below the brakes of that ravine it opened out into a sunny park where the snow melted off early, and the young shoots of grass had come up rich and green. Abe recalled that once before he had seen wild horses down there.

"How many of them?" asked Huett, becoming fired with possibilities.

"Big drove. I saw a hundred head. Some fine stock. There's a blue roan stallion in that bunch I'd like to catch."

"Well, I reckon if we trapped them we'd have a hell of a time catching them."

"But, Dad, they could never climb out of the canyon. And it'll be a long time before our herd grows so big as to need all the grass."

"Dad, it's sure a windfall of luck," put in George. "We need horses. We could cut out some of the best, catch them, break them. Breed them, too."

"What's your plan, Abe?" asked Huett, convinced.

"You go down the canyon in the morning, at daybreak, and tear down that pole fence half way up the draw. We'll ride on top, spread out and roll rocks off the rim. Then we'll pile down the several trails, yelling and shooting. I'll bet the whole bunch will break for the canyon."

"Supper's waiting, father," called Barbara, who stood by the table listening.

"All right, Barbara, I'll be there pronto," he called gayly. "Fetch me a little hot water. I've got axle-grease on my hands."

She brought it and stood by while he washed his hands. "Father, that's great—Abe's tracking wild horses into the draw, isn't it?"

"Yes, Barbara, it sure is. I reckon our luck has changed. A bunch of fine horses, all at once—almost too good to be true."

"Buck is old and lame now," went on Barbara. "He ought to be turned loose for good."

"He's sure earned it. . . . Barbara, I reckon what makes your eyes so bright is the chance for a new horse for you, eh?"

"Oh, yes. I'd love to have one of my own," replied Barbara.

Her earnest feeling touched Huett in that old sore spot —the poignant fact of his failure to give his loved ones the comforts, the pleasures, the rare luxuries which made life so much easier and happier. He had known some of these when a boy. Lucinda had never been without them until she came to him. And he had always shared her conviction that Barbara had come of fine stock, whatever the fatality and tragedy of her childhood.

"Abe, this girl Barbara is raving about a wild mustang broken for her," he said, a little huskily.

"Barbara, you shall have two and take your pick," replied Abe, with a warm soft glow in his gray eyes.

"Oh, grand!" she cried, ecstatically. "May I go with you to drive the wild horses down?"

"Aw now, ask me an easy one," said Abe, regretfully. "Babs, you're good on a horse, but this drive will take awful hard riding. Suppose you go with Dad. You can help him tear down the fence, then get back out of the way and watch those wild horses pile by out into the canyon. Watch for that blue roan stallion!"

"Come to supper," called Lucinda, impatiently. "It's getting cold."

Logan straddled the crude deerskin covered bench and sat down to the table that was likewise the work of his hands. It was laden with good wholesome food. He and his sons were too hungry to talk. The shades of the spring dusk fell upon them there.

Before daylight the next morning Logan arose, scraped the red coals out of the ashes and started a fire. He put the kettle on. Then he called Barbara.

"I'll be right down," she replied. "I heard you get up."

"Boil some coffee. And butter some biscuits. We might not get back in time for breakfast. I'll go milk—then saddle up."

It was dark outside and coyotes were wailing over the ridge. The lofty pines stood up black and still. Logan heard the boys coming in with the horses. He went out to find Buck and his steed saddled and haltered to the corral fence. Faint streaks of gray shone in the east, while the morning air was cold and raw. He could hear wild turkeys calling sleepily from their roost up in the forest. Returning, Logan found the boys had preceded him to the cabin. Barbara, clad in overalls and boots, looking like a lithe sturdy boy with a pretty brown face, was serving them with coffee and biscuits.

"Good. I reckoned you'd better have a snack of grub," said Logan, as they greeted him. "What's the deal, sons?"

"Dad, you'd better rustle," replied Abe. "We'll be at the head of Three Springs by sunrise."

"Don't worry, Abraham. We'll have a hole in that fence."

It was gray dawn when Logan set out riding down the canyon with Barbara. Five miles down the walled valley spread widest and then began to close in again. The walls grew more rugged and opened up with intersecting canyons, or draws, the boys called them. The gorge called Three Springs Draw was as deceiving as any ramification of this strange valley. Its opening appeared like a shallow cove in the east wall, but the inside soon spread out into a large area of grassy parks, groves of pine and maple, and thickets of oak. The fence of poles crossed the narrow neck between the open ova' valley and the rough-timbered, rock-strewn gorge beyond.

"Reckon this is a good place," said Logan, dismounting. "Barbara, pile off and tie Buck back a wavs. Wild horses have a peculiar effect upon tame horses. Abe says a tame horse gone wild is almost impossible to catch. . . . You climb on that flat rock. You can see everything from there and be safe."

"All right, that'll be jake," returned Barbara. "But can't I help you take down the fence?"

"Sure, and let's rustle. Abe will be letting out that Indian yell of his pronto. That'll be their signal."

Barbara did not have her wide shoulders and strong arms for nothing. She had done her share of the Huett labors. Logan found a strong satisfaction in watching her. How well he remembered Lucinda's pride in Barbara's good looks, which some time got the better of Lucinda's need of help. Barbara always wore gloves for heavy work, and Lucinda worried too much about sun and dirt. Logan was always amused at these evidences of Lucinda's lingering vanity. For his part he thought Barbara a pretty girl, and what was better, good, obedient, and lovable, who would make some settler as wonderful a wife as was Lucinda. But that last thought always worried Logan. He did not want to lose Barbara.

The pole fence was a makeshift affair, strong enough, but neither nailed nor wired, and it was so easily pushed over that Logan quickly saw the need of a new one.

"Oh—listen!" cried Barbara, suddenly, dropping the pole she had carried to one side.

On the instant a piercing yell rang down from the heights. It was Abe's call which he always used when they were hunting the canyons. In the early still morning, with the air cold and clear, the prolonged bugle note pealed down, to rebound with a clapping sound from wall to wall, to wind across the canyon and die in hollow echo.

"Wonderful!" cried Barbara. "Hasn't Abe a voice?"

"Yells like an Indian," replied Logan, with enthusiasm.

"Get up on your rock now. I'll answer. Then you'll hear some thunder."

Logan cupped his hands round his mouth, drew a deep breath, and expelled it in a stentorian: "*Wa—hoo-o!*"

His yell let loose a thousand weird and hollow echoes. Logan went back to have another look at the haltered horses, then he returned to mount the rock beside Barbara. He had scarcely sat down when from high up and far away a rock crashed from the rim, to start a rattling slide. It had scarcely ceased when a like sound came from the other side of the canyon.

"If I remember right there's a rocky weathered wall just at the head of Three Springs," said Logan. "A big rock rolled there will start an avalanche. The boys do that when they hunt bears. You bet if there are any bears below they come piling out. . . . By golly! I forgot my rifle. It wouldn't be so much fun if an old grizzly got routed out up there and came rumbling down here."

"I'll shinny up that tree," replied Barbara, gayly.

"Daughter, I'm a little heavy to run or shinny up trees. . . . *There!*"

"Oh my!" shrilled Barbara.

Thunder had burst under the rim. A sliding rattle soon drowned heavy crashes and thuds, until it swelled into a deep booming roar that filled the canyon. It was a tremendous sound that took moments to lose its power, to lessen and end in rattling slides and cracking rocks.

"Golly! Wasn't that a noise?" ejaculated Logan.

"Terrible. But oh, so thrilling!"

"Barbara, every four-legged animal up that draw will run wild down here. The boys won't need to waste their ammunition shooting or their voices either . . . Look! Deer coming."

"Oh! How strangely they bound! As if on springs. But so graceful. . . . There's a fawn. . . ."

"Barbara, I hear the trample of hoofs. Stampede! That's the sound to thrill me. Horses or cattle it's all the same."

"Look, Dad!—Flashing through the brush—under the trees—white, red, brown, black! . . . Look! Wild horses!"

Logan saw them burst out of the timber and yelled his delight. A wild shaggy drove of mustangs, long manes and tails flying, poured out of the draw like a flood. The vanguard passed Logan and Barbara in a cloud of dust, so swiftly as to be obscured from clear view, but this body was followed by strings of horses and then stragglers that could be seen distinctly. Logan discerned many a clean-limbed racy mustang that if well-broken would sell at a good price. His thrifty eager mind grasped at that. But Barbara was squealing over the beauty of this sorrel and that bay or buckskin. Suddenly she tugged at Logan.

"Look, Dad, look! Abe's blue stallion! . . . Did you ever see such a beautiful horse. Wild! Oh, he could never be tamed."

"Gosh, but he's a thoroughbred," returned Logan. "Lamed himself a little. Reckon that accounts for him being behind. . . . Bab, I'm afraid there's a horse Abe wouldn't give you."

"Abe would give me anything in the world," cried Barbara, her voice rich and sweet. "They're gone, Dad, out into the canyon. How many altogether?"

"Eighty or a hundred head. And I'll bet half of them good for something. This is not a bad morning's work!"

"Isn't that a bear?" queried Barbara, pointing up. "On the ledge—above the clump of firs. . . . Yes, it's a nice big shiny black bear."

"Sure is. Wish I had my gun."

"I don't. Dad, I never forgot my bear cubs. Oh, why

did they have to grow up, to be nuisances to *you*? Never to me!"

"Bab, your bears got too big. But it sure was interesting —the way they refused at first to go back to the wild and kept coming home. . . . That fellow, though, never belonged to you. He's part cinnamon. See the red shine on him in the sun. . . . *Wow!* the boys are shooting at him. Listen to the bullets crack on the rocks. Must be shooting at long range."

"Oh, I hope he gets away," cried Barbara.

"There he piles off the ledge, out of sight in the brush. When a bear runs down hill like that he's safe, Bab, even from as wonderful a shot as Abe."

Logan got off the rock to begin putting up the fence. While he was at this task George and Grant rode out of the draw, and came trotting up to Barbara, gay and excited over their successful venture.

"Hello, Babs," called Grant, as he leaped off, to brush the pine needles and bits of wood from his person. "Did you hear the rocks rolling? Wasn't that slide Abe started a humdinger of a roar?—Did you see the wild horses?"

"Grant, it was all wonderful," replied Barbara, her eyes fixed eagerly upon the draw.

The boys set to work helping Logan with the fence. By the time Abe rode out of the timber they had completed the job, at least to Logan's satisfaction.

"Paw, it's not high enough," said Abe. "Some of those wild horses would jump it. We'll cut some more poles and snake out some stumps. Build up the low places. Then we'll have them corralled."

"Abe, it was a slick job," said Logan, admiringly. "Talk about a windfall!"

"Funny how I hated to start that big slide. Guess I got soft-hearted at the last. . . . Barbara, what do you think?"

"Abe, those wild horses will be safer, happier, shut up in our canyon. . . . And I picked out two . . . Oh, we saw your blue stallion. He was a little lame. Prettiest horse I ever saw, Abe."

"Do you want him?" asked Abe, his eyes shining on her.

"I wouldn't be mean enough to take him," she replied.

George rode into the timber to drag out stumps. Grant walked off with the axe. Abe sat his horse watching Barbara with that slight pensive smile upon his tanned face. Logan found a seat to rest upon while the boys fetched more materials to raise the fence. He felt unusually exhilarated. Abe had solved the horse problem for some time to come. Nearer and nearer crept the actuality of that vision of years.

"Sons," said Logan Huett, to his boys. "Our hay is cut and stored. The corn and beans can wait. We've a hundred sacks of potatoes to haul to town. That leaves us the big job. Driving cattle in to sell!—The first time in twenty years!—By God, I can't believe it!"

"Dad, we could have sold quite a bunch last year, but you wouldn't," rejoined George.

"I hadn't the nerve. . . . Boys, we'll cut out all our old cows that haven't calved, and the steers and throw them into the pasture tonight. . . . Your mother and Barbara will go with me on the wagon. We'll leave at daybreak. I'll wait for you at Turkey Flat. Next day we'll camp from there."

Two hours later the boys had Huett's herd bunched under the wall in the west side of the canyon. Those several hundred head of cattle, that had appeared so few down on the wide range, now when bunched and milling, raising the dust and bawling, appeared to Huett an im-

posing and all-satisfying spectacle. They were the beginning of a great herd.

He rode out to meet the boys and have his share in the
round-up. Lucinda came out to watch. Barbara, astride
her spirited little buckskin mustang, flashed here and
there to drive stragglers back into the bunch.

"Logan Huett, you're holding a round-up," soliloquized the rancher. "Kick yourself and wake up. The
most important move on a cattleman's range is about to
take place for the first time in Sycamore Canyon."

He reined his horse beside the corral fence upon which
Lucinda had climbed to see.

"Luce, look at your sons. Cowboys!" he exclaimed,
with a thrill that was communicated to his voice. "Isn't
that a grand sight?"

"Dear, I—I can't see very well," faltered his wife.

"What you crying for, Luce? Didn't I always tell you
the day would come. . . . Look at Barbara ride!"

"She'll kill herself on that wild pony. . . . Oh, Logan,
need she be like the boys?"

"Lucinda, she can't be anything but what you made
her—the finest girl west of the Rockies."

"Logan!" He saw her eyes shine through her tears.
"Do you really mean that?"

"I sure do, wife. Let her ride."

He joined his sons and lent his big voice and his tireless energy to this task—the happiest and most important
that had ever been undertaken on his range.

Yet buoyant as they all were, they addressed themselves
to that task with intense seriousness.

The herd was not by any means tame. Crowded into
the triangle under the wall, with one corral fence pre-
venting escape from the other side they milled around
like a maelstrom, bawling loudly, knocking heads and
horns together. Barbara had the swiftest riding to do, as

her job was to overtake those that ran out of the circle, and drive them inside the pasture gate. Logan helped Abe cut out the cows and steers designated by George, whose job of selection was the one of great responsibility. Grant had to rope the cattle that could not be cut out of the herd, and drag them from the mêlée. He was left-handed, but extraordinarily unerring with a lasso. He could pitch a small loop over the horns of a steer that was fenced all about by a forest of horns, as well as throw clear across the herd and fasten it to a steer plunging out on the opposite side.

Logan reveled in the round-up. The sharp calls of the boys, Barbara's high-pitched cry, the pound of hoofs and grind of horns, the coarse bawls of the steers, the swaying straining mill of the whole herd, the dry acrid smell of rising dust, and the swift horses, running in, halting on a pivot, to wheel and hold hard—these were music and sweetness and incense to the longing ambition of Logan Huett.

At length George called the count.

"Eighty-seven—and that's aplenty," he announced. "Dad, cattle were seiling at thirty dollars on the hoof last spring. They'll fetch more now. What'll you do with all that money?"

"Lord—son," panted Logan, wiping his grimy face, "after I square myself with your mother and you-all, not forgetting Barbara, I'll not have enough left to pay my debts. . . . But, by thunder, once in our lives we'll ride high and handsome."

"*Whoopee!*" yelled George and Grant in unison. Abe bent thoughtful eyes upon the glowing Barbara.

"Luce, now supper and to bed," shouted Logan. "We'll be on our way before sun-up."

The snail's pace drive was not too slow for Logan. It could have been slower and yet have given him joy. Every windfall along the dusty road, every big pine and rock, swale and flat, in fact every landmark so well known to him that he could locate them in the dark, each and all seemed to greet him. "Wal, old timer, drivin' to the railroad at last!"

Holbert, at Mormon Lake, was frankly glad to see Huett come along at last with cattle to sell. He was full of news, much of it bad. At the peak of his cattle raising, the year before, his son-in-law had thrown in with a band of rustlers and had driven ten thousand head of stock out of the territory before Holbert knew a hoof was moving.

"Look out down your way, Huett," he advised, morosely. "When you begin to sell cattle you're a marked man. There'll be hell to pay on this range in five years."

Holbert's pessimism, which was corroborated by his neighbor Collier, in no wise dampened Huett's ardor. He had his heavy boot on the neck of the hydra-headed giant that had kept him poor for twenty years. That trip to Flagg, for him and his family, far outdid the one years before, when his beaver pelts had brought their first happy Christmas. He spent lavishly. He bought secret gifts for the Christmas soon to come. He paid his pressing debts and saw himself at last on the road to success.

The drive back home, with a second wagon and team, was in the nature of a jubilee. More than once Lucinda had Logan stop the wagon so that she could get out and gather purple asters and golden rod. She talked of their honeymoon ride through that dreary desolate forest. And before they got home Lucinda talked of other things—particularly about Barbara.

"Logan, you're blind as a bat to all except cattle," she said, tersely. "You never saw how the men at Flagg, young and old, flocked around Barbara. That girl could be the belle of Arizona. She could marry any one of them. Take her pick."

"Good Lord, Luce!" ejaculated Logan, surprised and stung. "Our Barbara leaving? Not to be thought of!"

"How can we help it?—But for Barbara's singular loyalty to us—her love for the boys—she would be having suitors *now*."

"Luce, you trouble me."

"No wonder. I'm troubled myself. Barbara loves George and Grant. And she worships Abe. But she doesn't know it. She thinks she's just a fond sister. Nature will out, Logan!—She's no kin of ours. She's not their sister. . . . And my trouble is this. Since she must marry—do her part for our West—she should marry one of our boys!"

"My God, Lucinda! you'd have to tell her you're not her mother. I'm not her Dad. Who could we tell her she is? We don't even know her name. . . . Aw, Luce, let's keep it secret long as we can. Not to break that sweet girl's heart!"

"There's the rub, Logan dear," returned Lucinda, soberly. "But the thing can't be overlooked forever."

Another autumn came. It was different from all the autumns, except one, that Huett remembered. It followed a hot summer remarkable for short dry electric storms. What little rain fell was up on the bluffs and the high rims. Not a drop descended in Sycamore Canyon.

That spring and summer the grass in the canyon had been thicker and richer than usual. Huett had dammed the brook into a small lake and had run many branches from it through the meadows, until it sank into the ground. The gardens, orchards, and alfalfa fields, having abundant water from the irrigation ditches, did not suffer from the scorching sun and dry wind.

Indian summer held off.

One day Abe met two cowboys out on the road, riding to Payson. They reported the worst grasshopper plague ever known in that section of Arizona. Ranchers all the way down had sent word along the line for Collier, Holbert, and Huett to look out for a river of grasshoppers flowing over the best of the range land.

When Abe reported that news to his father it was received seriously, but not in any anxiety. Sycamore was a deep hole in the forest and unlikely to be visited by a plague.

George Huett, the most studious and keenest of the Huetts, took a pessimistic view of the possibilities.

"But Dad, suppose the grasshoppers did happen to light down in Sycamore," he said, in reply to Logan's sanguine convictions. "They would absolutely eat us up, clean us out, ruin us."

"Son! How do you figure that?"

"Because our canyon is a narrow strip compared to the open range. They'd sweep right through, eating everything to the roots."

"But our stock can live on browse."

"In normal years, yes. But this is not normal. No acorns, no moss, none of that long tufted grass on the slopes, and very little leafage."

"Then it is serious," returned Logan, quickly troubled. "Just when our prospects are so bright! . . . God must be against me!"

"Nature is, that's sure."

"What can we do?"

"Dad, that's the hell of it. We can't do anything but hope and pray."

"Would you cut the alfalfa?"

"Sure, if we had time. But you know what a job that is. Usually we take a week to cut, dry, rake, and haul. And here those grasshoppers are right on top of us."

"You don't say?" Huett swore under his breath.

"Abe said he'd not worry you till he had to. He rode up the canyon, meaning to climb out and scout back toward the open range. You see our canyon is almost in a direct line with that flight of grasshoppers. The open country east of Mormon Lake sticks a spike down into this forest. And the point of it is not very far from the head of Sycamore. Grassy draws through the woods all the way. And, Dad, these damn grasshoppers don't hop! They *fly*."

"Sure grasshoppers can fly. I've seen the wild turkeys chase them. It's always good hunting when the turks are feeding on them. . . . Son, what you mean? Grasshoppers can't eat while they fly."

"No. But all the same, that's how they cover ground so fast. I've read in the Bible of the locust flights in Egypt. And I've heard of grasshoppers' flights in Kansas. Much the same, I reckon."

Huett, and his two sons waited anxiously for Abe's return. He rode in presently, dark of face and somber of eye.

"Bad news, son?" queried the cattleman.

"Dad, it couldn't be no worse," replied Abe, sliding out of his saddle, his glance like gray fire. "They're in the canyon."

"No!—Not our canyon?"

"Yes, our canyon. Half way down. A mile or two of grasshoppers, like a yellow carpet rolling down the grass. They leave the ground as bare as if it'd been burned. . . . Thousands, millions, billions. . . . Barbara," he called to the listening wide-eyed girl, "what's next after billions?"

"Trillions, you stupid boy!"

"Well, trillions of yellow-legged hoppers. They'll be on us pronto. . . . I'm so mad I'm sick. If we could only *do* something."

"My—God!" gasped Huett. "I can't feed our stock a

month this winter, even if we had the corn and alfalfa
cut."

Lucinda heard from the door. Her face appeared to
Logan to take on again the old sad cast. But she turned
indoors without speaking. Barbara, however, vented
enough amaze, disgust, and anger for the whole family.

"Babs, swear all you want," said Grant solemnly. "It
won't do us any good. We're going to be ruined by a mob
of bugs!"

"Oh no! You men can do something," she cried.

"What?"

"Set fire to the grass!"

"By golly, that's an idea, Dad," spoke up George.

"We can meet them with fire. That'll do the trick,
but. . . ." Abe broke off with a somber shake of his dark
sleek head.

"Not to be thought of!" boomed Huett. "We'd set the
forest afire, burn all the timber and grass in the country.
. . . But let's think of some other way."

"Dad, just wait till you see the air full of buzzing
grasshoppers and the ground yellow with them—then
you'll savvy we can't do a thing," averred Abe, tragically.

"Well, I won't see it till I have to," averred Logan,
gruffly, as he got up. "But no Huett ever showed yellow.
And we won't, even with a yellow plague upon us!—
Come, sons, we'll cut the alfalfa."

George and Grant followed him to the barn to get
scythes and rakes. But Abe sat looking at Barbara. Presently he mounted his horse and rode up the canyon.
Huett went ploddingly at the labor, his somber gaze bent
upon the rich green hay that he was mowing.

"Say!" called Grant, suddenly. "What'n hell can be
chasing Abe?"

"Dad—look!" shouted George.

Then Logan looked up to see Abe riding swiftly by the

cabin. He waved and shouted to Barbara as he passed. He headed his lean mustang across the gardens and came tearing up to Logan, scattering dust all over him.

"*Dad—we're saved!*" he panted hoarsely, his dark face alight, his eyes piercingly bright. "What you—think? . . . You'd never guess—in a thousand years."

"I reckon not—if you come ararin' at me like this. What ails you son?"

"He's loco, sure as our rotten luck!" declared George, which assertion corroborated Logan's. Abe was not the kind to show excitement in any event, let alone the intensity which radiated from him now.

"We haven't got rotten luck," he cried. "But the most—marvelous luck—in the world. . . . We're not going to be cleaned out. . . . I tell you—*we're saved!*"

"Son, I heard you the first time," replied Huett, soberly, not daring to accept Abe's strange excited statements. "If you're not crazy—tell me how we're saved."

"By God, you'll never believe me," declared Abe, with a deep laugh. "I couldn't believe my own eyes. But dang it—come and see. . . . Dad, I hope to die if I didn't see thousands of wild turkeys come flapping, sailing, running down out of the woods upon that swarm of grasshoppers."

"Wild turkeys!" burst out Huett, suddenly dazzled.

"Sure as you're alive," replied Abe, eagerly. "The regular fall round-up, you know, when the turks band together to come up-country for the pine nuts and acorns."

"Of all the miracles!" exclaimed George, beamingly. "Dad, one big gobbler can eat a bushel of hoppers!"

"I reckon I was wrong to say God had deserted me," declared Huett, in august self-reproach.

"Sight of my life," declared Abe. "Come on. You've got to see it. Maw and Bab, too. . . . But we must walk—slip along under the trees—so those turks won't catch a glimpse of us. I reckon, though, that wouldn't make no difference today. . . . Come, we'll take a short cut."

Soon all the Huetts were following Abe through the woods. Barbara slipped her hand into Logan's and ran to keep up with him. Abe hushed their exuberant talk. They crossed the timbered slope above the cabin, keeping to the left, climbing the rocky vine-covered ledges above the falls, and went rapidly through the thick belt of timber beyond. Abe led across the brook. Soon Logan saw through the scattering trees the brown open canyon again. Perhaps half a mile beyond Abe halted.

"Listen! Did you ever hear the like of that?" he queried.

A strange sound filled Logan's ears. Indeed he could not compare it to anything he had ever heard. It was a loud buzzing seething hum mixed with a thumping flapping roar.

"I'll be doggoned!" ejaculated Logan. "Hear it, Barbara?"

"Do I? Oh, what music! Come, let's hurry, Abe, so we can see!"

Abe led them to the edge of the woods. Out there in the grassy open of the canyon, under a dust cloud, was being enacted a onesided war—a massacre—a carnage. Clear across the flat stretched a wide, shifting, bronze, white, and black belt of wild turkeys in swift and ruthless action. Logan made no estimate of that huge flock. But in that country of wild turkeys, where he had seen large flocks for twenty years, this one surpassed all. Beyond the dust cloud, up the canyon, moved a yellow glassy mass in the air. It waved up and down. Behind it under the dust thumped and picked and darted the army of huge gay-plumaged birds. They moved forward in a stretched formation, yet dozens of great gobblers left the line to run back after grasshoppers that tried to escape to the rear. They were big fat slow grasshoppers and they could not fly far. Not a one escaped to the rear.

"Oh, Dad, isn't it grand?" cried Barbara, excitedly as she clung to him and they hurried along at the edge of the timber to keep up with the moving spectacle.

Manifestly Huett was entranced, enraptured by the scene. This was, if anything, the strange miracle of destiny prophesying his success. Nothing could halt him now.

"Wonderful, Barbara! I never saw the like," he said with a voice that shook. "Abe was right. . . . We're saved. And never so long as I live will I kill another turkey."

"Dad, it's all day with that bunch of grasshoppers," said George. "The turkeys will stick to them until they've gobbled every darned one. You know a gobbler likes a fat juicy hopper about the same as Abe does apple pie."

"In that case, goodbye to the hoppers!" laughed Barbara.

They came to where a point of the forestland projected out into the open. Abe halted there.

"I reckon this is far enough," he said, as they joined him. "Some of those wary old gobblers have begun to look back. It won't do to scare that bunch . . . isn't it a mess, Paw? Aren't those turks doing a great job for us?"

"So great, son, that I'll hang here a while longer," replied Huett, fervently. "Go back, all of you. Mother looks tired. We've come a couple of miles. All to watch a flock of wild turkeys!"

"Logan, nothing is ever as terrible as it seems—at first," returned Lucinda, and giving him a sweet smile she started back with Barbara, followed by the boys.

Abe halted and turned with one of his rare smiles: "Paw, would you like turkey for supper?"

Logan waved him on. Soon they passed out of sight under the pines. Then Logan once more turned his attention to the massacre of the grasshoppers. The action did not change. The cloud of insects kept flying and hopping up the canyon, while the turkeys ran thumping up the dust, pouncing and picking as before. But the sight grew somehow magnificent to Logan. It was nothing in raw nature but an incident. But to Logan it had vast significance.

The dust cloud moved along behind the yellow stream. And the colored throng of turkeys, their bronze backs bent, or their red heads high, with checkered wings flapping and feet pounding, kept surging, massing, disintegrating, running up the canyon. The loud seethe and buzz, with the roar of the feathered jackals, gradually diminished to a hum.

Logan watched them out of sight and sound. And then he lingered there in the dreaming silent forest. This unexpected and unparalleled accident that meant so much to him seemed inexplicable as a mere happening on the cattle range. Logan's pondering thought was not equal to the subtle intimations. What was his long toil, his ceaseless energy, reserved for? Had not Lucinda meant that this should be a lesson to him—that he had been too self-centered, too grimly fettered to his one task, too prone to doubt and fear? Something nameless and inevitable waited upon his years. A mournful stir in the great forest, a breath of the soul of that wilderness, had a counterpart in his emotion, a whisper, the meaning of which eluded him.

Chapter Eleven

LUCINDA allowed herself to be persuaded again by Barbara and Grant to attend a dance at Pine.

These occasions had been few and far between as the years flew by. In that country they were the only social gatherings of any kind and were attended by all the scant populace for fifty miles around, irrespective of character.

Whatever Lucinda's qualities—which Logan so often maintained with solid pride, were perfect for a pioneer's wife—she had never favored these country affairs until the children grew far beyond the age of the other young people who gave themselves so avidly to this one pleasure. Dances were the only means by which the older folk got acquainted and the youngsters had a chance to court each other. The drawbacks, from Lucinda's point of view, were the invariable and often serious fights among the young backwoodsmen, and the cowboys, not to mention the men of doubtful prestige.

So the time had come when Lucinda reluctantly was compelled to attend an occasional one of these functions. Logan enjoyed them immensely. He talked cattle to the other ranchers, and watched the young folk dance. It did not seem to worry him that the young bucks fought over Barbara. She was the prettiest and most popular girl between Flagg and the Matazels. Logan took vast pride in that. Nevertheless he did not encourage young men to call at Sycamore Canyon. He still clung jealously to the secret and the dream of his isolated range.

But Lucinda saw things differently. She had forestalled the courting of Barbara until the girl was older than most young mothers of that region. She would have put it off altogether, or indefinitely, if either had been possible.

A very beautiful relationship existed between Bar-

bara and Abe. If they thought about it at all they probably regarded it as sister and brother love, but Lucinda
believed their worship was deeper than they had conceived. Abe had paid little attention to other girls while
Barbara would have been content always to dance, ride,
work, and talk with Abe.

The respect and devotion Grant held for Barbara was
a joy to Lucinda, although it was purely of a brotherly
nature. Grant held no favorite among the country belles,
although he interested himself in many of them. George,
however, was different. He made no secret of his affection for Barbara, but his interest in other women was
more violent and possessive than either of his brothers.

Lucinda pondered over these things all morning of
the November day when the Huetts were preparing to
drive to Pine for the Thanksgiving turkey shoot and
dance. Logan was intent on loading more produce to sell
in Pine than one wagon would contain. Barbara labored
between ecstasy and despair over the white gown Lucinda had given her. Grant and George decked themselves out in all the cowboy finery they possessed. Abe
came in dressed in buckskin, carrying his rifle.

"Abe Huett!" exclaimed Barbara. "You're not going
to this dance in buckskin?"

"Bab, I'm going to a turkey shoot," replied Abe,
mildly.

"But you promised to come to the dance. . . . Abe,
I won't have any fun without you."

"Sure I'll come. You don't think I'd leave you to that
pack of hombres, do you? . . . But I don't want to wear
pants and boots when I can be comfortable in buckskin. Barbara, I'm going to win that turkey shoot."

"Win! Of course you'll win. But, Abe, please dress up,
and look like—like somebody. You can't dance in moccasins."

"I can't dance in boots, or shoes either."

"You can too."

"I never get much chance to dance with you, anyway."

"You shall tonight. I promise. Please, Abe."

"Say, you don't have to coax me. I'm tickled to death. But, darn it, Barbara, I'm no good as a dancer."

"You're not so bad, Abe. Sure, you're no dancing dude like George."

George took the sly dig as a compliment. Lucinda divined something untoward was brewing here. Barbara was not jealous of George's attentions to his other friends, but she took exception to a great many of them. Lucinda thought this an opportune moment to bring matters to a head.

"George, you're not going to take that Mil Campbell to this dance?" hazarded Lucinda, with pretended assurance.

"Why, yes, Maw—I'd thought of it," drawled George, as he carefully adjusted his scarf.

"No! . . . Not really?"

"Yes, really," retorted George, the red leaping to his cheek. "Mil can dance rings round that outfit. It's a mixed crowd, you know . . . and why shouldn't I?"

"I shouldn't think you'd need to be told," returned Lucinda, coldly.

"Now, Ma!"

"Brother, the reason you shouldn't take that hussy is because Ma and I will be there," spoke up Barbara, her eyes blazing."

"Aw, I don't see it!" ejaculated George. But he was aware of it and he was angry.

Abe eyed him penetratingly. "Say, don't look for me to help you fight that Campbell outfit again."

"You can all go to the devil," shouted George, furiously.

"If we did we'd meet you there, George Washington Huett," said Barbara, cuttingly. "But don't misunderstand me. . . . George, it's really none of my business whom you take—or what you do. Only I've blinded myself to your actions. Mil Campbell is handsome, and I'll bet she's lots of fun. She certainly can start fights among her beaus. But, you know, she's hardly a—a person to flaunt in front of Mother and me. . . . Don't expect me to speak to you, let alone dance with you."

George's tanned face turned white and his eyes held a passionate reproach. But he strode out silently, his head up.

"Aw, Babs, you raked him over pretty hard," said Grant. "After all, blood is thicker than water."

"Served the lady-killer just right," added Abe. "George has got some sense, but he doesn't use it until he's waked up by a jar. . . . And, Bab, don't you feel sorry. That Campbell outfit hate George because Mil is crazy about him. There'll be a fight. And George will come sloping home sure ashamed of himself and probably licked bad."

Lucinda reproached herself for this issue, yet could not but feel that good would come of it. No doubt George was more deeply involved with the Campbell girl than they had suspected.

"Say, the stuck-up hombre rode off by himself," said Abe, from the door. "Maw, I'll put my good clothes in the wagon and change down there. . . . Bab, I'll bet you'll just dazzle them tonight. . . . Sorry you won't be there in time to see me win that turkey shoot."

"Abe, you couldn't lose."

"All the crack shots of the Tonto will be there," he rejoined dubiously. "I'll have to do some tall shooting."

"Here," flashed Barbara, leaping up from her box of finery to tie a bit of bright ribbon upon his buckskin coat. "There. Abe Huett, you dare to lose now."

"Thanks, Bab. . . . I reckon I'd be kinda bad for some hombre if I was shooting at him."

Barbara watched them ride away up the canyon road.

"Ma, if I could only meet some fellow like Abe!" murmured Barbara.

"Abe is a real man, Barbara," replied Lucinda pridefully. At that moment the impulse welled up within her to reveal the truth about Barbara's past to the girl, but another more disturbing emotion thrust it back. Eventually Barbara must know the fact of her adoption, but Lucinda still dreaded the time when she would have to tell her.

"Well, I'll never marry till I do find some one like him," said Barbara, as if to herself.

Logan rushed them in order to be ready for the drive down to Pine before noonday. It was quite far, but down hill all the way, and they accomplished the journey by sunset. Logan let them out at the log schoolhouse in the woods just on the edge of the little hamlet.

Already a number of families had arrived. Children were making merry around a big fire, while women were carrying utensils and packs from the wagons. Lucinda and Barbara deposited their heavy donations on the rough clapboard table that looked as if it had done duty for many years of weathering. Then while Lucinda made herself agreeable to old and new acquaintances, Barbara, with her precious box, ran into the cabin to change, along with other young women who had journeyed far for this night's pleasure.

While the sun set and dusk gathered, one by one horsemen arrived, singly and in couples and groups, buckboards and wagons. The Holberts and Colliers had traveled sixty and seventy miles to attend this dance. Lucinda met several new families, now calling themselves neighbors, who had homesteaded between Mormon Lake and Sycamore Canyon. All of Pine and most of Payson was represented, and many from the Verdi and Tonto.

They thronged around the fires and tables, eating and talking and laughing, until the fiddler arrived. He was a lean old man who had played one tune on his instrument for thirty years. The only other variation in music the dancers received were the tones struck from another violin by the accompanist who beat rhythmically and monotonously on it with little pine sticks while the fiddler sawed with his squeaky bow.

Lamps at each end of the schoolroom shed a yellow glare upon the circling dancers. As before, Lucinda looked on curiously, wonderingly, not quite understandingly. How seriously these young people took their dancing! It might almost have been a solemn occasion. No smiles, no whispers, no coquettish glances nor lover-like embraces! There were pretty girls there, as well-dressed as Barbara, but none of them could equal her grace. She danced first with Grant, while Lucinda kept her eyes fastened upon them.

After a dance the young people would stream out into the firelight, some to slip off into the woods, the majority crowding first around the tables, then the fires. The big blazes were kept roaring by attendants. The November night was still, clear, cold. Between dances the older folk sauntered through the schoolroom, gossiping and meeting neighbors they had not seen for months. The children romped here, there, and everywhere until they fell of sheer exhaustion and were put to bed behind the stove where a generous space was allotted them. Thus the young people grew up in celebration.

Presently Abe approached Lucinda. She hardly knew his lithe powerful figure in the unaccustomed garb. How handsome he was! Lucinda thrilled at his clear, fine, tanned face, dark almost as an Indian's, at his shining eyes. He put his arm around her.

"Maw, I won the turkey shoot," he announced, proudly. "Best shooting I ever did. But I sure had to."

"I'm glad, Abe. What'd you win?"

"All three shoots. Three gobblers and fifty odd dollars."

"So much!—Have you told Dad?"

"Yes, he's bragging around. But I haven't told Barbara. She's been so corralled I couldn't even see her. . . . *Aw!* there she comes. She saw me. . . . Maw, she's just too lovely."

Barbara came running, her dark eyes beaming upon Abe.

"Oh Abe! I heard. It's just wonderful. But *I* knew you'd win," she cried, and embraced him shyly.

"Wal, if you ask me this is what made me win," he drawled, touching a bit of ribbon in his buttonhole. "What do I get for winning? 'Cause sure I'll spend most of that prize money on you?"

"What do you want, Abe?" she asked, wistfully.

"I reckon seeing you like this is enough."

"But Abe! You'll dance with me?"

"Sure. . . . Bab, I ran plump into George with his lady. Doggone, but she's handsome! Made eyes at me! But I didn't speak. I'll bet George will raise hell with me."

"Neither did I, Abe," replied Barbara. "George has danced only with her so far."

"Gosh, the fool is loco. That Campbell outfit will break loose pronto."

Lucinda intervened, troubled by these disclosures, and she begged Abe to warn George to avoid a fight.

"All right, Maw, I'll try," said Abe dubiously. "But it won't be no use. George is riding high and he's due for a spill. . . . Come, Barbara, see if you can make me dance as well as you made me shoot."

Affairs of this kind lasted all night, to break up at daylight. As the hours wore on the dancers grew more and more obsessed with something that Lucinda thought for most of them was physical contact. They swayed to the music, but it was only a means to an end. The young men outnumbered the young women and as a result the latter had little rest during the evening. The best girl dancer, in the estimation of the majority of men, was the one who could dance all the men down. Mil Campbell had enjoyed such reputation before she had become infatuated with George Huett. She was a strongly built, wiry young woman in her twenties, with a bold flashing kind of beauty and allurement that went to the heads of young swains like wine.

For that matter, few indeed were the boys who did not drink as the dance wore on. A local liquor, called white mule, distilled by moonshiners down in the wild Tonto, was far from being conducive to the peaceful continuance of the dance. On rare occasions Logan had indulged in a drink or two of this fiery liquid that was so disarmingly named. Lucinda thought it had rather an amusing and relaxing effect upon her husband Grant became exuberant under its influence. Abe never touched it, nor any other kind of drink. Fortunately for George and his family, dances and other festive occasions were rare, for he was fond of the sorghum juice, and it always acted subtly and oppositely on his genial temperament.

These reflections had passed through Lucinda's mind, and had been forgotten, at least for the period of agreeable intercourse with some new women acquaintances. But not all the conversations Lucinda happened upon, or could not avoid hearing, were agreeable. There were cliques in that section of Arizona—homesteaders, squatters, pioneers, cattlemen, ranchers, Mormons, and others of whom it was not safe to speak.

Lucinda heard a swarthy woman say, "Thet stuck-up Huett outfit," which remark gave violent check to her friendly feelings of the moment. When later her ears burned at innuendoes that could not have concerned anyone else but George and the Campbell girl, Lucinda thought her hopes of enjoying one dance without distress were futile.

There were few intermissions between dances. The fiddler and his accompanist played through long intervals, only stopping to wet their throats, before beginning again. When, however, there was excitement outside, those who were dancing and watching would rush madly from the cabin.

This inevitable circumstance held off so long that Lucinda's fears began to wane. They were revived quickly, however, when she encountered Barbara at the wide front door, attempting to drag Grant inside. Barbara was pale and her eyes were purple blazes.

"Now!" ejaculated Lucinda, her heart sinking like lead.

"Mother—don't go out," panted Barbara. "There's a fight—about ——"

"What's happened?" interrupted Lucinda, aghast.

"Oh, if it hadn't been one thing—it'd have been another. But they had to drag me into it. . . . All George's fault! . . . Jack Campbell just asked me to dance. He wasn't drunk. And he was decent about it. Said I might stop a fight if I'd dance with him. But I was confused—angry, and I said no. . . . Oh, I should have danced with him whether Abe liked it or not!"

"You did right to refuse him. How can that start a fight?"

"I don't know. But it will. He said so."

"You stay with Grant. I'll go out and get Abe. We'll go home."

"Maw, we can't do that," objected Grant, sharply. "George is a jackass. But Abe won't leave him here alone to be half beaten to death by that Campbell outfit. And neither will I."

"Where's Dad?"

"He went off to town with Holbert."

Lucinda pushed through the crowded door, followed by Grant and Barbara. The excitement of the jostling couples could have been felt even if it had been suppressed. Brush had been thrown upon the fires, and flames with great sparks leaped high toward the black pines. In the open space before the cabin it was as light as day. A circle of men and women extended from one fire to the other. The dancers were craning their necks to see, climbing up on tables, and stumps in the background, trying to edge through the cordon.

Lucinda scorched her gown squeezing near the fire into the circle. In the full glare of the twin blazes George stood confronted by the dark long-haired uncouth-appearing Jack Campbell. Behind them Mil Campbell was struggling with her other two brothers to keep from being dragged into the crowd. On the instant she broke loose to run and take hold of Jack, who fiercely shoved her back. Lucinda had the same impulse, but Abe, who came from behind, laid powerful hold on her.

"Too late, Maw," he whispered, tensely. "Just as well they have it out."

What Lucinda hated most at that instant was not to see George standing there, pale, with gimlet eyes of fire, plainly at the end of his tether, but the tension of the onlookers, the suspended whispers of eager specula-tion and passion that ran through them, the raw some-thing in their gleaming faces. Dance, drink, and fight were the only emotional outlets these backwoods and cattle people enjoyed in their lonely elemental lives.

"I told you to leave Mil to her own outfit," rasped out Campbell.

"Sure. But you're a damn fool! she didn't want that," replied George, hotly.

"All Mil wants is to make trouble. An' all you want, Huett, is to play fast an' loose with her. Wal, I'm callin' you right heah an' now."

"Holler your head off. It won't stop me. But if you had any decency you wouldn't drag your sister's name in the dirt," rejoined George, scornfully. He was roused to wrath, probably inflamed by drink, but hard, calculating, holding himself in check. On the other hand, Jack Campbell appeared to be under the influence of the liquor as well as a malignant purpose which he would not see thwarted. His swaggering, bold, front attested to an issue long desired. He had at last hounded this son of the exclusive Huetts into the open.

"George Huett, I'm gonna mess up yore dude clothes an' mash yore pretty mug," declared Campbell, with robust satisfaction.

"Like hell you are! But if you pick a fight with me I'm telling everybody it's just hate. You've no cause."

"Didn't I accuse you of playin' fast an' loose with Mil?" demanded Campbell.

"That's a lie, Jack. And I can prove it."

"Bah, you cain't prove nothin' to me."

"Ask Mil. Only tonight I told her I'd marry her if she'd turn her back on your rotten outfit."

Campbell wheeled in amaze and fury. "Mil, is thet so?"

"Yes, it's so," cried the young woman, wildly, divided between shame and fright. Her flashing dark beauty gained from genuine distress and the play of the fire-

light upon her face. "Jack, this—this deal is outrageous.
. . . For my sake ——"

"Aha. You can declare yourself, Mil Campbell, right
heah an' now. Are you playin' fast an' loose with Huett?"

"No—I'm not," she panted.

"Wal, how aboot Rich Harvey? You're thick with him.
You was gonna marry him till this dude Huett ——"

"Shut your dirty mouth!" screamed his sister, in her
rage and evident guilt. "You're drunk."

"I'm sober enough to see through you, Mil Campbell.
You're dishin' my pard Rich for this Huett guy. Wal, I'm
givin' you away to him."

Mil hissed like a snake at her brother and turning to
flee, she almost ran across the fire in her madness to
escape.

"Huett, I'm tellin' you," went on Campbell, somberly.
"If Mil dishes Rich Harvey it won't change the fact thet
she ought to marry him."

"Campbell, I wouldn't believe a word you said," declared George.

"Huett, mebbe you'll believe this," launched Campbell, craning his black ragged head at George. "I jest
asked *yore* sister to dance with me. She said no! an' she
drew back her white duds as if she might dirty them if
they touched me."

"Campbell, I can believe that last. But you leave her
name out of this," retorted George, subtly transformed.

"She's no better than Mil," burst out Campbell, surrendering to the passion he knew would break Huett's
restraint. "Some folks down heah hints she's onnatural
fond of her brothers ——"

George leaped to swing a terrific blow upon Campbell's
mouth. Loosened teeth rattled on the leaves as he fell.
The men onlookers shouted lustily; some of the women
screamed. Lucinda pressed behind Abe, against Barbara,

who was clinging to Grant. But Lucinda's instinct was only to get out of the open. A burning within her burst all bounds.

Campbell bounded up and with lowered head plunged at George like a bull. He swung both fists wildly. Then came a furious exchange of blows, finishing with a sodden thump upon Campbell's nose that spattered blood and upset him. The backwoodsman plumped down ridiculously to the hoarse guffaws of the men. He snarled like a beast, and leaping up tried again to beat down Huett's defense. But he was outmatched. His opponent's longer reach and cooler method put him at a disadvantage. The break in his confidence was manifest to all and it transformed him into a savage.

"Look out, George!" yelled Abe, piercingly. *"Knife!"*

Lucinda saw the bright glitter of a blade in the fire-light. She staggered back upon Grant crying out: "For God's sake stop them!" A husky acclaim from men and screams from women gave way to a strained silence.

"Huett, I'll cut yore heart out," hissed Campbell, crouching with his right hand low.

"Jack, thet ain't fair play," yelled some man from the crowd.

Huett appeared cornered between his assailant and the nearer fire. Campbell had so maneuvered as to be facing both George and Abe.

"George, if he swings grab his arm," whispered Abe, in a silence so deep that all heard. Then Abe turned to call caustically: "Somebody pass me a gun—if you're not all Campbells!"

"Jim—Sandy," shouted Campbell, manifestly to his brothers. "Copper any more there. . . . This's my deal an' I shore got a hand!"

The white-faced George swayed a little to and fro in

his intense wariness. Then Campbell leaped, whirling the blade so swiftly that only its glitter could be seen. He evidently cut George's right arm, for it fell limp. Then his next move was a downward stab that wrenched a cry of agony from George. But with left hand he held Campbell's wrist momentarily.

On that instant Abe sprang in to deal Campbell a blow that resounded suddenly through the woods lifting Campbell clear from his feet and knocking him into the fire. Screeching horribly the man rolled out, his clothes blazing, his visage ghastly, his hands beating like broken wings. The knife was gone. The nearest onlookers broke out of their trance to drag Campbell away from the fire. Then the hoarse cries and lamentations were suddenly hushed as Abe Huett flung himself upon Jack Campbell's brothers.

A battle began that drew wild delight from the watching men and turned the women's faces white and tense. Lucinda had almost fainted when George was stabbed, but she revived to an appalling interest in Abe's onslaught upon the other two. The three combatants moved so swiftly that Lucinda could not tell who was who, until one of them went down. But Abe was not that one. The crowd stilled to the heavy blows, the tearing of garments, the deep curses and pants of the fighting men. Then the smaller of the Campbells stumbled, and fell flat on his back. Groggily he staggered half way to his knees when a powerful kick under his chin flattened him again. This coup left Abe engaged with the larger Campbell, who, unable to keep his feet before his agile and powerful opponent, resorted to the backwoods rough and tumble fight, which went obviously, from the first, against Campbell. His wrestling, his beating grew less fierce until it was plain he had been bested. But when he bawled

enough Abe dragged him up to his knees and struck **one**
final blow at the distorted visage. Campbell's head struck
the ground with a thud and he lay prone like his brother.

The dance sustained a longer intermission than usual.
There was a woman among the guests who professed
skill with wounds, and who bound up George's gashes.
The cut on his arm was nothing to be concerned about,
but the stab high on his breast had just escaped the lung.
It would be painful, but not necessarily serious. According to talk in the cabin Jack Campbell had been hauled
away to the village, terribly burned, and in a critical
condition.

After some of the men carried George to the Huett
wagon the old musician began fiddling more engagingly
than ever, and the dance went on as if nothing had
happened. When Lucinda expressed wonder at this one
of her women listeners replied: "Shucks, there's been
more'n one dancer carried oot of heah feet first!"

Lucinda had not heard from Abe since the fight but
Barbara, pale and distraught, told her that she had seen
him run to bend over George, and that he had arisen to
say: "Not bad knifed. Tie him up and send him home."

"But Abe. . . . wasn't he hurt?" queried Lucinda,
poignantly.

"Hurt? I couldn't tell," replied the girl, tragically.
"But he slipped away—from me. Oh, he was all rags,
mud, blood!"

Logan soon appeared on the scene. He had heard all
about the fight. Lucinda had always feared what his wrath
might be, yet here as always he was calm, practical, apparently unfeeling.

"Come, Luce, we'll go home," he said. "Barbara, **stay**
with Grant if you want. The dance has hardly begun."

"Thanks, but I'll go with mother," declared Barbara, constrainedly. "No more Tonto dances for me!"

"Abe's horse is gone," said Grant, when they reached the wagon. "I reckon I'll fork mine and amble along."

George came out of his dazed state to ask from his bed in the wagon, "Dad, where's Abe?"

"Gone home, I reckon, which is where we're going pronto."

"Was he bad hurt?"

"Not so you'd notice it, Grant said," drawled Huett. "Ben Holbert saw the fight. According to Ben that Campbell outfit made a mistake to jump you when Abe was around."

"Abe saved my life. Aw, Dad, I've been such a—a fool."

"Well, son, they say you had cause, with that handsome black-eyed cat throwing herself at you. Let it be a lesson. Keep quiet now. . . . Lucinda, are you ready to leave?"

"Yes, unless Barbara wants to change her dress."

"I'll ride as I am. Give me a blanket," said the girl, and she climbed into the wagon upon the hay beside George. Grant rode behind leading George's horse.

Lucinda thought she would never forget the bonfires, blazing up anew, the square log cabin with its gleaming lights, the pioneers standing around discussing the fight, the young couples coming out of the dark woods to join the dancers, the monotonous squeak of the fiddle and the strange intense rhythmic tread of feet. How weird were the tall black pines! They reminded Lucinda of those she had seen first in Arizona, a score and more of years ago.

Logan wrapped a blanket around her and clucked to the horses.

"Well, home by sun-up," he said, cheerfully. "Maw, I tell you I made a good deal tonight. Holbert put me on to it. Pretty decent of him. But he's in no shape to take up any deal. Besides he couldn't find the browse. That's where Sycamore Canyon has all these ranges beat. My oak thickets, my maple thickets with all their browsing leafage—they'll sure make my fortune yet!"

Chapter Twelve

THE first snow had fallen, making ample amends in its white drifts and blanched trees for the tardiness of its arrival.

Just when the wintry twilight began to steal down from the rims Grant came stamping into the cabin with brimming pails of milk.

"Dad and Abe not home yet?" he stopped whistling to ask.

"When did they ever come back early from a hunt? And the first this fall!" returned his mother.

"Doggone it! Let's not wait supper for them. What say, George?"

The eldest son sat near the wall close to the red fire which shone ruddily on his thin cheek. He was mending from his wounds.

"Not very long, anyhow," he said.

"Where are your ears—you?" interposed Barbara. "I can hear Dad's deep voice."

Lucinda had often heard this welcome sound with gladness and relief. How many, many times! She could tell that Logan had had good hunting. Heavy footfalls on the porch preceded the opening of the door. Logan entered to set his rifle against the wall and throw off his snow-covered coat. His broad visage wore a bright smile of satisfaction at sight of them all and the cheery fire and steaming pots. Abe followed, burly in his buckskins, soft of step and still-faced, with glad eyes for Barbara and his mother. They brought cold air and the piney breath of the forest with them.

"What luck, Dad?" asked Grant, eagerly.

"Four point buck and two turks for me," replied his father, with immense gratification in the telling. "Ask Abe what he got."

"I couldn't hit a flock of barns today," replied Abe
ruefully. "But, Dad, I really didn't have a good shot."

"Ha! Ha! You had the same as I—at the buck anyway."

"Take care, father," taunted Barbara. "You know it's
happened that you and Abe shot at the same buck at the
same time—and *you* thought you hit when really you
missed."

"By thunder, you're right, Babs. I forgot. . . . It sure
was fine up on top today. 'Pears I can't walk as I used to.
Abe had my tongue hanging out. . . . Luce, it's good to
get home. Something smells awful good. My mouth has
begun to water. What you got for supper?"

"Beef and potato stew, for one thing," replied Lucinda.
"If you and Abe wash up a bit supper will be ready."

"Maw, how about that apple pie you promised if I'd
drag Dad home before dark?" queried Abe, gayly.

"Barbara baked one for you."

"Bab, you're just an old darling!"

"Whose darling?" asked the girl, wistfully.

"Well, the Huetts' yet, thank heaven!"

Lucinda saw her husband and their sons and Barbara
sit down to a lavish supper. They were a happy family.
George's dereliction had been forgiven if not forgotten.
And as soon as he frankly confessed his shame and regret,
as Lucinda knew he would do, they would forget that
one unfortunate episode. The hunters ate like men of
the open after long abstinence. George and Grant did
not show failing appetites.

"Abe, are you going to give me a piece of that pie?"
asked the latter.

"Couldn't think of it."

"Well you doggone stingy hawg!" asserted Grant, half
in jest and half in earnest.

"Why Grant! of course he'll give you a piece," expostulated Barbara. "Here, I'll cut it."

"Make it a small piece, Lady," said Abe, grudgingly.

Supper over Abe washed the dishes and utensils, while Lucinda and Barbara wiped them.

"Grant, fetch in a couple of chunks of oak and some pine cones," spoke up Logan, as he reached for his pipe and pouch. He filled it, lighted it with a red coal, and sat down in his big homemade arm chair with a sigh. "Doggone!—Snow at last and winter set in. Holed up till spring! Never before felt so good about that. Reckon the deal with Widow Steadman to feed her herd on half shares has a lot to do with it."

"Dad, you'll have to brand her calves," said George.

"Only half of them, son."

Abe sat down Indian fashion on the hearth and stretched his wet moccasins to the fire. They began to steam. Barbara, from the bench by the table in the background, watched him with eyes unconscious of their worship. George got down the little box with his tame baby chipmunks, scarcely larger than his thumbs, and like a boy in great glee let them run over his lap.

"I reckon that was a good business deal, Dad," went on George. "It insures you of two dozen and more calves next spring. Costs nothing. Double the calf count the following year. Sure does mount up when you get going. . . . What can stop us now?"

"Once I swore nothing could. But the years have made me leery. . . . I reckon only rustlers could."

"Rustlers!—Say, Dad, you're not long-headed. It'd take a mighty big and bold band of cattle thieves to cost us much here."

"I hear you, son. Powerful sweet talk. But how do you figure?"

"No rustlers would have the nerve to drive up the

road here, right under our very noses. They'd have to make a hole in one of the fenced gaps. No fun driving steers out that way. It just almost couldn't be done. But if they did—well, Abe could track them. That'd be a bad deal for them, Dad."

"I reckon," returned Logan, soberly. "Mebbe bad for us, too."

"Can't see it that way. We'd track them to a camp or a cabin, make sure they had our cattle—then shoot before we talked. . . . Dad, I've heard some dark hints about the Campbells. You know where there's smoke in these woods there's bound to be fire. . . . I'd told you before—only I—well, I was loco about Mil Campbell. I'd have been fool enough to go the whole way with her, if Jack hadn't squealed on her."

"Son, you got out of that lucky. The Campbells are on the wrong trail. We'll hear from them some day."

Abe looked up to speak: "Did I tell you I met a cowboy on the road last Wednesday—no, it was day before yesterday, Tuesday? He's one of Collier's riders. Told me Jack was burned bad, but lost nothing 'cept hair and hide. He was up and around."

"I'm glad to hear that," said George, with a ring in his voice. "When I meet Jack next I want him to have both eyes."

"George, you'll have to look pretty hard to see him before I do," rejoined Abe.

"Sons, we'll never look for trouble," interposed Huett. "But that outfit had better steer clear of us. Come to think of it, though, we've worse outfits to watch."

Lucinda sat across the hearth from Logan in the other armchair, her neglected knitting in her lap, her gaze on the glowing red coals of the fire. For once such conversation from her militant husband and sons failed to rouse her. The rising wind outside in the pines, the soft seep-ing of snow against the cabin, the crackle and sparkle of embers—these seemed to take more hold upon her imagination than the hard words she heard. These familiar sounds took her back through the long years to the time of which she was thinking.

"Barbara, come here. Sit by me," she said, sweetly.

The girl rose obediently from the shadow to recline on the bearskin rug at Lucinda's feet.

"Aw, now—Luce," protested Logan, in a strangled voice.

"I have something to tell Barbara and the boys," rejoined Lucinda, stroking the glossy flaxen head resting on her knee.

"But what's your hurry?" expostulated Logan.

"It should have been told long ago," answered Lucinda, sadly.

Logan sank back sighing, and puffed moodily at a pipe which had gone out.

"Barbara, what I have to confess will amaze and grieve you," began Lucinda, with grave tenderness. "But it is best for your happiness, for the future that I see can be yours. And surely best for all of us Huetts. It has taken me years—years to come to this decision—to break one aspect of our happy home life here for a possible fuller and better one."

"Why, mother!" exclaimed the girl in astonishment. She rose to her knees before Lucinda.

"That is just—the—the secret," Lucinda faltered. "Barbara, I am not your mother. You are not a sister to Abe and George and Grant. You are no relation to us at all."

For a moment Barbara was stunned.

"Ah! . . . how dreadful! Oh, mercy—what am I—*who* am I?" cried Barbara, in anguish.

"The first is easy to answer," replied Lucinda, gaining

strength to go on. "You are the sweetest and best girl I ever knew. You are as good as you are beautiful. But *who* you are is a mystery. You came of gentlefolk, surely. But what they were and where they came from we never found out."

"Oh—dear God! Then I'm—a waif—a nameless ——"

"Listen, Barbara. It is a tragedy, yes, but nothing to be heartbroken about."

"Then why did y-you ever—tell me?" sobbed the girl.

"Because it is the only way we can ever keep you with us always."

"I don't understand."

"Let me talk, dear. . . . My eyes were opened at the dance last month. You were the belle of that dance. Many of these Arizonians are in love with you. And despite the fact that you don't care for any particular one of them— and that you've been happy with my sons—you will be forced to marry some day. Some one will pack you off and make you his wife whether you like it or not. That is western."

"But I wouldn't—I wouldn't!" burst out Barbara, incredulously.

"Well, darling, I don't know exactly how it would happen. But a pretty and healthy girl can't stay unmarried out here. She just can't."

"Then—how *are* you going to keep me—with you?" queried Barbara, in wistful misery.

"Let that rest for a moment. I want to tell you how you came to us."

"Oh do—*do*—even though it'll hurt so terribly."

"Barbara, it's almost unbelievable. But it was seventeen years ago. You are a young woman of twenty, yet the years have gone so swiftly, so brightly, so happily that to us you are still a child. . . . George was four years old. Abe was three, and Grant two. At that immature age, Barbara, these youngsters were as bad as little boys can be. Abe was the naughtiest. I've always been glad since that he was, because if he hadn't been disobedient, a little savage who liked to run off and hunt in the woods —we might never have known and loved you. For it was Abe who found you, Barbara, a little lost babe in the woods. . . . Let me tell you. Seventeen years ago last October—the fourteenth—I shall never forget it—the boys ran away from the cabin. I was busy and upset. I forgot about the boys until I went outside for something and they were gone. I called. No answer. I left off work and ran to find them. At the corrals I came upon their tracks. Abe's barefoot prints led up the road, where I had expressly forbidden the boys to go. George and Grant followed him. It was nearing sunset. I ran, calling and panting—up the road, through the gate, on through the woods. By this time I was distracted. When I came upon them playing by some logs that have rotted away long ago, instead of three children there were four. The little stranger was a girl—flaxen-haired, with eyes of violet. She was shy and sweet. When I asked her who she was she said: 'Bar'bra' . . . And to this day we have never known more. Her dress was of fine material. She wore pretty little shoes, but no stockings. I have saved those things all these years, and I shall give them to you. . . . Abe had found you crying along the road. Wagons had passed there that day and in some strange way you had become lost from one of them. I looked for a camp and listened for voices. But darkness was close, and as there appeared to be no camp near, I brought you back here with the boys. Logan said there must be a camp out on the road. He went to look, but in vain. Next day he trailed the wagons down to Payson, making sure you had become lost from one of them, and that you would be hunted. But here is the most astounding and inexplicable part of the story. These wagons did not stop at Payson. They went through at night. No one ever heard of a little girl being lost. No one ever came back to hunt for you! . . . That's all, Barbara. And it's all we'll ever know. Logan and I adopted you as our own. The boys from that day to this have loved you more than any sister anyone could have had."

When Lucinda ceased the girl's flaxen head drooped and she wept unrestrainedly. Logan laid aside his pipe with a cough, and gazed at Barbara with wet eyes. Abe sat transfixed and rapt. Grant's tanned face was one ruddy beam in the firelight. George looked a stricken man. Lucinda saw amaze, incredulity, sudden joy, and then a shame of realization flash across his pale mobile face. He realized that in losing a sister he had not gained a sweetheart.

Barbara raised her head. "I'll always call you Mother. . . . You've been so—so good to me. . . . Oh, I must have been a—a child nobody wanted."

Logan spoke up huskily: "My dear, don't think that again. It's only torture. Maybe such a thought is all wrong. My idea from the first night was that your parents were dead. . . . But *we* wanted you. I remember that night, when you lay in the corner there, asleep, your curly head close to Abe's, how I had a feeling you had come to us—to bless us with the daughter we wanted. I told Lucinda so. . . . *We* wanted you, Barbara. And we've always wanted you. . . . What you've missed we can never tell. Perhaps riches, fine parents—all that go with them. But never love, Barbara. You have not missed that."

"Oh, Dad, I'd gladly have missed all them to have what you've given me. It's not that—that. . . . I'm shocked. . . . Never to know who I am!"

"But you are Barbara Huett," added Logan, with loving finality.

Then Grant came out of his spell. "Babs, *I* think it's just great. . . . Suppose you'd been found by that Jack Campbell, or some hombre like him! Think how much worse off you'd been. You sure had luck to fall in with Maw. Where'd you or any kid have found as grand a mother? . . . It was swell to have you for a sister, Barbara. But this—this is just wonderful. . . . *For now you can marry us!*"

That naïve remark broke the tragic strain, at least, and brought a faint blush to Barbara's cheek.

"My son, wonderful as that might be, it's impossible for Barbara to marry you all," interposed Lucinda, with a smile that rivaled Logan's. What a burden seemed lifted from her conscience! After all, now that the secret was out, it was not so terrible, so devastating. The absolute certainty of her place in that family had sustained Barbara. In time the grief would pass and perhaps even the memory of it.

"That'd be Mormonism on the woman's side," declared Grant, gayly. "I'd stand for that, Babs. Sure you can take your pick. But I'm beating Abe and George to it."

"Grant, you're a very wonderful boy, not yet grown up—and I'll always be a sister to you," replied Barbara, in a demure voice not quite compatible with her wet eyes.

"Ow—ow!" wailed Grant. "All right, Babs. You're a poor picker. But I'll always love you just the same."

"Barbara, we will never let you get away from us," spoke up George, gallantly, but his pale tense face betrayed emotion he tried to hide. A fugitive hope was fading before realization. "If I'd only known you were *not* my sister—then all that fool gallivanting of mine would never have been. But I always ——"

"Let her be, you sudden hombres," interrupted Abe, his voice strong and vibrant. "Here she's just learned a sad fact about her life—and you hound her to bestow herself upon one of you. Let her be. . . . Some day, sure, she'll take the one of us she loves best. But give her a long time. She's been a sister too many years to become a sweetheart pronto. . . . Barbara, it'll all come right. Don't let Grant or George rile you. We've all got a long hard job to raise that thirty thousand head of cattle Dad's heart is set on. I know *I* can work harder, and become a better man, in the hope I may win you some time. . . . I found you that day so far back. But I remember, Barbara, honest I remember your skinned knees, your dusty dress, your tear-wet cheeks, and sorrowful eyes. And I was only three. . . . Dear, don't feel unhappy. This must have been meant to be. Maybe you came to save the Huetts."

Lucinda's heart welled painfully in her breast. How she thrilled as the silent Abe, for once so eloquent, expressed his manliness, his fairness, his deep loyalty to Barbara and to all of them! He made it so easy for Lucinda to bless her intuition. Always she had known that Abe was the one for Barbara; always that had been her most secret cherished dream. And she read in Barbara's fascinated eyes, in the quickening and dilating changes in a marvelously soft and lovely glow, that the girl realized now how and why she had worshipped Abe all her life.

The only difference in Barbara that was manifest to Lucinda seemed to be a brooding pathos at times and a conscious realization that her status with the boys had vastly changed and heightened. The former gradually wore away and a deeper less girlish happiness prevailed.

Abe changed the least under this new order of life at Sycamore Canyon. It was evident that Barbara's possible attainment simply added bewilderingly to his affection. He showed no sign of having an advantage over his brothers with Barbara because he had found her and no doubt had saved her from wild animals or starvation. Lucinda particularly noted that if Abe was more kind, he was less demonstrative. He never teased nor playfully fought with her as had been his wont. He had realized her sex, her desirability and they were sacred. This seemed the more complete to Lucinda because Barbara was the only girl Abe had ever really known. What little leisure he had enjoyed he spent in the woods.

But this new relation of Barbara's changed the lives of the other brothers.

All at once, it seemed to Lucinda, Grant developed into a man. He had, fortunately, no serious faults nor weaknesses nor vices to correct. He lost nothing of his sunny temperament, his love of banter, his propensity to tease, his habit of sharing whatever he had with Barbara. But he openly and persistently courted her.

George exhibited more serious and profound evidence of a dividing line in his life. That winter he was confined to the cabin a good deal owing to danger of pneumonia that the wound in his breast occasioned. He read and studied, and discussed the cattle problem for hours with Huett. When spring came again and he regained his old strength he plunged into work as never before. He did not ride to Pine or Payson. He gave up drinking. A dance at Holbert's failed to tempt him, though Barbara went with Grant. Even a rodeo at Flagg on the Fourth of July failed to drag him back to the competitions and thrills of cowboy life.

Once George said to his mother: "I reckon I've no chance to win Bab now. Not with this handsome Indian Abe around and that lovable guy Grant! But I love her and I'll never stop trying to prove she's made a man of me. . . . And it won't make any difference if she picks Abe or Grant."

Early in the fall George prevailed upon his father to round up another bunch of cattle and drive them to the railroad.

"But, Dad, it's the thing to do now," he persuaded patiently. "If we cut out and sell the old stock, buy young stock with the money, or part of it, our herd will grow faster. You hang on too long. Besides we need repairs, new tools, supplies. And, Dad, we must get a car. Some of these other ranchers are getting the jump on us. A few of them have cars and some of them have trucks. Times are changing. We've gone to seed down here in our lonely canyon. We're old-fashioned. If we had a truck this fall we could haul five hundred sacks of potatoes to Flagg in a couple of trips."

The idea did not appeal to Huett. He hated the stinking, dangerous horseless vehicles that had begun to make unbelievable changes in the country. George argued that their use made the territory provide better roads and that the time saved more than the expense. Huett agreed to a limited sale of cattle, but vetoed the car idea.

"All right. I'll buy one with my own money," declared George stubbornly. "And I'll bet you see."

Wherefore George did not return home from Flagg with his father and Grant. When he did come back, however, his advent was proclaimed by rattling cracking noises long before he got down the hill. Lucinda heard Logan guffaw loudly, and Grant yell a wild, "Whoopee!" Then Barbara screamed in glee, which brought Lucinda out with an exclamation: "For the land's sake!"

She stared, first in wonder then in fright. George was driving down the hill in a black automobile that sounded rickety if it did not look so.

The Huetts were nothing if not spellbound. But

George made the grade without running off the road, and came whirling across the flat, to come to a halt before the cabin with a bang.

"Howdy, folks," he drawled, as he surveyed them all, with fire in his eyes and a smile on his lips.

"George Huett!—Where'd you get that contraption?" demanded his father.

"Bought it. Second hand. Never mind how much. . . . And have I had a hell of a time getting here? Well, I guess!"

"When'd you leave Flagg?"

"Before noon."

"Not today?"

"Sure today. Say, this car of mine isn't Buck—though by gosh! it bucked on me some. . . . Hop in, Dad. Let me give you a little spin."

"Not much," declared Huett.

"Take me, George," begged Barbara, her face eager and daring.

"Well, I guess. Pile in here."

George drove her around the bench and down across the brook, sending up great sheets of muddy water, out on the flat, and back again, in a cloud of dust. Barbara leaped out radiant and breathless.

"Oh—grand!" she cried. "You go so fast. . . . But I was—scared."

"Doggone these young people nowadays," complained Huett to Lucinda. "Our old way—too slow, too slow! . . . Reckon I'll come to it if these cars ever get safe."

George did not succeed in convincing his father that automobiles were to be trusted, but before winter came he proved they were marvelous to cover distance, to save time, to add wonderfully to the comfort and efficiency of a housewife, to bring mail and supplies quickly to the ranches. "You see, Dad," explained George. "You've been a pioneer for twenty-five years. From now on you're a rancher."

The driving of this new stock, the repairing of fences, the toil early and late in the fields, and the other manifold tasks of the growing ranch made days and seasons fly by on wings. The boys stacked a hundred tons of alfalfa and sold as many bushels of potatoes before the frosts hurried them to the game trails with their guns. Lucinda and Barbara were rushed with their labors—putting up endless jars of pears and peaches, of pickles and tomatoes, of apple-butter and mince-meat. Logan stored away in the cellar a load of the finest cabbages he had ever seen.

"Ha, Luce!" he exclaimed, heartily. "Remember when I used to say we'll not starve, anyhow? . . . Things are pretty good. . . . Well, well, it's been long coming."

While the seasons sped by Huett's herd of cattle had doubled, trebled, quadrupled. How amazingly they multiplied now! The calves came as if by magic. Widow Steadman died without any kin to whom to leave her cattle and her several thousand head gravitated to Huett.

George hit upon a plan to cut a track beyond Three Springs Wash to the canyon below and enclose that. It resembled Sycamore somewhat, but was larger and revealed more gaps to fence. George demonstrated, against his father's remonstrances, how two canyons rich in acorns and oak browse would raise a larger herd of stock more quickly than one; and Huett finally succumbed to facts and figures.

"But rustlers can steal from us down there very much easier than they have been able to in Sycamore," replied Huett, still the over-cautious and long-suffering cattle-man.

"We'll risk that. Besides we'll let what's left of **our**

wild horses drift down there. Those broom-tails eat a lot, Dad."

Lucinda divined anew how Logan had so inspired them all with his great idea, his driving passion, that long habit of work, of sacrifice had left them unable to slow down, to begin to see the prosperity that had really come. But what were ten thousand head of stock to Huett? He limited the sale to less than a thousand a year. He kept out of debt and bought more cattle.

But Lucinda did not fail to see their happiness. They were as busy as honey-storing bees. They were sufficient unto themselves. Several times a year Lucinda and Barbara went to town, finding more pleasure in these trips for their infrequency.

Seldom did Lucinda broach the subject of marriage to Barbara, and she finally stopped altogether after Barbara said:

"Oh, Mother, I am afraid Abe will ask me some day, and if he does I—I can't beg him to wait longer—I love him so. . . . But George loves me too—and Grant. I think Abe hates to hurt them. . . . We're all so happy. Why can't we go on this way longer?"

Chapter Thirteen

LOGAN HUETT lived to learn that he did not yet know the West.

Like wildfire in a wide-swept prairie the dramatic killing of Tim Mooney traveled over the range. Before the shock of his neighbors and fellow-ranchers had passed, the Mooney family left the locality and Dwight Collier sold out to Holbert to ride away. He was not backward in telling that of late he had suspected Mooney of deals in which he had no part. The range did not believe this, but they were quick to accept the rumor that Mooney's son drew a large amount from the bank at Flagg.

Then little by little, as cowboys compared notes, and cattlemen found time and freedom to talk, the guilt of Tim Mooney stood out indisputably. None of them patted Logan Huett on the back for his service in ridding the range of this crooked cattleman, but they exonerated him from any suspicion whatever. They called the fight an even break in which the better and the honest man came out on top. The good it did manifestly served to scare off any other lone and butchering rustler who might have followed in Mooney's footsteps. However, the harm it created was the tendency to focus attention of the predatory cattle interests—the rustlers and their queer ramifications—upon the fact that there were rich pickings in the Mogollons and from the Little Colorado to the Tonto Rim.

Huett's sons did not suffer any blight of spirit because their father had joined the ranks of Arizona killers. George and Grant grew a little harder, and Abe a little more silent. But Lucinda and Barbara did not leave the canyon, even to visit their nearest neighbor for over a year. When they did return to Flagg, they found that the incident had been swallowed up in the past, during which plenty of dark and considerably sterner deeds had transpired. No bar sinister or ban of ignominy had extended to their names during this period of seclusion. Their friends, the real born pioneers, amazed them with a warmer welcome and absolute reticence; as a result Lucinda and Barbara were not long in recovering from the shock.

Logan alone knew what havoc Mooney's killing had wrought in him. The great fear that he had given his sons a name they would never live down, that the success of his enterprise had been disrupted if not set back for many years, and that the genuine horror and remorse he had endured—all these futile apprehensions had been a senseless waste of mental strength, of nights of sleep and days of labor. He lived to discover this fact too late. Of the numberless vicissitudes of life by which he had been burdened, the killing of Mooney cost him the most anguish and left the hardest mark. To survive and to grow in that country required more than a great ambition, with commensurate strength, endurance, honesty, and indomitable pluck: a cattleman needed all these qualities and more to gain foothold and means; even when he had finally raised herds of cattle and many horses, it took vastly more courage to keep them. A prosperous cattle country had always developed or drawn the rustler, and as long as cattle were raised it would continue to do so. Wide unfenced ranges, the wilderness of forest and canyon would never see the day that cattle were not easy to steal and men of that ilk present who would not profit by it.

The ensuing period multiplied Huett's cattle and the labors incident to their care. He was keen enough to see that the habits ingrained by the long years of toil and poverty could not change on short notice, if they ever could at all. He was glad of this. He had brought his family up modestly, to know the value of money, to be happy working toward a definite end, to be little influenced by the outside world. Cars and magazines found their way down into Sycamore Canyon, to open the eyes of the wilderness-loving Huetts, to force upon them the progress of the modern world, but they did not change Huett's idea of cattle-raising, nor the eighteen-hour-day of the cowboy Huetts, nor the economy and industry of the women. The future had come almost to mean nothing: the present was full, all-satisfying.

The time came when the spider-shaped Sycamore Canyon, with its ten miles in length and its vast acreage in grass and browse, supported fifteen thousand head. It was a wall-fenced range, protected from storms and cold and heat and drought, and impractical for the operations of rustlers. Only wandering riders butchered a beef occasionally as they passed through. But Turkey Canyon, with twice the acreage, with its numberless rich grassy offshoots, became the bane of Huett's life. Sycamore should have been enough to look after for one man and his three sons, but they had undertaken the task and they would not falter. Despite the continuous stealing of stock by rustlers, horse-thieves, riders with no known homes or occupations, the Turkey Canyon herd increased. A few straggling steers driven off in the woods, a bunch of young stock cut out and stolen at night through one of the outlets impossible to close, or a daylight raid by a band of determined rustlers who operated when the Huetts were miles away—these kept the Turkey herd from climbing by leaps and bounds to equal that of Sycamore. And it wore on Huett year by year, until he grew implacable toward the thieves who kept him from his cherished goal.

"Dad, you're cussed short-sighted and bull-headed."

averred George repeatedly. "Let's sell the Turkey herd."

"Not yet," declared Huett doggedly, for the hundredth time.

"Well, then, let's pay no more attention to these two-bit thieves, let's lay for the real rustlers, who raid Turkey once or so a year. They're about due now. Last time they got three hundred head. . . . They grab a bigger bunch every time."

"Sense in that," agreed Huett, gruffly. "What's your plan?"

"Abe says we'll camp down there, hide out and watch."

"And leave Lucinda and Barbara alone? Nope to that."

"One of us will go home every night."

"I reckon that'll do. But what of the other work?"

"It'll have to go till we drive this outfit away for good, or kill them!"

"Ha! We've got to catch them first."

"Abe swears they keep a lookout on one of the high points or along the rim. They watch us. Then when we're gone they pull the raid."

"What's the use to camp near Turkey then? A better plan will be for you boys to pretend to drive to town, but come back after dark, and next day before sun-up we'll sneak down to Turkey."

Even this plan failed to trap the keen rustlers, as did also the hiding-out down in Turkey Canyon. No sooner had the Huetts returned to the necessary harvesting when the rustlers made off with the largest steal Huett had ever sustained. Abe reported the loss, which he estimated two days later from a broad cattle track heading down toward the Tonto.

"Sell that Turkey herd or see it fade before your very eyes," warned George Huett to the raging rancher.

"Dad, I've a hunch that outfit will come back," said

Abe, ponderingly. "They must have a safe sale for stock."

"Safe! If we trailed them and recognized every stolen steer, what could we do?" retorted George. "We have no brand. We're an easy mark for those buzzards."

"Boys, time was when our losses were less than what it'd have cost to hire a dozen riders. But that day has passed. My method never stood the test of years—I'm bound to admit that. All the same I won't change."

"It'd be wiser to weaken. Sell out or hire cowboys," advised George.

"Weaken? Hell no! . . . Grant, do you side with George?"

"I sure do, Dad. I hate to go against you. None of us ever did before. But this is getting too tough to stand. Maybe it never occurred to you to think how we boys need money. You never give us any money. And we've sure earned wages, if no more. . . . Well, you could sell that Turkey bunch for twenty dollars a head. Nigh on to ten thousand head. Almost two hundred thousand dollars! . . . We'd all be rich and you'd still have the Sycamore herd."

The amazing stand from the youngest son, heretofore the least asserting one of the Huetts, hurt Logan deeply and precipitated one of the few quarrels he had ever had with them. The argument did not end there. George and Grant took it to their mother and Barbara. When to Logan's consternation his women-folk promptly and vigorously took issue against him, for the first time in any serious stand, he discovered grievous doubts of himself, of his unchangeable passion and will. He argued, stormed, raged, all to no avail. He was wrong. Then as a last straw, Barbara appealed to the silent Abe and won him over. The Huetts' house was divided against itself.

The truth overcame his rage with himself and vexation with them. He sat down in his big chair and leaned his head on his hands. Lucinda came to touch his shoulder with sympathy.

"Folks," he said, laboriously, "allowing you're right, you don't see it from my side of the fence. I've spent my life—the best of it—fighting odds in this canyon. . . . Lack of money and help first—then the meat-eaters, and cold, wet, heat, drought, ignorance of farming—I had to learn—and a thousand other troubles, the last and worst of which is the cattle thief. For nearly thirty years I've fought these odds—and now I'm rich in stock—with my life's ambition in sight. . . . You ask me—and I acknowledge its justice—to quit now, to weaken in the face of a few lousy rustlers. I won't do it! Dammit I'd lose every head of stock in Turkey Canyon rather than show yellow. . . . But this is what I will do. As soon as I can count thirty thousand head, I'll sell, divide the money equally among you, and go back to civilization to live. . . . That's all. I'm boss here. And what I say goes."

Huett did not sell a single head that year, and thus avoided leaving the Turkey Canyon herd unprotected. He sent Grant, with Lucinda and Barbara, to town for supplies. They took their time about this trip. Upon their return Huett marveled anew at what a little visit outside would do for women. He did not need civilization, and in fact was better in mind without contacts with men. The times had changed but he did not change. Lucinda looked rested and averred that it had been good to go, but better to come home. Barbara returned rosy and fresh, handsomer than ever, raving about airplanes and motion-pictures. Logan had never seen either and was amazed. He asked Grant one question: "What's the price of cattle?"

"By golly, Dad. I-I forgot. I sure forgot to ask," replied Grant, mortified at his laxness.

"For the land's sake! What did you do all the while?"

"I bought all on your list," replied Grant, stoutly.

"Well, I'll see. The wagon looks loaded all right."

Abe looked with affectionate regard from Barbara's radiant face to Grant's. "Wal, Dad," he drawled, "reckon I'd better go next time—or lose my girl."

Barbara joined in the laugh, but she blushed becomingly. Huett made the mental reservation that she should be marrying one of his sons soon; and he could not see, as Lucinda averred, that Abe had the inside track. Pity there were not three Barbaras!

October was in its last golden decline. With November came the first snows and the movement of cattle ceased. Huett and Abe took to the woods and the game trails. Of late years game had gradually grown harder to find. There were plenty of deer and turkey far back in the forest, when once Sycamore Canyon and its adjacent ridges had been overrun with them. Hunters from the railroad towns had grown in number from year to year. Huett and Abe encountered some of these that season, roaming around, shooting at every rustle in the brush.

"Son," he said to Abe, as they rested on a log, "I reckon I'm unreasonable. But I don't like the new order of things. All these tenderfoot hunters banging around. Elk protected by law. Open season for deer and turkey one month. Forest under government supervision."

"Dad, you think only of your one object in life," replied Abe. "The President of the United States was thinking of our children's children when he made this a forest reserve. It's a good thing. We don't obey the laws any more than the Stillmans or the other backwoods people. We kill meat when we want it. But these laws were not made for natives who live in the woods."

"Humph! Why didn't he make laws against rustlers?"

"There are plenty of laws to govern cattle thieves, but who can enforce them way out here in this canyon country? It's up to us, Dad."

"Reckon I've owned these woods too long," said Logan, as he gazed lovingly down the timbered swale, where the noonday sun shone on patches of snow colored with russet oak leaves and scarlet maple. The great silver spruces vied with the yellow pines for supremacy over the forest glade. The aspens, almost wholly denuded of their golden fluttering leaves, stood out white-trunked against the dark green background. Windfalls massed on the ridge, and there was down timber everywhere. The air was cold, though the sun felt warm upon Logan's bare head; the old forest tang of pine was thick in his nostrils. The truth came to Logan that he hated to share this wilderness with anyone but his own.

"I reckon it'll last during my day," replied Abe, thoughtfully.

"Abe, you know we're going to live in town eventually. I wonder now."

"That'll be fine for the women, and for Barbara, when she has youngsters. But I'll spend half my time in these woods. When you sell our stock, Dad, keep Sycamore for me."

"For you and me, son."

They picked up their turkeys and venison, and went on down the ridge toward home. Huett had a strange thought that troubled him. More than twenty-five years ago he had taken Abe on his first hunt up that ridge. They had never missed a year since; but there would come a hunt together, perhaps this present one, that must be the last. Huett threw off the vague, sad presage.

The Turkey Canyon herd had gotten beyond handling by so few riders. It had multiplied exceedingly. Every spring rustlers tore down the fences to let the cattle stray into ravines and work out on top. That fall it would have taken an army of cowboys to prevent the theft of straggling steers and yearlings, but such loss was so insignificant that Huett could only guess at it; his sons never told him.

One night Abe did not come home from his scouting. It was not unusual for him to stay away over night during the hunting season, but this was early October. Logan was concerned, not for Abe's safety, because he knew that Abe had no equal in the Arizona woods, but for fear of the long expected cattle raid.

"Where'd you see Abe last?" asked Huett.

"He waved to me from the rim above Turkey Wash. The south point," replied Grant. "He made signs. The most I could make of them was that he'd gotten track of something down Turkey. His last signal I took to mean he'd come home."

"But suppose he doesn't return?" queried Logan.

George and Grant pondered for a while and at length were in accord about the wisdom of waiting until the next day and if Abe did not return then, of taking up his trail from the point where Grant had last seen him. Lucinda and Barbara grew worried and would not go to bed. Finally late in the evening Huett went outside with his sons and listened: The autumn night was solemnly quiet; then George, keen-eared, voiced a warning whisper. The group froze stone-like. Presently soft padded footsteps caught Huett's ear—he knew that quick tread. In another moment Abe loomed up at the porch.

"Howdy. Stayed awake late for me, huh? Just as well, for I shore would have rustled you out."

"Yes, we're up, son, and what else is up?" rejoined Huett, again his relieved and confident self.

"I reckon you'll think hell is up," said Abe frankly. "Cattle raid!"

"Nope, not yet. But we're in for a humdinger."

"Forewarned is forearmed, you know. Come out with it," replied Huett, gruffly.

"Dad, Jim Stillman and his brother, with Tobe Campbell, and two more men I didn't know, are going to raid us."

"Five of them, eh? Well, not if we see them first!" Logan replied grimly.

"All my hiding out for them wasted time!" ejaculated Abe, in disgust. "They didn't come down through the woods. They came up the road from Pine, and made no bones about piling right down into Turkey. I sneaked up as close as I could get. They camped in an open spot and weren't afraid of a bright fire but at that I heard a little and guessed a lot. . . . Would it surprise you to learn Tobe Campbell was Hillbrand's right hand man?"

"Wal, son, nothing can surprise me about that coyote," Logan drawled.

"It's so, and Campbell had taken hold of that Stillman outfit. Tobe is the meanest and the slickest of that Campbell bunch. . . . Tobe had to give it away that he was Hillbrand's man. I heard him. Jim didn't have the guts to hold out against this, and they got together right then and there. I heard your name, Dad, and mine, and something about Sycamore. Tobe drew a map on the ground. I jumped at conclusions and made up my mind about their deal hours before I found out. They sat there talking till long after midnight—didn't drink anything but coffee. Anybody could have told there was a big deal on. . . . Sure, Jim Stillman shook like a leaf. . . . They were all excited except Tobe. He was cool and bright, like a coiled greasy rattler."

"Ahuh. And what's his big deal?" queried Logan, sharply.

"Campbell aims to drive Sycamore."

"Sycamore!" exploded Huett. George smacked a hard fist in his palm, and Grant, who seldom used expletives, swore lustily. Then Logan found his tongue. "Abe, if *you're* not loco, that Campbell hombre is. Drive Sycamore? I never thought of such a thing. It couldn't be done."

"Yes, it could. Bold deal, you bet—but practical to a rustler like Hillbrand. Slow drive up Sycamore before dawn. Some rider will go up and open our gate. They'd have two thousand head climbing out before we got you. . . . You know, it's quite far to where our road starts up the slope. They figured we might not hear a slow drive. When we did come out—as Tobe is figuring—they'd smoke us up from the slope, and once on top with all the cattle they could drive, they'd be jake. They'd have all the advantage. A couple of men could hold us back and kill us if we tried to get out up the road. The others would drive the cattle hell bent on, once down in the Tonto. . . . And Paw, we could never prove those un-branded cattle belonged to us."

"My God! Just like that," ejaculated Huett, with a snap of his fingers.

"It might have been just like that, Dad," retorted Abe, cool and hard. "But I got on to them. Tobe Campbell will never turn that trick. And some of them won't get out of Sycamore."

"George, how'll we meet this deal?" queried Huett.

"Dad, this Tobe Campbell always was a crafty hombre. If he put a couple of his outfit close to the cabin here they could kill us or drive us back while the rest stole the cattle."

"I thought of that," spoke up Abe, quietly. "We won't be in there when it gets light enough to see. But Maw and Barbara will. And when the fight begins they can shoot out the window as fast as they can pull the trigger."

Huett nodded his shaggy head in approval of that. Plenty of rifle shots would help. "And do you reckon we ought to hide out—let them make the drive up here? . . . I don't like that plan."

"Neither do I—so damned much. But what're we gonna do better?" rejoined Abe, dubiously.

"It won't do to waste time. After all, my objection to your plan must be the idea of my stock being driven up here. Campbell's outfit will be behind them, and might make a drive up the road in spite of us."

"Dad, they'll walk the cattle, two riders behind, two on each side of the herd, and one—who you can gamble will be Tobe Campbell—out in front. He'll open the gate."

"Foxy Tobe!" ejaculated George, scornfully. "If we should happen to wake up *he'd* be out of gun-shot."

"Abe, figure the deal quick," said Huett, realizing the imperative need of prompt decision.

"All right," replied Abe, in quick eagerness, showing that he was ready. "Dad, you stay here in the cabin with Mother and Bab. Keep your eyes peeled. Have your rifles and six-guns loaded, with plenty of shells on hand. When the ball opens, shoot, whether you're in range or not. . . . George, you and Grant hide in the cow-shed. Don't let the cattle be started up the road. Don't wait for me to shoot. I'll go up, chain that gate so it can't be opened pronto. Then I'll work down on the rocky point that sticks farthest out in the canyon. I can cover every place from there. If they drive up under the west wall—

well, the ball will be over without any of you getting a dance. But they'll probably drive up the center. That means a thousand yard shot for me—pretty far for a moving target. My main object in taking that stand, though, is to make sure Campbell doesn't climb the slope below the road. You know there's only one place. He's sharp enough to know it. . . . I reckon that's all."

George and Grant went round the cabin to their quarters. Huett did not speak to Abe before they returned, rifles in hand, buckling on gun-belts. In the cool starlight they appeared formidable.

"Paw, it's been comin' a long time," said Abe significantly. The three tall forms vanished in the gloom of the corrals.

A dull fiery pang gnawed at Huett's vitals. After the many stealings of the rustlers, the consequent pursuits, the running encounters, brushes, and escapes, there was to be a crucial fight. Huett had always longed to get it over with, but now that the hour had come he had a dreadful premonition that one or more of them might be killed. He felt this the darkest hour in his spiritual life as well as his physical career as a cattleman. Huett gazed down the weird opaque canyon and cursed it with all the passion a strong man could feel in a moment of intense bitterness and regret. He had loved this wilderness valley, he had spent more than the better half of his life there; his early dream, his ambition, his love of Lucinda, and the days of toil and defeat, the coming one by one of his sons, the blessed gift of little Barbara, the years of rain and shine, of struggle and victory—all were inextricably, hopelessly woven of these complex, fateful fibers.

Then almost magically, it seemed, his old practical habit reasserted itself—the habit of facing an obstacle: so powerful had it grown that this rustler raid and the ruts that had seemed so fearful were discounted. Logan paced to and fro until a faint gray showed over the black forest to the east. Dawn was not far away. No doubt the rustlers were already on the move. He went back into the cabin.

"Luce—Babs, wake up," he called. They were asleep having lain down fully dressed, and both voiced the same query.

"Abe's all right. He got home long ago. We're in for a fight with that Stillman outfit. Tobe Campbell has thrown in with them. They're going to try to drive Sycamore."

Logan was to learn what a pioneer's daughter could say in the hour of greatest stress. He thrilled to his marrow.

"Tobe Campbell!" exclaimed Barbara, in hot amazement. "Why that hombre made violent love to me—called his brother Jack a low-down worthless backwoods loafer —begged me to marry him. And now he sneaks up here with those outcast Stillmans to rob us! . . . The damned rotten lousy Tonto villain! I hope Abe shoots one of his pop-eyes out!"

"You'll get that chance yourself, maybe," he replied. "I'll want you and Luce to do some shooting when they come. Abe's idea is for us to shoot as much as we can whether we see any rustlers or not."

"I hope we come right close," snapped Barbara, viciously. "Dad, it's just hideous to think that after all we've endured—now when we're earned peace and rest, we must fight for our cattle and our very lives."

"Hideous is right, Barbara. . . . No, Luce, don't strike a light. It's daybreak now. We'll be able to see pronto."

The open door and window let in the gray gloom. Logan placed a table under the window, and piled i high with firearms and ammunition. He made sure the guns were loaded.

"Stand here and don't talk," whispered Logan, taking his rifle. "I'll watch from the door."

He peered out. The rims of the canyon were black, the space between gray, with outlines of trees and walls dimly showing. Straining his ears Logan listened for sounds. At last he heard a light thud up in the woods, probably the fall of a pine cone. It quickened his sense. There was a strange oppressive silence mantling the forest. By looking back at the east he could discern the almost imperceptible brightening and spreading of the light.

Then the indistinct shapes began to take form and familiarity—the path, the bridge and brook, the tall pines to their right, the blur of corrals and sheds, the bulge of slope.

A whistle! It had a low piercing human quality. No bird or animal ever emitted a note like that. Barbara, peering out of the window, heard it, for she whispered something. Logan turned to reply: "Must have been George. Abe's too far away. . . . Reckon they hear the drive!"

Logan listened more calmly. As the hour approached its climax his mind and senses seemed to fix. The gray gloom perceptibly lifted or disintegrated. He saw the corrals, and the cow-barn, where George and Grant waited, and the pale yellow road leading up the slope. A blue jay broke the silence, heralding the dawn. Faint and far away sounded the chatter of a black squirrel. Then Logan heard another faint noise which he could not identify.

The ruddy color appeared over the eastern pine-fringed rim. A stone rattled down over the ledge opposite the cabin, giving Logan a start. It was not an unusual sound. Weathering of the cliffs was always going on. He peered up the trail, through the gap in the ledge. It was light enough now for him to see that the gate of peeled poles was open. Seldom of late had it been closed, but now it seemed an oversight. Still, cattle running up the canyon would never find that small steep opening. He turned toward the canyon.

A curtain of fog hung over the upper part, silvering in the light of breaking day. The ground was white with frost. On the moment he saw a dark moving line come from behind the jutting corner of wall.

"Dad—*there!*" whispered the sharp-eyed Barbara.

Logan did not reply nor turn. He had felt the gush of hot blood, the leap of passion, the stringing of his nerves. Doubt ceased. What brazen boldness these cattle-thieves showed! To raid a rancher's herd in front of his door! It seemed incredible; but there moved the dark line, ragged with heads and horns, not a half mile away; and a faint sound of hoofs thudded on the still air. Logan shut his eyes and tried to simulate sleep, to find if that faint trample would wake him. But it was hard to hear even now when he was awake. The cunning Tobe Campbell had learned much from Hillbrand. Cattlemen in that country lived too far apart; they were too indifferent to their neighbors, too jealously intent upon their own business; they made no concerted effort to get rid of rustlers—and this was the result.

"Oh, Dad, they're driving all our herd!" whispered Barbara, indignantly.

"No. But they're sure not stingy with this raid. . . . Barbara, you and Luce keep your nerve now. Hell will be popping pronto. I'll miss my guess though if it lasts long."

He watched. When he saw horsemen at each side of the herd and behind, his thoughts ceased whirling and settled into the one cold hard business at hand. The rustlers drove straight up the canyon, on the right of the brook, over the deeper grass. They had not missed any asset to help them in this raid. No hoof cracked a rock nor made a thud in that grass.

Logan counted eight riders. Abe had missed some. The herd drove easily. They were tame. They passed opposite Abe's stand surely out of rifle range—Still Logan listened grimly for a shot. How little these rustlers dreamed that the most unerring rifleman in Arizona had sharp, cold eyes upon them!

"Folks, get ready . . ." ordered Huett, turning to look at his family. Barbara stood with her rifle over the window sill, which was almost up to her shoulder. Her pale face, flashing eyes and compressed lips, showed resolute defiance and courage. Strangely Huett remembered her the first time he had ever seen her—a curly-haired, big-eyed little tot. Lucinda held her gun ready, locked in somber expectancy, as if she could see dreadful issues beyond Huett's ken.

A ringing rifle shot broke the silent canyon. It came from the wall beyond the corrals. Abe! Huett wheeled to gaze. He almost stepped outside in his eagerness. The herd was across the brook nearing the turn; riders were galloping up on both sides, swinging guns aloft, while hoarse shouts started the cattle into a run. Another sharp crack from the cliff! It brought puffs of white smoke from the mounted men. The crack of their guns right over the heads of the herd stampeded the cattle. Rapid rifle-fire burst from the sheds. Men appeared swallowed up in a trampling roar and cloud of dust.

Huett leveled his rifle at the mêlée and waited for a rider to break through the dust. A horse plunged into view, but it was riderless. As Huett stepped out on the porch, peering low, he saw a burst of red flame from the ledge above the cabin, and then simultaneously with a banging gunshot came a violent shock, a burning blow from a bullet that knocked him back against the wall.

"Get away—from window!" he shouted to the women inside. He raised himself on his elbows. Two riders, guns in hands, yelling like Indians, rode down at breakneck pace, and reaching a level, began to shoot. Bang-bang-bang! Bullets thudded into the logs of the cabin. As the two turned toward the corrals and galloped by, a stream of red fire burst from the cabin window. Huett dropped flat as Barbara's thirty barked spitefully. The foremost horse broke his fast pace, leaped high with horrid snorts and plunged down, unseating his rider, but as the horse lunged, the rustler hung on grimly to the pommel. He made a magnificent leap from flying feet and just missed the saddle. The crippled horse, mad with pain and fright, dragged him across the brook and kicked free to race among the bellowing scattering herd.

Barbara ran out of the cabin, working the lever of her rifle. She fired at the second horseman. He emitted a piercing yell of agony and sagging in his saddle, managed to guide his horse down the canyon on the left side of the brook.

Huett lurched upright from his knees, staggering, and seized hold of the porch post. Just then Barbara wheeled, her face like ashes, her eyes bright with a brilliant light.

"Dad! You're hurt!" she cried, piercingly, and rushed to support him.

"I don't know . . . reckon so," he replied, thickly. His senses were not clear. As she helped him over the high door-jam Lucinda gave him one horrified look and collapsed on the floor. Logan felt hot blood streaming down his face and neck. Barbara helped him to his big chair, and then dashed back to the door, working the lever of her rifle. She peered out.

"What's doing, Bab?" called Logan, hoarsely.

"Oh, I—can't tell," she panted. "Yes . . . cattle on the rim—down canyon. . . . Stampede! . . . I see riders—scattered . . . horses running hard. . . . Oh, Dad! I believe we've driven the rustlers off!"

"I'll bet we have—those that could ride! . . . Bab, come here. . . . Run your finger in this hole over my ear."

"Dad! I—I can't! Oh, the blood is pouring," cried Barbara, suddenly weak.

"Then I'll have to. . . . Augh! Talk about fire!— Aw, that hombre just creased me!"

"Dad, you're not—bad hurt?" faltered Barbara.

"I'm not hurt at all. Bullet ditched my scalp. Gosh, it burns! I'm bleeding like a stuck pig. Well, if the boys get off this easy we're jake. . . . Lucinda's only fainted, I reckon."

"She's coming to," cried Barbara, gladly. Then she ran to the door, and gazing out she cried: "George! He's crippled. Can't see the other boys . . . Oh, mercy, if they're only safe!"

Barbara bathed Lucinda's face, brought her back to consciousness and helped her to the bed. Logan averted his bloody face, and stood up with an effort. "Luce, I'm all right." He stamped out on the porch to encounter George, dragging his leg. The healthy tan was gone from his face. At sight of his father he halted short with a grimace.

"Just nicked over the ear, George," announced Logan.

"Aw, that's good. You sure look a sight to scare one into creeps. . . . I stopped a slug, worse luck."

"Grant?"

"God! . . . I'm afraid, Dad. I saw him get hit—fall— then jump up. Four or five of those thieves bolted for the road. Grant ran out to hold them back. They were using Colts. With his Winchester, Grant had the best of them. I ran out, too. That's when I got stung, from the other direction. I ducked behind the corral—had two shots at the other two. Didn't miss, either, but they got away. . . . Dad, I counted eight men altogether."

"Eight?—Yes, so did I. There's Abe. He's holding Grant up. They're coming. If he can walk at all he's not hard hit. . . . Aw, thank God! . . . I reckoned my lot could be no worse. But it could! George, tell the women we're jake, while I wash off this gore."

Logan took a survey of the canyon. The dust had settled. All down the grassy stretch cattle had begun to graze. In the square before the corrals Logan espied two prone figures, one of which moved. Half way up the road there lay another. Far down under the west wall he saw a crippled horse dragging its bridle.

Striding to the bench, Huett washed the blood from his head. He felt the hot, stinging furrow over his ear. What a narrow escape! Still, an inch or even less was as good as a mile—the Huetts had weathered another vicissitude of pioneer life. The terrible remorse that had clamped him before the fight came back with new strength, but it could not stand before his exultation at the successful repulse of this rustler raid. With this gang split and depleted, if merely of its leaders, there would nevertheless be a let-up in rustling for a long time.

Chapter Fourteen

IT WAS an evening in fall when the warmth of the Indian summer day and the pervading melancholy stillness of the season lingered long after darkness mantled the canyon.

George and Grant had returned from Flagg bursting with news of the war in Europe, which was now beginning its third year. At first it had hardly touched them, remote in their canyon. But as time went on and America seemed to become more and more involved, they discussed it with quickening interest.

Lucinda could not quite grasp why a war in far-off Europe held such interest for her sons and husband.

"It's because they're men, Barbara," she said to the listening young woman, who stood with great eyes like midnight gulfs fixed upon Abe. "It's even got Abe fascinated. . . . Men would rather fight than eat."

"But listen, Mother," replied Barbara.

Huett looked up from the newspaper he had spread over his knees. His gray eyes had the old keen flash. Lucinda noted that it was not the front page of the paper which had interested him.

"Cattle, wheat, cotton, corn—all keep going up," he boomed.

"Well, as to that, I'd forgotten," replied George. "Business all over the U. S. has had a tremendous boom. If the war keeps on we'll all get rich."

"Keeps on? Humph, when it started, we thought it would last a few months, and now it's in its third year. . . . Cattle at twenty-two dollars! Big price. What're the Babbitts doing?"

"They're holding on, Dad. Running eighty thousand head."

"That's what I'll do," declared the rancher, ponderingly.

"You'd have to, even if you wanted to sell. Too late this fall, Paw," said George, shortly, as if the matter of cattle was a secondary consideration. "Take a look at the front page of that paper."

"I don't read so well as I used to, son. And the war itself doesn't interest me. I reckon they're all crazy."

Grant interposed earnestly: "But, Dad, it's spreading. It *might* involve the whole world. Even America!"

"Shucks! That's ridiculous. Let 'em kill each other off over there. But the U. S. must keep out of it."

"Suppose Germany sinks American ships with her submarines?"

That query arrested Huett.

"Tell us more, George," put in Abe, quietly. He showed no excitement, but he was somber.

"The Germans have got the bit between their teeth," declared George, with pale face and flashing eyes. "And you bet they'll keep coming. It looks bad for France and England."

"Suppose Germany licks France and England. What'll she do then?" asked Abe.

"God only knows. But that outfit would sure be swelled. . . . If they tried to make a clean sweep, and tackled the U. S. ——"

"Hell! You boys are loco. That's not conceivable," interrupted Huett.

"There are a lot of brainy men who say it *is* possible," said Grant.

"Bab, I've a piece of news that will flabbergast you," went on George.

She did not encourage him. Evidently Barbara had come across a thought she could not surmount or get around.

"You know how loco Joe Hardy was over airplanes. First it was cars and then planes. Joe sure was a rotten horseman. . . . Well, Joe has left for France, where he's going in the air service."

"Doggone!" ejaculated Huett. "I've seen the day I'd have jumped at that. I was in the army three years."

"I'd want mine on foot," said Abe. "Never savvied what held those airplanes up."

"They don't all stay up, so I read," rejoined George. "Dad, I wish you'd been in town. You'd have found out there are more places in the world than Sycamore. And more things to think about than we ever dreamed of. I declare I felt like a hick. Mr. Little said if Teddy Roosevelt had been president he'd kept Europe from going to war. And the Kaiser warns the United States that if we send contraband goods abroad he'll sink the ships."

"That would be right," spoke up Abe, stoutly.

"Sure! But what if these grafters had power to get their contraband on passenger ships. And the Germans sunk them with Americans on board. What a hell of a mess that would make!"

"Americans should stay home," interposed Huett, with finality.

"Dad, haven't you taken sides yet?" asked Grant.

"No, I haven't. But if you press me I am for England. And France fought for the United States during the Revolution. That shouldn't be forgotten."

Lucinda went back to the neglected housework, but Barbara stood behind Abe, her hand on his shoulder, and listened. It was a new and strange kind of talk in that cabin. It troubled Lucinda. She tried to dismiss the vague unrest with an acceptance of Logan's failure to see aught for them to worry about, but she could not do it. Logan's thoughts revolved around cattle. Her sons were back-woods cowboys, but they had intelligence, education, and intense patriotism. Logan had patriotism, too; Lucinda used to think it the only religion he had. But during the long years of his struggle that had been relegated to oblivion. It would take a shock to wake up Logan. The boys, however, were quick to grasp how a great war, even far beyond the Atlantic shores, must affect all Americans. That was the realization which troubled Lucinda. Her consciousness refused to face the thought that had darkened Barbara's beautiful eyes. She hoped that with the hunting season nearer, and winter to follow, there would be no more news about war and her loved ones would forget.

But when this most desirable thing had almost happened, Logan and Abe met a party of hunters just in from town and they stirred anew the curious fire of interest. Snow fell in early December, assuring a white Christmas. Owing to increased automobile traffic from Flagg and Winslow to Phoenix and points south, the road was kept open. Occasionally one of the Huetts ran into travelers to hear more news. There came a respite, however, during the later months of winter and early spring. Lucinda's menfolk heard no more to augment their excitement, and it gradually subsided.

But the nameless something that had troubled Lucinda did not subside. It seemed to be a shadow without substance, a premonition of a vague and undefined trial of the future. She drove it away, but it continually returned. Lucinda feared the years of toil and worry had made her morbid. She divined, however, that this intangible recurring emotion was not morbidness. It was deep, primitive, mystic—a something inherited from the mother of the race, a whisper from the beyond.

Logan was reluctant to start for Flagg that spring. Lucinda and Barbara backed him up, overcoming the eagerness of the young men. They decided, however, that when

they did go George would drive the car with Lucinda and
Barbara, while Logan would go in the wagon with Abe
and Grant. Logan wanted to finish a stone-walled corral
before they left. It had long been his intention to utilize
the hundreds of rocks that had rolled down from the bluff
on the west side of the canyon. They lay everywhere near
the corrals and the shed for horses and cattle to stumble
over.

"Dad, it's too big a job," complained George, when
they had one wall half laid. "We'll never get it done."

Huett shook his shaggy gray head obstinately. "We've
more time now that we don't have to guard the cattle."

One sunny spring day when the wet slopes were drying
up and the turkeys had begun to gobble, Lucinda went
with Barbara out to see the men. Abe had prevailed upon
Barbara to coax Lucinda to make Logan leave off the
stone-wall work and go to town.

"We'll go," declared Lucinda. "A little more of this
uncertain dread will finish me."

"Mother! What uncertain dread?" asked Barbara
anxiously.

"I don't know." Lucinda untied her apron and laid it
aside.

As she left the cabin with Barbara she saw the sunflowers sprouting green from the brown soil and bladed
grass showing along the log wall. How many years had
she tended that garden with its homely flowers! Some
association full of sweet and pervading melancholy attended the observance.

When they arrived at the scene of Logan's new enterprise George and Grant were loading a sled with rocks
from the slope, and Abe and Logan were working on the
wall.

"Look who's here!" boomed Logan, and Abe, after a

steady glance at Barbara, slowly laid down the stone he had been about to set in place.

"Logan, we want to start at once for town," announced Lucinda.

"Doggone my pictures! George and Grant have pestered me. And now you womenfolk! Now what's. . . ."

"Hello!—Riders coming lickitty cut down the road," interrupted Abe. "Luke Flesher and that cowboy who used to ride for Mooney."

"Yes, that's Luke. . . . Something is up," rejoined Logan.

The horsemen reached the corral and reined their sweaty mounts. Lucinda knew Flesher to be a neighbor down the road. He doffed his sombrero to her and Barbara. The cowboy hung back a little, shy and silent.

"Howdy, Huett, an' you fellars," called Flesher, with flashing tawny eyes upon them. His sallow visage showed strong excitement. "Bet you my house you haven't heahed the news."

"Howdy, Luke. . . . What makes you reckon we haven't heard the news?" returned Huett, curiously. Abe leaned over the wall. George and Grant came striding up.

"Wal, if you had you'd shore not be layin' that wall," retorted Flesher, with a short laugh.

"No? It takes a heap to throw me off a job."

"Huett, cattle are sellin' at forty dollars on the hoof, an' goin' up."

"What?" boomed the rancher, his tanned face suddenly going red.

"Yes, what. But that ain't nothin' atall. . . . *United States has declared war on Germany!*"

In the blank pregnant silence that ensued Flesher lighted a cigarette while his keen hard eyes studied the effect of his terrible announcement. For an instant Lucinda was concerned with a blinding shock to her con-

sciousness. Then she saw Logan sit back utterly con-
founded. Under Abe's dark clear skin worked a miracle
of change. George greeted the news with a ringing whoop.
Grant stood transfixed and quivering. Barbara's strong
sweet face turned pearly white.

"That was three days ago," went on Flesher. "I was
in town before the wires came. Course everybody was
het-up about the Bochs sinkin' the *Lusitania* with hundreds of Americans on board. France is licked. England
is licked. An' if the good old U. S. don't step in to hell
with democracy an' freedom! Germany shore has her eye
on America. All the same, when the news came, Flagg
went loco. Arizona is buzzin' like a nest of mad yellow-
jackets. The draft is comin' for able-bodied young men
between twenty-one and thirty."

"Draft! . . . What's that?" queried Logan, huskily.

"Government order forcin' all fit young men to train
for war. . . . But a good many cowboys an' other fellars
are not waitin' on the draft. They're enlistin'. Jack Campbell was the first."

That information appeared to sting Logan. He might
as well have boomed out that if his sons had known they
would have been the first.

"My sons will not wait for the draft," he said stiffly.

"Good! There'll shore be a hell of a lot of speculation
on how many Huns yore Abe will bore. Haw! Haw!
Haw! . . . Arizona will send a regiment of riders an'
shots that couldn't be beat nowhere. . . . Wal, Huett,
heah's the papers I was commissioned to give you. I've
been ridin' all over to the outlyin' ranchers in the woods.
Don't like the job. Shore falls tough on women. I'm sorry,
Mrs. Huett, to have to tell you an' Miss Barbara. But it
strikes into every home. . . . We must be mozyin' on."

"Wait," called Logan, as Flesher gathered up his reins,
"are the Babbitts holding on to their stock?"

"They are not—an' cussin' themselves blue in the face. Sold out for thirty-three dollars a haid."

"Well!— Who's buying?"

"Stockmen in Kansas City and Chicago. Speculators. Big cattle barons. Stock movin' this last ten days. Santa Fé have wired for all available freight cars. Everybody figurin' that the government will begin to buy beef an' hides."

"They'll shove the price up?"

"Skyhigh, Huett. You want to be in on this. How much stock you runnin'?"

"I reckon—thirty thousand head," returned Logan, swallowing hard.

"Dad, the count will be more this spring," interposed George.

"My Gawd!" ejaculated the astonished Flesher. "Ain't you settin' pretty? Hang on, Huett, *but not too long.*"

Then the visitors wheeled their horses and made off up the road at a gallop. The Huetts did not soon rouse out of their trance. Lucinda felt herself to be a part of the stone wall upon which she leaned, numb, halted, dead except in her consciousness which was a maelstrom of conflicting thoughts.

Logan tumbled the stone off his knee that he had forgotten was there.

"Sons, we'll never finish this corral," he said, loud and clear. "We leave for town at once. . . . George, get out your car. Luce, you and Bab pack pronto. Abe, you and Grant rustle with the wagon."

Grant ran off with thudding boots. But Abe had not heard. He fixed a strained soft gaze from his wonderful gray eyes upon Barbara. She saw only him.

"Bab, will you—marry me—at once?" he asked trenchantly.

"Oh—yes—Abe!" she cried. A radiant transfixed face

attested to joy that overcame grief. Abe took her hand and put an arm around her. They forgot the others. Lucinda walked behind, leaving Logan by his unfinished stone corral.

Lucinda's perceptions magnified to startling clear and vivid reactions. She saw that a profound and tremendous excitement had seized upon her family, stultifying, inhibiting, blinding them to the incredible and insupportable truth. Her husband, after thirty years of the poverty and toil of a galley-slave, saw suddenly the grand rainbow of his dreams looming before him in an arch of gold. His sons would not wait to be drafted! Those sons, reared in the wilderness, red-blooded and virile as savages, to whom the world and cities and ships and armies had been but names, had rudely been shocked into a passion of patriotism, had flashed before their serene vision the kaleidoscopic train of great scenes, of brilliant images, of the glory of adventure, of the romance of war. As for Barbara, she had been staggered, and before her sensitive soul had grasped the significance of this catastrophe, love with its fulfillment, with the wifehood delayed so long, closed her mind for the time to all but the tumultuous truth.

But upon Lucinda descended the doom of the mother. She thought of her sons. She remembered the travail of their birth. She saw them from the beautiful moment to this fatal hour. They were a part of her flesh and blood, of her spirit; the inexplicable dread that had weighed upon her for months gathered strength yet never clarified its sinister meaning. The tall pines, black and old, moaned with the old voice that had been a bane to her all her life there; the looming walls, gray and silent, looked down upon her in pitiless knowledge of her plight.

Presently entering the cabin with this burden. Lucinda

was plunged into the vortex of her family's wild excite- ment. Logan was a young man again. George and Grant raved like two boys upset by prospect of an adventure too grand to grasp. Abe had gotten no farther than his mar- riage to Barbara. And Barbara, her eyes like stars, her thought and emotion meeting those of her lifelong play- mate and sweetheart, ran and packed and laughed without realizing her eyes were wet with tears.

"Folks, pack all your things and throw them into the wagon," said Logan. "We're leaving Sycamore for good. I'll keep the ranch. . . . We'll come back for a visit every fall, when the leaves color and the deer take on their blue coats. . . . At last—by God! . . . Thirty thousand head and more! . . . Forty dollars and going up!"

George drove the old Ford at a speed that would have appalled Lucinda during a less poignant time. She sat in the front seat with Barbara and held on tightly. The back of the car was loaded full with their baggage.

Every familiar landmark along the road gave Lucinda a pang. Barbara laughed at every bump. She saw some- thing beautiful, but not along the road. It never crossed George's absorbed mind that he might be passing the en- trance to Sycamore Canyon for the last time, and Turkey Flat and Cedar Ridge. He never saw them at all.

For once the Huetts did not stop at Mormon Lake. Lucinda saw with pity the run-down ranch of the Hol- berts, and she thought sadly of their disintegration, and the old man still living there, waiting for the prodigal son who would never come back.

It was dark when George ended the drive with a grand rattling flourish in front of Wetherington's Hotel. He engaged rooms, stored the baggage, and took Lucinda and Barbara to supper. Afterward they went out. The main street was bright with lights and thronged with people.

Cowboys in groups jangled their spurs along the sidewalks. They had heated faces and eyes that flashed.

"Kinda like July Fourth, circus day, *fiesta*, and Saturday night all messed up," said George. "Everybody going some place but don't know where!"

"Take us to the motion-pictures," entreated Barbara.

They went. The big barnlike hall was crowded with a noisy motley crowd of cowboys and lumbermen. When Lucinda's eyes grew accustomed to the dim light she saw a sprinkling of girls all over the theater. It seemed full of a charged atmosphere. Before the regular picture came on there were snown comic features, and then a kind of bulletin of war news and government propaganda, the first of which elicited roars of mirth from the audience and the second drew a fearful din of stamping boots, shrill whistles, and wild whoops. Lucinda felt the surge of feeling that was rampant. She wept over a screen drama which at a normal hour would have been as nauseous as sawdust.

After the show they squeezed out of the theater merging with the stream of excited humanity. Cowboys sidled up to Barbara and made bold advances. One of them said: "Sweetheart, I'm goin' to fight the Huns for you. Come out an' play with me." Barbara appeared bewildered, but not angry. George laughed at the cowboys, and placed Barbara between him and Lucinda.

"Town wide open. Everything goes. Bab, I reckon you'd better not run around alone."

"Oh, I can take care of myself. I like it."

But Lucinda probed deeper. She guessed a laxity, a levity, a hurried audacious haunting something in the crowd of young people. She had never known there were so many girls in and around Flagg. She had never seen them so unreserved, so silly, giggling, flirting, brazen. The old-time Western girls, except the dance-hall type and the street-walkers, had been noted for their poise, their dignity, but these virtues seemed gone. Something had let loose. The rows of saloons fronting the railroad were thronged with cowboys. Lucinda was relieved, and Barbara disappointed when George took them back to the hotel. Lucinda closed weary eyes on Barbara preening herself before the mirror, listening to the strange hum in the street.

Next morning Lucinda awoke to the tasks at hand. After breakfast she and Barbara called upon Mrs. Hardy to ask about a furnished house to rent. That worthy friend did not know of one and could not help them. She talked volubly about her son Joe who had gone to France and was flying an airplane in the famed Lafayette Escadrille. Lucinda could not understand the woman's pride, or Barbara's shining-eyed wonder!

Mr. Al Doyle, an old friend of Logan's whom they met on the street, directed them to a house that was to be had for renting. It had just become vacant, but would not be so for long. The town was full, the landlord said. Lucinda took it, mainly for the cosy sitting room with open fireplace, which she knew Logan would like when the cold nights came. Flagg stood at a high altitude and had bitter winters.

Lucinda sent Barbara down town to purchase many needed things for the house, while she set to work to clean the place and make it comfortable. George came presently with the baggage.

"This shack will do for the present, maw," he said. "But when Dad sells out you can afford the swellest house in town."

Lucinda could not accustom herself to the idea that they were rich and could afford everything. George moved furniture about, stowed the baggage where Lucinda wanted it, then drove down town for Barbara's purchases. By nightfall they were comfortable, but George dragged them down town to supper, and again to the movies. This was a Saturday night and for noise, crowd, hilarity, and a wild clinging of young men and women, eclipsed anything Lucinda had ever seen.

"When will Abe get in?" asked Barbara, for the hundredth time.

"I reckon tomorrow sure, maybe early," replied George. "Hope so. . . . Mother," he hesitated a moment. "Did I tell you I—I passed A Number One?"

"Passed! What?"

"Why, the army examination for soldiers."

"Ah—I see," murmured Lucinda, so low she was scarcely heard.

"Grant is as fit as I am," went on George. "And, of course, Abe could pass anything. . . . Grant and I want to go into the Cavalry or if not that the Light Artillery. Anything with horses!"

"What'll Abe go in for?" asked Barbara, tensely.

"He wants to be a sharpshooter, like Dad's father was in the Civil War. . . . God help the Huns that Abe draws a bead on!"

Lucinda thought there would be many beside the Germans in need of God's help. Mothers—wives—sweethearts deserted! Men had always, from the remote aboriginal days, loved to fight. But it was the women who bore sons and therefore the brunt of war. In that moment Lucinda regretted the lapse of her religion after her marriage to Logan. She had to face her soul now, and perhaps some day the final sacrifice of a mother, and she needed God.

Late on Sunday afternoon Logan arrived with Abe and Grant, having made a record trip from Sycamore. George, who hurried to the house to tell his mother and Barbara, declared: "Dad is hipped with his cattle prospects. Grant is crazy about war. Abe is sold on marriage. . . . Son-of-a-gun rushed off to fix it up with the pastor. Guess we're leaving tomorrow— Babs, *I* think you should wait until we come back from the war."

"Why?" interrupted Lucinda, softly.

"Aw, looks like Abe wanted to cinch her before he goes," declared George, not without bitterness. "Suppose he came back with a leg shot off? Bab would be tied to half a man all her life."

"I'd rather be tied to half of Abe than to the whole world of men."

"Bab! Forgive me. I reckon it still hurts. But I hope and pray Abe will come back and you'll be happy."

"Thank you, George," replied Barbara, with emotion. "You'll see us married?"

"Sure. I'll be game, Bab. So long as I can't have you I'm glad it's that lucky hombre, Abe. . . . I wish I had an anchor like you. My God, it seems a soldier needs one! I'm finding that out. These cowboys are loco. And the girls—clean out of their heads!"

Presently Abe strode in to fold both Lucinda and Barbara in a bearish hug. Rough-clad, unshaven, smelling of horses and dust and hay—how splendidly virile he was! A devoted spirit shone from his eyes.

"Darling, we're to be married at seven," he said, fervently. "Gosh, it's too wonderful to be true! . . . Mr. Haskell, the new pastor, can get a license for us, even if it is Sunday. You've got just an hour to make yourself the loveliest bride that ever was. I'll change at the hotel and be back pronto."

He was gone. Lucinda saw through dim eyes how Barbara faced the door by which he had left, with her quivering hands half outstretched.

"Hurry, dear," admonished Lucinda. "It's well you have everything ready to put on. I must rustle, too."

Logan did not appear. Lucinda thought impatiently that the man was so insane over his cattle project that he could not remember his wife or his children. Abe came, shining of face, his eyes bright as stars, with a white flower in the lapel of his dark coat. Barbara could well worship that young giant of the woods. He was like a superb pine. Lucinda lived over again in anguish the conception, the birth, the growth of this her favorite son, and at last, in that supreme moment, loved him so greatly she would not have had his life otherwise.

Grant arrived, gay and handsome.

"Oh, Bab, but you're sweet! You're a peach! How can Abe ever leave you? I couldn't."

Then George followed, pale, dark of eye, gallant of speech, the unaccepted lover who had come through the fires of relinquishment. But Logan did not come. They waited until seven; then Abe led Barbara out, followed by Lucinda with George and Grant. It was but a short walk to the pastor's house. How pleased Lucinda was to learn that Abe had thought of being married in church! Mr. Harkell's wife and sister accompanied the party. The church was brightly lighted, and Abe had thought to have flowers at the altar. The minister's deep voice, quavering a little, broke the silence. How quick the ceremony! Lucinda wanted it to be long. She scarcely heard the solemn queries of the pastor, Abe's deep affirmative, and Barbara's low and eloquent promises. The scene at the altar seemed to fade. Lucinda saw envisioned a little ragged boy leading a curly-haired girl along the lonely road. So long ago and far away! So appallingly sweet this picture. So tragic the reality of Abe bending to kiss the bride!

George snatched her away with a gay cry and leaned to kiss her. "One for me, Bab—one for Abe—and one for you. . . . God bless you and bring him back!"

Grant took his turn. "Barbara, you're a Huett at last."

Then Lucinda embraced Barbara, and held her close for a mute convulsive moment.

They went down town for dinner. No one would have thought that it was Sunday. The saloons, the dance-halls, the gambling halls, the theaters and restaurants were wide open. Among the stream of cowboys with their girls moved beaded and brick-colored Indians, dark of visage, sombre of eye.

"Bunch of Navajos from the Painted Desert in town to enlist," announced George, as the wedding-party found seats reserved for them in the restaurant. "Won't wait for the draft any more than we would! I call that just great. And say, won't there be hell along the German front when these Navvies slip out of the trenches at night to throw bombs? They'll just eat that job up . . . Redskins, niggers, greasers, all enlisting! Are they Americans? Well, I guess!"

"Brother, that'll do you," said Abe, shaking a brown fist at George. "Barbara and I have just been married. We don't know there's a war. Tomorrow is a thousand years away for us. Let us be happy at our wedding dinner. Let us think of Sycamore and the old days that will never return."

Logan came at last to join them, regretful, impressive in his felicitations to the bride and groom—a Logan Huett who had evidently found himself to be one of the state's big cattlemen. It seemed as if he had left off a plodding and unsuccessful character with his old clothes. Barbara beamed upon him. Lucinda forced her subtle and clairvoyant divinations into the background of her consciousness. She would be happy with them all this last time. And they all were happy, if to be happy was to rise above and forget their agony, to eat and talk and laugh, to tease the bride with reminiscences of the past, to speak lovingly of Sycamore and the days that were no more.

Lucinda lay awake long hours that night, praying to bear up, hoping the dawn would never arrive. But it did come—a gray cold breaking of day at the window.

She heard trotting horses and whistling cowboys go by, and the creak of wagon wheels and hum of motors. The business of the world did not halt for heart-broken mothers.

At breakfast Logan talked about the cattle market. Lucinda at last, in desperation, turned upon him.

"Logan Huett, are you mad about cattle? . . . Good God, man, don't you realize your sons are leaving today for the war?"

"Why Luce! . . . What the hell? . . . Aw, don't be so cut up. Sure the boys are going to enlist. And it's the proudest day of my life. But it doesn't faze me, wife. You women jump at conclusions. America will never get in this war. Once our army reaches Europe, if it ever does, those Germans will quit like yellow dogs. They're licked right now. Well, then, what of that? Our boys will get some military work—a good thing in itself—they'll see some of the U. S. if not France, and they'll come back all the better for service. We'll have our new house then, and a couple of nice girls picked out for George and Grant."

Thus the practical cattleman dismissed the dreadful thing, which, like a poisonous lichen, was eating into Lucinda's heart. For a while after Logan was gone, Lucinda attended to the housework, and she derived some comfort from his deductions. But this did not last long under the pitiless light of her intuition. She was a woman —a mother—and she could not explain what she knew. There seemed to be a sixth sense in her, an intelligence that had not yet clarified for her its subtlety.

Barbara came at noon, transformed into a woman, her face lovely with its pale pearl color, her eyes shadowed, the exquisite violet dark and dim.

"Mother—he—they leave at two," she sobbed. "It's a special train—westbound. . . . They go to some place in Washington state—a training camp for soldiers. . . . I've had my last moment alone with Abe. He's rushed to get through. But they accepted him pronto. . . . Dad is down there bragging about how many Germans my—my husband will kill. . . . Yes, dad is, mother. He's smoking a big cigar, his chest swelled out, his thumbs in the armholes of his vest. Oh, it's disgusting! . . . It's terrible! Dad can't see. George is drinking and doesn't care. Grant is on fire with some strange passion that I think is false. . . . But Abe, he is different—his heart is breaking too."

"Then why does he go?" asked Lucinda, stern in her judgment.

"He'd *have* to go, anyway. But Abe wants to. Down street he pointed out a war poster on the billboard. It was a picture of a gorilla making off with a white woman. It said in big black letter: *'Save your sweetheart from the Huns!'* Abe wants to go because of that. Oh, mother, I—I *can't* endure it!" She seemed on the verge of collapse.

"You must, Barbara. At least until after they go. We must not let them carry away memories of miserable faces. Our woman's lot is harder. Men fight and women weep, you know."

At two o'clock that day, when the special train pulled into the station, all the people of Flagg and its environs were present. Banners and flags waved from the windows. Young faces, keen, tanned, somehow raw and primitive, flashed upon the spectators. These young men joked and made witty remarks to the girls present.

Lucinda's little party was only one of a dozen such groups. They could not be alone, even if they thought of such a thing. The crowd was loud in its good cheer, its well-wishing, its farewell to its youthful champions. All along the front of that line Lucinda saw the wet eyes of women. They were all mothers, all sisters, all sweethearts of these boys going away to war. That light of glory in their eyes, dimmed by tears, told the secret of that sacrifice. This woman acclaim of the soldier was in the race.

"*All aboard!*" yelled the conductor.

Grant put his arms around Barbara and Lucinda. Tears coursed down his cheeks.

"Goodbye, Bab. . . . Goodbye, mother. . . . Don't take it—hard. Ten to one we'll never get to France. . . . So long, Dad! Good luck with the herd!" He snatched up his luggage and ran to board the train.

Abe stood aside to let George at Barbara. The parting had sobered him. His farewell was a kiss and a gallant smile. "Barbara, if I make a good soldier I'll owe it to you." And he turned to Lucinda: "*Mother!*" That was all he said, but he clasped her close. As he kissed her Lucinda suffered the ghastly illumination of her dark forebodings. *George would never come back to her.* But he, young, physical, elemental, never divined that awful truth. He broke from her, wrung Logan's hand, and rushed away. The train was moving. Abe let go of his mother, pressed Barbara's rapt face to his breast, then followed his brothers. Logan ran along the car-step from which Abe was waving

"Son," he shouted, huskily, "you gotta be at that turkey shootin' at Pine!"

The long sustained cheer of the watchers died into a strange sobbing breath as the train pulled out and left them standing there.

Chapter Fifteen

HUETT met his old friend Al Doyle in the bank. As a young man Al had helped build the Union Pacific Railroad and the Santa Fe. He had been pioneer, cattleman, lumberman, teamster, and guide. If there was one Arizonian who knew the West it was Doyle. Of late years Doyle had been guiding geologists and archeologists into the canyon country, and hunters down over the Tonto Rim.

"Howdy, Al," said Huett.

"Wal, hullo, old timer," replied Doyle. "What do you hear from your sons?"

"Not much lately. Letters few and far between, and all cut up. Makes me tired. Abe's at the front. They shoved him along pronto. George and Grant among the reserves."

"They'll smoke up that Boche outfit before the snow flies. Hell of a war, Logan! We got in just in time to save France and England. With Hindenburg falling back and the Yanks arriving by shiploads it won't be long now."

"Al, I haven't sold out my cattle yet."

"Say, old timer, you don't have to tell me that. You've ootfiggered all the big blokes who reckoned they was smart. But, Logan, don't be a hawg. Don't wait too long. There's bound to be a slump when winter sets in. On the q.t. I'll give you a tip I got from Charteris. The government has ordered cattle from the Argentine."

"You don't say!" ejaculated Huett, astonished and impressed.

"If the war ended in November, say, you fellows who're hanging on to your cattle would be left holding the sack. After the war the bottom will drop out of everything. I went through the Civil War, Logan. I know. If we had hard times after that Civil War, what'll we have after this World War?"

"Hard times! Why, Al, that's not conceivable. Take Flagg. The place is lousy with money. You see money sticking round loose. No one would stop to pick up a greenback from the gutter."

"Shore. And that's just why, Logan. This war has made the U. S. enormously rich. Seventeen thousand new millionaires! Everybody is rich. The value of money has been lost sight of. An orgy of spending, gambling, wasting will follow this. And then just you wait!"

"Al, are you giving me a tip or a hunch?" queried Logan, good-humoredly, though he began to take the old westerner seriously.

"Both. . . . How's your stock making oot? It's a dry season."

"They're O.K. I sent some cowboys down last month to keep tab on them. If everything wasn't jake I'd have heard."

"Best canyon ranges in Arizona. And you're running thirty thousand head?"

"Thereabouts. Some over that, George counted."

"Huett, are you getting dotty in your old age? Cattle selling now at forty dollars on the hoof! Good God, what *do* you want?"

"I been holding out. Was offered forty-two a while back. Reckon I can get more from Mitchell, the government buyer."

"Wal, Logan, if I was you I'd take what I could get while the army is shelling oot greenbacks by the car-load. It won't last. Not in the face of Argentine cattle! Shore, the price might and probably will go up. But don't take the risk. Anyway, you and your family will have more money than you can spend all the rest of your lives. . . . Logan, yours has been a long hard uphill pull. You've done great. . . . It's thirty-three years ago since I met you at Payson, while you were soldiering with Crook, and tipped you off about Sycamore Canyon. Remember?"

"You bet I do, Al. And there's been a hundred times in that thirty-three years when I wanted to murder you."

"Ha! Ha! . . . Wal, all's well that ends well. I shore gave you a good hunch. Thirty thousand head at forty or over? . . . Lord, I can't figure it up."

"One good hunch deserves another. Maybe I can return it some day."

"Huett, have you reckoned what a hell of a mess Mitchell will make of that drive up from Sycamore?" queried Al, seriously.

"Have I? Well, I should smile. But I reckon I can make this deal without delivery at the railroad."

"All the same you don't want a thousand head lamed and lost. Mitchell will make some kind of a count."

"That's what George advised. I'd better have some say in the drive."

"You want a lot of say. Those cattle will be fat. They mustn't be drove hard. You're lucky that no herds have come up from the Tonto all summer. Grass will be enough. Water scarce. Drive ten days—six miles a day. *And* fifty good cowboys, old timer, red rookies from the camp. There were a lot turned down. Failed to qualify. And that's funny, Logan. Where's the cowboy who never broke a bone?"

"Damn if I know. Al, what'll I do about such a big outfit?"

"Wal, reckon we'd better get my son Lee on the job. Mitchell won't swiggle at five dollars a day. And that'll be easy picking for a lot of boys. Let me see. Joe Arbell, Jack Ray, Hal McDonald, Con Sullivan, Bill Smith, all the Rider boys, except Al, who went to France. And

Wetherill would let his son fetch a bunch of Navajos. . . .
Logan, that ootfit, with some other riders thrown in, can
do the job O.K."

"Fine. . . . Al, by gosh, I reckon you've pushed me
off. I was tilting on the fence. Will you make an offer to
Lee for me?"

"Shore will. I can almost guarantee it a go."

"I'll look you up tonight. . . . Now, what'n hell did
I come in here for?"

"Money, same as me, I'll bet. There's still some left.
While we've been talking here I've seen stacks of long-
green pass out of that window. Beats me where it comes
from. . . . So long, Logan. Don't get weak-kneed now.
Sell!"

Logan finally remembered that his errand in the bank
was to draw money for Lucinda and Barbara. He wrote
out a check and noted the amount of his balance had
dropped below ten thousand dollars. He had had much
more than that, the accumulation from years of sales of
small herds. Where had so much money gone? Cashing
the check Logan wended his way home.

All through late spring and summer, since the boys
had gone, Lucinda and Barbara had worried Logan more
and more. Lucinda had altered, broken, greatly. She suffered under a hallucination that her sons would never
come back from the war. She was queer sometimes. She
wept at night when she thought he lay asleep. Barbara,
mentally at least, appeared to be worse than Lucinda.
Losing Abe with no certainty of his return had proved
a terrific strain. Logan could only judge of her state of
mind by her pale face, her great burning eyes, her courage, her restless energy and insatiate passion for all forms
of war relief service.

Both she and Lucinda had plunged into work with all

the other women of Flagg, and particularly those who had sons, brothers, sweethearts, cousins, friends who had gone to France, or to the training-camps. They organized bazaars, concerts, socials, knitting-circles. They were persistent and relentless about raising money for their soldier boys, for relief work, particularly the Red Cross. Logan swore he had contributed a pretty penny to that cause. He had come to fume a little about all this crazy obsession. From morning till late at night his women folk ran and worked and harangued themselves until they were so tired, so nervous, so upset that they could not sleep.

But when Logan got home to lunch, to see Lucinda's sad face and Barbara's strained eyes, he reproached himself for his impatience and irritation. When all was said, his women were the least carried away by this infernal war mania. At least Lucinda did not quite make a fool of herself and Barbara did not forget that she was the wife of Abe Huett.

"Any news, Dad?" asked Barbara.

"About the same, Bab. The bulletin said 'All quiet on the Western front.'"

"All quiet! Oh, the liars! I get so sick reading that line."

"Why sick, my dear?"

"Because it's false. Just think how hideous! You read that down town—and Mrs. Hardy reads a wire from Washington that Joe had been killed in action. Crashed over the German lines! Cited for bravery! . . . Oh-h— poor Joe! That boy, who loved machines. . . . He couldn't fight!"

"Aw! . . . That's a punch below the belt. . . . That's real. . . . I'm sorry—awful sorry. I'll drop in to see Mrs. Hardy."

"Logan, did you remember to get the money?"

"Yes, Luce, I did—finally. Here. . . . Folks, we've been spending a lot of money somehow."

"Money doesn't mean anything these days," said Lucinda.

"I reckon not. But it took a long time to earn some. . . . I'm not kicking, maw. I was just telling you."

"Dad, could you let me have a—a hundred?" asked Barbara, hesitatingly.

"I reckon so—if you promise to rest once in a while, and stop that damned knitting. Every time I come home, even at meals, you knit, knit, knit. It's getting on my nerves, honey."

"It's not the knitting, Dad. But I'll have to quit for a while. My fingers are raw."

"Well, after all, I have got some news," declared Logan, sitting down and slapping a big hand on each knee. "I reckon I'll sell out."

"Your cattle?" cried Barbara, eagerly.

"Logan, how often you've said that," added his wife incredulously.

"I reckon I'll sell at forty. Might get more, if I stuck it out. But Al Doyle called me a hawg, and darn me if he wasn't near right."

"Daddy! Sell at forty! And you have thirty thousand head? . . . Why, that's over a million!"

"Sure. And if I waited to get one dollar more a head—why that'd be five thousand more for each of the Huetts. Can you see now why I've hung on so tight?"

"Oh Dad!—It's too good to be true!"

"Not much. It *is* true. . . . Set out some lunch, Luce, and the sooner I'll mozy down town while I'm in this humor."

"Mother, think how we can help the Red Cross," murmured Barbara.

Logan grunted forcibly. "Yes, my girl, but there'll be a limit. The war has got you both hipped."

Mitchell, buyer for the government, suavely welcomed Logan into his office and moved a chair for him. Mitchell was a man over forty, with stern smooth face, and shrewd cold eyes.

"Good day, Huett. You certainly have taken your time about giving me an answer."

Logan returned his greeting and drawled: "I'm never in a hurry with cattle deals."

"You'd have done well if you had been in a hurry," returned Mitchell, curtly. "The price of cattle went up. You cattlemen lost your heads. You could have sold once for forty dollars a head—then thirty-eight. When it was thirty-two I warned you—advised you to close. But you knew it all. Yesterday I bought the last of Babbit's for twenty-eight. Today I wouldn't give you twenty-five."

Huett took that for a crafty greedy bluff. Nevertheless it added to his concern. Doyle had been right—he had waited too long.

"I can sell to Kansas City buyers for more than that."

"Go out and try it. The stockyards there are flooded."

Huett got up slowly and clapped on his sombrero. "Good day, Mitchell," he said gruffly, and stamped out.

Mitchell called after him: "Your family will suffer for your pig-headedness!"

That surprising sally added anger to Huett's amazed concern. It happened to hit an extremely sore spot. In the next hour he was to learn that the market for cattle had closed, so far as it pertained to Flagg. Babbitt, Charteris, Wilson, Little, all the cattle barons confirmed this, and admitted frankly that they had gambled for too high stakes. But Huett could not be convinced. A man who had thirty thousand head of cattle to sell held a fortune

in his hands. The boom might be past, but beef and
hides represented gold more or less. He wired to Kansas
City for an offer, and then hunted up Doyle.

"Let's have a drink, old timer," suggested Al. "We
need it."

"Don't care if I do. . . . Mitchell turned me down
cold. Wouldn't give me twenty-five!"

"Logan, I don't like that girl-chasin' dude," replied the
old Arizonian, bluntly. "I just had a talk with my son
Lee. He was keen about your offer, and he can get a
dozen or more good cowboys and fifty Navvies."

"Humph! If I can't sell I can't drive."

"Sell? Of course you can sell. It's tough to come down,
but you must reckon on the large number of cattle in your
herd. The three hundred thousand head sold here since
early May averaged only twenty dollars a head. Some
went for thirty and most of them for fifteen or less."

"So I reckoned. Just wired to Kansas City."

"Logan, Lee thinks this buyer is hot after Barbara.
It's pretty well known, Lee says, among the young people. Mitchell has been playing high jinks among the
Flagg girls. But Barbara snubbed him, which made him
mad about her."

"Most young men and older ones too fall for Barbara.
She had to give up the dances because of the fights over
her."

"Shore. But this is different, Logan," rejoined Al, seriously. "In war time women are not responsible. Or else
they're inspired about somethin'. I remember during the
Civil War that officers in uniform just played hell with
women. It's worse now, for this is a hell of a war."

"But Al . . . my God, Barbara is——"

"Just like all the other young women, thrown off her
balance. My daughter is only fifteen, but she's loco. She
despises cowboys that were not accepted for draft. To

sum it up, women are not themselves nowadays. Wal, war plays hell with men, too. . . . The hunch I want to make about Barbara is this. You can't keep her out of this war relief work, but you can keep her away from Mitchell."

"I sure can, if it's necessary," returned Logan, his surprise succeeding to grimness.

"Mitchell thinks he has you in a corner now. His refusal to buy was a bluff. He might be low-down enough to work on Barbara with this cattle deal."

"Ah-huh. I wouldn't put it above him. Thanks, Al," replied Logan, soberly, and went his way.

From that hour he meant to take interest in what was going on in Flagg. But he resisted his desire to interrogate Lucinda and Barbara. Next day he received an answer to his telegram. His Kansas buyer offered ten dollars on the hoof. That did not interest Logan. But he accepted the fact of a slump in the market price of cattle and that he had lost considerably by holding on. That was the gamble of cattle-raising. The gamble still applied. He had a week or two yet that he could wait, and still make the cattle drive that fall. Meanwhile he walked the streets, talked war and cattle, read the bulletins and the papers, and had a keen eye for all forms of relief work.

One night Barbara presented herself late at the supper table, most becomingly dressed, very handsome indeed. Logan particularly noted the red spots in her white cheeks and the brilliancy of her eyes.

"Bab, you sure look good for sore eyes. . . . Where are you going all togged up?"

"I have a date with Mr. Mitchell," replied Barbara, frankly.

"Some bazaar or Red Cross affair?"

"No. He wants me to see a war picture at the theater."

"Ever go with him before?"

"No. He never asked me."

"Barbara, it's all over town that Mitchell is hot after you," said Logan, gravely.

"Oh Dad!" she cried. "I didn't think you listened to gossip."

"I didn't until lately. . . . Has Mitchell made love to you?"

"He tried. He's gallant, like a romantic soldier. Likes all the girls and they like him. But since I told him I was married he's been very—nice."

"Has he mentioned my cattle to you?"

"Yes. He intimated you were a greedy old cowman who'd hang on to his cattle and let his family starve. He predicts that cattle and hides will have no value after the war. I told him I could persuade you to sell. Indeed I was going to talk to you presently."

"My girl, had this slick hombre hinted that he'd buy my cattle if you were very—nice to him?"

"What do you mean?" asked Barbara hotly.

"Bab, I knew you were an innocent unworldly girl, but I didn't think you could be so green."

"Father! You've insulted Mr. Mitchell and now you insult me," protested Barbara, hotly.

"No, honey. And I swear I think more of you for your innocence. But don't be a little fool, Bab."

"Oh, I can't believe what you hint about Mr. Mitchell."

"Barbara, you women couldn't see the devil himself if he had on a uniform. . . . Now you take my word for it until you see for yourself. . . . Let's slip one over on this fellow, as the saying goes here. You go to the movies with him, but come home pronto. Be sweet to the lady-killer. Give him a dose of his own medicine. Tell him you are afraid your Dad will go broke hanging on to his cattle herd. Tell him if he'll only buy it you'll be very—*very* nice to him."

"Logan Huett!" burst out Lucinda, red in the face.

"Dad, I'm surprised," added Barbara, hotly.

"You'll be a damn sight more surprised if you do as I ask," declared Logan, bluntly.

"I'll do it and I'll—I'll mean it," returned Barbara, spiritedly. "I think you're suspicious, unjust, old-fashioned. I think you're ——"

"Never mind what I am," interrupted Logan, in the first stern tone he had ever used to her. "I know what you mean by being nice. You'd be yourself. Mitchell will take it another way. But after tonight you are never to go anywhere with him again or ask him in here if he calls or lay yourself open to any occasion with him alone. Do you understand me, young lady?"

"I—I couldn't help it."

"You'll obey me?"

"Yes, father."

That ended the discussion, though not the confusion and resentment Logan's women-folk felt. As for Logan he had taken pains to find out all about Mitchell and he felt not only justified, but quite elated. He attended that motion-picture, to his regret. The scenes of marching soldiers and embarking marines, the long lines of moving artillery, the endless streams of trucks, the soldiers, miserable and begrimed in muddy trenches, the tanks belching fire, and the cannons puffing smoke, the great holes blown in the ground by bursting shells— all these scenes purported to have actually been filmed at the front made Logan sick and dazed.

"So that's war?" he muttered, jostling through the noisy crowd emerging into the street. "And I sent my sons into that. . . . Good God! I reckoned they'd have a chance. Man to man, with rifles, behind trees and rocks, where the sharp eye and crack shot would prove who was best! But *that*—God Almighty—what would you call that?"

Logan went home to find Lucinda out, as usual. He lighted the lamp and building a fire in the open fireplace he composed himself to his pipe when Barbara entered quickly. Her beautiful face was white instead of pale and her great eyes appeared to flare lightnings.

"Hello, Bab. Glad you got home so early. What upset you?"

"Dad, I don't know which was the worse, Mr. Mitchell or that ghastly motion-picture," she replied, with suppressed agitation.

"Humph. That picture was pretty damn bad. It made me sick."

Barbara threw off her coat and hat, and stood in the open door of her room, facing Logan. He had never seen her as she was now, and he felt a surge of elation.

"Dad, I apologize," she said, her dark eyes on him. "You were right about Mitchell. I started out to be very sweet and nice, as I had bragged to you I'd be. . . . I'm afraid I overdid it. On the way home, just now, he— he. . . . Well, I'd have been happier and safer with Jack Campbell. . . . But I got away from your lady-killer without destroying his illusion that he'd made an easy conquest of the simple little country-jake. Which I was!"

"Ha! Ha! Well, I'll be doggoned. . . . I hope he didn't insult you, Bab. It takes me off my feed for weeks to kill a man."

"Hush, Dad. He insulted me, but he didn't guess that. I reckon he thinks it his charming, masterly way with women."

"Humph. I'm not so stuck on that— Did Mitchell mention cattle?"

"He did. He'll send for you tomorrow. And he'll buy. It's up to you now, Dad. I'll never let him come near me again."

Logan sat up, smoking, and waiting for Lucinda to come in. He would sell his thirty thousand head. Then what? Wait for the boys to come home. He would miss the brown game trails and the lovely colored woods this fall. What strange inexplicable creatures women were! But wonderful, good, faithful—most of them! And men? He was not learning so much to make him proud of his sex these days. War, greed, lust—they seemed to go together.

Next morning Logan had a stroke of good fortune in the shape of an offer from a Chicago firm, through its local buyer who had arrived in Flagg, of twenty-five dollars a head for his cattle, delivered at the company's cost at the railroad. When, therefore, Logan received a verbal message to call upon the government official he felt pretty self-assured. He would get more than twenty-five, and anything more he felt was a windfall.

Mitchell was cool, calculating, business-like when Logan entered his presence. Logan's last vestige of respect fled before this smooth mask-faced man who had only the night before insulted his daughter. Logan sensed something he had never encountered before in his deals with men, and it baffled him. But he divined what an infinitesimal figure he cut in the machinations of this suave gentleman. It affected Logan accordingly.

"Morning, Huett. I hear Blair made you an offer."

"Yep. He came across pretty good."

"Twenty-five a head and expenses of delivery. He told me Al Doyle had prompted the offer and that you'd accept."

"Wal, that was fine of Al. But I couldn't think of it."

"No, you wouldn't," retorted Mitchell tartly. "What do you want this morning?"

Logan conceived the idea that Mitchell really did not care what the cattle cost, once he made up his mind to buy. It was an unusual deduction for Logan to make, and he shrewdly thought he would test it out by asking a high figure from which he could come down considerably and still make a big deal.

"I want expense for the drive and full charge of it. Thirty-five dollars a head, paid on delivery at the railroad—in cash."

"In cash?" repeated Mitchell in amazement.

"Yes, in cash. I might have to wait on a bank draft for so much money. It'll take two weeks or more to drive. That'd give you plenty of time to get the cash."

Mitchell waved a deprecatory hand, which meant that it was no matter of importance how the debt was paid. But before he averted his eyes Logan caught a fleeting glimpse of an extraordinarily steely flash. Also the man crushed a piece of paper that he held in his hand. These evidences of feeling puzzled Logan until Mitchell turned with a light on his face. Then Logan imagined the singular reaction had to do with Barbara.

"Expenses and management of delivery o.k.," said Mitchell, blandly. "But thirty-five dollars is too high. I can't pay it."

They argued. Logan certainly felt the buyer's flinty edge, yet he did not seem to grasp sincerity. Logan distrusted his own deductions. He had made too many blunders. Here he meant to hold out a little, then capitulate for anything above twenty-five.

"Twenty-eight dollars on the hoof!" launched Mitchell, out of a doubtful sky.

Logan shook at the tigerish leap of hot blood. After all his stubborn resistance and the flex and reflex of prices to call so much was balm to his wounded pride, gratification to his greed.

"Sold!" he boomed, and extended a great horny hand. But the army official was writing and appeared not to notice the gesture.

"Logan Huett. Flagg, Arizona. Thirty thousand on the hoof. Twenty-eight dollars a head. Pay in cash on delivery. Expense of drive extra," he droned crisply, while he wrote rapidly. He shoved the paper back and his sleek head came erect with a hawk-like swiftness. "Huett, the deal is on. Drive under your personal supervision. Get a move on!"

At highnoon, five days later, Huett stood on an elevated part of the rim at the confluence of Turkey and Sycamore Canyons.

The resonant yells of cowboys floated up to his tingling ears; the weird wild cries of Indians whipped back in echo from wall to wall.

"Sight of your life, old timer!" called Doyle, hoarsely in Huett's ear.

"It is, Al, and thirty-three years' wait makes it sweeter."

Far as eye could see, across the floor of Turkey Canyon and up its six mile length, spread a living restless mosaic of cattle. The yells that pealed from cowboy to cowboy and Indian to Indian were the relays down to Huett. His answering shout was to start the drive. The cowboys had taken three days moving the cattle in Turkey over to Sycamore. Huett's arrival on the rim was the signal that Lee Doyle and Jess Smith waited for.

"Blow your horn, Gabriel," called Al, with gusto.

Huett began to draw in breath, to fill his wide lungs and expand his deep chest; and when he was full to bursting, he expelled it all in one stupendous stentorian explosion. *"Waa-hoo-ooo!"*

Abe's old hunting call, augmented to grand volume by Huett's passion, boomed across the canyon and banged back. All the hope and failure, the ambition and discouragement, the endless toil and unceasing trouble, all Huett's life as a cattleman, the terrible years at last crowned with victory, success, wealth, pealed out in that long wonderful yell. Before the echoes ceased the Indians below on each side of the herd relayed the signal one to another up the canyon until their voices were lost in the distance. The head of that magnificent herd was out of sight round the bend, probably far beyond the cabin.

Huett watched in silence. He could hear his heart beating. At last far up the canyon the mass of cattle began to move. Like a turgid current of stream, congested by tossing driftwood and roots of stumps, the movement came on down slowly through the herd until all the cattle were on the move.

"The drive's on, old timer," shouted Al, waving his sombrero. "Goodbye old bulls and long-horns—goodbye to Sycamore."

Huett lingered. The herd moved at a slow walk, gradually going faster as the forward mass broke into free action. The old cattleman waved to them a farewell to Sycamore. There was a lump in his throat. His eyes grew dim so that the red and white and black checkered carpet of cows and steers blurred in his sight. This was the most exceedingly full, the greatest moment of Logan Huett's life.

"Wal—Al, they're off," he said, in husky accents. "My cup is almost full. . . . If only my sons could see!"

They left the rim, climbed over the rough ledges to the open woods, and out to the road and the waiting car.

Huett had the driver run the six miles up to Long Valley, and stop at the forks of the road, where the branch led down to his ranch. But instead of going down to a vantage point on the wall below, Huett, this time alone, climbed the steep bluff and got out on the edge above his cabin. He gazed, and an irresistible yell escaped his panting lips.

His cabin appeared to be a little moss-roofed, green-logged island in a river of many colors and jostling waves and milling eddies. The narrow construction of the canyon here was packed solidly with wagging bawling cattle. *"Whoopee! . . . Ki-yi-ki-yi!"* rang up the piercing yells of the cowboys. Their echoes mingled with the sing-song chant of the Navajo riders. The trample of thousands of hoofs made a low subdued roar. Dust rose in puffs and patches, rolling back on the slight breeze to merge into a cloud that obscured the wide mass of the herd below.

This scene was intimate and beautiful. Huett could smell the cattle, the manure, the dust, the hoof-ploughed earth of his corn and alfalfa fields. What of his great patch of potatoes? He could see the burly bulls, the wide-horned cows, the thick-necked steers, the yearlings and heifers, crowding along the corrals, obliterating the brook, coloring the bench, surrounding the cabin, passing on under the pines. Huett thought he reveled in bliss, but there was a pang in his breast. His cattle were going. Something was passing. It seemed almost like the end of life.

Soon the vast volume of animals down around the corner in the wide stretch from wall to wall by their very momentum forced those ahead in the constricted neck of the canyon into a lumbering gallop. And then the trample grew deafening, the dust rose to hide the motley stream. Huett stood a while longer above the ranch he could not see and the cattle that thundered by under a yellow pall. Then he retraced his steps back down off the bluff and out to the road where Doyle and the driver awaited him.

"Makes me think of the old buffalo days," said Al. "Hope that run doesn't develop into a stampede."

"Nothing to—worry us," panted Huett. "They're crowding—through that narrow neck. . . . She opens out soon. Before sunset they'll be—up on the range."

They drove up to the end of Long Valley, and leaving the road, bumped and swayed over rough going through the woods until compelled to stop. Then they dismounted and walked. Two chuck-wagons, widely separated, awaited the drivers at the point where the open range sent a gray wedge into the woods. Huett and Doyle were not far ahead of the vanguard of the herd. For three hours Huett sat on a chuck-wagon seat, watching his cattle flow like a magic colorful river out of the forest and spread across the wide corner of range. Those hours might have been minutes.

Before sunset the entire herd was up on the level and halted for the night. Cowboys came swinging in on dust-caked horses. Soon Lee, Bill, Jack Ray, Con Sullivan, and other drivers rode up to pay their happy respects to the cattleman. They were all as black as the nigger Johnson, but not so shiny of face.

"Mr. Huett—Dad," called Lee, cheerfully, as with a scarf he wiped his begrimed face to show it red and wet, "it was easy as duck-soup."

"Wal, old timer," drawled Bill Smith, with the dust rolling off him in little streams, "we shore piled along high, wide, and handsome."

"Mister Huett, it waz graa-ndd," boomed the Irishman.

Johnson's eyes rolled to show their contrasting whites. "Boss, we done it. Yas suh, we sho did."

"From now on," said Jack Ray, "it'll be sing an' roll on, little dogies."

When Huett got a chance he shouted: "I'd rather be a cowboy than President!"

"Come an' git it before I pitch it out!" yelled the cook.

During the drive Logan went three times from Flagg to cheer the boys and feed his insatiate love of all which pertained to cattle. As luck would have it the good fall weather persisted and on the afternoon of the tenth day the herd rolled tired and slow but in fine condition into the railroad pastures. Lee Doyle and Bill Smith, astride their horses, one on each side of the gate, counted the cattle. Lee gave the number to the thirty-one thousand and sixty odd.

A counter for Mitchell did not attend, much to Huett's dissatisfaction. The erstwhile suave government buyer struck Huett as being sore under the collar. Barbara, upon being questioned, made the reason perfectly clear to Huett: the man, so far as women were concerned, was brazen, unscrupulous, and extraordinarily vain.

Five hundred and more cattle cars cluttered up the side tracks and yards of the Santa Fé. For the first several days Mitchell loaded and shipped an average of fifteen hundred head every twenty-four hours. After that, with cowboys and railroad men working in double shifts, he shipped three train-loads every day until the great herd was gone. At his office that night he informed the waiting cowboys and Indians that he would pay off next morning. For some reason or other he was inaccessible to Huett.

Sleep did not soon visit Huett's eyelids that night.

The November wind sang paeans under the eaves. And the morning sunlight danced for the rancher's magnifying eyes. He was prodigal in promises to his wife and daughter. And he went down street with boots ringing on the frosty sidewalks. Mitchell, urging press of settling his affairs, put him off until two o'clock.

It was a Saturday afternoon—a half holiday for the bank. Huett had hoped to bank his cash upon receipt of it. Nevertheless nothing could concern him this day. On the sunny sidewalk he waited the government man's pleasure. Holbert and Doyle were with him, loyal, proud, excited. They both took some share of credit for Huett's dramatic finish with the cattle.

"Al, did I ever tell you about Abe's shooting at the training camp?" asked Logan, fully aware of other listeners.

"Not that I recollect," replied Al.

"Wal, it was sure great. . . . The first day when Abe was marched out on the shooting range with a lot of green recruits a red-headed cuss of a sergeant shoved Abe up to the mark, and handed him a thirty government rifle: 'Hey, long legs, do you know one end of this from the other?' . . . Abe said he reckoned he did. 'All right, then take your turn. Shoot,' ordered the drill sergeant. 'What at?' asked Abe. 'At the target, you dumb head!' . . . Then Abe saw a lot of white targets with black center and rings. Fifty yards, a hundred, two hundred, and so on up to a thousand. Abe asked which one he should shoot at. 'Rooky, look here. *Can* you shoot?' yelled the sergeant and Abe modestly replied that he reckoned he could not shoot very well. 'But I wouldn't want to shoot at this first target,' added Abe. . . . Then he threw up the rifle. Gosh! It always was wonderful to see Abe get set and aim. When he was a little boy he took to guns. . . . Well, Abe took five shots at the thousand yard target, off hand. The flag man waved back three bull's eyes and two shots inside the first circle. . . . Ha! That red-headed sergeant got red in the face. 'Hell, you said you couldn't shoot.' And Abe kind of kidded him cool and easy: 'Wal, my ole man says I can't.' "

Mitchell finally called Huett into his office. Another official in khaki sat on the other side of a table containing a few papers and two large neatly wrapped packages, identical in size and appearance.

"Huett, my man's count was thirty thousand nine hundred," began Mitchell, cold of voice and mien.

"All right. That's near enough."

"Sign here," went on the buyer, indicating a dotted line on an official looking document. Huett bent over the table, and taking the proffered pen wrote his name with a fine flourish. "Witness his signature, Lieutenant."

When the official had done this Mitchell folded the document and put it in his pocket. Then he handed one of the packages to Huett.

"Here's your money," he said, brusquely, and shoved it into Huett's hands as if it burned him. "I don't need to tell an old Westerner like you that the town's full of bums, redskins, greasers. . . . Good day."

Huett found himself out in the street, light-headed, with a heavy compellingly-pregnant parcel under his arm.

"Let's have a drink," he said, gayly to Holbert and Doyle.

They went into the corner saloon and sat at a table. Huett placed his parcel between his knees out of sight. They drank. Huett would not hear of his friends' returning the compliment—not on that day of days. Then he ordered another drink. Scarcely had they set down their glasses when Mitchell, accompanied by a stranger in civilian garb, entered the saloon. Mitchell espied Huett and his friends, and with a direct gesture and an elated laugh he drew the attention of his companions to them. They turned abruptly on their heels and went out.

"Them Eastern army men are queer hombres," remarked Holbert.

"Wal, if you ask me," drawled the shrewd Doyle, "that swelled-up galoot got took in by a plain Westerner and snubbed by his daughter."

"Let's have another drink," said Huett, chuckling with a deep grin.

Holbert and Doyle were the first to make a move. One on each side of Huett they steered him through the crowd. The short fall day had almost closed. Cold wind slipped down from the dark peaks and the dust swirled. Huett's comrades made sure no one was following them. They left him at the gate.

"Wal, old timer, cache that little windfall tonight and sleep with one eye open," advised Doyle.

"An' have yore guns layin' around," added Holbert. "Some hombre might have seen you comin' out of that office."

Logan went in and locked the door. The sitting room was cheerful with lighted lamp and fire. A smell of ham and coffee was wafted in from the kitchen. Lucinda appeared wiping her hands on her apron and Barbara ran from her room.

"Wal, Babs, have you seen your soldier admirer today?" asked Logan, cheerily. as he laid the parcel on the table.

"Have I? Dad, not half an hour ago he sneered at me and laughed in my face. I didn't know what to make of it."

"Luce, pull down the blinds—and shut the kitchen door. . . . I've something to show you."

His big hands shook as he stripped the tight rubber bands from the heavy parcel. "Thirty thousand nine hundred at twenty-eight!" he whispered tensely.

"Oh Dad—hurry. . . . I feel. . . ."

Logan rasped the stiff paper covers flat. A neat pile of cut newspaper and tin foil pieces spread out over the table.

Chapter Sixteen

IT WAS dusk when Huett stamped out of the cottage, deaf to Lucinda's entreaties and Barbara's cries, his big fist tight about a ragged wad of the bogus paper money, his mind blocked at what he thought could be only a stupendous joke.

Yet his breast seemed to be crushed with a paralyzing fear.

The night watchman was lighting the street lamps. Huett strode on faster. He found Mitchell's office empty and vacated. Then he remembered that the cattle-buyer and his associate in the saloon had been carrying hand baggage. They were leaving Flagg. Then on the moment he heard a distant shrill whistle of the East-bound train. Whereupon Huett, who had not run for years, broke into a dash for the station. He arrived there strangled for breath, his great chest heaving like a bellows. In the waiting room he found a woman at the ticket-window. He stamped through to the platform.

The usual loungers were there, and hurrying station-men, and waiting passengers. Down the railroad track shone the headlight of the train entering Flagg. Huett rushed on. At last, under one of the yellow street-lamps, he espied Mitchell, the lieutenant who had been in the office, and two other men, and several young women. Huett broke into the circle to confront Mitchell.

"You—you. . . . What do you mean?" exploded Huett, in a husky almost incoherent voice, and he extended the big fist still clutching the cut papers.

"Hello, Huett," replied the government man, in cool irritation. "No time for you. I'm saying goodbye to friends."

"By God—you've time—for me! . . . That package

you—gave me. . . . Cut newspaper and tin foil. . . . *Not money!* . . . Damn poor joke."

"Man, you must be drunk," flashed Mitchell, his piercing eyes like cold steel.

"Drunk? . . . Hellsfire!" thundered Huett. "You gave me paper—instead of cash. . . . Look!"

Huett opened his huge fist to disclose pieces of shiny tin foil and crumpled cuts of paper. Some of them fell to the platform.

"You're either drunk or crazy," replied Mitchell, sharply. "I paid you in cash. I have your receipt. Lieutenant Caddell witnessed your signature. We warned you to be careful with all that cash. But you didn't heed. We saw you drinking in that dive."

Huett stood transfixed and mute, his spread hand still outheld, the fingers shaking, while Mitchell looked to his Lieutenant for confirmation of his claims.

"That's right, Huett," declared Mitchell's companion, crisply. "I saw Mr. Mitchell pay you cash. I saw you take the money and sign the receipt, and I witnessed it. Later I understand you were drinking with your cronies in the worst joint in town. But what happened to you after you left our office with the money is no concern of ours. That's all."

"Mistake—wrong package!" gasped Huett, suffocatingly.

Caddell made a gesture of scornful dismissal. Mitchell turned to the black-eyed staring girl who held his arm. The train rumbled into the station, with puffing engine and grinding wheels. Baggage and mail-cars passed on down the platform. Then with a jerk the train stopped.

Huett's mind cleared. A terrible flash of truth swept away the fog of stupefaction. This man had cheated him.

Like an imbecile he had walked into a hellishly clever trap inspired by his demand for payment in cash.

This swift deduction gave way to a slow metamorphosis in Huett's feeling. Violent release of dammed-up blood forced spasmodic expansion and movement of muscles. As he stood there, with that great hand outstretched, the quivering calloused fingers like a claw, he felt the rise of a maelstrom of fury. In all his life Huett had never been subjected to a full storm of passion. It transformed him. An expulsion of breath whistled through his teeth. His sight filmed with a tinge of red, coloring the pretty faces of the young women, the paling visage of Caddell, and the averted one of Mitchell. Disjointed thoughts blocked Huett's mind . . . to rend—to beat down these baffling foes—to kill—to tear from them his money, which surely they had.

He shut that spread hand into a ponderous fist. His bellow brought Mitchell around just in time to meet a blow like that from a battering-ram. Blood squirted as Mitchell went down, dragging two of the screaming girls with him. Caddell shouted lustily for help, and leaped to avoid Huett's fist. The other two men seized Huett from behind. He threw them sprawling and lunged upon the prostrate Mitchell, to half strip him of clothing. Then a crowd of men dragged Huett off his victim, back from the platform to the road. At length Huett stopped surging like a lassoed bull, and stood quiet in the grip of many hands, to see Mitchell carried on the train and his baggage thrown on after him. Caddell stood on the car-step, trying to rid himself of the clinging hysterical young women. The train started with a jerk, gathered momentum and passed on out of the station. Then the excitement of the crowd centered upon Huett.

"Let go of me," he rumbled.

"All right, men," called the sheriff. "Huett, you don't

'pear to be drunk. What'n hell was the matter? Who was
you tryin' to kill? I didn't get there in time to see."

"Mitchell, the government cattle-buyer. I sold him
thirty thousand and nine hundred head. . . . He was
to pay me in cash. . . . Gave me a package. Got my receipt. . . . I didn't open that package at once. Had some
drinks with Doyle and Holbert. . . . When I got home
—I opened it—found I'd been swindled. . . . My cash
was cut newspaper and tin foil!"

"For cripe's sake!" ejaculated the sheriff, while the
circle of men gave vent to like exclamations. "Huett,
are you out of your haid?"

"I was there, for a little . . . I'd have killed him.
Glad you pulled me off."

"You look queer, but I guess you're not loco. Huett,
can you prove what you say? I'll wire Slocum at Holbrook and have him stop that train an' arrest Mitchell.
We mustn't let him get out of the State."

"Prove it?" labored Huett, ponderingly. "I've that
package—and all the bogus money—except the handful
I grabbed."

"But somebody else who was on to this cash pay-off
might have switched packages on you. . . . Let's go see
Mr. Little. This deal has a damn queer look, but it's
too big for me to buck alone."

Huett passed through the murmuring crowd with the
sheriff and up town toward where the lawyer lived.
They found him at supper. This time Huett told the
story of the hoax more lucidly and in detail. Little's
black eyes snapped.

"Wire Holbrook to stop that train and hold both
men," he ordered.

"I'll do that pronto," replied the sheriff and hurried
away.

"Huett, this story of yours confirms suspicions I got

today," went on the lawyer. "Mitchell has been buying horses and cattle for the government. Charteris, who did some of his banking, told me Mitchell paid so much for stock and padded his report to the government. If we can stop him we'll sure make him sweat. But this is war time, Huett, rampant with greed, graft, crookedness. Mitchell has pulled a slick one on you. Good God, man, why did you demand cash?"

"I didn't want to wait for my money. Charteris said a government draft would be good, but there wasn't that much cash in his bank. He'd have to wait for the money."

"Eight hundred and sixty-five thousand dollars! Whew! A fortune! Huett I'm damned sorry, while I could cuss you for being such a fool. Certainly we ought to get that money. The case is flagrant enough. But these times! . . . Your drinking with Al and Holbert would hold against you. It's serious. . . . Go home now. Don't make the mistake of drinking any more. If we can get Mitchell back here tomorrow, we want you sober."

Huett went home in a daze. Little's evident concern put him right back where he had been before he was sure of the trick. But his consciousness would not harbor any doubt of his securing payment for his cattle. He told Lucinda and Barbara what had transpired at the railroad station. Lucinda wept. "I never—thought—we'd get all—that money," she said. But Barbara reacted differently. "You bet your life we'll get it," she cried, hotly, and flared into a passionate denunciation of Mitchell.

Huett paced the floor for hours, went out into the night to plod up and down the walk, and when at last he went to bed, it was not to sleep. Morning came, cold and drab, with wind moaning in the trees presaging winter. Huett built the fires. The women arose to get breakfast. He forced down a little food and a drink of coffee, then went down town.

That day Huett was to learn that the Holbrook officers had flagged the train designated, but Mitchell could not be found aboard. Lawyer Little took this news with grave disquiet.

"Why did you let the man get on that train?" he demanded.

"Hell! I knocked him flat. I had his clothes half torn off when they dragged me away. If I'd been packing a gun I'd have shot him. And that'd have been better."

"Yes, it would. The man's a crook and if we had him here, dead or alive, we could prove it. . . . Now we'll have to resort to the slow offices of the law."

Impatient days and weeks of waiting destined Huett to realize the law's delay. But Mr. Little was nothing if not energetic and persistent in his efforts to get some court action. In this he labored in vain, so far as Flagg was concerned. Then he went to Prescott. the capital, in Huett's interest, and finally got the State congressman at Washington interested in the case.

Meanwhile Flagg settled down and holed-in, as the old timers called it, to a real Arizona winter at high altitude. Huett spent most of his daylight hours chopping wood and the rest sitting before a warm fire. He received some meager comfort out of this, as it brought back so much of his life that had been spent gazing into the heart of a log fire. When he spread his broad hands to the heat something soothing and quieting happened to him. But he never enjoyed his strong-smelling black pipe after this loss, and finally ceased smoking altogether.

The war went on, now of secondary interest to Huett. He had three sons at the front and that was doing more than his share toward whipping Germany. His whole thought was taken up by this treachery of the government cattle-buyer and the recovery of his money. When Barbara received a letter—and she haunted the post-office—Huett would lift out of his gloom to listen to her reading it. This letter would be from Abe and it would be most exasperatingly censored and cut. Huett always cursed at this. "Since I've got three boys over there why the hell can't I hear what they're doing? I declare I'm getting queer notions about this government."

Lucinda's letters would be from George and Grant, and they came regularly once or twice a month. If it were needed, those epistles always spurred Huett's women folk to greater efforts in the war relief work. They were not needed to acquaint Lucinda and Barbara with the havoc the war was doing to American boys. Lucinda grew somber and calm. Barbara became a pale ghost of her old self, with haunted eyes and nerves at high tension.

Huett did not give up. All this might have made more impression upon him but for his obsession with what the government owed him. Thus far in his life of vicissitudes he had not yet been beaten down by adversity. He kept waiting, hoping, fighting on.

Late in January his lawyer received an important letter from Washington. Through the Arizona congressman the matter of a purchase of one Logan Huett's cattle had been thoroughly investigated. The sum of money for cattle had been paid in cash by the government buyer, Mitchell, and that transfer of cash, and the signature of the seller, had been witnessed by Lieutenant Caddell. The receipt was in the government's hands, along with information that said Logan Huett was addicted to the bottle and questionably associated.

"I feared it," declared Little, hoarsely, white of face. "They've got us nailed. Only one chance in a million, and that is to carry the case to Washington. But I can't give up my work here. And, Logan, you can't afford a trial there. With the U. S. government at war! My God! It'd be worse than folly."

"All the same, I'll go," declared Huett, and bidding Little write out all suggestions as to how he should proceed, he went home to tell Lucinda and Barbara. His wife thought it a forlorn hope. "If we were only back at Sycamore!" she exclaimed. But Barbara was keen to have him go and begged to be taken along. "Mother, you can forward Abe's letters. Oh, Dad, take me!" she cried.

"No, I reckon you'd better stay here with Maw," replied Huett, ponderingly.

"Barbara, have you forgotten that you're with child?" queried Lucinda, in amazement.

"Oh! I had forgotten," replied Barbara, her white face flaming scarlet. "I'm ashamed . . . this war has almost driven me mad."

So it came about that Logan Huett went to Washington, D. C.

As a young man Huett had been to Chicago, and at that period he had lived in Kansas City. But Washington was a magnificent city, the nation's capital, and at this time of the war it struck Huett as being bedlam.

He forgot what he had come for and when he remembered he realized sickeningly that his hope was no more than a drop of rain in a storm. The city was thronged with civilians, soldiers, and strangers of many nations. A ceaseless stream of automobiles passed up and down the streets. Huett came to a dozen huge hotels before he found one that he thought of entering. Having secured a room, he went out again, and before he knew what was happening he had been shoved aboard a sight-seeing bus.

During that ride Huett's love and pride of country welled up again. The impressive government buildings, the Capitol, the White House, the Soldier's Monument filled him with awe and delight. His sons were fighting for what they represented.

Once more on his feet in the crowds Huett came down to earth. Accosted by beggars, hawk-eyed men, and suave strangers who offered to pilot him around, Huett came to see with chagrin that he was as much of a tenderfoot as any one of them would have been in his country. Then the loss of his watch awakened him to another aspect of the great city. He buttoned his wallet inside his vest and resolved to have his eyes about him.

About midafternoon Huett found the Army Building. It was immense. Men in uniform and civilian dress buzzed in and out like bees. Cars whizzed by. Overhead, airplanes droned about like monstrous bees. Despite Huett's grim strength, he had his first glimmering of the futility of his errand there. Uniformed attendants listened to him courteously and put him off with excuses. At length he was forced to leave the building without having seen a single army official.

Outside, in the rush of the closing hour, the traffic astonished and alienated Huett. A city was no place for him. And it seemed to him that across a dirty snow-piled park he passed there came a vision of his clean sweet silent Arizona forest. A sick longing such as he had never before experienced overwhelmed him. What was he doing there, just a miserable outsider among this swarm of grabbing humanity? It was long after dark when Huett, after getting lost twice, found his hotel. The hard pavements made his legs weak, he found his nostrils clogged with dirt, and he marveled that people could breathe and live in such an atmosphere. Night was as hideous to him as day had been: the roar of automobiles and electric cars murdered sleep.

For days Huett haunted the Army Building. He had patience and stubbornness. He resented being taken for a crank, for an old geezer from the West, for a lunatic who raved about thirty thousand head of cattle. But such was Huett's persistence that at last he was ushered through one office after another into the presence of some army official connected with the commissary department.

"My name is Logan Huett," replied Huett, in answer to a curt query as to what was his business. "I'm a cattleman from Flagg, Arizona. I sold thirty thousand head of cattle to your buyer, named Mitchell. He cheated me out of the money."

"How did he cheat you?" asked the official.

"I asked for cash. He got me to sign the receipt, had it witnessed by his man Caddell, then gave me a package of bogus money."

"Well, Mr. Huett, I can do nothing for you. It will be necessary for you to take court action against the government and prove your claim. Good day, sir."

Huett went out, a slow fire of wrath burning deep within him. He began to appreciate what a wall obstructed him in his just hopes and demands. Then in reading over Little's instructions he found that he had forgotten an important one—to call on the congressman from Arizona. At once Huett set out upon that mission. He was told that Senator Spellman had left the city, during the adjournment of Congress, and would not be back for some weeks.

Thus baffled at every turn Huett set out to put his case in the hands of a lawyer. Little's advice in this regard was to engage some reliable lawyer recommended by Spellman. Upon inquiry Huett discovered that Washington was full of lawyers of every degree. He took the bull by the horns, making a blind choice of counsel.

A retainer's fee of five thousand dollars was asked. Huett could not pay that, unless his money was recovered. The deal was compromised on half that sum. Huett left the office of the high-sounding firm, Highgate and Stanfield, cheered by a promise to recover his money soon, and worried over the fact that his bank account in Flagg had dwindled to less than two thousand dollars.

Then began a test of Huett's patience. He had to wait. And while waiting he read the war news, walked the streets, sat on park benches. Only his dogged indomitable spirit sustained him.

Huett received disturbing letters from Lucinda and Barbara. His wife begged him to come home without giving any reason, and Barbara wrote pitifully that they had not had any word from the boys in over a month.

Spring came early in Washington, D. C. Huett sat on a park bench, listening to the sparrows, feeling the welcome warmth of the sun, watching the slow green tinge the grass and trees.

Every day he called at his lawyer's office to inquire if his suit had begun. The last time he distinctly heard himself announced as "that farmer from Arizona," and when an answer was brought to him by the girl that his suit would be delayed until September, then Huett became a victim of helpless rage and bewilderment. September! If he stayed in Washington that long he would go crazy. Still—his money—his fortune—payment for his thirty thousand cattle and his years of toil—he could not abandon that.

Then Senator Spellman returned. He received Huett warmly. He was Western; he had been a cattleman himself; he heard Huett's long story with strong feeling, at the conclusion of which he emitted some genuine Arizona range profanity.

"Huett, I regret to say your case is hopeless. Absolutely hopeless," he went on. "Little should have made that clear to you. He has not the slightest doubt that you have been robbed. Bilked! . . . Nor have I. The whole country is rampant with graft and crooked work. Your case is one in a thousand. According to these buyers you signed for the cash. You received it, and were seen drinking in an Arizona joint. You'd stand no chance in court."

"I've started a suit already," replied Huett, heavily. "Paid two thousand five hundred as a fee."

"My word! Huett, you sure are a Western lamb among Eastern wolves. Who gipped you out of that much money?"

"Gipped?"

"Yes. You're a sucker. Washington is full of shyster lawyers. It's a hundred to one you fell into the hands of some of them. Who?"

"Highgate and Stanfield. Here's their card. One of them—I don't know which—guaranteed recovery of my money. I've been waiting weeks. Yesterday I was told the suit had been delayed until September."

"Humph," grunted the Senator, and taking the card he resorted to the telephone. He called one number after another. Huett did not listen. He was too sick and dazed to listen. Finally Senator Spellman hung up the receiver and took up his cigar.

"That firm is not rated among Washington's reliable lawyers. And no suit has been registered under your name. You've been duped again."

"Ahuh. . . . I'd begun to feel a hunch."

"Huett, this is a hell of a break. It'd kill most men. But you're a Westerner. One of Arizona's old hard pioneers! It won't kill you. It's just another knock—the toughest of your life, sure. But it involves only loss of cattle. That's nothing to an Arizona range man. Go back to your range and your cows. Cattle prices will climb sky-high. A few good seasons of rain and grass—and you're jake, old timer!"

After the blow fell Huett felt calm and strange. "Luce was right," he soliloquized, as he sat down on a park bench. "We're ruined."

"Boss, could you stake me to a nickel?" came in an oily voice from a man beside him. Huett turned to see a ragged tramp sitting there. His hard blue eyes expressed a humorous curiosity.

"Nickel? How much's that?" asked Huett, fingering in his vest pocket.

"Five cents. But if you don't happen to have it I'll take a dime."

"Two-bits. Smallest I've got, friend," replied Huett, handing the beggar a quarter.

"Thanks. Two-bits, eh? . . . Then you're from the West?" he returned, curiously.

"Arizona."

"You're kinder than you look, mister. Are you sick or in trouble?"

"Wal, so help me Gawd!" exclaimed Huett. "Somebody down here has seen that at last! . . . Here's a dollar, my friend. If you come to Arizona I'll give you a job."

"I'll bet you would at that. . . . What's ailing you, Mister?"

But Logan had left.

He went back to his hotel, beginning a desperate fight against his stubborn bulldog desire to stay in Washington and never give up his demand for that money owed him. There was a telegram on the floor of his room just inside the door. He took it to the window.

the better to see, and tore it open. The message was
from Flagg and read:

"George and Grant killed in action Abe missing.
                                    Lucinda."

Huett watched the dark hours pale and the dawn
break with soft rosy grayness behind the grand spire of
the Soldier's Monument.

He hated the light of day. Beaten down, crushed by
an unexpected blow that dwarfed the sum of all his
life's calamities, he had paced the endless black hours
away at last to sink on a park bench, realizing that as he
had forsaken God in his wild youth, now God had forsaken him in his troubled age.

The flush of sunrise, clear and bright with spring
radiance, grew like the illumination of his mind.

In the very beginning of that Western range career
he had started with a driving passion, a single selfish
purpose to which all else was subservient. He had sacrificed his wife, his sons, and Barbara. This tragedy, this
devastation of his life in one crushing blow must have
been just punishment, just retribution. He confessed
it with anguish, and an exceeding bitterness flooded his
soul.

That noble spire of stone, sunrise-flushed, rising sheer
against the rosy sky, an imperishable monument of honor
to a nation's dead—how empty and futile its meaning
to Logan Huett in that hour! It was a symbol of the
great government. Of the man of zealots, of patriots like
himself, blinded by the leaders of powerful cliques and
parties, who played politics as Westerners played poker,
who fostered war because their war lords wanted war.
Huett saw that the men who furnished the money to
waste and the young men for gun-fodder were patriotic

fools like himself. These boys had flashed up like fire, virile, trenchant, wonderful, imbued with the glory of fighting for their country. They had been misled. War in modern times held no glory for the boys who faced the firing line.

All these weeks in Washington, watching, listening, reading, had been working imperceptibly on Huett's mind, summing up incredible and bewildering changes in his thoughts that did not clarify until this rending bolt of death.

His strong heart broke.

The scene before his eyes strangely altered. The lofty shiny shaft, the faint tinge of foliage, the wide park and the gleam of water, the early cats and pedestrians that had begun to appear—these all faded. And in their place shone a stone-walled pine-rimmed canyon, with winding ribbon of stream and herds of browsing cattle, and a gray moss-roofed log cabin nestling on the wooded bench, all dim and unreal like the remembered scenes of a dream.

Nevertheless it was home. And his pang of agony was appalling. He should have lived for his family and not for cattle. His great ambition had been a blunder. His greed had broken him. He had been clubbed down in the prime of his marvelous physical manhood. And as his vision sharpened he saw three dirty-faced ragged little boys playing beside the brook. And he cried out in his soul: Oh my sons, my sons! Would God I had died for you! Oh, my sons, my sons!

Huett had telegraphed his wife the day he would arrive in Flagg, which no doubt accounted for his being met at the train by Al Doyle, Holbert, Hardy, and other friends. But Lucinda did not come. No observer could have discerned from their greetings that they thought the world had come to an end for Logan Huett. Arizonians took hard knocks as incidents of range experience. They did not mention the loss of Huett's three sons.

"Old timer, how'd you make out in Washington?" asked Al, hopefully.

"No good, Al," replied Huett, wearily. "Senator Spellman said my case against the government was useless. When I signed that receipt and took that package I ruined myself. . . . Some shyster lawyer down there said he could recover my money, and he fleeced me out of twenty-five hundred."

"By God, Logan, I was agin thet trip East," said Holbert glumly.

"It's over—and I'm done," said Logan, aware of their close scrutiny of his face.

"Wal, you reckon so now," returned Doyle, sagely wagging his gray head, "but a cowman who has bucked the Tonto for thirty years gets habits that can't be changed over night."

"How are my women folk?" asked Huett.

"Lucinda shows surprisin' strength. She must have known it was comin'. But I heah Barbara took it bad."

"Aghh!" grunted Huett, clearing his throat, and moved to leave the platform. Doyle and Holbert walked up street with him.

"Logan, what you reckon about this?" queried Holbert. "None of us, an' shore not one of the cattle buyers, had the prices of beef on the hoof figgered. Cattle are up to forty dollars a haid, an' goin' up."

"What did I say?" exclaimed Huett, stung out of his apathy. "*I* had it figured. I wanted to hold on for another year. My Gawd, if I only had!"

"Too late. But heah's somethin'. Cattle prices will **not** go down for years."

"Ha! Too late for me, in more ways than one."

"Aw no! Why Logan, you're far younger'n me, an'
I'm hangin' on," said Holbert, earnestly. "You know the
cattle game. Twenty-five years ago I was rich. Then I
was poor for twenty years. Now with these high prices an'
a growin' herd I'm sittin' pretty."

"*Quien sabe*, Logan," added Al. "You can never tell.
But I reckon how cattle gossip makes you sick. So we'll
cut it."

"Thanks, Al. There are some words I never want to
hear again, so long as I live. They are cattle, money,
government, war."

"Wal then, you'll have to get back into the woods
again. For this burg is full of war news. It's been hard
hit, Logan. . . . Last Tonto cowboy to go was Jack
Campbell. He crawled up on a nest-hole of machine-
guns, an' threw a bomb in on the Boches, just as they
riddled him. That was Jack's finish. We're all forgettin'
what once was his bad name."

"Well we may!" sighed Huett.

At the gate of Huett's yard Al and Holbert bade him
good day and hurried away. Logan went in slowly, like
a man walking a narrow log over a deep gulch, and who
dreaded the opposite side. He mounted the porch, and
as he hesitated, wiping his clammy face, the door opened
to disclose Lucinda.

"*Luce!*" he cried, in tremendous relief and gladness
that she did not look as he expected. And he staggered
in, dropping his bag to reach for her. Lucinda closed
the door and then took him in her arms.

"Poor old darling Logan!" she murmured, and held
him close and kissed him and wept over him.

"Wife," he replied, huskily, as he held her away to
gaze into her face. It was like marble, thinner, showing
traces of havoc, sad and marvelously strong. Huett found

home, love, understanding, mother, in her deep dark eyes. "I—I don't know just how I expected to see you, but not like this."

"Logan dear, I always knew. It was a relief of torture when the news came. . . . No other word about Abe. Missing. That was all."

"Missing! What does it mean?"

"Almost hopeless. They say it means a soldier might be blown to bits, or buried in a trench, or lost in a river."

"Ah! . . . No chance of having been made prisoner?"

"In that case we'd have known long since."

"Where's Barbara?—Al said it went bad with her."

"Wait dear, a little. . . . It's hard to tell."

Logan sat down heavily and averted his eyes from Lucinda's intense and pitiful gaze. She came close and pressed his head against her. "I'm so glad you're back," she said. "There is something serious to talk over. . . . Would you take us back to Sycamore?"

A keen blade could not have made Logan wince more violently. How terribly the question hurt! But Logan let it sink in before he asked her why.

"There are a number of reasons. We can earn our living there. We'll be away from this hot-pressed war news day and night. . . . Back in our quiet canyon! . . . I can garden again. And you can farm. It's not so cold down there. We nearly froze here. . . . I think Barbara might get better there. And the baby would thrive."

"Baby!"

"Yes. Barbara's baby. A lovely boy like Abe. But not so dark and he has Barbara's eyes."

"Ah. I forgot about Bab. I forgot. . . . Abe's boy! Well, now, isn't that just fine? . . . Luce, it makes me a grandfather."

"Logan, I'm afraid it was high time. . . . Will you take us back?"

"Sure I will, Lucinda," returned Huett, his mind halting ponderingly at practical ideas. "It's a good idea. We got to stay somewhere. . . . Mebbe it wouldn't hurt for long—going back to Sycamore. . . . Let's see. Hardy has my wagon. My horses are running in Doyle's pasture. We can pack the stuff here that's ours. And buy what we need along with supplies. . . . *Supplies!* My Gawd, what does that make you think of, Luce? . . . How about money?"

"I have over a thousand of what you left me."

Huett took out his check book and looked at his balance. "I've about the same. Ha! That's a fortune for us homesteaders. When shall we ———"

A piercingly-sweet, droning little song interrupted Huett.

"Is that—the new baby?" he whispered, with a thrill.

"No, dear. That is Barbara. She sings a good deal of the time. . . . You see—*she has lost her mind!*"

Chapter Seventeen

LUCINDA was no less shocked at Logan's aberration of mind than at his changed appearance. He appeared a ghost of his old stalwart virile giant self. And he forgot even the errands she sent him on. When he came home from down town she smelled liquor on his breath. She realized then in deep alarm that Logan had cracked. All his life he had leaned too far over on one side; now in this major catastrophe of his life he had toppled over the other way to collapse.

She had divined something of this upon his return and had at once appealed to him to take her and Barbara back to Sycamore. If anything could save Logan it was action—something to do with his hands—some labors to draw his mind back to the old channels of habit. Before this blow, despite his sixty years, he had been at the peak of a magnificent physical life. If he stayed in Flagg, to idle away the hours in saloons and on corners, to sit blankly staring at nothing, he would not live out the year.

When the days had passed into weeks without his having done anything in regard to their return to Sycamore she resolved to make the arrangements herself. She got Hardy to have a look at the big wagon, to grease the axles, and repair the harness; and she hired a negro to drive in the team and put them on grain.

Then she set about the dubious task of supplies and utensils. Al Doyle, who was as keen as Lucinda to get Logan out in the open again, declared vehemently: "There won't be one single damn thing left on that ranch. Logan forgot to leave a man on the place. All the tools, and furniture left in the cabin, will be gone. Stole!"

"Oh dear me! Al, it's beginning to pioneer all over again!"

"It shore is. But that's good, Lucinda, 'cause it'll raise Logan out of this bog he's in. . . . I advise you to take two wagonloads. I'll borrow one for you, and hire a driver, an' I'll buy all the necessary tools, an' have them packed. The grub supply is easy to figure out. We'll put our heads together on the cabin an' the needs of you women folk. . . . Don't worry Lucinda. It'll all be jake. The thing to do is to be arustlin'."

Only once did Lucinda's heart faint within her, and that was when she came home to find Logan and Barbara in the sitting room, with little Abe crawling half naked and dirty around the floor. Logan was trying again to get some coherent response from Barbara. And she sat hunched in a chair, her great dark eyes the windows of a clouded mind. They struck terribly at Lucinda's heart.

She could not endure to stay there on the moment, so she went into the kitchen, where she grappled with fear and doubt. Was she mad to take these two broken wrecks back to the wilderness? Possible illness, accident, loneliness, Barbara's obsession to wander around, would be infinitely more difficult to combat down in the canyon than in town. Here she could call in women neighbors or the doctor. Despite the strong appeal of reason supporting her fears, she succumbed to her first intuition. If there were any hopes left for Barbara and Logan, not to say bringing up the child, they might rise down in Sycamore Canyon. The labor did not appall Lucinda. Well she knew that upon the pioneer wife and mother fell the greater burdens. A strange subtle voice cried down her misgivings. And with resurging heart she plunged into the immediate tasks of getting ready.

They left Flagg with two wagons next morning before sunrise. Only faithful old Al Doyle saw them off.

His last words were—and they were the last they ever heard him speak—"Wal, old timer, it's the long road again an' the canyon in the woods. That's good. Adios!"

Lucinda rode on the driver's seat with Logan. Barbara and the boy had a little place behind, under the canvas. Evidently the movement, the grind of wheels and clip-clop of heavy hoofs had excited Barbara, who knelt on the hay to peer out with strained eyes no mortal could have read. The second wagon, driven by the negro, contained the farm tools, furniture, and utensils.

After a while Lucinda's eyes cleared so that she could see. She was glad to get out of Flagg. The black stumps, the gray flats, the green lines of pines and blue bluffs in the distance seemed to welcome her. They had not quite reached the timber belt six miles from town when Lucinda sustained a thrilling relief and joy in Logan's response to the winding road, the reins once more in his hands, the team of big horses, the rolling wheels and the beckoning range. These had been so great a part of his life that only insanity or paralysis or death could have wholly eradicated them. They began to call upon old associations. Lucinda's loving divination had been Godsent. Logan's heart and spirit had been broken, and the splendid rush of his life at maturity had been stemmed, stagnated, sunk in the sands of grief and hopelessness. Her great task was to keep him physically busy until this ghastly climax of tragedy wore into the past. Life held strange recompense for the plodder.

Logan spoke at intervals, especially when they passed old camp-sites, now homesteads and ranches. Cedar Ridge, Turkey Flat, Rock Waterhole still existed in their pristine loneliness. Logan halted at the Waterhole for lunch and to rest the horses. Then he drove on till sunset, to stop at a small brook which drained into Mormon Lake.

They camped. The negro turned out to be a helpful fellow, and between him and Logan, with Lucinda cooking, they soon had camp made and supper ready. Barbara walked around, her staring dark eyes as groping as her actions. She ate, fed the boy, and helped Lucinda. Sometimes she broke out into soft hurried speech, half coherent, and again she stood gazing into the pine forest. Logan sat beside the campfire, but he did not smoke. Lucinda spread her blankets under a tarpaulin pegged down from the wagon-top and lay down with weary, aching body. The campfire sputtered, the wind blew—then while she was fearing the old lonely sounds, her eyelids closed as if with glue and she faded into oblivion.

Next day Logan made another long drive, to the deserted cabin half way between the south end of Mormon Lake and Sycamore Canyon. Logan might not have even thought of their nearness to the old ranch, but Lucinda, during the supper tasks and afterward, kept talking and asking questions until he became aroused.

Before noon the next day Logan turned off the main road at the end of Long Valley and drove down through the forest toward Sycamore.

What stinging beautiful emotions flashed over her as they passed the open glade where she had first seen Barbara playing with the boys! From then on she was blinded by tears. They struck the down-grade. The old gate had not been closed since the cattle-drive. Logan emitted a strange hard cough, almost like a sob. He drove on, applying the brake. The wheels squeaked, the heavy wagon pushed the horses on. And then they reached a level.

"Same as always, Luce—just the same!" exclaimed Logan, huskily. "Only we are changed."

Lucinda wiped her eyes so that she could see to get off.

"Drive up to the cabin, Logan," she said, "and spread

a blanket in the shade for Barbara and the baby. . . .
What shall I tell the teamster to do with his load?"

"Unload it, I reckon, here by the barn," rejoined
Logan, whipping his reins. "Gedap there!"

The negro arrived while Lucinda was looking around.
The barn was stripped, proving how wise Al Doyle had
been to advise a new outfit. Lucinda directed the driver
to unload the farming equipment and pack it into the
barn, then come on up to the cabin with the furniture.

That done, Lucinda turned to the old hollow-worn
path. Her feet seemed leaden. There was a pang in her
breast and a constriction in her throat. The joy she had
anticipated failed to come at once. But she knew something would break the deadlock.

The brook was bank-full of snow-fed water, the old log
bridge as it had been. Then she espied Logan. He had
halted the wagon and was looking across at the unfinished stone corral. One look at his tortured visage was
enough. The very stone Lucinda remembered seeing
Logan put down on the wall sat there, mute yet trenchant
with memory of the three sons who had helped build
that wall with Logan, and who could not finish it because
they had gone to war.

Logan drove on up to the cabin. Lucinda, lagging
behind, fighting her own anguish, came to the long row
of her sunflowers. They were blooming, great golden-
leaved, brown-centered flowers, facing the sun. With
sight of them the joy of home-coming flooded her being.
She caressed the big blossoms and pressed them to her
breast; then she found early golden rod and purple
asters along the path. She gazed down the canyon for the
first time. The high walls, the black ruins, seemed to
gaze down protectingly upon her. Home! They assured
her of that and they gave austere and solemn promise of
the future.

Lucinda found the baby rolling and crawling on a blanket; Barbara, wildly excited by familiar scenes and objects that must have pierced close to reason, was running around in and out of the cabin. Logan was inside.

The flat flagstone lay under the hollowed log threshold. Lucinda knew both as well as her right hand. Wan bluebells smiled up at her out of the grassy margins. She peered into the cabin conscious of a clogged breast and pounding heart. Her emotions had not prepared her for practical facts. That cabin, hallowed by so much of sad and beautiful life, was a dingy dusty spiderwebbed barn. The rude table and bench-seats and the old rustic armchair, relics of Logan's master hand so many years ago, were the only articles left inside. The bough-bed had been torn apart, no doubt for firewood; all the deer and elk horns and skins were gone from the walls. In places the yellow stones of the fireplace were crumbling. An Indian or some cowboy artist had drawn crude but striking images on the smooth surfaces.

Logan was cursing, which sounds for once Lucinda heard with delight.

". . . —— —— dirty hole not fit for cattle. This here home of ours has been a camp for low-down hunters and loafers, and later a den for skunks, wild-cats, coyotes, and Lord knows what else! . . . There's a hole in the shingles. Some of the chinks are out between the logs. That door is hanging loose and won't shut. And dirt! Say, it's dirtier than all outdoors. Just one hell of a dump!"

"Yes, Logan—but home," rejoined Lucinda softly, as much overcome by his practical reaction as by the fact she expressed.

"Huh! . . . Home?—Aw, thet's so, Luce."

"I'll be practical, too, husband," said Lucinda, inspired to action. "Get out the broom and mop. And water buckets. And soap. We'll sweep and brush and scrape and scrub. . . . Mend the hinge on the door. Have the driver put a canvas over the hole in the roof. Have him cut a lot of spruce boughs. After that's done you can unpack and carry everything in. After that, Logan, if you're able to, see if you can chop some wood."

"Hell! I can chop wood," declared Logan, in gruff resentment.

Lucinda set to work, and she kept the two men, and Barbara also, busy at various tasks. When Logan flagged and Barbara drifted off into space, Lucinda prompted them again. They could not apply themselves for long. When sunset came, and at that season of early summer the golden rays shone through door and window, Lucinda surveyed the interior of the cabin with incredulous eyes and swelling heart. The den of hunters and beasts had been transformed. It was home once more, and more comfortable and colorful than ever before. Barbara had her old corner, where she sat on her bed with vague gaze trying to pierce a veil of mystery. Little Abe crawled around delighted with this new abode. Logan sat in his old chair, watching the fire, apparently lost to any of the grateful and beautiful feelings that stirred Lucinda.

Darkness stole up the canyon while she prepared supper. The night-hawks and the insects began their familiar choruses. A glorious rose and gold after-glow slowly paled above the western rim. The brook babbled as of old. Nature had not changed. Lucinda recalled the prayers of her youth. Her task was infinite, almost insurmountable, but her faith grew stronger. When night came, while she lay awake by Logan's side, with Barbara's corner silent as the grave, and the old wind-song mourning in the tips of the pines, then she seemed divided between hope and terror. In the hours when she

wooed slumber she became prey to the past, to her early
years here, to memory of her awakening to real love for
her pioneer husband, to the coming of their first born,
to that terrible and fascinating Matazel, to Abe's birth
in a cow-manger, and so on through all the succeeding
years of trial down to this agonizing end for the Huetts.

However, when morning came and the sun shone and
the canyon smiled in its early summer dress, Lucinda
did not fall prey to such memories. Her hope for the
future battled with realism, with the thought of age and
poverty, of her insupportable task with Logan and Barbara.

Night and day then for a week her mind worked from
the somber to the bright, from the material fact to the
spiritual belief, before she noted a gain for the latter.
She grasped something to her soul that she could not
explain. She no longer pondered over the inscrutable
ways of God. She forgot the horror of war and the crawling maggots of men who fostered it. Her work lay here
in this wild canyon and was still a long way from being
finished.

Lucinda soon began her labors in the garden. About
the only thing she could keep Logan steadily at was
chopping wood. He seemed to enjoy that, and his swing
of axe had much of its old vigor; but when she sent him
to the pasture to bring in one of the horses, saddle and
snake down dead aspen and oak to chop, he seldom mate-
rialized unless she hunted him up. Manifestly this was
what she must do! Mostly she found Logan beside the
old unfinished stone corral. At these sad times she hated
to break in on his reveries, and some days she could
not bring herself to this cruelty, and she left him alone
with his memories. Nevertheless it was forced on her to
see that she must keep him working.

With Barbara she had less trouble. Barbara would

obey as long as the idea of work lingered in her mind, but when sooner or later it faded, she would wander away. She always wanted to go into the woods. There seemed to be something beckoning to her off under the dark pines. She would sit by the door on the old porch bench and watch the canyon trail, a habit appearing to Lucinda to be the one nearest rationality. It had to do, Lucinda thought, with vague mind pictures of Abe riding up the canyon. It was heart-rending to watch, but Lucinda found some inexplicable grain of hope in it.

Little Abe had improved and grew like a weed. Sometimes Barbara neglected to nurse him, but he never forgot when he was hungry. When Lucinda told Logan that they must have a milk cow very soon, Logan agreed and almost instantly let the need slip from his mind.

Lucinda, with some help from Logan and Barbara, succeeded in planting her garden patch by the end of June. This time, in a normal season, was not too late to insure a crop before the severe frosts came, and with their supplies and the meat she hoped Logan would provide, they could live well through even a fairly severe winter.

"Logan," she said one night as he sat by the fire, "summer is getting along. You must snake down a lot of firewood and chop it for winter."

"Plenty of time, wife," he said. "Why, it can't be June yet."

"June has passed, husband," she replied patiently. "You should have all the wood cut and stowed before Indian-summer comes."

"Why ought I?"

"Because at that season you roam around the forest locating the game. Getting ready for your fall hunt! You forget. There never was anything you'd let interfere with that. We must have plenty of venison hung up and frozen, a lot of turkeys, an elk haunch or two—and some of those nice juicy bear-ribs that always pleased you."

She did not betray her intense hope for his reception of these suggestions. Long she had refrained from urging them. If he showed no interest—if he failed to respond . . . She dared not follow out her train of thought.

"Huntin' season!—By gosh, I never thought of that," he ejaculated, lifting his shaggy head with a flare of gray-stone eyes. She had struck fire from him and was overjoyed. Next instant he sagged back. "Aw hell!—Huntin' without Abe?—I don't know. . . . I reckon I couldn't."

"Logan, you must feed Abe's boy so that he can grow up fast and hunt with you," replied Lucinda, sagely.

"My Gawd, Luce, do you expect me to live that long?" he asked, haggardly.

"Of course I do."

"Humph. I reckon I don't want to," he said gloomily. But he seemed to be disturbed and haunted by the idea. "Wal, there won't be any game when little Abe gets big enough to pack a gun."

"You once said there would always be turkey and deer in the breaks of the canyons."

"That's so, Luce. I'll think it over. . . . Have you seen my rifles?"

"Yes. I rolled them in canvas. And Al bought a new stock of shells."

"Ahuh. . . . Doggone me!" he added mildly.

Lucinda wept that night while Logan slept heavily beside her. It was not from exhaustion and pain, although after she lay down she could not move, and her raw blistered hands and aching limbs hurt her excruciatingly, that Lucinda shed slow hot tears. They were tears of joy at some little reward to her prayers for Logan.

But Logan never unrolled the canvas bundle of rifles

which Lucinda leaned against the fireplace, nor did he take down the pipe and tobacco which she placed in plain sight on the jutting corner of chimney, where he had always kept them.

Lucinda toiled on, unquenchable in faith that Logan would rise out of his gloom of despondency, and that Barbara was not permanently deprived of her sanity. If there were not daily almost imperceptible things to keep this hope alive in her, then she suffered under a delusion. Work was a blessing. It sustained Lucinda in this period which tried her soul.

One summer morning, towards noon, when the great forest was so still that a dropping pine-cone could be heard far away, Lucinda bent over her work at the table under the back window of the cabin.

Occasionally she looked out to peer down the brook at Logan who sat beside the unfinished stone wall staring at space. He made a pathetic figure. All about him expressed the catastrophe in which the labor of a lifetime, fortune, comfort, his sons, his patriotism, his faith in man and God, had vanished.

Lucinda sighed. She had moments of despair, in which she had to fight like a tigress for her young. It was ever-present, the stark, naked fact; against which she had only mother love, an ineradicable faith, and a nameless, groundless hope. Yet in the last analysis of her terrible predicament she had the profoundest of all reasons to fight and never to yield, never to lose faith—the task of bringing up Abe's son. When gloom lay thick upon her soul she was carried ahead by that duty.

Barbara was outside on the porch, in her favorite place facing the canyon and the trail, and the fact that she was humming a little song to the boy indicated that she was in one of her placid states of apathy.

All at once Lucinda ceased her work to gaze out up the forested canyon. No differing sounds had caused this. She was puzzled. The brook murmured on, the soft wind moaned on, a stillness pervaded the canyon. The sun was directly overhead, as she ascertained by the shadows of the pines. Something had checked her actions, stopped her train of thought. It did not come from outside.

Suddenly a stentorian yell burst the silence.

"*Waa-hoo-oo!*"

That was Logan's hunting yell. Had he gone mad? Lucinda became rooted to the spot. Then her ears strung to the swift hard hoof-beats of a running horse. Who was riding in? What had happened? Logan's whoop to a visiting cowboy? It seemed unnatural. The charged moment augmented unnaturally. How that horse was running! His hoofs rang on the hard trail up the bench. A grind of iron on stone, a sliding scrape and a pattering of gravel—then a thud of jangling boots!

"*Bab, old girl—here I am!*" called a trenchant voice, deep and rich and sweet.

Lucinda recognized it; and her frightened heart leaped pulsingly to her throat.

Barbara's piercing shriek followed. It had the same wild note that had characterized Logan's, and above and beyond that a high-keyed exquisite rapture which could only have burst from recognition.

"*Abe! . . . Abe!*"

"Yes, darling. It's Abe. Alive and well. Didn't you get my telegram from New York? . . . My God, I—I expected to see you . . . but not—not so thin, so white. Dad must be okay—the way he yelled. And. . . . Aw, my boy! . . . So this is little Abe? He has your eyes, Barbara. . . . Brace up, honey. I'm home. It'll all be jake pronto."

"*Abe!* . . . You've come back—to me," cried Barbara, in solemn bewilderment.

Lucinda heard Abe's kisses but not his incoherent words. She lost all sensation from her head down. Her body seemed stone. She could not move. Abe had come home and the shock had restored Barbara's mind. Lucinda felt that she was dying: joy had saved, but joy could also kill.

"Mother!" cried Abe. "Come out!"

If Lucinda had been on the verge of death itself his call at that moment would have drawn her back, imbued her through and through with revivifying life. She rushed out. There stood Abe in uniform, splendid as she had never seen him, bronzed and changed, with one arm clasping Barbara and the boy, the other outstretched for her, and his gray eyes marvelously alight.

"Doggone! Here we are again," Logan kept saying.

It was an hour later. The incredible and insupportable transport of the reunion had yielded to some semblance of deep, calm joy. Logan seemed utterly carried out of his apathetic self. Barbara had recovered her reason; there was no doubt of that. Spent and white she lay back against Abe, but her eyes shone with a wondrous love and gratitude and intelligence. Lucinda knew herself to be the weakest of the four. She had just escaped collapse. The hope of this resurrection, though she had not divined it, had been upholding her for weeks.

"Some day—not soon—I'll tell you about George and Grant," Abe was saying gently. "When you hear what they did—what their buddies and officers thought of them—you won't feel their loss so terribly. . . . My case was simple. I had shell-shock and lay weeks in the hospital unidentified. When I came to my senses I proved who I was and got invalided home. I was in bad shape then. Once started homeward I got well pronto. That's all. The Germans are licked. They'll never last another winter."

"Abe, I reckon you smoked 'em up," said Logan, intensely.

"Dad—I knew you'd ask me that," replied Abe, a gray convulsion distorting his face, aging and changing it horribly. "Yes, I did. At first I had a savage joy in my skill. . . . It was sheer murder for me to shoot at those poor devils. A hard-nosed thirty government bullet would get right through their metal helmets. . . . But in time I grew sick of it. . . . And now—well, let's bury it forever."

"Sorry, son. Just the same it's good for me to know. I'm holding on by an eyelash."

"Abe, did any one in Flagg or on the way out, tell you what happened to your father?" asked Lucinda.

"No. I got in late, borrowed a horse and came araring. . . . What happened?"

"He sold out to the army cattle buyers. Thirty thousand and nine hundred, at twenty-eight dollars a head. . . . They swindled him. Not one dollar did he ever receive of that money."

"Good God!" exclaimed Abe, furiously.

It was for Logan then to confess shamefacedly his monstrous carelessness and trust.

"Aw Dad!—Then we're back in the old rut again?"

"Poor as Job's turkey, son," replied Logan, huskily.

"I don't care on my own account," said Abe, dubiously. "But for mother and Bab—it'll be tough to begin all over again."

"Darling, I needed only you," whispered Barbara.

"Dad, I forgot to tell you," went on Abe, brightening. "You'll never believe it. Cattle are selling at fifty dollars a head, and going up."

"For the land's sake! . . . Who's buying?"

"Kansas City and Chicago."

"Did I ever hear the likes of that . . . My Gawd, why didn't I wait!" ejaculated Logan, with a spasm working his visage.

"Never mind, Dad," returned Abe, slowly. "We're not licked yet."

Abe's return acted miraculously not alone upon Barbara. Logan hung around him as if fascinated; as if he could not believe the evidence of his senses. Lucinda knew they were all saved. The war had not impaired Abe physically. And spiritually she thought he was finer, stronger. Abe was of the wilderness. The old potent loneliness and solitude, the trails and trees, the cliff walls, and home with Barbara and his boy—these would soon blot out whatever horror it was that haunted him.

The family sat together for hours until late afternoon.

"By gum, I forgot to unsaddle that nag," said Abe. "Bab, if you'll let go of me for a spell I'll ride down the old trail a ways."

"Abe, are you really home?" she asked, eloquently.

"What do *you* say, sweet?"

"This is not a dream? You are not among the missing?"

Abe stood upright to swing her aloft and clasp her endearingly.

"Bab, I've caught you looking at me—I believe you've been a little loco. Dad seems kind of daffy, too. But I *am* home. I'm well. I'm so happy I—I— . . . there's no words to express how I feel."

He strode across the garden to the field where the horse was grazing, dragging its bridle; and mounting with the old incomparable cowboy step into the saddle he rode down the canyon.

They all watched him disappear around the jutting corner.

"Gosh, Luce," ejaculated Logan, coming out of a trance. "I must rustle some firewood. I don't want Abe knowing. . . ."

He shook his head ponderingly and slowly made for the empty space around the chopping-block.

"Hurry. I must get supper. Abe will be starved," called Lucinda.

"Just as little Abe is this moment," declared Barbara, as she took up the crying boy.

Verily, thought Lucinda with fervent thanksgiving, the return of the lost soldier had reclaimed that family.

Barbara watched for Abe from her old waiting place on the porch. The afternoon waned, the sun set in golden splendor, the purple shadows fell, and twilight came with its lingering after-glow.

"He's coming, mother," Barbara called joyfully from outside, and she ran down the path to meet him. Presently they came in, with arms around each other. Barbara's face was flushed and rosy.

"Maw, I'm starved," yelped Abe, at sight of the steaming pots.

"Come and get it, boy," she replied happily.

"Dad, just wait till I eat, and I'll sure take a fall out of you," declared Abe, as he straddled the bench. "I've a swell joke on you."

"You have, huh?" said Logan. "Wal, son, if you can make anythin' in this God-forsaken world of mine look like a joke, come out with it pronto."

"Wal, I shore can, old timer," drawled Abe.

It was not a bountiful supper, to Lucinda's regret; she had been caught unprepared. But never under that cabin roof, where Abe had grown to manhood, where he had sat hundreds of times after a grueling drive or two days hunt, had he eaten so ravenously. Lucinda waited on him, Barbara hung over him, Logan watched him, and they all forgot their own suppers. Their feelings transcended happiness.

"How about that joke?" demanded Logan, impatiently.

"I'm afraid I'm too full to talk," declared Abe, as he threw off the snug-fitting khaki jacket and unloosened his belt. His powerful shoulders had lost their brawn. "Dad, you were telling me this afternoon how poor we are. One team, one wagon, a few tools, no horses, no help—and only a little money left. Wasn't that it?"

"Yes, son. I wish to heaven I didn't have to confess it. But we're as bad off as ever in our lives."

"Dad, you sure are a rotten cattleman," went on Abe, with a smile and a fine flash of eyes upon his father.

Logan took that amiss. Manifestly it hurt him deeply, for he crushed his big hands between his knees and almost rocked double. That was one of the moments when Lucinda could not look at him.

"*Dad!* . . . I was talking in fun. That's my joke," cried Abe, contritely.

"Wal, I can't see it—son."

"Listen. And you will darned pronto. . . . Do you remember Three Spring Wash?"

"I reckon so. Why?" rejoined Logan, lifting his head.

"Do you remember the time we trapped the wild horses there?"

"Sure do."

"Oh, Abe, I remember that," cried Barbara, wonderingly.

"Well, Dad, do you remember we had a bunch of cattle running in there before the big drive?"

"I reckon we had, same as in those other side canyons."

"Do you remember that Grant and I, with the help of some Indians, had the job of tearing down that fence in

Three Springs and driving the cattle out into the main
herd?"

"I remember that, too," declared Logan.

"We didn't tear it down."

"Huh!" grunted Logan, stupidly.

"Grant forgot, and I missed that job on purpose. I
knew there were more than thirty thousand head in the
main canyons. So I left that bunch in Three Springs.
We never tore the fence down. Nobody tore it down for
that drive. It has not been torn down since."

"My Gawd, son—what you—sayin'?"

"Dad, the fence is there still. . . . And I counted
around fifteen hundred head of cattle, all fine and fat.
And you can bet that's a short count, for I didn't ride up
in the oak draws and pine swales."

Logan's big square jaw wobbled and dropped over a
query he could not enunciate.

"That's my joke on you, Dad. And I think it's a peach."

"Abe!" cried Barbara.

"You sure are a locoed old cattleman. Here you've
been moping around Sycamore, heart-broke and pocket-
broke when you've got sixteen or eighteen hundred head
of stock worth fifty dollars a head."

"For God's sake, son, you wouldn't play a joke—like
that—on your poor old Dad?" implored Logan.

"I wouldn't if it were a lie, Dad, but this is true.
Absolutely true. I'll show you tomorrow."

It seemed to Lucinda that while she watched with
beating heart and bated breath, a slow change worked in
her husband. He stared into the fire. A rumbling cough
issued from his broad breast. Then he stood up, apparently seeing straight through the cabin wall. He ex-
panded. His shoulders squared. His gray eyes began to
kindle and gleam, and all the slack lines and leaden
shades vanished ruddily from his visage. When Logan

reached for the old black pipe and the little buckskin bag, and began to stuff tobacco in the bowl, then Lucinda realized she was witness to a miracle. She stifled a sob which only Barbara heard, for she came swiftly to Lucinda whispering the very truth that seemed so beautiful and so distracting. Logan bent down to pick up a half burnt ember which he placed upon his pipe. Then he puffed huge clouds of smoke, out of which presently stood his shaggy erect head, his shining face, his eagle look. Lucinda saw her old Logan Huett with something infinite and indescribable added.

"Wal, son," he drawled in his old cool easy way. "You can't never tell about this here cattle business. *Quien sabe,* as Al used to say. . . . I reckon I was kinda sick in my gizzard. . . . Now let me see. A few cattle makes a hell of a difference. Say we got fifteen or sixteen hundred head. All right. You'll rustle some cowboys and cut out all except the youngest stock. I reckon that'd be half, say eight hundred head. You'll drive them to Flagg and sell. . . . Eight hundred at fifty?—Forty thousand dollars, son! . . . You'll bank that money. You'll buy a truck and a car—and all you can think of—and Luce can think of—and Bab can think of—and new guns for me. *Aghh!* . . . Then you rustle the cars and all that stuff home. . . . Abe, we'll begin cattle raising again. And we'll bring little Abe up to know the game. We'll never make the mistakes I made. . . . The ways of God are inscrutable. I reckon I'll never forget again. . . . And after all I'll never miss that thirty thousand head."